Trophies

Trophies

HEATHER THOMAS

WILLIAM MORROW

An Imprint of HarperCollins*Publishers*

Trophies is a work of fiction. All places, things, names, and characters are invented—or used fictitiously—and any similarity to real places, things, names, or persons existing, living, or dead is purely coincidental. Hear that, girls? *Coincidental. No,* it's not all about *you!*

HarperCollins books may be purchased for educational, business, or sales promotional use. For information please write: Special Markets Department, HarperCollins Publishers, 10 East 53rd Street, New York, NY 10022.

FIRST EDITION

Designed by Chris Welch

Library of Congress Cataloging-in-Publication Data

Thomas, Heather, 1957-
   Trophies / Heather Thomas. — 1st ed.
      p.   cm.
ISBN 978-0-06-112624-6
1. Women—California—Los Angeles—Fiction.   2. Wives—Fiction.   3. Self-realization—Fiction.   4. Hollywood (Los Angeles, Calif.)—Fiction.   I. Title.

PS3620.H6279T76 2008
813'.6—dc22   2007049143

---

08   09   10   11   12   WBC/RRD   10   9   8   7   6   5   4   3   2   1

For my husband, Skip,
who with every day
creates new reasons for me to fall crazy in love with him

And for India:
Mommy has more time now

ACKNOWLEDGMENTS

Thank you, Ellen Vein, for reminding me that I am a writer and for your masterful nagging, loyalty, and mad skills. Thank you, Frank Coffey, for unending assistance, patient wisdom, and ability to joke under torture. Thank you, Lucia Macro, for weathering the storm and making this happen. Thank you, my wonderful daughters, Kristina, Shauna, and India, and my magnificent mother, Gladdy Lou Ryder, for maintaining family joy, order, nurture, and ritual, despite my work schedule.

Thank you to the finest staff in the world, Deborah Stenard, DeVonne Stallworth, Douglas Dingee, Kristin Dahl, Max Amaya, Teresa Vasquez, Suyapa Amaya, Antonio Flores-Parra, Mary Ellen Ciminera, Tawnya Ahlgren, and Jim Simmerman for putting up with me and keeping it together. (And for not killing me in my sleep.) Thank you, Dr. Barry Kaye, for putting my carcass together, again and again and again. Thank you, hospital fundraising whisperer, Dr. Gary Gitnick. Thank you, Mark Allen, for inspiring me to create your evil twin. Thank you to my girlfriends, who are *all* Trophies: No, it's not about you but it couldn't exist *without* you! Thank you to Madaline Blau, for giving me wings. And thank you again, my loving husband, from whom all things flow . . .

Trophies

PROLOGUE

Marion Zane hadn't realized how long it had been since she was in a department store, or any shop for that matter, until she entered Barneys New York in Beverly Hills. Years of stylists, personal shoppers, assistants, on-call makeup and hair artists, salaried valet and home delivery service had eliminated the need to drag her ass out of the house and purchase freakin' anything with her own two hands. Sure, she *talked* to store managers and salespeople over the phone, but it wasn't the same as the actual shopping experience. Restaurants, private schools, but especially stores were the marketplaces of Beverly Hills. Places where you would run into people you knew without prearrangement. Catch up. Have an unplanned conversation.

She'd definitely been separated.

It had been so long, Marion almost suffered visual overload. All the stuff. Case upon case of delectable "it" bags to her left, candy counters of makeup and glistening jewelry in front of her, mannequins slouching around in showstopping gowns above, and to her left a garden of couture shoes that would give cocaine, crystal meth, and American cigarettes a run for their money in an addiction race. It had been so long, it felt like a *treat*. Make that a bittersweet treat, because although she could purchase as much of anything as her heart desired, she had no time; unless she were willing to look like a contestant on *Supermarket Beat the Clock.*

She used to watch that show as a kid. Didn't she?

(Okay, time to stop consumer-culture brainwash. You're late.)

She waded into the busy shoe department, located her favorite salesman, John, and asked him to stretch out the toes of her slingbacks. As she started to take a seat, he made a game-show-model gesture toward a pair of buttery-soft suede Chloé boots.

"Gotta stay on task. I'm giving Patti Fink's stepdaughter's seventh-grade class a LACMA tour in twenty minutes."

"Not even time for these, hon?" John asked above the shopping din.

(The first hit's free.)

"It'll just be a second to stretch these. I can send anything you like to the house."

Already, two women had noticed Marion inspecting the boots and were pointing them out to their own salespeople.

"Okay, the boots. Thanks."

John bustled away. Marion sat down and wiggled her liberated, grateful toes. What was she thinking? Wearing new four-inch Louboutins for a lunch at Chow's followed by an afternoon of walking? She'd been on the museum board for years, giving hundreds of tours, and had a whole closet section of cute walking kicks. Must've been the quid pro quo nature of the lunch that had thrown her off her game.

Joan Hoyard had said she'd come to Marion's political reception if, in return, they could lunch, in public. Joan said she needed to up her "cool-ness factor." The idea made Marion feel like a gigantic a-hole, but Joan was a major Democratic donor and she needed her on the RSVP list.

Her husband was expecting it.

And if ya got down to cut-the-crap bone honest, Joan Hoyard was right. Being spotted lunching with Marion Zane would definitely punch up any-one's status.

Marion had MAJOR INFLUENCE.

Who'd've ever thunk it?

(Enough of that.)

To avoid further temptation, Marion stared at the floor. White dot at two o'clock. She wasn't the only one who saw the small white pill lying on the floor of the shoe department. Craig-the-stylist saw it too.

"And what have we here?" he said, snatching it up and holding it pin-cered, for all to see. "Look, Marion, someone dropped a pill!"

Marion immediately noticed the cacophony of lusty foraging begin to die down.

Craig plopped down beside her, scrutinizing the tiny tablet, like a jeweler. "Think it's a Benzo?"

Around them, various purses were discreetly unsnapped and unzipped.

"Or maybe an Adrerol?"

Pockets were patted, glasses cases looked into; one woman quietly unfolded a tissue from her pocket.

"Oooh. It might be an Oxy!"

Several necks craned. Some women stared directly.

Weary of the amateur *PDR* talk, Marion leaned over and took a look. "It's melatonin, Craig."

Craig frowned and tossed the pill back in the bullpen, where it remained unclaimed. Shopping and socializing resumed. He remained squished in beside her.

"Yeah, but did you check out the panic? Talk about a suspended moment in time. Frozen Trophy Wives, as far as the eye could see. Just look at 'em, Marion! The most pampered poodles on Earth and wealthy beyond a care in the world. Why the fuck do any of you need to medicate?"

Marion was used to the prejudice. It went with the territory. She also knew Craig was trying to embarrass her because he was still pissed that she'd dumped him for that genius girl Anna Wintour had recommended to her. She didn't give a rat's ass. The pill wasn't hers and Craig wasn't that witty.

At that moment there were at least four women in the shoe department who passed gossip faster than semiconductors. Marion smiled and matched Craig's volume. "Wow. You really *do* hate your clients, Craig."

"I never said that."

"You implied it. You went straight for the doofus generalization: you think any wealthy wife is a useless consuming asshole, incapable of ever comprehending human suffering."

She could tell he wanted to clap his hand over her mouth and shove her beneath the seat cushions, but store security would be on him in seconds. Craig could only contort his face and hiss for mercy.

She lowered her volume. After all, she'd changed clothes in front of him hundreds of times. Being naked with a guy had to count for something. "Whatever keeps you warm at night."

"Housebound shopaholics keep me warm at night. But ya gotta admit, if there was ever a poster child for schadenfreude, it would be an unhappy

Beverly Hills Trophy wife. I mean, you guys *chose* the gilded cage; no real power, ironclad prenups and all."

Not that witty at all.

" 'No real power' . . . mmm," Marion answered. "Let's just take a second to think about all the politicians, environmental causes, social programs and legislation, spiritual leaders, medical treatments and research, schools, universities, libraries, hospitals, museums, performing arts centers, preserved architecture, disaster relief, artists trends, schools of thought, and moral causes that would never have gained traction without the attention, influence, and seed money from powerless Trophy Wives. I'd call any demographic group which directs billions of dollars in charitable funds kinda powerful."

"Ah, yes. The Late Thirties Hyperdrive. I really must publish my theory. It's the other biological clock."

"Oh, please."

"Oh, yes, think: no matter how many bras you burn, women are still socialized to compete against each other for attention from men. The richer the man, the more vicious the competition. You Trophies possess a monstrous competitive hyperdrive when it comes to beating out other broads for billionaires. But what does a Trophy do with her humongous competitive force once she's snagged her man, popped out the kids, and placed them in private status schools? 'Make the World a Better Place.' Why? Because you're all either losing sexual attraction, overentitled, or looking for an excuse to dress up and throw yourselves a party."

Poor Craig. He never scratched deep enough.

"Losing sexual attraction? As in, trading wolf whistles for service props?"

Marion slowly stretched and recrossed legs that could have been hand-tooled by a sex maniac. There were only three straight men (husbands) in the vicinity; all automatically gaped. One even bumbled into the Prada display, sending boots, slingbacks, pumps, and satin dress sandals clacking onto the floor.

"Your hypothesis has more holes than Dick Cheney's heart," she continued. "One, this is Los Angeles and the women you've chosen to malign are all rich with a capital *R,* meaning unlimited access to the best of the best." (Marion knew of several bodies and faces in this town with a

longer half-life than uranium. But she wasn't about to name names.)
"Two, most Trophies, as you call them, are unfairly genetically gifted to
begin with." (A-hole smug but he'd asked for it.) "Three, there are
enough ass-kissing personal shoppers/florists/designers/trainers/party
planners/agents/salesmen/journalists/assistants/hairdressers/gigolos/
stylists, and if need be, construction sites to make any of us feel attractive into our graves."

"Okay, smarty thong, you've got to admit you're overentitled."

"I admit nothing. I *do* believe I can achieve anything I want if I really go
for it. Isn't that what the feminist movement taught us? The money might
come from a patriarchal source, but charitable donations are almost always directed from a *matriarchal* source."

"Because you want to dance, yak, and compare Vera Wangs."

"Honey, some of us throw parties when we change the color of our
highlights." (Patti Fink.) "I've *never* needed an excuse to make a good
time, thank you very much. But back to your crack about 'no real power.'
Motivation aside, a pretty big chunk of the world goes 'round, thanks to us
poodles."

"You're only as powerful as your prenuptial is weak."

(Take a second to relish favorite sentence in the universe.)

"What prenup?" she asked.

Craig sat back, impressed.

"Powerful and bulletproof. But about the hyperdrive—" she said.

John reappeared. "Here you go, babycakes. Hey, Craig, you're sitting.
Those antibiotics must've cleared everything up."

He presented Marion with her (fierce), and now comfortable, Louboutin slingbacks.

"Cute, John. By the way, your mom came in for a fitting. You might not
recognize her, I shaved her back. So, Marion, the new genius girl has you
doing your own shopping?" Craig sneered without taking his eyes off her
shoes.

"Hardly. I lunched at Chow's, across the street. It's a Chinese—"

"I've been to Mr. Chow!" snapped Craig.

"—the food's perfect but salty so I popped in to have John stretch my
new shoes so I can survive a museum tour this afternoon. Thanks. They're
perfect."

John smooched her, then left to put the Prada display back together. "Stay outta those public bathrooms, Craiggers. Ya only get three strikes."

Marion pointed her toe for Craig and coughed for his attention since he was futilely scanning the Louboutin shelves for her shoes.

(Aaand turn the knife.)

"'My new girl' sent these, last week. They're not even in the stores yet."

"Department-store buyers don't always order the more garish styles in a collection."

"Those sour grapes taste good?" She stood to go but didn't get two steps.

"But we're not finished with the vicious competition part of my theory."

(Don't like the way he's smiling.)

"With charities? Don't quit your day job, Craig. Maybe there's competition for fund-raiser calendar dates or young wives for junior boards, but it's not as ruthless as you're fantasizing. We're all pretty much friends who support each other's concerns."

(Lie-lie-lie-lie-lie-lie-lie!)

"Always the secret keeper, Marion. If you're not gonna gossip, let's go hypothetical: What would any of your friends do if you pulled their charity identity out from under them? As you said, this is Los Angeles. Home of name-above-the-title. What if you just ran over their little public-and-self-esteem face, moved in on their 'cause,' and got more credit than they did?"

"Now you're just being bizarre."

(And it was too scary to even think about.)

"Okay, not a close friend."

"Craig!"

"And let's say, just for fun, you *did* have a prenup. How many of your *friend*s would stay your *friends* if Richard divorced you and you wound up with zip? How many of your *friends* would leap like gazelles at the chance to take a crack at him the minute you moved out?"

(How many?)

"This isn't about charity anymore, is it?"

"It never was."

"Now I remember the reason I fired you. It wasn't just your mediocre skills."

(Run. Away.)

Marion swanned out of the shoe department and toward the exit. She didn't even glance at the case of Fendi clutches. Not for a second.

She never thought lunging into a Wilshire Boulevard intersection exhaust could feel like a breath of fresh air. Her new onyx Maybach, gleaming like her first pair of patent-leather maryjanes, was purring at the curb. She dove into the back. So much for the marketplace.

"Carl, we need to stop at the first drugstore on the way."

"Sure, Mrs. Zane. There's one over on Beverly."

Marion's stomach was churning like a darkened sea before a hurricane.

1

Marion

The bar crystal was wrong. It had cuts. Marion fingered the rocks glass and figured it was probably from the Tiffany set. And she didn't need to wear her glasses to recognize the Buccellati ice bucket, which meant that the whole shebang was way *too much*—the biggest mistake you could make at a political event. Donors like to think every penny of their money is going into boots-on-the-ground media campaigns for the average working Joe and other rolled-up-sleeves stuff. This bar said the pope and Queen Elizabeth were coming over to burn dollar bills. (Yeah, yeah, you could choke on the irony.) There was also that McCain-Lieberman-thing law about not spending too much. Bottom line: it was wrong.

People would notice and talk.

(And she'd be a target.)

Marion felt the ghost of an all-too-familiar yip in her stomach.

(Oh, no you don't.)

This was totally fixable.

"Ivan!"

"Yes, Mrs. Zane?" said a soft German voice at her elbow.

Marion almost knocked over the portable bar. You'd think that after fifteen years, she'd be used to her assistant's spooky habit of appearing before she could even speak his name, but it still jigged the bejesus out of her. The foyer was the size of a small church with vaulted ceilings and freakin' marble floors. How'd he sneak up so quietly in hard soles?

Ivan's James Bond face was neutral, but she could feel him smirking on the inside as he offered her her reading glasses. Eerie. At least he wasn't in a tux.

From the first day she'd met him, Marion had always imagined Ivan in an advertisement for expensive shirts (or on cheery days, expensive underwear). His sculpted good looks, perfect grooming, grace, and efficiency led everyone to assume, at first, that he was gay. For a while every rich, gay power player in town was descending on the Zane compound, armed with fictitious reasons to speak with "Marion's Aryan."

He never, though, responded to their entreaties. Yet, she realized, Ivan didn't respond to any of Marion's trampier girlfriends' advances either. Nowadays she just regarded him as a preternatural, asexual being and wrote off his sixth sense about dress as part of the package.

"We gotta dull this down," she told him. "Where's Jeff?"

"Here, Mrs. Zane," a voice promptly answered, and Jeff, her tuxedoed (yikes) majordomo, came bustling in, trailed ten paces by a silent six-year-old boy who was doing his best to appear invisible.

"Okay, it's a *political* event, so on all the bars: plain crystal instead of cut—use that Baccarat; plain silver bar accessories, plain cocktail linens, not jacquard—use that French set, plain serving trays, quiet flowers. Jeff, way too dashing in the tux. Just coat and tie, like Ivan, and shirtsleeves and bow for waitstaff. You guys know how to do this."

Jeff shot a look at Ivan.

"What?" Marion asked.

Jeff hesitated. "Mr. Zane said to use the good stuff."

"Ah, Jeffery, there are about twenty different sets of crystal in the basement."

"Twenty-four."

"Right, but in my husband's mind, we've got two: jelly jars and 'good stuff.' Warn me the next time he wants to take a hand in choosing the dishes. I'm sorry you had to drag this up."

Jeff smiled and bounced a nod. He got it. She wouldn't have to explain it again. "I'll change everything right away, Mrs. Zane," he said.

"Thanks."

Jeff gasped as he spotted the boy leaning on one of the Louis XVI gilt and alabaster console tables and started to shoo him back to the kitchen.

"Is that Peter?" Marion asked.

"Um, yes, Mrs. Zane. I apologize, but Karen had to work . . ."

Marion whipped off her readers, walked over to the boy, and squatted so as not to freak him out. Good thing she was in her uniform of jeans, a white shirt, and bare feet. If she'd been glammed, he'd probably have recoiled. "Hey, I'm Marion. You met me when you were three. Your parents let you watch cartoons?"

The boy looked at his father's raised eyebrow, then made the sign for "a little" with his fingers.

"What's your favorite?"

"*SpongeBob*," he whispered.

Marion nodded. "I've got that. C'mon."

She took him by the hand. He came without pulling.

"Mrs. Zane, you don't have to . . ."

"Please. At least there'll be *one* person in this house tonight who isn't bored to tears."

Marion led the boy out of the foyer, toward the north wing. She watched his head tilt up as they passed the Rodin bronze. Twelve feet tall and armored with defiant breasts and wide hips, the nude made a formidable guard before the carved stone archway to the family wing.

"Caught ya lookin'."

The boy giggled.

As she set Peter up before the giant flat screen and called for juice and popcorn, Marion had to admit she was kind of pissed at Richard's latest request: "Honey, I need you to give a reception on Thursday for a Senate candidate. He wants something intimate. Use your good list."

Translation: she had less than five days to round up no fewer than fifty (campaign manager's idea of "intimate") billionaires, tastemakers, and A-list movie stars who would probably donate to a newcomer.

That she'd done it in four was beside the point.

Did her husband think she just pulled these people out of her butt?

And here she was ragging on the finest staff in the world about *bar stuff*. All so Richard could seduce and place some millionaire-who-was-bought-out-of-his-company-but-still-wanted-to-wield into a position to change some law. It had to be zoning because Richard already had the media consolidation thing locked. That, coupled with above-normal libidinal demands, could mean only one thing:

Richard was building again.

Land development did the same thing for her husband as scrapbooking did for grandmas. He was always happiest when he had a project. Richard had made his first millions in land development. It was sentimental creativity.

Marion padded back to the foyer with Ivan at her elbow. She waited to make sure Henri and the waiters hadn't confused the crates of plain Baccarat with the ones of cut patterns. They hadn't. Make that the *fuckin'* finest staff in the world.

"Mrs. Erhardt's gardener's niece was ecstatic with the Sting tickets," Ivan told her. "Mr. Sting is sorry you'll have to miss tonight's concert."

"It's what I do for love, Ivan."

"Mr. Zane is building again," he added.

"No shit. Are you all packed?"

Tonight, Ivan was taking his first real vacation in fifteen years. He was committing to a three-month stay at a monastery in the Canary Islands. The order observed a strict code of silence. Guests had to turn in their electronics at the door and couldn't retrieve them until their departure date. Recreation consisted of thrice-daily silent vespers and meditative walks.

Ivan's idea of the "perfect sabbatical."

Marion gave him three days before he'd run screaming for a cabana in Ibiza. If not, she'd make him her charades teammate for life.

"Yes. My flight is at midnight. The event should be over by then."

"In the name of all that is holy, Ivan, it better be. And speak of the devil . . ."

"Hi, honey. This is perfect. Almost too good for that weenie Powell."

Marion winked at Jeff as her tall, salt-and-pepper-haired, handsome-for-a-billionaire husband rolled into the foyer, clutching the RSVP list. He snaked out an arm, coiled her in by the waist, and smooched her neck. Enveloped in her husband, Marion felt her stomach relax—and "pissed" turned into "miffed."

She was in the safest place in the universe.

And her "place" had on a surprisingly great choice of tie! Richard Zane was the most successful media mogul aside from Rupert Murdoch and a legendary real-estate titan, but he rarely made unpainful wardrobe decisions—and refused to work with a valet.

"I'll make this up to you tonight," he murmured in her ear.

She was about to ask her husband not to squeeze her ass in front of the staff, but before she could speak, in strode Zephyr—known as Marion's younger-and-taller-but-not-prettier-because-she-doesn't-do-anything-with-herself sister—who slammed a peck on her cheek so hard Marion made a mental note to call her chiropractor. Tonight, Zephyr's signature aggressive pantsuit was navy instead of black, leading Marion to assume she was in a wildly fanciful mood.

"He might be a weenie," said Zephyr, "but once Jack Powell's in the Senate, we use his appropriations influence to kill the zoning restrictions."

Yep, Richard was building again.

"That's a pretty enormous assumption for a junior senator," said Marion. (Shit. Did it again.)

The woman was over twenty-one. Marion *had* to stop correcting her.

Thankfully, Zephyr was in too buoyant a mood to take offense—not that her facial expressions revealed anything, anyway. Marion could tell by the relaxed jaw muscles and hands.

"He'll get on the committee," replied Zephyr, with professionally dry assurance. "Or we'll trade him *on* with a 'green' favor. The man's a guaranteed zoning change."

"And that means 'downtown' is moving again!" chirped Richard. "Throw in a school or some green space and we'll have—"

"—instant desirable housing and unlimited office," Zephyr added, reflexively flipping her hand out for Richard to low-five.

Zephyr had followed Marion's lead in moving to California then raised the family bar by passing the bar exam. She was the Zane empire's real-estate attorney.

"Why would Powell want to influence rezoning in downtown L.A.?" Marion asked. "Isn't he running as a Democrat?"

Richard and Zephyr exchanged a look.

What was that about?

"Powell is a *Blue Dog* Democrat, where development's concerned," corrected Zephyr.

Richard immediately caught the negative reaction on Marion's face and squeezed her tight. He knew she regarded Blue Dog Democrats as a farm team for the Republican Party and believed they needed to be closely monitored. "But he's *our* Blue Dog, sweetheart," he said.

Okay, now she was being patronized. As far as Marion was concerned, tonight's event was just a big ol' waste of MAJOR INFLUENCE. They could be fund-raising aid to Africa or clean energy development or . . . well, Richard *did* mention something about a school. Plus, if he built any greener, he'd be on the front of a package of frozen vegetables. All of his projects used green materials and were environmentally sensitive. Hell, they were just building, not invading a country. And building projects made Richard so happy. There was an old saying in the talent agency business: "Sell 'em, don't smell 'em." It was good advice for her marriage. And tonight, her husband wanted her to sell Jack Powell.

So be it. Squirming out of Richard's embrace, she left him and Zephyr talking about stages of investment.

"She's over six feet tall. Her pussy is like a *montagne!* Oh, *mon Dieu!* I beg your pardon, Mrs. Zane—I didn't realize you were in the kitchen."

"No need to, Roger, I'm under six feet."

Marion swept across her hotel-size kitchen, passed her mammoth (and now apoplectic) culinary genius, and plunged a greedy finger into one of his perfect mini chocolate cakes. Mmm. The melted center rivaled orgasm. She briefly flashed on being a teen and putting away about twenty of these. Then she remembered trying to wear jeans as a teen. Well, this was all she was getting tonight. She smacked her hand on the white, time-polished marble countertop, punctuating her resolve.

"Damn good. Don't frost it."

Surveying the identical countertops that rivaled an apartment in square footage, she took stock of the evening's fare. "Serve the miniburgers, crudités, empanadas, and pot stickers. No garnish. They look gorgeous, but we have to give the shrimp to the shelter."

Roger's big red buffalo head swiveled and fixed Jeff with a boiling glare. "Three hours of steaming. I *told* you it was politics." Two hundred pounds of tyrannical, temperament-challenged perfectionist were coming around the counter. Marion threw herself protectively in front of Jeff.

"No blame. Richard messed him up."

Roger snorted, further cementing the buffalo image in Marion's mind. After a second he went back to chef's station and started chopping green onions like an ax murderer. "Did they change the bar service?" he growled.

"Already done. Thank you, Roger, and so sorry about the shrimp. The rest is perfect, as usual. And you can shower off the fishy smell in the guesthouse if you're going out after."

Now he was violently dumping sour cream into a huge steel bowl. "It is I who apologize for listening to a moron."

Roger disappeared below counter and rummaged through dried herbs. He wasn't cooled down, but at least he was out of murderous mode.

Seeing Jeff had already slipped out of the kitchen, Marion thought it was a good idea to join him.

Roger was the only employee she ass-kissed, knowing since childhood that it was a bad idea to displease the person who touches what you swallow. Besides, the guy made five-star spa food. Who cared that she'd been blackballed at the Plaza Athénée, the Paris hotel from which she'd poached him. He was worth the trouble.

Shit. She hadn't checked the last-minute RSVPs.

Ivan came around the corner with the list. Make that *fuckin'* eerie.

She took note of the last-minute add-ons.

"So now the mayor *is* coming. He'll bring no less than six, so tell the girls at check-in. That makes only three regrets. Not bad for a last-minute."

"Two out of town. Donald Blum attending his brother's funeral. We sent a donation to the memorial fund," added Ivan.

Marion's gaze stalled at a name on the list. "Oh no! Alan Hertz. You have to call."

"Hertz wasn't on invites. He's a Republican."

"But he switch-hits for Blue Dogs. Zephyr said Powell was Blue Dog. He'll be insulted. Say 'Terrible mistake, Marion's horrified, blah, blah.' Go, go, go."

Ivan was off like a phantom.

More important, Zane Enterprises had just acquired Swift Technological Research Corporation, and Alan Hertz was the CFO. Powell, no doubt, had a publicist, so Alan might find out about the event and wonder why he hadn't been invited. Bad faux pas to begin a marriage. Most

A prescription for a healthier you!

Patient Name: _____

☑ As your doctor, I care about your health and ADVISE you to quit smoking

☑ I recommend these STRATEGIES to help you quit:

☐ **Freedom From Tobacco Program (7 Session Class)**
To sign-up for this program, call Health Education at 323-298-3300
* Program is free and medications are available at a reduced co-pay

☐ HealthMedia® BREATHE™
Visit us at: www.kaiserpermanente.org/healthylifestyles

☐ **Healthy Living Helpline**
To speak to a trained health care professional call 1-866-402-4320

☐ Set a Quit Date: ___/___/___

X _____ Date: ___/___/___

KAISER PERMANENTE.

Anne

310- 502 203 1991   310
                        456-4935

310 - 354-8042   carroxd

310-260 -8744 Pac.Pak - 253 proue

30
15
45D

perilous of all was the fact that Marion knew Kimble, Alan's wife, quite well.

Kimble Hertz was social. *Ambitiously* social. Slight a woman like that and she could become a dangerous enemy.

Or an even more dangerous friend.

For over a decade, Marion had reigned from a social position that appeared rock solid, but she didn't want to tempt fate. She'd witnessed what happened when the herd turned on its own. The memory of Verna Hale was still vivid.

And speaking of Blue Dogs, there was something she remembered reading about Jack Powell. Something she had taken the time to record. Something unsavory.

Not remembering started her stomach tightening. After all, they were endorsing this guy. Actually, *she* was endorsing him because she made the calls. It was on her head. What else had she forgotten?

Marion headed upstairs.

She needed her *Black Book*.

She skipped up the Malibu-tiled, circular servants' stairs that led to each floor, ending at the tower parapet. Since it was dusk, she sneaked a glance up to the top, hoping to catch a glimpse of Gilda the Ghost, the supposedly joyful child bride of Rutherford Wilson, who'd built the main mansion and gardens of the Zane compound for himself and his young wife. Gilda had leaped to her death from the tower parapet at exactly this time of day. The dowager who sold the Zanes the property claimed to have encountered Gilda more than once at several locations in the mansion—including this staircase. Marion hoped to do the same one day.

She wasn't the airy-fairy type. She'd failed catechism class and had no time to suffer through any new dogma. She just felt driven to know the reason behind the seemingly senseless suicide of Gilda Rutherford. Records left a total mystery. One evening the girl went upstairs to dress for a lavish dinner party in honer of Rutherford's birthday and instead took a swan dive into the reflecting pool. No note. No evidence of depression or foul play.

Tonight, Marion had her own theory.

"He only gave you five days to get the whole thing together, right?" she whispered.

No answer. No time. She got off on the second floor.

———

Marion rushed along the colonnaded marble corridor that framed the inner second story of the conservatory, marveling that she had never broken her ass in the place. She hooked a right at the family-wing hallway and broke into a trot. Pausing only to adjust the Picasso outside the master suite (knowing full well that her maid, Xiocena, would adjust it back), she entered her inner sanctum.

"Xio?"

Her maid had been invisible all afternoon. It was a first for the robust Latina, who hovered over Marion like a mother hen. Squishing across the pillowy-plush silk carpet, she passed through the elegantly-appointed-yet-not-too-feminine sitting room and lavishly-appointed-yet-not-too-feminine bedroom (no husband wants to sleep in Girlie-Foofy World) and into her dressing rooms (Definitely Girlie-Foofy). At least Xiocena had remembered to lay out her evening ensemble before she turned invisible. The silver velvet fainting couch was adorned with an appropriately-quiet-yet-arrestingly-chic-yet-doesn't-look-like-you're-trying-too-hard little black Chanel dress, La Perla bra, G-string, Louboutin slingbacks, and double-strand pearls. Xiocena knew her shit. For a half second it struck Marion that the clothes looked like her body had melted out of them. Like she'd been *absorbed* by the mansion.

In the last closet, she reached through sable and cashmere, pressed a panel on the back wall, and it sprang open. She touched her thumb to the screen on the safe and *click*, the steel door slid back and Marion extracted her *Black Book*.

It contained everything she needed to know. *Everything.*

She flipped through to the political listings and found Jack Powell's name. She had already edited it from the corporate section when he was bought out of his Internet venture-capital firm, Crane Partners. Now next to his name she wrote:

Running for and sure to win open California seat as Democrat—with a Zane endorsement, safe Democratic state, and homely opponents in both the primary and general, it was a given. Blue Dog—probable no vote on Environmental Regulations, All Tax Break/Subsidies, Rollbacks, and Nationalized Health Care. Swing on Women's issues, Separation of Church and State. Contact advantage for all things Business/Land Development. Future Earmark King. Hosted Fund-raising.

She made a note of the date.

(Aha!)

Marion found what had been troubling her. She was glad she'd recorded it.

There was another, older notation. One from Powell's days as top dog at Crane; a secretary had brought a sexual-harassment and *battery* suit against him. Depositions revealed that Powell had a reputation for putting his arm a little too far around women. By the end of a workday, Jack could give an exact account of who was and who wasn't wearing an underwire bra. Ugh. Better put Ivan on perv watch tonight.

But the notation didn't end there.

She'd also recorded the fact that six months later, the secretary had dropped the lawsuit. Coincidentally, at the same time Powell allowed himself to be bought out of Crane. In other words, the top dog had become a liability.

And now he was a *politician*? Talk about throwing grease on the liability fire!

(Too much smelling, Marion.)

Still, she made a note to call the Senate Majority Leader and Speaker of the House to warn them before she moved on.

In a lighter vein, she also noted that producer Billy Price had fallen in love with a local girl while filming on location and married her on the spot. A *twenty-five*-year-old beauty queen who gave tours of town hall. Must've been some tour, she thought.

A quick scan of some names from the guest list proved she was well prepped, after all.

Marion slapped the book shut with an exhale. Nineteen years. No yips.

The *Black Book* had started out as a method for dealing with black-hole baboon-screaming panic at the notion of social interaction. And as she grew, it grew. Now, her *Black Book* was the best goddamned sourcebook on the planet.

And the old Marion was dead. She'd never have to feel that social panic again.

She'd rather take a carving knife to her throat.

The *Black Book* went back into the wall safe. Her life was excellent.

Marion stripped down, slathered on a custom body cream that simultaneously moisturized, exfoliated, and performed heroic Preparation H dermis tightening, and buzzed downstairs to send up hair and makeup while she admired her silky hide.

Turning around, she came face-to-face with Ivan. Marion didn't cover up. She'd been changing in front of her assistant for years and he'd never batted an eye.

More confirmation for her asexual theory.

Ivan's conduct was so nonreactive to her nudity that even her Richard didn't give a shit if Ivan saw bod. Of course she drew the line at waxing and other private ablutions, but having an open door to the closet really made things efficient, especially when they needed to discuss matters that couldn't be blared over the intercom system.

"Mrs. Zane," he said without batting an eye. "We tracked down Xiocena. Her niece woke up with terrible stomach pains that wouldn't go away, so she's taking her to the trauma center at Mercy, downtown."

"Oh no! Why didn't she tell me? Downtown hospitals could take *hours*. I would've set her up with Lyndy."

"I'll check in for updates at fifteen-minute intervals."

"Yes, please. Xió adores that girl; she's all the family she's got."

"Right. Very good." Ivan exited as silently as he'd come.

Damn! She should be with Xiocena, helping her not Jack Powell.

Hair and makeup arrived. No choice but to wait.

An hour later, Marion was in complete battle dress. Alone, she regarded the package:

The dress was constructed, yet easy-to-undress soft. The heeled slingbacks gave a bare effect while providing proper political modesty. She wore the pearls but no other jewelry besides an eleven-carat, cushion-cut, D-color, flawless Key to the Kingdom. Thick, dark auburn locks fell long enough past her shoulders to advertise sexuality. Brazilian surgeons, in the eighties, had given her a perfect "Suzy Parker." (At the time Marion had no idea who Suzy Parker was, only that she was somebody beautiful, and that was an improvement.) Assorted exclusive face whisperers protected it from succumbing to thinned, over-Botoxed muscles or formula-heavy balloon lips that stretched the skin below women's noses until their faces resembled those of great apes. The faint smattering of freckles across her upper cheeks and nose tended to put both men and women at ease. Her breasts were wide rather than deep, allowing Marion to simultaneously wear fashion without looking matronly and thrill every man who ever took off her bra. Body sculptors had created her tiny waist without allowing the obliques to build out into "column body." Modern science, in the form of a vicious vacuum cleaner/laser blaster, forbade cellulite from even considering encroachment on her taut thighs, and thanks to Pilates, Power Plates, squats, and the "evil ham-curl machine," you could serve a martini off her ass. At forty-five, she could pass for barely thirty. Make that a *damn good-looking* barely thirty. The fat little outcast from Cleveland was now a Total Trophy. Marion couldn't help but chuckle.

Her own mother wouldn't recognize her.

Downstairs for one final check. And a perfect little blended margarita waiting for her in the kitchen, courtesy of Jeff.

Thank God, they started making Porfidio again. No hangover whatsoever.

Ivan stuck his head into the kitchen. "Any minute, Mrs. Zane."

He tossed her a breath mint and disappeared.

As she risked brain freeze gulping down the rest of her drink, a waitress, exiting the kitchen, caused Marion to do a double take. The woman wasn't on their regular catering crew, but that wasn't what struck her.

She looked familiar, but not as a waitress.

It wasn't so much the woman's face she recognized, it was her . . . what? *Being?* She tried to grasp the impression but it was fading like a phantom cramp. A past life? Had she contracted hyperspiritual hysteria from her pal Patti Fink? Nah. Nobody but Patti held a passport to that disassociated locale.

Anyway, personal fortunes undulated wildly in this town. The waitress may very well have had dealings with Marion in a different capacity. Maybe she'd assisted her at a store or a restaurant or maybe she was a long-forgotten client back in the eighties when Marion was a young real-estate Turk.

But it must have ended badly . . .

The hair on her neck was prickling and her arms were doing an imitation of raw chicken. This wasn't a yip. It felt . . . *dangerous*? She frowned and set her glass down.

"Marion."

Richard was searching her out, via intercom. No time for "once upon a time."

But it took almost a minute to shake off the chicken skin.

2

Lyndy

"Suzie Stein wants the number of my *what*? Is she retarded? First of all, nobody *styles* me, and second . . . hello . . . hello?"

The iPhone flashed CALL TERMINATED BY NETWORK. "Communication by Cell Phone" instantly rose in rank on Lyndy's interminable and constantly distended list of life's disappointments.

"Driver!"

Lyndy banged on the limo's partition, making furious spasmodic gestures, which included shaking the iPhone as if it were a can of hairspray at their chauffeur. "NO RE-CEP-TION! TAKE SUN-SET!" she bawled.

The chauffeur, impressed yet again by the soundproofing efficiency of the Bentley manufacturer's choice of glass, changed course without batting an eye. His turning was smooth, yet precisely abrupt enough to cause Lyndy to lap-slosh her goblet full of Armed Response, an immune-system supercharger and crucial prerequisite to any activities that bore the distinct possibility of leading to human contact.

Lyndy's "disappointment" ratcheted up into a state of ground-glass agitation.

Didn't the moron see she was on the phone? With a beverage? That's three times this week he'd been completely oblivious to her needs. He'd be gone by morning.

And no more drivers. (Unless it was to an awards show, or an event with a red carpet, or an evening where they wanted to drink, or anywhere without valet.) She'd buy a Jaguar Vanden Plas in aquamarine to match the color of her contacts and chauffeur herself.

And give the finger to all those self-satisfied little Prius jockeys!

Lyndy's lips stretched tight while she IM'ed instructions to her personal assistant, Jojo, to play dumb to the Stein woman's pathetic request. New-money vampires. This town was thick with them. She hated the way they thought they could just suck up the details of your life and use them to replicate like a bad horror-movie creature. Her hand moved reactively to the collar of her perfect Brioni casual-yet-regal suit as if it were about to be snatched away.

Stylist! Like some twaddling actress. She didn't have a *look*. She had an . . . air. Yes, an *air* into which one had to be born. She was a *Montgomery*, for heaven's sake. Since California had achieved statehood, the name had been synonymous with privilege, refinement, and social hegemony. Montgomerys had graced polo fields, governor's mansions, ballrooms, and country clubs from Humboldt to San Diego. Few California cities of note were without a museum or municipal building that bore the family name. The Montgomery lifestyle was a culture unto itself. There was no formula for the clothes they wore on their tall, *sportif* frames. It was they *way* they wore them.

The whole thing was so upsetting . . . she dove into the recesses of her brown croc Birkin for her treasured silver cigarette case. Years of use had nearly worn away the gold-filigreed *M*, but Lyndy wouldn't dream of reengraving it, wouldn't dream of tampering with the case's magic. She snapped it open, withdrew one of her grandmother's handkerchiefs, scented with rose and lavender oil, and putting the lacy swatch to her face, breathed deeply. When her father moved out, he had discarded the case in the trash, but little Lyndy rescued it in childish hopes of possessing at least a piece of the parent who'd abandoned her in such haste. Through the years, the story of its origin had evolved and blurred until she referred to it as a family heirloom, passed down by a great-grandparent.

The case, handkerchief, and oil worked like a talisman. Huffing the pheromones of birthright transported her to a balmy night from her childhood:

She was in the summer gardens of Rancho del Rey, the Montgomery family estate in Santa Barbara. The oaks, sycamores, and Monterey pines had been garlanded with hundreds of rainbow-hued paper lanterns. To her six-year-old eyes, it looked as if a door had been opened to Faerie. Earlier, they had witnessed Uncle Clyde score the winning goal astride his magnifi-cent polo pony, Xanadu, with only seconds left in the final chucker. Now ev-eryone was celebrating in high Montgomery style! She remembered the heady perfume of fine cigars and horse manure. Les Brown's band had thrown cau-tion to the wind, playing a scandalous rendition of "Light My Fire." Gaucho-clad waiters running back and forth to a buffet table groaning un-der iced lobster and caviar. Players, still in their jodhpurs and team shirts, backslapped handsome young men in madras jackets. Pastel summer frocks and upswept hair for the girls, each sporting an important piece of family jewelry, like an afterthought. Lyndy's grandmother had bought her a dress from Bullocks Wilshire and the petticoat rustled with every step of her pert white Keds with no laces. Uncle Clyde sneaked her a sip of his Pims. Ronald Reagan laughing and dancing with her great-aunt. So casual. So effortlessly elegant. Swish! Swish!

Memories reserved for only a precious few.

"Suzie Stein's practically forty—a little late to change one's breeding and history. Let those Trophy wives cannibalize each other," she pro-claimed, triumphant.

Lyndy's husband, Max, who resembled one of those fantastic fairy-tale illustrations of a palace guard with a human body and the head of a toad (and in Max's case, the *face* of a mournful toad), patted her thigh while remaining entranced with the evening's gridlock. "Tough break, sweet-heart. You wanna pill?" he asked.

He didn't see her shake her head or hear her proudly declare that her case was "comfort enough." For Max, in the tradition of all wealthy hus-bands who found themselves decades into a marriage unblemished by a prenuptial contract, had developed shamanistic powers of detachment that would rival those of the most potent of mystics.

Right now Max was having an out-of-the-body experience in Rio by the Sea-o. Actually he'd *brought* his body along with him for this one: nu-bile topless girls of all possible racial combinations were attending him as he broiled upon a padded poolside chaise outside a mountaintop casino. He could see the statue of Christ, embracing the azure bay, taste the sugar-rimmed mojito, smell the coconut massage oil administered by a lush and lusty minx with emerald eyes and skin the color of chocolate crème brûlée.

"... not the first time and surely won't be the last I have to deal with such women," Lyndy was saying. "I'm just going to concentrate on making it through this evening."

Lyndera Montgomery Wallert, socialite-philanthropist wife of Max Wallert—creator of two long-dead-yet-still-syndicated action series, producer of numerous lukewarm-domestic-but-overseas-hit action films, and undisclosed Dry Cleaning King of West Covina—was never one to confuse Reality with Facts:

Reality: Suzie Stein had phoned Jojo for the number of Lyndy's *hair*stylist. Her grandmother was coming in from Boca that week and Lyndy's sensible chestnut coif was a dead ringer for dear Nana's.

Fact: As a member of the stately Montgomery family, Lyndy's perpetual burden was to gracefully endure spirit-sucking hordes of new-money vampires if she wanted to be successful in her return to the TOP.

And right now she was headed for an endurance marathon at the home of the Queen of the Vampires: Marion Zane.

When the Zanes had rolled into town, they were awful Orange County. It didn't matter that they had billions, they were practically rubes. Naturally, Lyndy took pity on them and out of the goodness of her heart introduced them to her sophisticated Westside lifestyle, inviting Marion to private trunk-show luncheons at Barneys and a Civic Preservation Society dinner at Mr. Chow's. Lyndy even went so far as to offer Marion a coveted seat on her beloved fund-raising board for Beverly Hills Central Hospital. She had been so disappointed when it was declined. Looking back, she now realized Marion had actually been *feeding* off her, using her exclusive connections as a launchpad to rocket herself up the social ladder. The moment of liftoff was forever seared into Lyndy's consciousness:

She had given a large, star-studded dinner party in honor of Oscar de la Renta. She'd spent weeks planning every aspect of the affair, even personally shopping for the Venetian-glass Neapolitan dishes. Lyndy had plans to become buddies with Oscar. She even indulged in fantasies of a front-row seat at the Paris shows, gift boxes of gowns, and big, white, lacy blouses arriving at her home.

Instead she'd staged her own downfall.

When one guest couple developed the flu, she'd replaced them with a last-minute mercy invite to the friendless newcomer Zanes. What a dipshit mistake. The designer, who was seated beside her and obligated to be *her* dinner partner, barely said two words to his hostess all evening. He'd been too busy fielding a bombardment of conversational vomit fired by Marion Zane. The stupid, brazen wannabe even had the horrifically bad taste to engage Oscar in a *political* discussion. Forcing the man to explain himself in complicated anecdotes that left no room for any of Lyndy's signature witticisms. Valiantly, she tried to change the subject, but it was like trying to cut vanilla pudding, so seamless was Marion's theft. When Oscar abruptly checked his watch and said he was late for a flight, Lyndy thought: Poor man, he must be dying to get away from the bigmouth redhead. But when Oscar bid farewell to Marion, he *invited her to visit him at his villa on Lake Como.*

Lyndy would have given her left tit for a vacation invitation from Oscar de la Renta.

All she'd received was a pat on the arm and a hasty, "Thank-you-lovely-evening."

He then turned back to Marion and embraced her. *Embraced her!* Oscar was *into* Marion.

Everyone else heard. Everyone else took note.

Lyndy Montgomery Wallert had been publicly humiliated.

And Marion Zane had been crowned.

Without remorse, the little bitch had actually sent a thank-you note the next day to rub Lyndy's nose in her larceny. Next, she copied Lyndy and Max's glamour and muscled her way into Hollywood. Lyndy *knew* Marion was behind the Zane Enterprises purchase of Quantum Studios. Horror-movie replication. *Check under your beds for pods.*

Suddenly it was Marion, instead of Lyndy, whose invitations were "unregrettable." Marion whose charities had the thickest tribute books and most glamorous guest lists. Marion who had first crack at everything from designer collections (even before actresses) to insider trading tips. Marion who was the darling of great world and spiritual leaders. Marion who stole my goddamn spot at the TOP. Marion-the-new-money-vampire skank whose reception tonight is the A-list-place-to-be-I-can't-miss-even-though-it's-for-a-fucking-Democrat.

Marion the-Orange-County-Scuz-New-Money-Whore-Trophy-Wife- Cunt-Who-Stole-My-Oscar-Como-Vacation-and-My-Big-White-Blouses!

Lyndy realized she was digging her nails into the gel-padded seat of her custom ass-enhancing panties. She watched the blue anacondas disappear from the top of her hands as she used her handkerchief to return to the present, taking note that she had already spent her two-hour allotment that day dreaming of intricate and ultimate rat-fuck plans for Miz Zane. Plans that would culminate in perfect Unforgivable Humiliation. For years, she had bided her time, pretending to be one of that maroon-headed narcissist's loyal inner circle of ninnies, but all the while she'd known that eventually Marion would leave herself vulnerable. And now a plan was in place. The Beast of Revenge was salivating.

This time would be different. This time Lyndy wasn't alone.

And starting tonight, Marion Zane *was wide open*.

I-hope-I-hope-I-hope-I-hope-I-hope-I-hope-I-hope-I-hope-I-hope-I-hope!

Enough energy spent . . . soon she'd regain her rightful throne. And when she did, she'd treat herself to ass implants, resplendent and high. Lyndy, the hot girl on the dance floor, giving all the boys whiplash . . .

Lyndy used her ass dream as incentive to persevere her way back up to the TOP.

Entranced beside her, Max dreamed of nineteen-year-old girls who didn't speak English.

3

Pepper

The girl at the bus stop at Wilshire and Westwood was using the *same pen*. Funny, the things that catch your eye while you're waiting for a light to change. From behind the wheel of her custom, emerald green, metallic-fleck Porsche Illusion, Pepper Papadopoulos had to be at least twenty feet away; but there was no mistaking the blue plastic stem with the band of red above the white eraser. She remembered staring at that red, white, and blue pen for hours before she actually used its eraser. That's what the girl was doing in her UCLA Bruins notebook. Erasing. The gritty white nub worked better than Wite-Out. Handwritten records and numbers could be altered. Or eliminated as if they'd never existed. Seven years ago, Pepper had erased every worry in her grimy and broken little world. And crash-landed in love. She would have saluted, but the light was changing and she was already steering in second gear, with her knees.

That pen ruled.

That pen had snagged her the handsome devil currently pitchin' a fit in her passenger seat.

"Why do we have to kiss-ass the Greek minister a' shippin' if he's squeezin' yer brothers for bribes? What's his name, Co-socks?" she asked him.

"Kousakis! Not Co-socks! Kou-sa-kis! Gray hair, very, very short, with tight little fists that open only for stealing. He'll be the only one at Richard's reception tonight with a Greek accent besides me, my baby, and we must make him our friend. No Greek jokes. No short jokes. One wrong word, my family loses a port territory!"

"Hoth's Marion and Rithard know 'im?"

Pepper was lick-sealing the joint she'd just rolled in half a Tampax wrapper. (Growing up in a double-wide full of sisters, one acquires basic survival skills.) She stuffed the other half of the wrapper into the left bra cup of her dress and lit up. Pot temporarily stopped her gushing. After five children, six years of nursing, and hundreds of flow-control remedies, getting a teensy bit baked seemed to work best. Her husband was so used to it, he fished a roach clip out of her purse and handed it over without missing a beat.

"They met him at some conference in Malta. Naturally, he hounds them every time he's in town," he replied.

Pepper freed her right hand just in time to swerve and avoid a Jaguar driver who was defying the laws of physics by moving into her lane. L.A. drivers. They hurl themselves 'round town like they're in little metal uteruses. Like they're the only ones on the road tryin' to get somewhere. And everyone's late.

"Fucking idiot!" Ari screamed, nearly banging his head on the glass of the car window. "You almost killed us with that piece of English shit!"

Pepper was glad she'd insisted on driving. This Kousakis guy had her husband in a tizzy. Anything involving the family biz sent Ari into a tizzy.

Aristotle Papadopoulos was a music mogul, owning the rights to the largest online free downloading network, four labels, catalog rights to fifty platinum artists and groups, and was currently developing an encryption system that might end software piracy. But his start-up dough came from the family shipping empire, which was controlled by his big brothers. In his mind, he was still the young screwup who'd almost crashed the family business and got banished to Hollywood. Tonight, he'd put on a tie, for Lord's sake!

"I still don't understand," he said. "Why invite him if they think he's a pest?"

Pepper gave him a look. "You owe Marion, big-time."

"Yes *we* do, my baby. So tonight, we must do justice to Marion's thoughtful effort and keep your ferocious wit in a box so—"

"No little-midget-dick jokes in front of Kosacks?"

"Pepper!"

Pepper wasted her toke, laughing.

So easy to tease. His brothers must've tortured him.

"Relax. I'll take care of him," she soothed.

"No, no. *I* will take care of him. You, have only to—"

"Behave. Yessir."

Pepper suppressed her guffaw. She *always* took care of everything. Ever since she was a kid when her mother worked double shifts.

"Good." Ari sighed and Pepper noticed that his long legs were folding up toward his chest as if his drawers were too tight. If he messed with his hair anymore, he might snatch hisself bald. Did he get into the Red Bull again? She'd *told* Nanny to stash it in the garage.

Now it was her turn to heave a great big sigh, drawing Ari's eyes to her breasts. To the horror of every woman she met, childbearing had had no negative effects on Pepper's Barbie-doll figure and breathtaking face. If Ari was within ten feet of her, he became aroused. Pepper had her own theory about the onset of puberty causing the male brain to shed its frontal lobe and develop, in its place, a thick, dish-shaped, boob/butt magnet.

"Are the bosoms dry?" he asked.

"Dry as a bone."

"Hmm. Speaking of bones . . ." Ari moved her hand to his appreciative groin.

She was happy to oblige. Hand jobs calmed him down and she'd finished her joint. Pepper calculated their rate of speed and distance to destination then compared it to Ari's average hand-job start-to-climax duration and knew they were cool. Might freak out a few truckers and SUV moms, but who gave a shit? She had plenty of diaper wipes for cleanup.

Pepper had never dreamed she'd end up married to a European, much less a Greek. All the European boys she'd met as an exchange student in Brussels, and later at Stanford, seemed like sexless pipe cleaners, with their prissy manners and geeky music. But something happened to them around forty-five. The pipe cleaners filled out and prissy became suave, even worldly. Still, she'd expected anyone named Aristotle Papadopoulos to be a squat, hairy bully, not Antonio Banderas's taller, courtlier brother. He had her from the get-go. From the moment she walked into that deposition.

"Oh, my baby . . . will this make you leak?" Ari worried.

"If it does, I'll bum a dress from Marion."

Pepper had five inches and at least twenty pounds on Marion. Yet ever since she'd dropped her first "pup," Pepper-size, late-model designer dresses and tops had been "mistakenly" delivered to the Zane compound. And stored in Marion's closet. She was that kinda gal.

Marion had befriended Pepper while everybody else was shunning her as a dumbfuck-bimbo-hick-who-destroyed-Ari's-marriage. Well, she did steal Ari from his first wife. But she stole him from bloated-and-crazy-pain-medication-addicted-with-no-kids.

It was really more like carrying out a jail break than wrecking a marriage.

And Pepper was no dumbfuck.

At least the FBI, the SEC, and the United States Trade Commission didn't think so. Pepper had worked for all three as a code breaker. But that was pre-Ari. Nowadays her math skills only showed themselves when she was speaking with their business manager. Freaked the poor sucker out.

Anyway, socialite wives in L.A. had avoided her like head lice those first few months. Marion made it possible for Pepper to remain in Los Angeles—and in her marriage.

Having been introduced only once, they'd accidentally busted each other at the Westwood In-N-Out Burger and bonded over forbidden fare. Well, forbidden to Marion, who limited herself to one bunless burger (a lone patty framed by iceberg lettuce with one slice of cheese and light sauce) a month. Pregnant Pepper was wolfing down a double-double (two cheese-and-meat patties and three buns) with extra sauce, pickles, and a chocolate shake as a pre-lunch snack. She didn't have the heart to tell Marion it was her second. Ari had been introducing her to L.A. women for three months. This was her first lunch invitation. Still, she figured Marion had invited her to sit with her out of courtesy to Ari.

Actually, Marion had been curious. She'd studied Pepper for a few bites, then asked, "Why didn't you walk out last night?"

Point-blank! Pepper nearly choked on her burger. "Beg your pardon?"

"Last night," Marion explained. "At the benefit. Those assholes gave you more shit than the guy who sweeps behind the elephant at the circus parade gets. Speaking to you in monosyllabic words. Sniggering at tasteless jokes about 'country' and 'incest.' They worked the word *adultery* into every other sentence. Why didn't you walk out?"

Pepper took a long hit of her shake. Those wives at the benefit table weren't assholes. They were poisonous bile-spitting vipers. They'd been lying in wait for her and abused her all night. So mean . . . she'd toyed with ideas of packing a suitcase. She decided that Marion Zane was either the cruelest woman on earth or she was one of those "fixers" looking for tears. And well, Pepper hadn't been in a generous mood.

"I could've played along and said, ' 'Scuse me, I gotta go check the still an' have anal sex wit' m' brother.' I could've walked out. But then those twats might stop feeling fat, ugly, an' dull. No sport 'n that."

For a second Pepper expected Marion to grab her skinny-ass sandwich and flounce out of the franchise; instead, she threw back her head, laughed like a jackal, then said, "Ari said you were smart. He has no idea. Now save me the trouble of leaping across the table and hand over that burger."

Three hours, two shakes, and two double-doubles later, they were friends for life. Marion introduced her to Patti and Maya, who also practiced noncompetitive female bonding.

That was enough to cause the other socialite wives to take note and retract their claws. Everyone sucked up to Marion. She was an alpha with moolah. And a heart. In L.A., that equaled MAJOR INFLUENCE.

And Marion had no truck with gossip.

If she had, Pepper knew she and Ari would be roastin' in one of those Dante circles of hell her hometown pastor had always mixed up.

Meanwhile, after climaxing, Ari was reconfiguring his clothing and smoothing back his Euro-long locks while he considered the reception they were going to. Richard Zane wanted everyone to meet and, hopefully, donate to the Senate campaign of Jack Powell, an Internet venture-capital millionaire. Ari had done business with the man and found him untrustworthy. Surely, George Kousakis would be intrigued by any inside information he'd learn about a future senator who might end up on a trade committee.

Ari also wondered what Richard was building this time.

Pepper wondered if Marion would serve those little pigs in a blanket.

And if she'd remembered to wear underwear.

4

Patti

As Patti Fink leaned across her eighty-two-year-old husband, Lou, to adjust the custom Louis Vuitton cover on his oxygen tank, one of her big perfect breasts flopped out. Lou twinkled awake and stole a playful nipple nip. This so shocked Felix Vasquez, the driver of their Rolls, he blew through the red light at Sunset and Whittier and barely avoided a four-car wreck by doing a one-eighty slide to the curb of the opposing lane.

He'd thought Lou was semi-catatonic.

Ass up across Lou's lap, Patti giggled at the excitement. She was always up for excitement. It was the next best thing to passion.

"Madre de Dios!" whispered Felix, who crossed himself then felt his chest to make sure his heart had restarted.

Lou gave Patti's three-hundred-dollar Agent Provocateur turquoise panties a fanny smack. "Don't kill me yet!" he bellowed at Felix. "I want another piece of this before I kick."

"I'm very, very sorry, Mrs. Fink! I did not expect . . . are you all right?" Felix asked.

The chunky, whipped-butter highlights in Patti's caramel mane joggled like agreeable sea anemones as her carpet-muffled voice bubbled up from the backseat floor. "Yes, yes. We're fine, Felix. It's only your second day. You'll get the hang of it, *muy pronto*."

Felix was Patti's gardener's nephew. When a terrible landslide wiped out his Honduran village, Patti insisted on spiriting all seven members of his family into the United States. The population of their tent camp, in the backyard of her Beverly Park estate, had swelled to eighteen. Right now Felix was wishing he had continued trying to dig his moped out of the jungle mud instead of emigrating.

"Thank you, Mrs. Fink."

"*Erhardt,*" barked Lou. "She's mine now."

The Rolls lurched forward as Felix searched for a suitable place to U-turn. "Yes, I'm sorry, Mrs. *Erhardt.*"

When Patti had spotted Lou's third wife's obituary in the *Mercury News* (she always subscribed to the Silicone Valley local between husbands), she took it as a sign from Mother/Father God. *The woman had died on Patti's thirty-ninth birthday.* She flew up for the funeral that afternoon to pay her condolences. Two months later, she and Lou wed in Palm Springs.

Patti'd already used up all the Vegas chapels.

"Which one is he?" asked Lou, refering to Felix in a little-too-loud whisper as he helped Patti right herself.

"Felix. He's the sister's oldest boy," said Patti, who never remembered to whisper.

"So damn many of 'em. Tell him to stay out of the tequila."

"Pay no attention to him, Felix," Patti called out while jabbing Lou in the ribs (very, *very* lightly).

Lou was Louis Erhardt III, holder of multiple microchip patents and legend of Silicone Valley. He was one of the original Cal Poly Five, and his inventions were cited in textbooks from Harvard to Berkeley. He was the only manufacturer to beat back military brass and insist on co-patents on directional missile systems. Lou had survived six earthquakes, ten lawsuits, two fires, umpteen bar brawls, three wives, syphilis, and cancer to become the principal shareholder of the largest microcomputer component manufacturer in the world.

Or, in Patti's words, "He pretty much invented tiny chips and stuff."

Patti Fink Finnegan McKay de Beers Suzuki Erhardt had been permanently christened Patti Fink by her girlfriends, who got tired of constantly updating their contact and invitation lists. Eleven of Patti's thirteen stepchildren were also referred to as "Finks." (Lou's kids, at fifty and forty-eight, were older than Patti, and therefore were allowed to retain their surnames.) At any given time, at least five of her stepchildren were warring with their respective birth mothers and residing at Lou and Patti's house. To keep track, Patti had had the names and birthdays of the children, whose ages ranged from eleven to twenty-two, tattooed on the inside of her left wrist.

She pretty much invented "Gang Waxing."

She would gladly have taken in Lou's children, too, but since they were currently suing her husband for their former shares of his $9 billion estate, it would've been "awkward."

Moments later it was Patti's turn to cross herself as the Rolls careened past the big white wrought-iron-festooned Mediterranean on the corner of Lexington and Benedict Canyon. She and Finnegan (number two) bought the house from Xavier Cugat (former husband of Charo). Finn called it their "coochie-coochie" nest. Patti wasn't Catholic. She just made the gesture whenever she passed real estate she'd inhabited with late husbands. It felt respectful.

Aside from the tank and wheelchair, Lou was pretty frisky for eighty-two. He loved snapping Patti's frothy garter belts while singing "Yes, We Have No Bananas." And he hardly ever needed a soft diet.

"Where are we going again, sweet stuff?" he asked.

Lou was crackers for Patti.

After disentangling her Marni sandal's five-inch heel from the seat belt, Patti refluffed her Marni jacket, Marni tank, Marni skirt, and Marni beads—it was always best to get the entire runway look so it was clear what went with what—then opened Lou's shirt button, blew him a tummy raspberry, and replied, "Marion's."

"What for?"

"I think it's Richard's thing. Marion called, I said we'd come."

Lou was cool with the vagueness. Patti always took him to fun events with great food. He was happy to be aboveground. Shoving a hand under her bum (for circulation), he nodded off as Patti whipped out a mirror to check her makeup.

Lou always told her he loved her "crazy green eyes."

They didn't always look crazy.

Patti was not crackers for Lou.

He was number five. Number four died of a heart attack. Three from an aneurysm. Two was a mountain-climbing fall, and her first husband died from a hit-and-run while jogging.

She got half price at Vera Wang. And Forest Lawn.

Although Lou was the object of all her wifely devotion and affection, the last time Patti had married for love—mad, passionate, I'll-work-while-you-get-your-master's love—was number one, Barry Fink.

And his will left everything to his *former* wife, the one who refused to have kids and ran off with the mold inspector.

Patti sighed and wiped the spittle from Lou's chin. What a sweetie. She'd let him sleep a bit before taking another run at the tank cover.

She checked her Louis Vuitton–covered (to match Lou's oxygen tank) BlackBerry to see what tonight's affair was about.

Whoo! Her schedule was packed. It made her eyeballs ache. (Or was it the lash extensions?) There were dinner parties, doctors' appointments, shrink, trainer, facials, hair, tailor, healer, doctor, chiropractor, Rolfer, dentist, Chinese medicine, homeopath, stylist, tarot, Pilates, Power Plates, contractor, decorator, college counselor for the youngest stepson from her third marriage, Lou's cardiologist, dermatologist for the gardener's nephew (so the poor child could develop some self-confidence), travel agent, Spanish tutor, and, of course, her own parties and girlfriend dates.

Then there were the RSVP'd events. This month alone, she had the Valentino Spring Collection Against Breast Cancer, the Mercedes Drives to Cure Aids, a séance given by a jeweler who wanted to speak with the late Dadaist Beatrice Woods to get the secret of her ceramic glazes for beads, six trunk shows, Rock Meets Gaultier, her fourth stepdaughter's school fund-raising gala, LACMA Fashion Pioneers Week, the Kenneth J. Lane Luncheon of Hope and a dinner party for the latest revolutionary dog psychiatrist.

So much cool stuff . . . and she'd need new outfits for each one. Patti hoped that Marion wouldn't mind her inviting Craig-the-stylist to Richard's thing tonight.

But what *was* Richard's thing? There was no info in the BlackBerry. Guess she'd forgotten to give the info to her middle stepdaughter to enter. (Who has time to learn all these toys? By the time you do, they've invented a new one.) Oh well, no matter. She'd do anything for Marion.

Their friendship went back to the days when they were kids; two young and clueless wives, facing the world together. Patti didn't have enough fingers and toes to count the times the woman had pulled her tush out of the fire; without judgment, only support. Marion knew more about Patti than anyone on earth . . . alive. Yep, Marion Zane was a true girlfriend's girlfriend.

Marion Zane knew how to shut the fuck up.

After dabbing on some of the-fabulous-new-gloss-that-plumps-your-lips-but-doesn't-burn, Patti reached across Lou and unscrewed, then rescrewed, his oxygen tank in order to get it better situated inside the custom cover.

He only turned blue for a second.

5

Maya

"No. No, that brand is *toxic chemical* pesticide. I tell you *organic only.* Ohhhhhhhh! There's a big difference. When you spray bush with chemical, it goes into groundwater and washes to sea and poisons fish and evaporates into air and ends up in breast milk and testiclesssssssssss."

As she spoke, Maya shifted her hips, which were sticking to the backseat of the vegetable-oil-powered Escalade, so her husband, Tom, had a better angle to continue the enthusiastic cunnilingus. But the conversation with her gardeners was still distracting her focus.

"You spray that shit and you are giving women breast cancer and men ball cancer and children small penis and bad brains so they can't learn and turn into criminals who mug me in my driveway when I'm eighty-two. *Ahhhhhh!* . . . Yes, I know Bel Air Garden Tour is not for two months . . . Yes, the garden has to be perfect. But unpolluted . . . *mmm* . . . so don't be bad boys no more. Use Neem oil . . . good . . . byyyyyeee . . . ! You can smell that chemical stuff. Iiieeee smelled it. If even one woman smells chemicals during the tour, *ahhh,* one hour later, we are in every blog and newsstand as environmentalist-hypocrites. As . . . as . . . 'Polluuuuuuut-erssssssss.'"

Having spent almost half of her life as one of the most famous supermodels on the planet, Maya was at an age when gals in her profession started scrambling for a reality-TV gig. Yet her rock-star sashay was still the most desired and highest-priced of the catwalks, her selling power without peer. If you lived in civilization, you couldn't go through a day without seeing her exotic, six-foot Chechen self on a billboard, TV, periodical cover, or Web site.

Yes, *Chechen*. Maya was the offspring of an Afro-Asian basketball player and a Ural Mountains beauty. She had won the Pick-Six genetic code of all three races. Plastic surgeons gave seminars on the elongated construction of "Maya Eyes." Dermatologists plunged oceans of collagen into faces yearning for "Maya Mouth" or "Maya Cheeks." Wigmakers developed special methods for copying the pounds of blue-black silk that cascaded to her improbably tiny waist.

Her very essence had been dissected and analyzed and marketed to the point of absurdity. If she forgot to button a button, it started an international fashion trend. Television programs, magazines, and coffee-table books were devoted to her beauty secrets and style. No drag-queen revue was complete without a "Maya."

Marrying mega–movie star Tom Hanson five years earlier had only added to her heat. Maya had grown so accustomed to the daily overreportage and false accusations of bizarre behavior that she hadn't even blinked at the "Pope-Sex" headline.

But she'd care if they called her a polluter. It was the dirtiest word in her vocabulary.

Maya equated polluters with mass murderers and said so at every public opportunity. Environmentalism was her cause célèbre. It wasn't that she didn't care about other human rights issues. She and Tom donated to dozens of legitimate organizations and movements—but howling in outrage for news cameras at, for example, a Special Olympics match just didn't work. Anyway, as far as Maya was concerned, global warming was the mother of all moral issues; all other causes would become moot if life ceased to exist on earth. Because polluters refused to reduce greenhouse gases, temperatures, extinctions and fatalities from catastrophic weather were rising at an alarming rate with no end in sight. Maya's natural temperament and the enormity of the crisis were a perfect fit.

Given her below-average acceptance capacity for crummy excuses, she scared the crap out of people at parties.

In Maya's eyes, you either "walked-like-talk" or you were "polluter."

Patti Fink had taken to carrying copies of her carbon-offsetting contracts in her wallet, next to her driver's license, out of sheer terror.

"Nobody's going to smell it in two months," Tom now said, arresting the rhythm of his lingual movements and raising the tousled blond head that had graced a dozen blockbusters.

"How do you know?" Maya retorted. "Were you professional smell expert? Before you were big-shit movie star?"

"I know what everyone's gonna smell on *my* face at the reception," Tom concluded, and dove back in as the Escalade turned from Stone Canyon Road and chugged up Sunset Boulevard.

Maya wasn't appeased. She'd hit up every power player in town to gain support for various environmental causes. Power players whose looky-loo wives would surely sign up for the Bel Air Garden Tour and a chance to march across the grounds of Maya's home with their treasured purses and judgmental eyeballs. Wives who would give up their entire handbag collection for five minutes of her husband between their thighs.

Or a chance to call her a hypocrite.

"I don't trusssst thosssssssse biiiiiitches," she moaned.

"Those bitches are your friends," gurgled Tom. "Stop squirming, you won't get away."

Maya didn't trust many women.

Marion was the exception. She would physically attack anyone who dared to dis her friend. Maya also adored the other wives in their circle, preferring Trophy-wife company to her contemporaries in the fashion world. She never caught Pepper or Patti staring at her, wishing she'd get her face into a car accident so they could steal her big-name accounts. (Still, Lyndy's fake ass was just plain sad.)

But she *trusted* Marion. And being a hostess's wet dream of a glamorous guest, Maya made sure she was on hand for all of her dear friend's fetes. It was the least she could do. Marion was the closest thing she had to a mother.

And Marion's confidence kept her out of the loony bin.

Or even darker places.

Maya stared at her left arm, outstretched and clinging to the handle above the blacked-out passenger window, and remembered her first meeting with Marion at a birthday bash for someone's forty-turning wife.

She was eighteen at the time and on regrettable advice from her agent had flown to Beverly Hills to serve as the hapless arm charm of Blancharde CEO Alvin Tessler. He was thirty years her senior and popped breath mints every three minutes. Maya was in negotiations to be the launch face for the cosmetic giant's Moonsilk foundation campaign, but Alvin hadn't once mentioned Blancharde. He was too busy showing her off like a prize pony.

After cocktails in the Arabian-themed dinner tent (the guest of honor was raised in Laguna but had just *loved* her trip to Morocco that summer), the Zanes had been seated two silk pallets across from Maya and Alvin. Every time Maya deflected Alvin's wandering hands or tactfully shifted from under his arm, she felt Marion's eyes on her. When their host invited everyone into yet another tent for dancing, Alvin was inspired to make a sickening purring sound—and suddenly Marion had materialized at her side and invited her to the ladies' room.

Maya practically bolted out of her seat.

As they scuffed their stilettos along the decomposed garden path to the main mansion, Marion linked her arm to Maya's and said, "You don't want to go that route." Then she firmly guided Maya past the waiting line for the loo and out the front door, where she whistled up a silver Ferrari and jumped in to the driver's seat. "Take this route instead."

Confused as she was, Maya's instinct was to resist the advice. A Blancharde campaign was worth millions. Economic freedom trumped self-hatred in those days. "I cannot leave. I lose Moonsilk campaign."

"Oh, bullshit. Alvin's just the CEO. I play poker with Margrite Blancharde."

Maya got into the Ferrari.

Two blocks away, she burst into tears.

Marion drove her to Diaghilev, where she didn't even wait for Maya to finish her second shot of iced vodka. "I know he's an ass, but those tears in your eyes weren't for Alvin."

Maya had no reply. She wasn't used to women giving a shit about how she felt.

Marion reached across the table, grabbed Maya's left wrist, and shoved up the sleeve to reveal ten tiny scars and two fresh-healing cuts, just below the crook of her elbow. "Those tears are about this."

Maya started to wonder if the bright-eyed, prying American was a witch. She'd been careful. The gauzy Gucci blouse had stayed buttoned to the wrist all night.

"Don't look so surprised, eighty degrees, you're under twenty, and you don't look like a heroin addict. I mean, this *is* Los Angeles. Plus, you winced every time Alvin grabbed your elbow. And by the way, you can see right through that blouse."

Maya yanked down her sleeve. "Are you seeing with eyes or very long nose?" she demanded.

"Fine, I'll back off. Good thing you're not up for a sunscreen account."

They drank another round in silence then Marion ordered a phone brought to the table and dialed.

"Who do you call?" Maya asked.

"My husband. I'm not fit to drive and I don't want him to use himself up on the dance floor, if you know what I mean. Hello? Will you find Mr. Richard Zane, please? Hey, baby. I'm at Diaghilev with three shots inside me, going for four. No, finish your cigar and make sure to dance with the birthday girl. Just remember, it's *Wednesday* night. Mmm . . . bye."

Maya's amazing face screwed up, then burst into laughter.

"What?" Marion asked in surprise.

"I am . . . ah . . . relief. I thought you were dyke."

Marion blew vodka out of her nose then squealed at the burn.

It didn't take long before Maya told her everything. She talked until Richard collected them at 1 A.M. What she shared Marion never told a soul.

That year, Maya landed not only the Moonsilk account, but the covers of *Sports Illustrated* and the *Victoria's Secret* catalog. Her arms healed completely.

Though they rarely got as shit-faced as they'd gotten on their first encounter, Marion and Maya became permanent fixtures at Diaghilev's Wednesday Night Happy Hour.

Eighteenth-century French-wrought iron gates swung open—the guards knew the car—revealing the Beverly Hills golden-age splendor of the Zane compound. The SUV rolled through, leaving the caravan of paparazzi outside.

"We are here," said a muffled Slavic voice behind a black partition.

"I'm not. Not yet." Maya giggled.

Tom also giggled, sending volts of pleasure up her spine. "Do that laugh, again!"

Vlad, Maya's ferocious personal assistant and bodyguard, who resembled a mirthless Mr. Clean, got out and waved off valets as his employers finished.

6

Claire

The Mansion Moment! As her husband of three weeks, producer Billy Price drove their Bentley (Moment Car) through the magical gates of Zane, Claire got so excited her teeth bit the hangnail she'd been worrying down to the quick. She didn't feel it. She was too busy experiencing tingles. There was the Spanish-tile fountain, the sculpture garden, and there was the tower. She'd read up on this Moorish castle, mentioned in California architectural guides alongside Hearst. And they'd been *invited* inside. She savored her view like good gravy as they crawled up the drive, lined with stone urns of overflowing succulents under old-growth sycamores and pines.

The Mansion Moment was part of the "Secret Rainbow Princess Promise" that Claire cultivated during her disappointing childhood in Winamac, Indiana. It fell under the category of "Glamorous Parties and Balls."

"It's not 'magical thinking,' it's *your* bottom line. They pushed back the play-offs. It's the weekend of Final Four!"

Billy was still on the phone, arguing about a release date with someone named Barry who did something at Quantum Studios. Claire made a mental note to learn more names and histories of the players in her new town. Back home, she knew everything about everybody. Billy and his friends might as well have been speaking Chinese at the restaurant last night. Even the waitress smirked at their in-jokes. She hated feeling left out.

Like right now.

"Kids? Sammy, are you hearing this? Barry thinks kids'll still go. Maybe little *girls,* but who'll drive them? Mommy and big sis are too busy making nachos and onion dip for the guys in the living room. Hey, there's a coveted demographic. Little-girls-with-chauffeurs-or-homely-single-mothers . . . don't start with the 'sexist,' you know that I'm right."

"You are right, sweetheart. I always made snacks for guys during Final Four," offered Claire. "Pizza rolls, steak bites, and deviled—"

"Honey, *please.* I gotta listen." Billy covered his tiny microphone stick.

She wasn't used to him being this sharp. Back home, he was a pussycat.

Diving back into her Mansion Moment, Claire craned her neck to view the backyard, but the buildings were so vast they blocked her view. She recognized the old stable and barn, now converted into underground parking. Two men stood on a side driveway that must have once been the bridal path. They wore beautiful suits.

Did Billy own suits? She'd seen none so far. So much to learn.

Claire got the impression that the suit men were arguing. They didn't look happy and they weren't speaking to each other.

"Warner's switched for Paul Greengrass. His date was on Elite Eight."

When Billy argued, his lip stuck out and reminded Claire of her mother's Siamese purebred. She'd miss that slinky kitty.

But she wasn't homesick. Not for a second.

Who'd miss cold slushy sidewalks and fried onion blossoms?

Claire had hooked up with Billy while his production company was "shooting on location." As Festival Queen, she was Pulaski County's Ambassador Hostess.

The crown was a dime.

"Ambassador Hostess" really meant lost hours from work, babysitting boring, fat business associates of some councilman who didn't want drunks in his house. Not one foreign dignitary. There *was* that Toyota executive from Osaka, but it didn't matter how rich he was; Asian guys reminded Claire of science fiction. She'd been so discouraged she was beginning to regret turning down Kelly Hardemann, the Beaver City College football star, whose dad owned the bottling plant.

Kelly had eczema *and* halitosis.

Then Billy came along.

When she got the call to go down to the county seat, Claire dragged her heels and almost forgot to lip-gloss. Two years of college and she was still the lowest-paid manager at the Bi-Rite. Would this waste-of-time year never end?

When she first laid eyes on the tan, antsy guy in a sweatshirt—who didn't have the class to remove his ball cap indoors—Claire knew she'd hit bottom. Now they were making her escort a hunting outfitter. He probably reeked of deer piss.

When she heard he was doing a movie for Hollywood (home of *American Idol*), she almost knocked over the mayor in her haste to make the acquaintance of such a glamorous, powerful person.

"Winamac is an Indian term for catfish."

Claire spent the entire day giving Billy her best "Points of Interest" tour. He found her "points" interesting.

The minute she dropped Billy off at his hotel, she rushed home to her parents' apartment above the bank-turned-cell-phone-store, locked herself in her bedroom, and went to work.

Claire didn't make a move without Google. Her eyes became sponges for any site that mentioned Billy Price's name. So many listings. So much to read.

By midnight, she knew she would marry him.

William Price made blockbusters.

William Price had a three-picture deal with Quantum Studios.

William Price lived in a Holmby Hills classic that had sold for upward of $12 million.

William Price took his daughters to the Golden Globes.

William Price made eight figures off his last movie.

William Price took his mother to the Oscars.

William Price was *divorced*!

Claire made up for low Bi-Rite wages by working as the "civic liaison" for Billy's production company. Hollywood paid so well! Within a month, Billy grew tired of coming up with questions about ordinances concerning Winnebago parking and asked her out on a date.

She still remembered their first; sharing a submarine and watching the technicians blow up a mini mall. Her "Rainbow Princess Promise" had said there'd be fireworks.

But did Billy feel them? She couldn't tell jack from his chaste good-night kiss.

After three dates with chaste kisses, she began to feel fat.

Claire was a devoted "rules girl," but she was also no fool. This prudish producer was probably her last shot at fulfilling her "promise." Next year's birthday would be number twenty-six. So she bet the farm, seducing him in the Arby's parking lot. She even did that "special trick" she learned from last June's issue of *Cosmo*.

The one she had been saving for her marriage bed.

It worked.

They wed at the wrap party.

Even though she never got the "Great Big Wedding" of her "Promise" fulfilled, Billy was a fairy tale come true.

Even if she was his *second wife*.

Claire was the real and final Mrs. Billy Price now. And she could hardly wait to become a "lotus-eater."

"Fuck."

Claire banged out of her reverie. Billy had never cursed before.

"Honey, I lost the signal. I gotta go down to the gate and get this done. I need you to go inside. We both can't be late."

The valet opened her door, unsealing the newlyweds like a fresh jar of pickles.

Go inside alone? This was worse than left out.

"But . . ."

"Marion's a sweetheart. She'll take great care of you. I'll only be a minute. Gimme kiss."

Claire already knew just how long a Hollywood "minute" could stretch. But she put on a brave face for her guy. She'd make her Entrance Moment alone, a mysterious beauty.

Claire had dwelled in the prettiest-girl-in-the-room comfort zone ever since she could walk.

Playing the theme to Disney's *Cinderella* in her head, she wafted up the time-polished steps, which were wide enough for a marching band. She had on her best suit—to set off her deep navy eyes and hug her swimsuit-competition curves without looking slutty. Thanks to egg yolks and one thousand brushstrokes before bed, her minky-brown hair was as shiny and bouncy as a Pantene ad. Light makeup, Mentos breath.

She was a beautiful maiden arriving at the ball.

As a black-suited butler answered the door, a woman with huge amber eyes and a waterfall of spun-gold hair hooked her chin over his shoulder and drawled, "Hi. Who the hell are you?"

Pepper, lithe and lovely in a white wool Dolce & Gabbana sheath, was the most beautiful woman Claire had ever seen.

Inside the cavernous foyer, the place was lousy with "most beautiful" women.

Claire was a plastic plant in the garden of Versailles.

She removed her small-gauge pearls in the powder room.

7

Deer in the Headlights

Out of the corner of her eye, Marion saw "his" and "hers" matching eye jobs advancing her way. Ah, the Cuscos (huge Democratic donors). She'd introduce them to her favorite new congresswoman, Maxine Dahl (in need of filing dough), who was hovering near Max Wallert (waste of time, he's red).

She snagged Jeff by the sleeve and was about to direct him to go generous on the Cuscos' drink orders when he took her aside.

"Xiocena called. Angel's Hope is overloaded, so they're still waiting to be seen."

"What are they doing at Angel's Hope? Xio lives two blocks away from Mercy."

"Mercy's trauma center was shut down. They were referred to Angel's."

"Has the girl seen a doctor yet?" she asked.

"Don't know. Xiocena had to get back inside so they wouldn't lose their place in line."

"The *second* she calls back, let me talk to her."

"Yes, Mrs. Zane."

"*Shit.*"

"Was there anything else?"

"Yeah. Um. Please use fat fingers with the Cusco drinks. Oh, Jeff. This is awful."

"Got it."

Marion took a second to switch modes then spun around and took both of the Cuscos' hands in her own.

"I adore you for coming on such short notice."

(French double air-kisses.)

"So, Jack Powell was bought out of Crane," whispered Ron Cusco.

(More like *forced* out.)

But Marion didn't take the bait. "As long as he hands the gavel to our side."

"Here, here."

"Have you met the new congresswoman representing the fourteenth district? The Honorable Maxine Dahl, Ron and Janet Cusco."

(And handoff.)

She felt like a friggin' social director on a cruise ship, pairing up people and conjuring up games so no one would notice that there was still no Jack Powell. She wouldn't give a shit if this was a dinner party; her chef, Roger, knew better than to have meals ready until an hour after arrival time, but Angelenos were uncharacteristically on time for political events. (Because they wanted them to *end* on time. Several of her guests had agreed to come on the condition that the reception was "hour and a half—tops.") She wanted to go ask Powell's campaign manager what was up, but the main wave of arrivals was flowing in fast. A quick room scan for Ivan found only Patti Fink, wedging between two pin-striped backsides.

(Give eyes a moment to recover from Patti's hair and wardrobe.)

Patti Fink was the only human Marion knew who could air-kiss, speak, and calculate net worth at the same time.

"Who's the woman in Armani?" Patti asked.

"Joan Hoyard."

(Did Joan look cooler since their lunch? Hard to tell.)

"Sold Cal-Con at two-point-one billion. That short man's Greg Dutcher?" Patti asked.

"Yep."

"F&T Offshore." Patti nodded. "Four-point-seven, going up. I know you won't gossip but his wife is boinking her trainer and it's just a matter of time, so I think you could invite Lou's spinster daughter to an intimate dinner with—"

Marion had her hands over her ears. "La-la-la-la-la-la . . ."

(Anyway, she knew, through her sources, that Lou's daughter was a lesbian.)

"Right. And the guy in vintage Matsuda?" Patti asked.

"Ramos Sanchez."

"The muralist?"

"Just for you. Tell me, is Lou's tank well connected?"

But Patti was already making a beeline for the artist. She beelined back and yanked Marion close. "Gina Greenberg's husband has a fake glass eye, so talk to his left one or you'll get dizzy and scared. I forgot his name."

"Paul. Thanks."

"And Jorge got into Brown. Thanks."

"Glad to help."

Marion had written so many college recommendation letters for Patti's stepchildren that she'd finally developed a standard form and filled in the blanks.

Patti beelined away.

(Sneak attack. Air-kiss Lyndy.) "No one should look so gorgeous for a Democrat's event. I see you're wearing my dress."

"I'll trade you for that purse," said Marion.

"From my cold, dead hand. Seriously, where's your boy wonder? Time's a-wastin' and I've got a chauffeur to fire."

"Jeez. If I didn't know you better, I'd say you were almost cheery," Marion marveled. (Fake searching around the crowd and pretending to spot Powell.) "Over there talking strategy with Nancy Bren."

"Then with any luck, we'll be home for sunrise. Waiter! Gin and tonic, rocks, with a squeeze of lime and no tonic."

Marion greeted three more couples, then noticed everyone's head turning left in unison.

The Hansons were in the house.

"Oh, wow! You got fat!" boomed Tom Hanson.

After giving Marion his customary greeting and squishes (reset hair), Tom busied himself with a drink order while Marion towed Maya over to a man who looked like a tired magician.

"Maya, have you met Marshall Perry?" Marion asked her friend.

Marshall kissed Maya's hand. "You partake in politics, my dear? How shockingly delightful."

(And shockingly lame.)

After his latest script, *East of Hades*, an action thriller set in Chechnya, went over $120 million at the box office, Marshall Perry had adopted a pseudo-intellectual-gent persona and looked down his nose at everyone.

When Marion screened *East of Hades,* Maya had practically thrown rocks at the projectionist. Evidently, the film was pathetically inaccurate, clichéd, and bigoted to boot. Basically, Perry bugged the shit out of Marion. She didn't invite Marshall as a guest. He was the entertainment. As in Colosseum.

"Marshall wrote *East of Hades,* Maya."

"The one set in Chechnya?"

Marshall puffed proudly. Maya broke into a huge, toothy smile. Like all Chechens do just before they kill somebody.

"Your movie is bullshit."

"I beg you pardon?" he asked.

"You misportray people, culture, and history. The dialogue is shit. It's the work of a hack."

Shock and insult rendered Marshall's face into something resembling an angry Cabbage Patch doll. "Pardon my frank analysis, honey, but what the fuck would a rag mannequin know about Russian dialogue, let alone Chechnya?"

(Annnd over the falls!)

Marion believed such carefully staged "incidents" as this one made parties successful, and from the looks on everyone's face within earshot, she was right. They looked like kids at a birthday party before the piñata broke. She couldn't name a political reception where folks had looked this happy.

"Douche bag didn't even recognize the accent," she said, taking Tom's arm and walking away.

"Soaking wet, she looks Persian," quipped Tom. He was used to this.

While Maya reduced Marshall to pulp in English, Chechen, Ingush, *and* Russian, Marion directed Tom to go flirt with Constance Ross. She was the estranged wife of Willard Ross, the leveraged buyout specialist. Marion knew for a fact that Willie cheated; anything with tits and a pulse. Connie needed kind words and an ego boost.

(Another donation, assured.)

If Jack-Powell-the-Rude ever chose to show up.

Twenty minutes late. The Marshall smack-down was supposed to be his opening act. The campaign manager was on his second drink. That couldn't be good.

Marion took a search lap, wading through snatches of conversation.

A hostess's welcome was glazed on her face, but her *ears* were set on "Reap."

"Did you hear about Broadcom? The *real* story is . . ."

". . . daughter got arrested."

"He's overleveraged. It's over."

". . . was picked up by Sony. It's crap but don't tell."

"Just between you and me . . ."

". . . strictly confidential."

"It's true."

Some of it was. Once gleaned, threshed, and ground down, the information harvest around her was surprisingly bountiful. Of course, Marion had an ironclad rule not to pass gossip. *Never. Ever.* But the *Black Book* *remembered* everything. A girl's gotta keep up . . .

"Marion, should I buy Cal Nova?"

"No. Talk to Marvin Freeland and learn why."

"Marion, do you have a good tree service?"

"Jim Scott in Santa Monica."

"Marion, we're going to India."

"You want the Kohinoor suite at the Oberoi. I'll send you the manager's number."

"Marion, who do you know in Dubai?"

"Call me tomorrow."

"Marion, who's Maya callin' hog afterbirth?"

(Air-kiss Pepper and Ari.)

"Marshall Perry. But I wish she would beat the crap out of Jack Powell instead. Have you seen him anywhere?"

"Wouldn't know 'im if he sat on m' lap," Pepper replied.

"Have you met George Kousakis yet?"

"Do we have to?"

"Pepper!" warned Ari.

"He's right over here," Marion said, and steered the couple over to a very short, scowling fellow who seemed to be boring the hell out of Drake Volger, the architect. Upon seeing Marion, Kousakis forgot the space-and-form genius existed.

"Here is my beautiful hostess. You know, I was telling Richard a while ago that you two must visit me this summer."

(French double air-kiss from eight-inch minimum.)

"George, have you met the fabulous Aristotle and Pepper Papado-poulos?"

Kousakis looked at Ari like he'd smelled a fart. Pepper shifted uncomfortably.

"Oh, yes. You're the one that got caught," said Kousakis.

Marion spoke so quickly she thought her tongue would catch fire. "Don't tell me you played fool to *that* old rumor, George. *Everybody's* known better for years. Next you'll be asking about gerbils . . ."

Kousakis's phone rang. It didn't vibrate. It *rang*. Loudly.

(Could he get any more rude?)

(Yes. He was answering it.)

"If you'll excuse me, Marion. Papadopouloses."

He smooshed past Pepper and headed to the front door. Just like that.

"Ari, I'm sorry . . ."

"No, darling. We'll speak later. It's fine."

Ari didn't linger in shame. He pivoted and immediately joined Drake Volger in teasing Tom about being offered the part of Robin Hood in a new movie.

Marion turned to Pepper and squeezed her hand. "I'll set up another go, later."

"That'll go nowhere. You saw 'im, Marion. He hates the Papadopoulos brothers. They won't pay his bribes and now he's askin' for shares. Li'l midget felt my ass as he pushed past! I'd say that's a dominance gesture. He knows I'll do nothin' cuz he's got the family by the balls."

"Two words: *Natura Thesally*," Marion said.

"Who's she?"

Marion winked.

Richard didn't look flustered at all. He was gabbing and laughing with Billy Price—where was his bride?

But before she could reach him, the mayor blindsided Marion with a hug. She hugged back. He was one of the good guys.

(Reset hair.)

"Good evening, Your Honor. How is Elena's hip doing?"

"My mother is fine, thank you. A new woman. Your surgeon did wonders. You've got quite a crowd here."

Yeah, just about every full wallet in town. You could almost see the little dollar signs in the mayor's eyes go *ching-ching*. Who could blame him? In politics, it's either fund-raise or die.

"Where's Jack?" the mayor asked.

"On my way to find out. Allow me to introduce you to my dashing friend . . ."

(Air-kiss Ramos Sanchez.)

"Oh, my God, the muralist?"

"Ramos, the mayor is obviously a fan and he's about to dedicate a long-overdue park, next to Chinatown, that is just screaming for one of your works."

(And handoff!)

Marion sidled up to her husband. He was trying to follow Ron Cusco's story about Warren Buffett, but she only needed one-third of his attention anyway.

"You say 'hey' to the mayor?"

"Hugged, backslapped, and thanked."

"Then maybe you can get him to deliver a speech before our guests switch political parties. Powell's thirty minutes late."

"He'll be back in a minute."

"From where?"

"Service driveway. He had to talk to some guy about business. Ivan's with him . . ."

(???????)

". . . Clinton was always late."

"Clinton was *Clinton*!"

Without waiting for Ron's punch line, she hauled ass toward the kitchen.

By chance, Marion glanced in the ladies'-powder-room foyer and saw a pretty young woman (out-of-state) adjusting and readjusting herself.

Suit jacket open, suit jacket closed, lip gloss on, lip gloss off, refluff hair. Oh, no. Sweating. Repowder, reblush . . .

The girl was getting rough with herself.

She recognized the panic, not an unusual state for first-timers to contract at Westside parties. This must be Billy's missing bride. Better stop her before she melts into a puddle of wet cosmetics and self-loathing. She slipped into the powder room and shut the door.

Claire almost jumped out of her skin.

"Hi. I'm Marion and you must be Claire."

"Oh, God. I'm usually not . . ."

(Like a shiny deer, caught in the headlights?)

"You look lovely. Really."

She looked like she was going to cry. Claire was already comparing their features in the mirror. This neural pathway had to be broken. Fast.

"Most of the women here started out as shopgirls or whores."

(Lie. Okay, partial lie.)

"And most of them are so self-absorbed that they'll only notice your face as a beautiful younger-than-themselves blur. So don't waste the Lancôme."

"Huh?"

"But they're all very nice. Well, one's a bit crabby but you don't have to meet her."

(Lyndy.)

Claire gave a little smile. "This bathroom is very . . . nice."

Marion looked around the room as if she were noticing the lacquered walls with inlaid mother-of-pearl Tree of Life designs for the first time. The ceiling had a small fresco of Venus looking down from sun-rosied clouds with smirking Cupids fluttering around her hips. The vanity was carved rose quartz. When she and Richard had first looked at the 1920s mansion, she had seen the possibilities, but it was this little jewel of a bathroom that had sold her on the house. It told her that it was built at a time when people still believed in magic and romance.

"Why, thank you," she said. "It's my favorite room in the house. Now put down the puff and let me introduce you around."

Claire lowered her compact.

"They don't bite."

(Well, maybe Lyndy. But only after her third gin and tonic and the evening's young.)

Claire haltingly put her makeup bag in her purse.

(Slowly now, or she'll bolt.)

"That's right. Come on . . . . come on . . ."

Claire allowed herself to be led out of the powder room. Marion grabbed her arm, spied Patti, Pepper, and Maya cliquing up near the Rodin, and hauled Claire over.

"Have you met dear Claire? She's the beauty who stole Billy Price's heart."

"Oh. Congratulations. We loooove Billy. So talented. His hair is all real," trilled Patti. "I'm Patti Fink!"

"Th-thanks. Nicetomeetyou."

Marion gave them all a look that said, *Gentle with the newbie.* "Claire was a consultant for local government back in Indiana, so she'll have a lot in common with you, Pepper."

Claire looked shocked and heartbreakingly appreciative for the euphemism.

Pepper gave a wide Southern smile. "Well, I'm sure we do. Pepper Papadopoulos. Billy's got half custody, right? Two girls?"

"Three. Six, nine, and thirteen. They're adorable. You have children?"

"Six, five, four, two, an' ten months."

Pepper's pancake-flat belly wasn't lost on Claire. "Maybe our sixes could playdate?" she asked.

"Your six is a masochist?"

Patti, meanwhile, was reviewing the list on her wrist. "I've got two fourteens, two fifteens . . . oh, here's a sixteen."

"Is it hard raising twins?" Claire asked.

"Huh? I don't have any twins," said Patti. But she checked her wrist again, to be sure.

"I fucking hated his ex-wife," offered Maya.

"Beg your pardon?" Claire gulped.

Marion excused herself.

She stepped out the kitchen side door, looked around, and suddenly regretted never having dropped acid in her youth. She had no excuse but to accept the scene before her as reality.

In the service driveway, Jack Powell was scowling at some guy in a too-tight jacket.

Ivan was handing Too-Tight-Jacket cash.

A lot of cash.

"I take it this man's not your cabbie," Marion announced.

When he saw her, Jack Powell shimmied like he wished to disappear, making Marion think of a *Star Trek* episode when the transporter wasn't working. Jack finally managed a politician's grin but couldn't find his voice.

(So many deer tonight.)

Before she could get out a good sailor's curse, Ivan gestured toward Too-Tight-Jacket. "This individual is a business associate of Mr. Powell's and he's blackmailing him for fifty thousand dollars in exchange for a disk which contains incriminating digital images which could deep-six his senatorial—"

"Marion, I was set up. I had no idea—" Jack protested.

"Images of what?"

"Gambling," barked Jack.

What a crappy lie. Internet guys were supposed to be creative.

"It does not matter," said Ivan in his soft German accent. "This individual is now paid off in cash and we will deposit this reimbursement check from Mr. Powell in the morning. Mr. Powell is going to go inside and stop embarrassing his fine hosts, and this individual whose name you do not wish know is going to hand over his home movie and vanish back into the shadows from whence he came."

On cue, Too-Tight-Jacket handed a memory stick to Ivan. Jack clutched for it, but Ivan tucked it in his inside breast pocket. Jack immediately looked for something to do with his hands.

Nobody ever argued with Ivan. It wasn't physicality; he was barely six feet and trim. And his face was more male model than bouncer. Yet when he was serious, most people went docile. She'd seen trainers who brought vicious dogs to heel with the same effortless, dominance mojo. Pepper always said men were dogs.

"I will destroy this immediately," announced Ivan.

"What if he made copies?" mewled Jack.

"He will not because he knows I will find him."

Too-Tight-Jacket twitched, blinked, and made for the gate.

What had he recorded Jack doing? Marion wondered. It had to be sex. The guy didn't look clever enough to deal drugs, let alone document bribery or fraud.

"I apologize for the delay, Mrs. Zane," Ivan told her. "The reception can now proceed as planned."

"Thank you for taking care of this, Ivan."

"You don't want to know." Ivan turned to Jack. "Please return to the party, Mr. Powell; there are many guests waiting to hear why they should give you their money."

Marion latched a steel grip on Jack Powell's arm and steered him away. Jack stopped outside the kitchen door.

"Marion, I never meant for you to—"

"Yes, I regret it too, Jack. And I'm certainly not going to press you for the ugly details, but I am going to tell you that if you are ever so pathetically stupid as to engage in *anything* that could compromise your election and our stellar endorsement again, I'll personally see to it that you get elected as chicken-head latrine bitch of L.A. County Jail. Now get your ass inside and stop embarrassing my husband."

Mumbling something about "freshening up," Jack dashed off, dodging past the kitchen staff like a tailback.

(Ugh. Thank God for Ivan.)

If anyone deserved a three-month vacation, it was him.

Marion and Ivan's stars had first crossed when she and Richard took her stepkids to Guatemala for a tour of Tikal with Conservation International. They were staying in the jungle, at a charming camp that also served as a way station for injured animals; taking meals in the company of gorgeous tame parrots and toucans and touring the majestic temples and plazas with renamed experts in the fields of anthropology, primatology, and ethnobotany. When Marion first laid eyes on the dangerously handsome man chatting quietly in German at the camp owner's table one evening, she naturally assumed there was a fashion shoot going on in the neighborhood. She never dreamed he'd been summoned as protection from ex-paramilitary groups who had no civilian skills aside from kidnapping for ransom. That sort of thing only went on in Colombia or Mexico.

The trip had been going as well as expected. Dickie Jr., ten at the time, was thrilled by the excursion and behaving like an angel—they didn't find out about his theft of the tourist center's fifteen-hundred-year-old skull until they returned home. True to form, eight-year-old Crystal kept up a constant litany of complaints about the jungle being "too green," the animals "probably diseased," and the ruins "totally ghetto" from the moment they landed. When she failed to show up for breakfast on the third day, everyone considered it a blessing and gave thanks to the gods of anorexia. The scene outside Crystal's hut told another story.

The front door had been smashed into firewood and three men in ski masks and camouflage lay dead on the ground. Two with broken necks, one stabbed through the heart. Ivan was untying the nanny and Crystal was unharmed, hopping around, and delightedly squealing about how "the German dude got medieval on the punks with bad cargo pants." It was first time the child had smiled all week.

Marion never was sure how Ivan disposed of the bodies and ushered the Zanes straight to their plane without having to deal with local or national police authorities. All she knew was he got them back in time for the beginning of classes after Harvard Westlake's spring break. No customs, no nothin'. As Crystal said, the man had "mad skills."

Marion repaid him with a job for life. Ivan miraculously obtained his own green card and citizenship. Marion hadn't regretted her offer for a moment and never questioned Ivan's methods of operation. Things just always worked out so well.

As Jack disappeared into the house, Marion realized that witnessing an actual blackmail payoff left her not only pissed and appalled but also a little bit amped, and she decided she had time for one more perfect margarita in the kitchen.

Alone in the driveway, Ivan whipped out a disposable phone, punched a speed-dial key, and gave the party on the other end a detailed description of Powell's blackmailer and the vehicle in which he departed. As he dictated specific instructions, his dark eyes grew merry and bright.

8

Sunk Ships and Loose Lips

Pepper sneaked into the dining room, where Roger had left her a tray of mini pigs in a blanket. She'd been the chef's crush ever since he caught her last Thanksgiving using his turkey baster bulb as a makeshift breast pump. Midchew, she felt a hand on the small of her back, working downward. A fat, tiny hand.

"Mr. Kousakis!" she yelped, spinning away. She was alone with him.

"I apologize for my brusque demeanor earlier, my dear. The Papadopoulos brothers can be quite . . . difficult. They do not possess the same negotiating skills as their father and tend to make decisions against their own best interests."

"Meanin' they won't raise yer bribes."

This only made Kousakis grin. So much for her appetite.

"Perhaps you could employ your own *skills* to persuade your husband to understand that compliance with custom will prove to be to his advantage."

He was talking to her chest.

Keeping her cool, Pepper leaned down low enough for him to almost get a clear view. Her drawl was pure honey-drip velvet. "You wanna see my skills?"

Kousakis made a stupid face and nodded like a schoolboy.

Pepper took a good down-grip on his tie. The same grip she used on Jed and Cooter when they tried to run in a parking lot.

———

Lyndy was holding court with a few captive wives in the foyer. The floor was navy-dyed marble, inlaid with a brass map of the constellations. Lyndy chose to stand at the center of the universe.

". . . oh, please. Anyone can get their picture in those new faux society magazines. They cater to the vanity of those who think they should have stature and fame merely because they have wealth. I mean, how grotesque. It's not journalism; it's commercial exploitation. Those magazines were conceived in order to draw revenue from hawkers of luxury goods placing advertisements. It's a brilliant concept from a business point of view, but that niche market has contributed to the sorry state we find ourselves in now—where there is no longer any distinction between new money and real class."

Most of Lyndy's listeners appeared to have been struck by a sudden, intense interest in astronomy. Except Maya. The editors of those lifestyle magazines had always been kind to her.

"You mean your *old California money* kind of class, Lyndy?" Maya asked. "There is no fortune in America that did not start with a cheat or a thief. Your family stole land from naked Indians. How *classy* is that?"

"The Indians? No. No, that land was newly, ah, annexed United States property, or territory. Or whatever they called a piece of land that wasn't a state yet. Open to homesteading by brave and courageous . . . homesteadering pioneers. Indians held no legal claim. And technically, they didn't even believe in ownership of any land."

But the wives had all gratefully drifted into new conversations.

Maya planted a big kiss on Lyndy's cheek, then joined Tom, who was regaling a group of non-industry types (who'd smile and nod if he recited the phone book) with Marion stories.

". . . sometimes courage and sometimes because she just didn't know any better. One year she ran all the dangerous gossip columnists out of town because she didn't like the way they picked on her friends. Like Verna Hale. Remember her, Maya?"

Maya nodded and almost felt queasy at the memory of an interview she'd had with the notorious gossip columnist.

An editor had set her up on a lunch date with Verna Hale for a "friendly interview," friendly like the Spanish Inquisition. Before she could say hello, Verna asked her if she was "boinking" Tom (yes), who was still very married at the time (yes) and kept asking straight through dessert, trying to wear her down. Maya was so scared she had to excuse herself three times to go puke in the ladies' room.

". . . nothing was off-limits," Tom went on. "She'd do a story on somebody's kid who was institutionalized or publish doctors' records. AIDS-test results! Her genius was that she wrote just enough truthful stories to enable her to mix in false ones. People believed her. She ruined marriages, careers; she caused suicides. Honey, you remember that kid-show host Verna accused of making anti-Semitic remarks?"

Maya nodded again.

"He lost everything and jumped off the roof of his accountant's building. And the story was a lie. In those days, Verna Hale totally owned the gossip market: national column, TV show, and radio. She'd destroy anyone on a whim. The studios were terrified of her."

"She always wore this heavy gold bracelet," added Maya. "A wolf's head sinking fangs into a rabbit."

"Giving her an interview made you feel like you were the bunny," said Tom. "Nobody did jack until Marion hired her own investigators to dig up Verna's 'sources' on the kid-show host and get their confessions. Richard had just bought a studio and local network and she had them feature the evidence until the nationals picked it up. That was the tipping point. People found their balls and started a class-action suit that put Verna Hale out of business."

"What happened to her?" asked Lucy Wai, who, along with her partner and husband, Satung, had recently crested a hundred million through their exclusive, luxury destination club, Castlespaces.

"Hasn't been seen in years. Maybe she went to work for Karl Rove," Tom finished.

There were big guffaws, which quickly died down to uncomfortable silence as the notion sank in. Max Wallert joined the crowd.

"Verna was married to Fred Bowman, the securities king, in my day," he put in. "Did that gossip thing after he dumped 'er without a dime."

"You're kidding?" Tom said. "Verna Hale was a Trophy wife?"

"How do you think she learned her trade?" said Max.

After comfortably dozing in his chair during the entire exchange, Lou Erhardt raised his head. "Verna Hale? I balled her back in '78 . . . she wasn't much."

Lou was an instant hit.

Patti had committed a cardinal sin. She'd left Claire alone with Craig-the-stylist. It wasn't her fault. She couldn't help it that national-treasure actress Helen Alexander was wearing an *amazing* vintage squash-blossom necklace. Patti had been to the Bean Dances at the First Mesa . . .

Craig had always wanted a young society star as a client. He was tired of being run ragged by manic-depressive underage actresses with thinning malnutrition hair and the eyes of bush babies. There were only so many size zeros available to wear without underpants. And his Trophy wives were worse. Five feet of legs topped off by D-cups—a tailoring nightmare. Those spoiled, giant geishas were already set in their "personal" style. No room for creativity. He was merely their rag gofer.

Claire was a peach-fresh lump of raw clay. One he could mold.

"Mr. Carlip, I read about you in *InStyle* magazine," Claire told him.

Meaning she'd missed that horrible *Harper's* piece where he was compared to Starbucks, may-that-columnist-burn-in-hell. Yes.

"How would you style me?" she continued.

Craig eyed her like a lion eyed a baby impala. "By leaving you alone. You're perfect."

"No, really."

"Really. Look around you. These broads have been done to death. Like they all came out of the same *Vanity Fair* layout. But *you*, Claire, are stylistically courageous."

"Me?"

This was too easy. He pretended to study her sad little suit ensemble. "A fresh young bride, clad like a blocky Republican matron. It's genius!" He gestured toward Maya. (Okay, he didn't *actually* style her, but *dreamed* he did, once.) "She'd never have the balls. All she wants me to get her is 'chic' and 'hot' . . . have you always dressed asexually?"

Claire made a consultation appointment for the next morning.

———

Marion entered the dining room from the kitchen in time to witness George Kousakis's head rock back like a bobble doll as Pepper released his tie. The man took off faster than the first customer allowed inside Barneys warehouse sale. Pepper straightened, snagged a white wine from a waiter, cruised over to where Marion was peeking out at the reception, and downed the whole glass.

"What'd you say?" Marion asked.

"Back the fuck off my family or you'll be readin' 'bout *Natura Thesally* on every front page in Athens."

"That should work."

"So tell me about her, Marion. Did he get the girl pregnant? Was she underage?"

"Actually, she was leaking."

"Come again?"

Marion decided to clear up Pepper's confusion about *Natura Thesally*. "Kousakis got his start running black-market oil back in the seventies. One night the supposedly empty tanker he was captaining sprung a leak, so rather than face jail time, he locked the six-man crew belowdecks, set some dynamite charges, and booked off in a Zodiac. He told authorities his mutinous crew was involved in smuggling oil and explosives—and no one was alive to dispute the cover-up. Problem was, when they raised the wreck, only *five* bodies showed up. Kousakis must've been haunted for years thinking that one guy might have escaped and could show up at any time to put him behind bars."

Pepper grabbed another wine from a waiter. "Okay, I know you got good sources for that *Black Book*—"

"What *Black Book*?"

"—but who on earth told you—"

"The *sixth* crew member of the *Natura Thesally*. We met Kousakis when we attended this trade conference on Malta last summer and he tagged along with a group for a dinner, on board our boat, *Triumphant*. Well, the first mate took one look at him and went for a flare gun. Our captain had to confine him to quarters. We didn't find out for two days that the mate had crewed on that tanker."

"Shut up! Why didn't he tell his story to the authorities?"

"As an oil smuggler or a mutineer? Good thing Kousakis didn't see him or he might have tried to sink *our* boat too. Anyway, since Kousakis controls a good portion of Mediterranean trade, I decided to file that info away."

"In your *Black Book!*"

"Oh, look. Jack Powell's decided to join us."

Pepper turned in time to see her husband almost knock the politician over plowing his way toward them.

He was that upset.

"What did you do to Kousakis?" Ari asked. "Don't play stupid. He joins you for hot dogs, and now he's my ass boy. *Apologizing* for bad manners! Saying my brothers misunderstood his position and that all ports in France are no charge. Did you two slip him a drug?"

"Aristotle!" cried Marion.

"Really, babe, it's all good," Pepper told him. "You just need to call Marion's first mate—"

"What?"

Marion chose that moment to bugger off.

Jack Powell was fifty minutes late and just now starting to greet the guests. That meant he wouldn't commence speaking for another twenty, meaning that the reception was going to go almost an *hour* longer than expected. His campaign manager was morbidly leaning on Lou's wheelchair, and the rest of his crew had abandoned the party to snoop around in Marion's home. The evening was stretching so long Marion caught herself spacing out. For a second she thought she saw Craig-the-stylist helping himself to the pot stickers.

Maybe she shouldn't have canceled the shrimp.

At least Martha Shelling, the orotund-voiced coastal development queen, hadn't lost her enthusiasm. Fueled by her third vodka soda, she was blabbing away with Zephyr, who appeared to be well on the road to pie-eyed herself. Marion frowned. This was hardly an occasion to get sloppy with an amplified voice.

"I am so sick of the term *gentrification*," Martha brayed. "It's not about 'gentry,' it's about believing our city centers shouldn't be carpeted with bums and urine. And that eighteen people living in one apartment just might be unsanitary. But I'll tell you, City Hall will be *thrilled* if you force up the property values without getting their hands dirty. All that new revenue? If you're successful, they just might claim eminent domain on the rest of it. It could launch a domino effect."

"We'd call that an early Christmas present," quipped Zephyr.

"I'm hoping it works; Oxnard's ripe for the picking," added Martha.

So *that's* what this party was about, thought Marion, putting someone in office in order to drive the poor from their homes. Martha's little speech didn't surprise her, but how on earth did Zephyr's generation become so callous? So cruel?

Her eyes found Richard, smiling and pitching Jack Powell to Terrence and Lilly O'Shea. They'd used their software fortune to create a nonprofit that helped inner-city working poor to develop literacy and computer skills. She wondered how the O'Sheas would react when the people they served became homeless.

Zephyr was still smirking at the "Oxnard/picking" joke when Marion leaned to whisper in her ear. "Tell your alchy-pal to dial down the volume on your evil empire plans. You're in a room full of people who still possess human hearts."

She didn't care when Zephyr shot daggers her way. It wasn't the first time. She was about to tell Martha that the top of her panty hose had snuck up until it was exposed above the waistband of her skirt, then decided against it. No favors for a-holes.

Marion knew that for Richard this was all a game of big-boy Legos, where he thought no further than replacing the old, red bricks with stacks of shiny, new blue ones. That didn't let him off the hook, but he certainly wasn't acting in full consciousness. Well, he'd be fully conscious soon. She'd make sure of it. She was his wife.

And legally, half of the Zane downtown property was hers.

"I have news that is worse than your candidate."

She turned at hearing the words. It was Ivan.

"Xiocena's niece Carita lost consciousness while she was waiting at Angel's Hope, so they sent her by ambulance to UCLA," he said.

"Why the fuck didn't they treat her at Angel's Hope?" Marion asked.

"There was no room."

For the first time in her life, Marion Zane bailed on her own event.

9

Pickup and Delivery

They saw the blacked-out Chevy Tahoe, with a visible dent over the left front wheel well, drive past the bars of the automatic security gate a second time and knew their target was casing the street for predators or a tail.

A reasonable precaution when carrying fifty thousand dollars in cash.

The Tahoe had already spent one hour on city streets, most likely circumventing the fifteen-minute direct route from last known location to this address. It would probably drive past the gate two or three more times.

They hadn't even bothered to follow it.

The Patriot Act had eliminated so many time-consuming investigative steps that their assignments were now executed in record speed with relative ease—even moonlighting assignments, conducted over disposable phones.

Running the Tahoe's plates through ClearPoint's NSA database had produced a confirmed residence at 243 North Mesa. The Tahoe would be pulling into the parking garage, eventually.

It arrived ten minutes later.

Their target exhibited heightened awareness and defensive posturing—namely, raising a cocked, .22-caliber pistol in his right hand and turning periodically toward the still-closing automatic security gate while exiting the Tahoe and proceeding toward the apartment-complex entrance.

As the automatic security gate closed and their target reached the lobby-entrance door, he relaxed to the extent of lowering his weapon to a position of ninety degrees while simultaneously reaching into his left pocket and producing a key card. As the recognition system responded to the key card, unlocking the lobby door, their target pocketed the key card and reached forward to grasp the door handle. Through this action, their target left himself vulnerable for the second it took them to drop down like two bogeymen out of the overhead air vent and plunge a hypodermic into his neck.

At an approximate height of five feet ten inches and weighing approximately 170 pounds, their target easily fit under the false bottom of their Lexus hybrid SUV's rear-seat bench. Their target would fit even more easily into the air-transport container trunk, once he was relieved of all clothing and possessions, including that leather jacket, which appeared to be two sizes too small. Both the SUV and the airplane's containment receptacles were well ventilated and their target was exhibiting regular heart and respiration rates. This was good. Although their target, according to ClearPoint's NSA database, had no familial ties and performed a procurement service so odious that his death would assuredly produce celebration, their assignment did not include termination.

Their target was to be deposited at remote coordinates within the Amazon River basin, alive and fully alert.

Aggressive fungal infestations, ants whose saliva produced an effect akin to leprosy, poisonous snakes, piranha, giant catfish, jaguars, and if their target was lucky, Kapayo Indian machetes would do the termination work for free.

In record speed, with relative ease.

The Patriot Act was turning them into fat asses.

10

The High Cost of Living

The young women, who lived in the big, yellow sorority house with an *X* and a horseshoe over the door, seemed oblivious to the fact that their front-yard landscaping was being trampled by seventy-five sport-coated young men.

In fact, they looked stoked.

The young men, each clutching white roses in their strong, well-scrubbed hands, were singing to them in respectful, three-part harmony. Traffic had backed up on Hillgard as drivers braked and lingered in order to witness this phenomenon.

Now the young women were singing back, but the sugary melody was lost on Marion. All she saw was ritual and dogma that would forever remain a mystery. There had been no sororities at the night school where she'd gotten her real-estate license. Looking at the shining, mostly white faces of the women clustered on the balcony and hanging out of windows, Marion knew the protocols of serenading would probably remain a mystery to people like Xiocena's niece as well.

No *cholas* in sight.

A dimpled sorority blossom opened the front door and smiled at the young men with the roses. Her clear pink cheeks, shiny, fresh-clipped hair, straight white teeth, rounded yet toned body, and crisp designer frock trumpeted a carefully attended, expensive upbringing. If this girl ever experienced excruciating pain, a tender-mannered family physician would summon an army of experts within minutes. She would never have to worry about losing consciousness after waiting unseen, hour upon hour, in an ER ward.

Marion's Maybach pulled forward on Hillgard toward its destination, the UCLA Medical Center's emergency driveway across the street, as the young men filed inside the sorority house. They were on their best behavior.

Marion always hated the queer yellow glow of streetlamps. Besides making her look like Liza Minnelli, yellow light just felt inherently *wrong,* like something nuclear or poisonous had been unleashed upon the land, turning everything the shade of illness. It felt like the world was dying. Those streetlamps lit the UCLA hospital parking lot. Seeing Xiocena in the toxic lamplight outside the emergency entrance confirmed her instincts. Something was horrifically wrong. Her housekeeper was motionless except for hands that fingered rosary beads.

"Get a blanket, Carl," Marion told her chauffeur.

She gathered Xiocena up, and hugged her close, so she wouldn't have to look into her eyes when she asked the question: "Where's Carita?"

"She died in the ambulance. Her stomach was bleeding inside her. Nobody knew."

"Angel's Hope didn't even examine her?" Marion realized that was an asshole question before she finished asking it.

"There were no angels. Angels only come to people like you, Mrs. Zane. I promised my sister on her deathbed . . . I *promised!*"

"Oh, Xio! I'm so sorry . . . !" She could have gone on, but spewing conciliatory bullshit was an insult to the niece. This wasn't God's plan. It was man's fuckup! Marion tightened her embrace.

Xiocena shuddered as the shock took her deeper. Carl wrapped the car blanket around her and ran into the emergency room, leaving Marion alone, holding her friend in the yellow light.

Marion had never processed helplessness well. She was a fixer. Marion Zane had no problems, just momentary delays that were easily alleviated with a request, phone call, or note. Helplessness hadn't entered her world since . . . well, since even before Richard. She didn't allow it to enter her friends' or even well-liked acquaintances' worlds. She'd constructed a life that allowed her to fix anything at any time.

But she couldn't fix this. No amount of money or connections could fix this.

There were no angels. At least not if you lived in the wrong zip code. They were all across the street at the sorority house.

Floating away from herself. That's what helplessness did to her. Marion hadn't felt it in twenty-three years, but it was instantly familiar. Floating away . . . behind a glass pane . . . away from the whole shitty situation . . . the horror . . . the needless waste . . . she wasn't holding Xio . . . she was glassed in . . . she could look at everything from a nice, numb place . . . she saw them wrest Xio from her arms and roll her inside . . . she saw herself in the Liza Minnelli light, alone . . . grasping and speechless . . . just like the *other* helpless time . . . somebody was taken away from her that time too . . .

(Careful, now.)

. . . she looked the same as the *other* time . . . she looked like a mime doing a seaweed impression that time too . . . of course this time, she was a mime with . . . MAJOR INFLUENCE.

Marion galvanized back into herself. A taxi was dropping a couple off at the Student Health Center and she hailed it.

11

Throw-Down

Marion strode into her foyer just as Jack Powell finished speaking. She couldn't tell whether her guests were applauding his speech because it impressed and inspired them or because it was over. Who cared? They were still here. There was still time. Marion headed for the podium.

She passed Jack Powell, basking in the enthusiastic warbling from a clutch of guests. He must've taken that politicians' public-appearance course because he was listening with a style that made every one of them believe that his or her advice would have a direct influence on the Powell campaign and senatorial policy.

Right.

She grabbed a goblet and, lacking a spoon, plucked out Patti's rosewood chopstick that was holding up her hair.

Ting. Ting. Ting.

Unison head swivel. So many eyes. But no yips. Yips didn't even enter her consciousness.

"I know you've all come here for a political reception," Marion began, "a reception that's gone on rather long, at this point."

Knowing chuckles. Instant stink eye from Jack Powell. Tough beans.

"But I need you to bear with me for a few more minutes. Thanks. Many of you know our housekeeper, Xiocena. At four o'clock today, her niece Carita was experiencing severe stomach pains. Since the girl lived downtown, Xiocena drove her straight to Mercy General. But they were told Mercy's Trauma Center was closed due to budget cuts, and although Carita was clearly in pain, they were directed to Angel's Hope Trauma Center—forty-five minutes away. But Angel's Hope was handling *three hospitals'* worth of trauma cases and Carita just had stomach pains. No amount of begging from Xiocena could change the fact that they had to get in line behind car accidents and gunshot wounds. So Carita waited. For hours. The only reason she received any attention was because she lost consciousness. And even then, the trauma center had no available beds or doctors. Angel's Hope was forced to put her in an ambulance bound for UCLA. That was the closest trauma center willing to take someone without insurance. Halfway to UCLA, the ambulance paramedics discovered Carita had internal bleeding. But it was too late. She died before they even reached Westwood."

Collective response of shock and dismay. Good.

(Name the problem.)

"Carita died because we live in a city where immediate health care is only available to the wealthy."

Collective response of moral outrage. Good.

(Start with a tease.)

"Now, I don't know about you, but I don't want to live in that city anymore."

The only sound louder than the guests' collective anticipatory inhalation was the plasticky clicking of Patti's Marni necklace as she craned her neck to take in everyone's reactions. Good.

(Name the solution.)

"Richard and I happen to own property in Carita's neighborhood that's earmarked for development. And, forgive me for springing this on you, darling . . ."

She could only look at Richard for a nanosecond.

". . . we're going to build a hospital on that land. A hospital with a large, well-staffed, state-of-the-art trauma center. Carita Memorial."

Wah-wah mummers of approval erupting into clapping. Good.

Richard spilled his drink on himself, but that was to be expected. At least it hadn't shattered in his hand.

(Make it about them.)

"Thank you, but I didn't announce this for applause. I announced this because of you."

Patti wedged in next to Maya and squeezed her hand purple. "Holy shit. Holy shit. She's going to do it."

"Ow. Do what?" Maya asked.

"The very riskiest move in the entire world of fund-raising," breathed Patti in reverence.

(Name their power.)

"You're all people who believe in equality and community. You're all people devoted to fighting injustice. You're also all people who can give or raise a million dollars toward this hospital without losing a wink of sleep."

"She's doing a Throw-Down!" squeaked Patti.

"A what?" asked Maya.

"Marion just bet the farm," Pepper said, now flanking Patti and Maya. "A Throw-Down is askin' for big donations from a captive audience. Without warnin'."

"It hasn't been done since the eighties," said Patti.

"Why not?" asked Maya.

"Because it pissed people off. 'Specially people who bullshitted about their income." Pepper looked worried.

"Throw-Downs practically crashed nonprofits back then," whispered Patti.

Maya bit her lip. "What will happen to Marion if her Throw-Down doesn't work?"

Patti swatted her.

"Social suicide," said Lyndy, sliding in beside them and remaining very, very still.

(Open heart. Be a leader. Ask.)

"In the name of human dignity," Marion continued, "I'm asking for your help . . . so, who's with me?"

Frozen audience. Like a photograph. Bad. Really, really, bad.

(You little fool.)

Marion flashed on her future self at a C-list Oscar party, seated with reality-show contestants. The ones who lost. She saw future birthday parties of empty rooms with wind and tumbleweeds.

The next step in a Throw-Down would be to single people out and cajole them to give.

What if they refused?

(Was that a baboon screaming? Or was it just Lyndy smiling?)

Why was she smiling?

It took every fiber in Marion's body to keep her knees from buckling as the yip hit her. She'd never survive the next one.

"Five million dollars," screamed Patti. She couldn't stand the suspense. It was either pledge or wet her pants. (Plus, she loved being first.) Lou didn't even blink at the amount. He was focusing on her jiggly bosom and it made his head nod. Patti was so grateful she vaulted over Maya and covered him in kisses.

"We'll give two million," said Ari. He didn't want to give Pepper a chance to pledge more.

"And I'll raise fifty," hollered Pepper.

"Xio is best woman on earth. It's a fucking disgrace. Two million," growled Maya as she disentangled Patti's earring from her hair.

"Thanks, Marion, now I'll be wearing tights all summer!" joked Tom.

It was a well-publicized fact that Tom was wanted for a Robin Hood remake, and his words started an avalanche of pledges and competing attempts at humor. After that, the room caught fire. No one noticed Craig-the-stylist as he crept out the front door. They were too caught up in the giving fever. Even the most jaded and cynical were standing on tiptoes, straining to be next, as if pledging would redeem their very souls.

The Throw-Down was working.

The second yip was less severe than the first and Marion was able to release her death grip on the podium. Good ol' Patti. Her pledge totally made up for the time Marion and Ivan had to fly out to Kansas and rescue her from that colony. The one that had degenerated from "Conscious Biblical Living" into bunkers, polygamy, and automatic weapons. The one that exchanged Patti for her weight in meth. Blessings upon *all* her girls. Pepper, Maya . . . where did Lyndy go?

Less than two months ago, Claire was cutting coupons for panty hose. Hearing the heady monetary amounts of the pledges made her feel strangely exhilarated and sparkly. This was now *her* crowd. *The Wealthy.* Luxuriating in that notion, she wanted to sing out a pledge so bad her arm ached, but Billy beat her to it.

"Three million. Now I won't have to buy that pesky boat."

Claire chuckled along with *her* crowd.

"My wife's in the head but she's gonna do this, anyway. One million," said Max.

He was glad Lyndy wasn't there to hear the laughter.

Jeff was a professional to the core, but Xiocena was like a sister to him. What if it had been his boy instead of her niece? He shot up his hand. "One hundred dollars. This is my city too." To his relief, Marion smiled gratefully.

"Hell, then, I'll add another hundred for each of my staff," countered Ron Cusco.

That started an avalanche of household representation. And finger counting.

Pepper was working the calculator function on her BlackBerry like a demon. (Well, somebody had to keep track. This was a ton of dough.) Patti was watching so closely Pepper had to bat her head out of the way more than once.

"We should form a committee," Patti offered. "There's tons of people who weren't here tonight who would love to give to this." Pepper nodded. Patti looked at Maya, who pointed to Pepper.

"As long as she does the math," Maya quipped.

"Marion, we're officially forming your fund-raising crew," shouted Patti. "Carita United Memorial."

"Patti Fink, you just spelled *CUM*," Pepper said as she thumbed in calculations.

"Oh. 'Fund-raising United for Carita'?" Patti offered.

"We're going to be called *FUC*?" asked Maya.

"How about—*eeeeeeeeeeeeeeeeeeeeeeeeeeeeeeie!*" Patti had just seen the Throw-Down total on Pepper's BlackBerry screen.

"Fifty-eight million!" sang out Pepper as they all charged Marion, bouncing her in a squealing scrum for joy.

"In twenty minutes, with no event, no dinner committee, no invitations. With a Throw-Down!" shrieked Patti. "You just made Westside fund-raising historyyyyyyy!"

"If any of you ever . . . need a body part, a kidney . . ." Marion was too choked up to continue.

It was good to be queen.

12

Left Wide Open

A tentative knock interrupted Lyndy's tantrum in the men's powder room. She scared off the inquiry with a Kentucky-mule kick to the door.

How dare she! How dare she!

Hospitals were *hers*!

There was an unwritten law among socialites. Do not step upon one another's turf.

Marion hadn't stepped on her turf, she'd fucking torn into it with a backhoe.

With a friggin' *Throw-Down*.

Over the years (especially the ones when she was still at the TOP) Lyndy had harnessed her status to create a three-hundred-bed wing and research lab (both bearing her maiden name of Montgomery) at Beverly Hills Central. Whenever Lyndy thought of BHC, she imagined herself as its beautiful yet powerful angel of mercy. The Dispenser of Health for the Westside. She held such sway over the hospital they allowed her to dictate which new project would reap the benefits of the Winter Gala profits. This year she'd chosen the Rapid Response Viral Detection and Containment Team. In the event of plague, mobile units of doctors and police could swoop down on the infected and cart them away to quarantine centers, effectively stopping a virus in its tracks. Especially bird flu or anything else from China. Especially in Lyndy's neighborhood. It was the perfect target program for the gala. Who doesn't worry about flu in the winter?

What would happen now? None of those bitches had ever given Lyndy such sizable donations for BHC! Would BHC court Marion now? Would Marion now be the one who was procuring specialists and private rooms with one-touch speed dialing?

Who would Lyndy be then?

As fearful tears threatened to ruin her carefully applied mascara, Lyndy reached for a wad of toilet tissue and found herself face-to-face with an exquisite seventeenth-century Dutch landscape. A fine manor house glowed pink at sunset. Below, in the fields, faithful peasants herded cows in to make evening cream and butter for the master. When Lyndy had first laid eyes on this painting, entitled *Dusk,* she'd thought it sublime. A perfect, peaceful world. She'd fought like a tiger for this painting at Sotheby's last month. With every raise in the bidding, she'd envisioned it hanging in a place of honor in her home. Over the fireplace in her study, to inspire contemplation. On the wall next to her side of the bed, to encourage gentle repose. Finally being outbid was so crushing, she couldn't look at her bedroom wall for a week. Finding out that Marion Zane was the one who'd outbid her was too much to bear.

And she'd hung the fucker above a goddamn urinal.

With a cry like a wounded animal, Lyndy lurched around, looking for something with which to mar the painting. She spied an ornamental soap dispenser and lunged forward, but the sight of herself in the mirror caused her to freeze in midflight. What she saw shocked her.

She was unkempt.

Suddenly she heard her grandmother's voice: "Remember, no matter what, you're a Montgomery. Remember . . ."

Lyndy pulled herself together. Yes, she remembered.

And she also remembered what was in store for Marion Zane.

After she ground Marion into dust, she'd take this lovely Dutch landscape off the shattered Zanes' hands for a price *below* auction. With one hand on the painting and the other touching the monogrammed *M* on the on the right breast of her lacy chemise, she made a mortal vow to rescue *Dusk.*

Marion only saw Zephyr's untamable hair as she went out the front door. But the hair looked pissed (and inappropriately inebriated). Oh, shit.

Richard looked to be okay with the whole thing, which meant nothing because he had a better public mask than Marion. After she broke away from the Trophy love-scrum, Marion burrowed into his arms. Richard smiled affectionately and hugged her back for all to see and acknowledge. She was the only soul in the room who knew his embrace was lighter and stiffer than a sincere one.

"I-know-you-hate-my-guts-but-if-you-could-only-see-Xio's-face-that-girl-didn't-have-to-die," she chanted into his chest.

Richard ground his smile into the top of her head and spoke through his teeth. "Don't talk to me yet."

(He was beyond furious.)

He smoothly separated them (squeezing her arms a little too hard) and held her at his side (very firmly) as they accepted congratulatory hand-shakes and kisses. They stayed like that, she and her smoldering Siamese twin, for what seemed like hours. The philanthropic orgy had worked on their guests' systems like dopamine and everybody lingered. Marion felt guilty for wishing the very folks who had just handed her $58 million would get the hell out, but she wished it just the same.

Between well-wishing heads, Marion watched Ivan hand Jack Powell the shattered pieces of the memory stick. Powell pocketed them quickly as his campaign manager stumbled over and attempted to slur out a pep talk. Jack snarled something and the man staggered backward, almost becoming a third wheel in a Renaissance painting of Mercury and Psyche embracing.

"Carl has Xiocena in the service driveway."

Ivan had managed to materialize close to her ear. As Marion jigged, Richard's hand fell away and again he spoke through his smile.

"Go on, Marion, go out."

Over the twenty years they'd been married, Richard and Marion had fought as much as any couple.

Hadn't they?

Definitely. When she thought about it, Marion could recall more than a few silent and frosty evenings spent in separate wings of the compound and several nasty name-calling rows. She didn't even want to think about that terrible night when every strappy sandal she owned ended up in the pool—along with his ugly-ass Leroy Neiman painting. But they always knew when to reassure each other through their rage. It was almost instinctual. They even had a code for when tempers were at a fever pitch and they were in danger of speaking what Marion referred to as "unmaking spells," words that once out, could never be rescinded and would eventually destroy any partnership or trust. Their code told them, "Even though I'd like to rip your head off, right now, I'll love you till I die and we're rock solid." Marion thought it timely to employ that code now.

"Are we still booked for the cruise?" she asked softly.

Nothing. Richard didn't even look at her.

He'd never been too pissed off to reply to the code.

Marion realized that this was the first time she had ever screwed with his land-developing business, or any of his businesses for that matter. Sure, she made suggestions. She sat on all the Zane empire boards and the majority of her ideas, like urging the purchase of the Spanish Language Radio Network, had yielded spectacular results.

But she wasn't stupid.

She knew her suggestions had been made in order to give Richard more clout. No matter how astute her business acumen, Marion would always be regarded as a token wifey on the board, expected to vote along her husband's wishes. This was the first time she had ever sprung a business decision on him in which he had no choice. And in public.

Richard really cared about "in public."

Springing a business decision on Richard would have been unthinkable earlier in their marriage, when her every move had been calculated to make him happy. And to make herself bulletproof. Of course that was when she was a breathlessly subservient Stage I Trophy. She'd passed the tests of time and was well into Stage III now. A Stage III Trophy had to be able to exert some power. It wasn't as if her and Richard's livelihood was at stake.

Come to think about it, the Zane Enterprises Internet acquisitions had been her ideas too. Shit, she was the freaking broker who'd brought Richard into the Irvine project. That project made him a billionaire. She had *earned* Stage III clout!

But she *wanted* reassurance.

All this ricocheted around her head in about three blood-draining seconds. Marion finally turned and started walking toward the kitchen.

"Marion."

She turned to face her husband.

"*Yes, we're still booked.*" He spat it out. But spat or not, it was out. (Yessssssssssss!)

Blood flowed back into her upper body. She'd be paying for the Throw-Down for a while (on her knees and various other positions), but they were okay.

She was okay.

Jack Powell was not okay. He looked like a guy with erectile failure.

"I'm sorry, Jack. This was totally unplanned." Marion believed in making amends swiftly, eye to eye. He might be a perv but she'd screwed him over. Royally. He'd come to her home hoping to establish relationships that might result in checks and instead ended up writing one himself. He couldn't avoid it. Everyone in the room knew that only millionaires could afford to run for high office in California.

"I'm sure Richard will arrange and host another reception." (She sure as hell wouldn't.) She wasn't even sure that Richard would, but it seemed like a smooth exit line.

"Hey, life happens," slurred Jack's campaign manager, who now qualified as shit-faced. "We made some good contacts, we'll be following up . . ."

Jack said nothing. He just nodded at Marion with weirdly closed eyes and sort of sidearm-smacked her shoulder. Did he learn that in Little League?

Marion sidearm-smacked him back, in case it was expected. He felt unusually rigid.

Okay, she was getting creeped out.

"Glad you understand, Jack."

With that, she turned and clicked briskly off to the kitchen, driven by a sudden urge to wash her hands.

Jack Powell had been wise to keep his eyes closed. He knew that if he had actually looked at her fucking face, he would smash it in. Nosy judgmental bitch just screwed his whole FEC filing plan. He'd have to scrape and hustle over the phone now, like a beggar, to make the deadline. All so she could glorify herself with a hospital. Stupid bitch. Hospitals were financial catastrophes. He'd be sure to mention that to Richard Zane when he got him alone.

She actually *threatened* him. Bitch had that same smug look his mother used to get when she was ordering him around like a dog. The look that said, *Obey me or I'll have my husband beat the daylights out of you.*

Women like that needed to be brought to heel . . .

While his retinue packed it in, Jack stared at his hands, his mind filling with violent fantasies.

"Carita's being taken to the funeral home."

"Pierce Brothers?" asked Marion as she scooped up her purse and coat from the kitchen.

Ivan nodded. "Mid-Wilshire. Xio can take care of everything in the morning."

"Good. I'll make sure to request the older embalmer. The guy who did Mavis Parish must've smoked a fatty before coming to work because he overinflated her and they couldn't get her into any of her clothes. Two hours before the service, her cheapo nephew finally coughed up for something at the closest mall in her new size. Imagine, being buried in mall clothes, looking twenty pounds overweight! 'Course, all that fluid did pop out her wrinkles."

"Right. I left all the information on the office desk for the morning. Your calendar's double backed up on the discs above the back desk . . ."

"Yes, that's the thirty-thousandth time you've briefed me. Hon, we're gonna be fine. We're doing only domestic travel and I'm locked into a local project. It's the slowest time of the year; believe me, I'd join you if you were going somewhere less horrific."

"Right. Are you sure I can't escort Xio home . . ."

"Ah! Not another word, Ivan! That's how you lost all the other vacations. You are going straight to the airport and making your flight to shut-up island. We've got a big fat betting pool going on in the house about which day you'll break, and I intend to win."

Ivan actually smiled as he held the kitchen door open for her. "Yes, Mrs. Zane."

The sight of the idling Maybach in the service driveway was sobering.

"What did they give Xio for shock?" Marion asked.

"Light dose of Valium. Carl said she's stable and Roger made sure she ate. There's a margarita in the back for you."

Marion stared at the Maybach's black-tinted backseat windows and turned to her assistant. "Funny, you know, in so many circumstances, you could say, 'Grace of God, it could have been me.' Or, 'It could have happened to anybody.' But not this time."

"You took the first step toward changing that, tonight," Ivan told her.

Marion begrudged him a nod. "Fifty-eight million dollars. Only a hundred million to go. At least none of it's going to Powell."

"Since you mention the distasteful subject, I had the unfortunate experience of viewing a portion of the contents of Mr. Powell's ransomed memory stick and I strongly recommend avoiding any future association with him. The man's a hyena."

"What was he doing?" Marion asked.

"Something grisly and unmentionable."

"Ugh! Wait a minute, what did you hand Jack Powell?"

"Roger's topless sunbather diary from Portofino."

Roger had compiled his peeping vid during the last Zane Mediterranean trip and for months had been playing it relentlessly on his laptop as he cooked. It was set to last summer's beyond-obnoxious Euro-disco hits, the kind of tunes that implant themselves in your head for days. Several employees had risked bodily harm and deleted the diary from the laptop hard drive. But Roger kept the memory stick locked up and always re-downloaded it.

"Congratulations. You are hereby the official patron saint of my kitchen. So, all business is buttoned up."

"Yes. Do you want to know the location of the memory stick?" Ivan asked.

"Not now," whispered Marion.

Xiocena was looking up at them through the car window.

Ivan opened the driver's-side door, reached in, squeezed Xio's hand, then stood back so Marion could enter. Marion suddenly felt a rush of affection for her strange, stoic employee. And a little pang of trepidation.

"Well," she told him, "I'd say have a wildly fabulous vacation, but since you're not going anywhere wildly fabulous, I'll just say have a very, very well-deserved rest."

"Thank you, Mrs. Zane."

Ivan must have vibed on her feelings because he wasn't shutting the door.

"Ivan, stop it! Nothing's going to go wrong!"

At that moment they heard the fingernails-on-a-blackboard sound of terra-cotta against terra-cotta above their heads. They looked up in time to see but not avoid the roof tile that was plummeting toward them from the parapet. It shattered less than a yard away from Ivan's left foot.

The Zane compound was almost one hundred years old and it was commonplace for bits to crumble and deteriorate every so often, but the timing of this accident felt almost too perfect. It was almost as if the mansion were issuing an ominous threat. Or just screwing with their heads.

Thinking fast, Marion waggled her finger at the cupola. "Gilda, that wasn't funny!" she chided the ghost of the Mansion.

Then she grabbed the door herself and spoke to Ivan. "Remember to stay on the island for at least three days or you'll make Roger rich!"

With that, she shut the door. Through the darkened window, she could see Ivan watching her and Xio pull away and got the sudden image of him in a monk's habit.

Was he thinking about starting a new life in the brotherhood? Free from all the minutiae of schedules and the need to conceal privileged depravity?

Still, she just couldn't reconcile Brother Ivan, ringing the bell for choir practice, with her memory of ass-whupping Ivan, casually stepping over the corpses of Crystal's would-be kidnappers. Monastic life didn't contain enough action or well-tailored clothes. Besides, Ivan wasn't into boys.

Marion reached for her margarita and embraced Xio with her free arm as the tears resumed.

Ivan watched the Maybach pull out the gate and returned to the kitchen, where Jeff and Carter, one of the security guards, were overseeing the cleanup. Richard had already gone upstairs. Roger, showered, spiffed up, and lounging with a glass of Pernod, was alternating between cooing into his cell phone and growling for everyone to hurry up. Time to burst his bubble.

"Good night, Roger. I'll see you in three months."

Roger looked at his reflection in the cell-phone screen and patted his hair. "I'm right behind you, as soon as these fools finish."

"I'm afraid not. Tonight is Thursday. Mr. Zane has his ten-thirty massage."

"But he fired the masseuse!"

"He's trying a new one. She'll need to be shown in and let out. He'll need waitstaff."

"I have a motherfucking date! Can't Jeff or Carter do it? All they ever need is water or tea. Ivan, you should see this girl. She's over—"

". . . yes, like a mountain. Carter has security duties and Jeff has his child. I left a memo."

Roger never read the memos.

He let out a string of French curses and threw his phone into the sink.

"And if there's nothing further . . ." Ivan began.

The entire kitchen resounded with a hearty, *"Get out!"*

Before he got into his Porsche, Ivan took a last look at the Zane compound. He wondered if he'd ever see it again.

Roger was on his third glass of Pernod when Gary, another security guard, came into the kitchen.

"Spare some leftovers, bud?" Gary asked.

A blade flew past his head and stuck into Ivan's memo on the cork message board.

"I've got blue balls, you fuck!" Roger spat.

Gary developed a sudden craving for Jacopo's pizza delivery and ducked out.

Suddenly Roger heard a voice say, "I'll stay for you."

He turned to see a uniformed woman who was obviously a waitress from the catering staff. One he'd never seen before. That was odd because the catering staff had packed up their van and split twenty minutes ago. Granted, she was rather unremarkable-looking and moved like a mouse, but she wasn't invisible. How long had she been standing there?

"Who the fuck are you and why are you still here?"

"Okay, I won't stay. Just trying to help out," the woman offered.

She hurried to the employees' closet and fished out her coat.

Roger had always considered himself an excellent judge of woman flesh.

Probably the reason he hadn't noticed this waitress was that she was way over his age limit for sex. This one he guessed to be in her late forties. Her unmade-up face was pleasant and unlined but her hands were old and the ass had slightly dropped. Plus, her brown hair was well coiffed but couldn't hide the coarse texture of its natural gray. That could only mean one thing: bad divorce attorney and now catering to make ends meet because she'd spent all the alimony on face work and hairdressing to catch another husband. Not an uncommon experience on the Westside. It also meant she wasn't a flaky kid, looking to rip off the Zanes. She'd want to do a good job so her services would be requested again.

Roger looked at his watch. He could either leave now or spend the rest of the evening with a jar of Vaseline.

"Fifty dollars, no more. And I want to photocopy your ID."

She almost jumped at the sound of his voice. Mousy broad must really need the money.

"That's fine."

After he copied the waitress's driver's license, Roger whipped up two gorgeous steak sandwiches for Gary and Carter. They'd go along with it.

Once she was alone, the waitress straightened the employee dining room and set two very special water bottles in the bucket of ice Roger had left out. She placed the ice bucket on a tray, added napkins, and left it ready, by the kitchen door. Unbuttoning the collar of her uniform, she took a peek into the dining room to make sure she was alone. Satisfied, she straightened her shoulders and seemed to grow taller and wider. Even her gait changed as she slowly sauntered into the foyer, coming to a stop in front of the grand staircase.

Now she could properly greet Marion's home. "Guess who's guarding the henhouse," she muttered, peeling back a grin and exposing sharp gleaming canines as she licked her lips.

13

A Not-So-Soft Underbelly

Not wanting Marion's cocktail to go lonely, Ivan had left a two-quart thermos of margaritas in the backseat of the Maybach. Since crying leaves you thirsty, the ladies helped themselves, more than once, which led to the discovery that the combination of Valium and tequila stimulated the oratorical centers in Xiocena's brain.

A flood of words began rising from her mouth. "I miss my sister so much; I keep hoping Carita become like her. But my sister an' me, we grow up on a farm in Chiapas, with no gangs, no horny stepfather. Carita . . . she grow up sad. The minute my sister die, she go straight to gang and she get hard. She want money to get away from stepfather, but American kids—they no want to work. They want *easy money*. Big money fast. I tell her don't be asshole! Come live with me! Gangs are not family and gang money is from drugs and stealing. But she have to see for herself, and when she want to stop, they jump her out with a bad beating. She show up at my door, two years later, I no recognize. Torn clothes and purple all over. She only fifteen. Then she live with me an' go to school an' we get her emancipated. She stay with me two years but she no happy. She grow eyebrows back but nice girls see tattoos and don't want to be her friend. So she want to quit school an' get a job. She sad an' again think money will make her happy. I tell her money okay but is not your mama. I tell her the jobs pay shit with no college."

Xiocena caught herself and looked at Marion, who knew Xio made triple the average housekeeper's pay, well above what many college graduates were learning.

"You are the only one who pays good," Xio was quick to add.

Marion briefly considered mentioning the Honduran tent village in Patti's backyard and Pepper's well-bribed nannies, but Xio was on a roll.

"I offer to change her school but she say she no wanna wait an' she quit. Then she start to make money an' move out. I never know what her job is. She say she sell stuff on the Internet, but in school, she make F in computer. And she live inna shit apartment inna bad neighborhood. I say come home; your mama, she would not want you to live like this, but she say the money will get better. Then she get hurt."

Xio grabbed Marion's wrist. "You know what I think?"

Marion almost said, *Do I have a choice?* but remembered she was bearing witness to a tragedy and admonished herself back into listening. Still, she was beginning to tire of the monologue.

"I think Carita was *puta*! Or maybe she go back with gangs. The doctors say she no fall on bedpost. They say the bruises and bleeding were from fists."

"Honey, you did what you could," Marion soothed. She hated the generic condolence, but she'd exhausted her repertoire of original expressions and was too wasted to come up with new ones. As Xiocena finished her drink, she discreetly set the thermos out of reach.

"Ah, we were not mother and daughter. You have Dickie Jr. and Crystal, Mrs. Zane. You are all so lucky!"

"Lucky?" Did Xiocena mean "lucky" like saying, "Hey, that's lucky!" when someone stepped in dog poop and you wanted to make them feel better?

Marion thought Dickie Jr.'s *lawyer* was the luckiest of all. He'd just purchased a Sun Valley ski condo with fees earned keeping the little shit out of jail. The boy was six months graduated from business school and already screwing with SEC regulations. It was on Dickie's account that the only truly expensive items displayed in her houses were over one hundred pounds and unliftable. Last time he was home, her Fabergé eggs went on walkabout.

And Crystal, who only called her when she wanted to borrow the boat, the plane, or a vacation home, had yet to make a discernible contribution to the human race. She thought tipping the doorman of her Fifth Avenue apartment was community service. And then there were the paparazzi photos.

You'd think that if a person planned to have her cootchie photographed in public, she'd at least get a decent wax. If Marion saw one more photo of her stepdaughter's privates on the Internet, she was going to apply for a gynecology license. Pepper had e-mailed the girl's latest portrait with the caption, *Hurray! Crystal's finally got a job—spokesmodel for Taco Bell.*

Both kids were a chip off the block of their birth mother. Marion really should have forced Richard to fight harder for full custody. But back then, she was only a Stage I . . .

"Too bad we never had our own kids, eh, Mrs. Zane?" Xio asked. "They would have been fierce. You ever miss not having?"

Marion bit down hard on a chunk of ice. It took her a second to recover. "Not really."

Then she snatched up the thermos and took a long pull. Glasses were for pussies.

14

Stepchildren of the Night

Claire could feel Billy's body stiffen within her dozy postcoital embrace and she knew he wanted to make a call. One minute later, he patted her flank and eased out of bed.

"They're wrapping in Manila. Gotta call Terry . . ."

"Can I get you some tea or—?"

"No, Cookie, I'm fine."

Throwing on a robe, he padded off to the study.

"Cookie"? He'd never used that term of endearment before. Weird. Claire caught her reflection in a silver frame on her nightstand. Did she look like a "Cookie"? Wasn't that what they called the greasy old man who fixed beans in the cowboy movies? Next to all those gorgeous women at the Zanes' tonight, she sure felt like a "cookie."

Well, not for long. Starting tomorrow, she was going to be *styled*! And not just her look. Craig had contacts for *everything*, from party planners to travel agents. Craig-the-stylist was going to be her guide to her new lifestyle of lotus-eating.

Ignited with anticipation, she rolled onto her back, relishing the high-thread-count sheet beneath her body. The room was decorated with the quiet elegance and cool colors, with fruitwood furniture and sumptuous fabrics, of the entire house. Definitely tasteful. Billy's choice of a classic Holmby Hills mansion, with its white brick exterior, shutters, and boxwood hedges confirmed that he was the perfect match for a Secret Rainbow Princess. Claire might have grown up above retail space but she practically had a degree in Tasteful Stuff, thanks to the Web. Her new life was perfect. Almost like a Brooks Brothers ad!

Was something breathing next to her head?

Six-year-old Eva popped up an inch from her face. "Are you naked?" she asked.

"No! What kind of question is that?"

Claire quickly slipped into her wrapper under the sheets. The excitement of the Zanes' reception had caused her to forget that Billy's daughters were spending their first night with their new stepmother. She had even torn out that recipe for breakfast waffles to surprise her new brood.

"Get out of my daddy's bed!" Eva yelled.

Not exactly "Welcome to the family." Surely, the child was confused.

"Sweetie, did you have a bad dream?" Claire asked tenderly.

Eva stumped her foot. "I'm not going back to sleep until you get out of my daddy's bed!"

Claire sat up and fluffed the sheets. If there was one thing she knew how to do, it was kill with kindness. "This comforter is so yummy," she crooned. "Do you want to come up and join me?"

Eva got in at once. "I know it's yummy. I used to get to cuddle before you came."

Ahhh. Eva was feeling *displaced*. Claire had read about this issue in the child psychology paperback she'd bought at the airport in anticipation of living with children. She would reassure her. "Well, who says you can't now?"

"Katia," Eva replied.

That would be the nanny. The one who reminded Claire of a dark-haired Ann Coulter, without the legs. She'd barely met the woman when she was introduced to the girls at the restaurant. Katia had insisted on sitting alone in the back, where she ordered stuffed cabbage and a Jagermeister. Yuk!

"Well, what she doesn't know won't hurt her. You know, I think there's a *Strawberry Shortcake* on the TiVo in here."

"Oh, I love that show!"

"Me too!"

Claire turned on the TV, and within minutes, she felt the little girl nestle into her side. How sweet! She'd never thought as far ahead as children in her Secret Rainbow Princess Promise, but this was nice. Except . . .

Eva was sucking her thumb.

Claire had cut her teeth on the kiddie pageant circuit, where facial symmetry outweighed even figure and talent with judges' scoring. If there was anything that could turn a smiling winner into a loser with braces, it was thumb sucking. Besides, Eva was *six*. Time to have outgrown that habit. What would people think?

Slowly, gently, she pulled the thumb out of the sleeping girl's mouth.

"DON'T!" cried a stern voice.

Katia was standing inside the doorway. When the heck did she come in?

"Never draw attention to the thumb. *Never.*"

Like a bad dream, the nanny came closer and closer to Claire until her lips brushed her ear. The woman smelled like one of those pine-tree air fresheners that they sell at the car wash. It took all of Claire's willpower not to recoil.

"Her mother doesn't want her getting a complex."

"Does her mother want expensive orthodontia?" Claire whispered back.

With a preternatural jerk, Katia straightened and blared, "So, you think Eva's mother is an idiot!"

Stung, Eva looked at Claire. "I—I never said . . ."

"My mommy's not an idiot! That's mean!" the child cried.

"I never said she was, sweetheart . . ." Claire soothed.

"But you are choosing to ignore bedtime and other parenting decisions," interrupted Katia. "You think you know better."

"Eva came in here herself," Claire explained. "We were just bonding and having fun. Why are you so worked?" *And why aren't you working at Guantánamo?*

Katia turned on Eva, who was now sucking away to beat the band. "Ignoring bedtime is *unhealthy*. Do you want to get sick? Do you want to have green mucus and sore throat and miss all the birthday parties and fall behind at school so you are ashamed when you get left back a grade and all your little friends advance without you? When little girls miss their sleep, they don't grow properly and their bodies become stunted like trolls. Do you want to work in a circus when you grow up? That is the only place where trolls are welcome."

Now Eva was crying in earnest.

And Claire wanted to borrow her thumb. "Katia! Enough with the scare tactics. Nobody's turning into—"

Just then, nine-year-old Haley flounced in, yelling, "People are trying to sleep!" Eva sprang from the bed into her arms.

"Claire was making me sick in the bed!" she announced.

Haley gasped and looked at Claire like she was a monster. "Stranger danger," she croaked to her sister.

"Wait a minute, I'm not a—"

"I can hear you guys through my headphones!" cried thirteen-year-old Brooke as she stormed into the room. The two younger girls ran into her arms. Claire shot out of bed a little too fast, catching her wrapper in the covers, exposing a breast. Haley screamed before Claire could readjust it.

"You keep your hands off my sisters!" hissed Brooke.

Claire felt as though she were being sucked into a whirlpool. "Okay, everybody, this is a giant misunderstanding. Eva came in here and—"

Eva broke for the hall, crying, "I don't want to be a troll!"

Haley followed on her heels. "I'm telling Daddy!"

Claire tried to continue. "—didn't want me sleeping with your dad . . ."

Whoops, bad image.

Horrified, Brooke clapped her hands over her ears and ran out screaming, *"Daddy!"*

After remaining perfectly still during the delirium she'd set off, Katia swiveled her head and shot Claire a ghastly smirk. "I've been here a long time," was all she said.

15

Who's Yer Daddy?

Pepper gave a silent prayer of thanks as she stepped onto the solid ground of her driveway and realized she was still in one piece. Ari, smarting from the Kousakis encounter at the Zanes', had bolted out of the reception and beaten her to the valet. The kid in the white shirt and clip-on tie had no idea he was handing the keys over to Mr. Toad. She didn't mind when Ari took out that curlicue address marker at bitchy Kathy Kutcher's house on Doheny when he was outrunning the cop but she'd always liked the yard lighting at the Greenes' and those hibiscus trees on Coldwater were just about to bloom. Like her, they didn't deserve to die so young.

Ari couldn't let go of the fact that she'd been the one to deal with Kousakis. He didn't let up about it the whole drive home.

"Why didn't Marion tell *me* about *Natura Thessaly*?"

(Because Kousakis didn't feel *your* ass!)

But Pepper didn't dare divulge that George Kousakis had propositioned her. Greeks killed one another over that sort of shit and she didn't fancy the idea of conjugal visits at Soledad. "I dunno, Ari, maybe she forgot. There were a jillion folks comin' in her front door and we, um, just missed our turn."

"I was going to handle him. I had a plan."

"I know, Ari, must've been the wine. I'm so sorry . . . and that was a stop sign back there."

"I specifically asked you not to handle him."

"I know, Ari. I was wrong, wrong, wrong. Do you hear a siren?"

"I am a grown man! A businessman! This was *my* family and *my* problem to fix. I love you and appreciate your wanting to help, and in fact, you did help where four grown men had failed, but *I* hadn't failed, yet. *I* could have handled him!"

"Of course you could, Ari. I'll never do it again . . . Is that a cat on the windshield?"

The kitty caused the car to spin a perfect 360-degree doughnut-turn. (Pepper would have upchucked but centrifugal force kept it in.)

Two more doughnuts, three fishtails, and multiple ornamental-property casualties later, they were home.

She and Ari lived in a spectacular, expanded midcentury modern, built in the era of Sinatra-style entertaining. It occupied two acres of prime hilltop, flat pad. After Pepper finished thanking god she was still alive, she staggered out onto the lawn, bent over, and gulped air to make the world stop spinning. Ari ambled over to her and felt her butt.

They never miss a chance, do they? Did he think she was stretching?

"Oh, my baby. You know I can never stay mad at you for long," he said.

At least he'd worked his tanty out on the road. His skin had returned to a human shade and he was rocking on his heels with his hands in his pockets. Or were his hands rocking and his heels in his pockets? Pepper straightened up and gave him a whap.

"Just remembered the bottom line, didn't you? Kousakis is now your bitch."

Dang! Ari was so hot when he smiled.

"You are lucky you are exquisite," he said. "As a matter of fact, yes, I remembered, and I can hardly wait to tell my brothers."

With that, he chirped along the walk to the house, towing Pepper behind him like a blown-out speedboat as he spoke.

"They will dance like little girls in spring when I tell them about the *Natura Thessally*. Nicholas might even take his head out of his ass and congratulate me."

Pepper was, of course, exactly right, Ari thought. Yes, I remembered the bottom line.

He also remembered that his brothers would have no way of knowing that Pepper was the one who'd reined in Kousakis. Tomorrow he would be a god in their eyes.

He practically skipped into the house.

Ahhh. The living room always put him at peace. Two and a half stories of floor-to-ceiling glass gave a dazzling 180-degree view of Los Angeles. Unfortunately, it also gave a dazzling fishbowl view of six-year-old Jerry and five-year-old Cooter shooting Orange Crush cans off the back of the couch with an air rifle.

Ari let loose an obligatory parental bellow then spun around, assuming his lovely wife would seize the reins and administer the rest of the up-braiding. But Pepper was gone. Stiletto clicking on the stairs told him she was already hauling ass to let the nanny out of the bathroom in which she was surely blockaded.

Ari was alone in the lions' den.

Better to come on strong, take them by surprise.

He crossed the living room in two strides, grabbed Jerry by the collar, and ripped the rifle out of his son's hands. "Guns! In my house! In the living room!"

Wait a minute. He *knew* this gun. This was the exact Crossman air rifle he'd thrown out two months ago. Here was the mark where Jerry scratched the stock when he tried to club his brother and hit the coffee table instead. How did they get it back? He'd personally handed it to the garbage man!

That blink of a thought was, unfortunately, enough of a break in the rhythm of his berating for Cooter to squirt past him and dash upstairs.

"Paris! Come back here!" Ari called out after him, but Cooter never responded to his christened name. His own mother refused to use it as long as they resided in Beverly Hills. In the same fashion, Janos was "Jerry" and Marta was "Maybelle." Ari had given up by the time they had Chevelle and Jed.

Yet one in the hand was better than none. He glared down at Jerry. "Janos! I don't know where to begin. The gun? The damage? The disrespect for my home and wishes? Ignoring you bedtime? Imprisoning nanny? You put a chair against the door again when she made pee-pee, didn't you?"

Jerry cracked a grin that would put Peter Pan to shame. "Two-time chump . . ." he muttered.

"Silence! I am very, very disappointed in your behavior!"

Ari gave himself silent kudos for remembering to say "your behavior" instead of "you" so his son would not identify himself as a bad person. He was going to continue his talk by discussing the "other choices of behavior" his son could have made in order to set a good example for his younger brother, but the boy's eyes were filling with tears.

"What now? Tears? Are you a little girl?"

The tears became a waterfall as Jerry trembled and shrank back.

Was that fear?

Ari couldn't remember the parenting class he had taken covering anything like this, but he knew fear was bad. Fear meant children stopped listening and started running to other adults. He'd never laid a finger on his children, but other adults might not believe it. He envisioned Jerry calling Child Services from a psychiatrist's office. After all, this was America . . . He decided to change tactics.

"I mean, ah, it's okay to be sorry. But don't be scared, honey. Janos? I'm not going to hurt you."

Jerry timidly peeked up at Ari, his beautiful eyes glistening.

"Papa loves you. There, there. It's all right," Ari soothed.

Jerry flung his arms around his father's legs and sobbed a baboon squall that would have drowned out a jackhammer. Ari could only pat the child's back and wait for him to feel reassured.

At least his son would know he was loved. He'd never be able to tell a psychiatrist his father had never said "I love you."

Just then Pepper returned to the room. "Dadgum it, Jerry! Quit bullshitting yer daddy an' git that butt upstairs so I can beat it!"

Children always brought out the "country" in Pepper.

Before Ari could open his mouth to ask if those were really flames coming out of Mommy's eyes, Jerry let go of his legs and casually wiped his nose on his arm. His angelic face instantly transformed into a defiant scowl.

"Shoot! 'Night, Daddy."

Jerry stomped away toward the stairs with Pepper clicking ominously behind him and saying, "An' you can fork over that box a' shot I see stickin' outta yer back pocket!"

"Aw, Mommy!"

"Don't 'aw, Mommy' me! I had to promise Lucille another three hundred a month because of you burrheads! I swear, she quits an' I'm shoppin' fer yer next nanny in Baghdad. An' you can fergit about Little League till you an' Cooter dig every pellet outta that couch! Now hand me my brush an' drop them drawers."

Outside the glass walls, an acre of lawn dropped away into a twinkling treasure chest of city lights. Out there, Ari was a giant. Young executives practically knelt at his feet in the hope of hearing a chance tidbit of wisdom from the Master of the Music. He'd triumphed during one of the toughest periods in recording history by intuiting consumer habits and desires. Grammy winners leaped out of *their* seats at restaurants to come pay respects at his table.

Upstairs, his son made no cry of protest as he received his punishment. He had the same blood as his mother.

This reverie was broken when Ari's foot nudged against something on the floor. Moving aside pierced aluminum cans, he discovered a framed print of the family portrait he and Pepper had sent out as this year's holiday card. He picked it up and started to set it back on the red-lacquered side table, but something in the photo caught his eye.

The portrait showed him, Pepper, and the kids wearing matching reindeer antlers and hugging one another like happy maniacs. A rifle pellet had cleanly penetrated the frame's glass and lodged in the center of Ari's forehead.

Open season on Daddy.

Looking into the faces of his offspring, Ari found no trace of himself.

16

Off to Bed

All twenty-eight thousand square feet of the Beverly Park Tuscan Villa were finally quiet. Even the haughty Roman emperor statuary near the guest entrance looked grateful. Stepdaughters Katsume and Mary Margaret, both fourteen, had retired after an evening of dueling cheerleader try-out routines (with dueling deafening-volume musical scores, Nelly vs. The Killers). Stepsons Jorge and Finnegan, eighteen and twenty-two, were hopefully back at college and not throwing parties at the Innsbruck chalet, as they did the last time they were there. Fifteen-year-old Günter had finally put the tuba down (band practice plus self-defense against the cheerleaders) and whatever argument the gardener's family was screaming about in the tents in the backyard seemed to have been resolved without bloodshed.

Sighing with relief, Patti was sitting on the edge of her tub, flipping through the British edition of *Harper's* as she waited for her moisturizer (and aphrodisiac!) to soak into her body. (She had a proper bathroom "tuffet," but it was made out of hot pink suede, so she never sat on it wet or creamy.) The alchemist's cream, blended under the light of a waxing moon, was designed to break down any fear or grief blockages in her chi flow so that Patti would experience blockbuster orgasms. The handwritten label on her little brown jar read *Patti's Oooh-la-la Rub.* Very personalized.

And very surprising. Who knew she needed to smell like peanut butter cookies and Vick's VapoRub in order to come like a freight train?

A hosiery ad in the magazine compelled her to assess her own endowments, and, of course, she stopped at her breasts. Her perfect, *natural* breasts.

Their perfection brought Patti to a place of regret for never having posed for *Playboy* when, as a semiregular on *Star Trek,* she'd had the chance.

In those days, everybody from casting agents to studio suits read *Playboy.* A layout might have separated Patti from the actress herd and made her career take a different turn. She might have been discovered by a director. She might have been a star.

And she would never have taken up with the likes of Barry Fink, owner of an on-set catering franchise.

She'd had a shoot date and everything lined up, but Larry-the-grip, her sort-of fiancé at the time, had suddenly turned prude and begged her to cancel, saying, "It would just kill my mother!" Two years later, that same sort-of fiancé had a sex-change operation and started calling himself "Laura." He moved up to the Bay Area and was last seen exotic-dancing at Teddy's End-of-the-Line. Patti figured his mom would jump up and down praising Jesus for a Playmate girlfriend now.

"I should have done the spread," she said to no one in particular.

Taking a deep whiff of her arm to get over the grief, she dove back into her magazine.

She was happy to see that supermodel and wife of Keith Richards, Patti Hansen, was still beautiful. She didn't actually know Patti, but she'd worshipped her as a teen and shared the same first name, so she felt a certain kinship. If Patti was still cool, all was right with the world. Patti Hansen *always* flashed tit in those layouts in *Vogue.* Bet Keith Richards's mom was thrilled to see them.

Another whiff of her arm told her that full absorption had taken place, so she donned her La Perla ensemble. La Perla really wasn't her usual brand because they rarely made any wild bras in D-cup, but this set was an exception. Nothing made men harder than black French lace. And the G-string and garter belts weren't so bumpy that they screamed out from under a clingy dress. Slipping on and clipping in Fogel stockings, she straightened the seam and scanned her shoe closets.

"Fuck-me? Fuck-me? Fuck-me? Fuck-me? . . . Aha!"

All of her "fuck-me" shoes had been switched to the bottom half of the third closet. Wanting to help out the backyard refugees, Patti had asked

Wanda, her housekeeper, to train one of the gardener's nieces in the Art of Valet. The girl was very creative and was constantly rearranging Patti's clothes-filing categories. Patti didn't usually wear peep toes with stockings, but they were featured that way on all the spring runways, so she threw caution to the winds and selected a formidable pair of red patent-leather slingbacks with peep toes and five-inch heels. The shoes caused her to yearn for something stretchy, so she shimmied into a tight-bodiced scarlet Alaia dress that she topped off with fire-engine-red lipstick and a red fox stole.

Patti took another whiff of her forearm then swept out of her dressing room and struck a pose in the bedroom doorway. She could feel the seductive energy emanating from her body. She was an irresistible force of nature. Oooh-la-la!

Lou was lying in their bed, sleeping. Deeply.

Patti sighed and checked his oxygen connections.

Then she grabbed her red croc Hermès (not the Birkin, the other one) purse and drove down to her suite at Shutters Hotel on the Santa Monica beach for her midnight date with internationally-ranked-but-without-a-sponsor-so-far surfer and favorite paramour, Ricky.

You'd think, because of the ocean and all, Ricky's favorite color would be blue, but it was definitely red.

17

Days of Yore

Lyndy was performing her unfortunate evening ritual of checking the locks on the doors and windows of her historic Bel Air hacienda, Nedio del Sol. How many times did she have to explain to the housekeeper that these old windows didn't truly lock until the latch was pushed "fully to the left"?

Forgetful cow!

Her gracious abode was constructed in a double-decker square around a courtyard with wings jutting out from two ends. Built long before the age of air-conditioning, it boasted over one hundred windows and twenty doors that opened outside. That made one hundred and twenty Achilles' heels.

She padded down the north courtyard hall, turning to her right, every so often, to peer through the floor-to-ceiling plate glass, the only thing separating her from the pressing darkness outside. She and Max had glassed in the open sides of the covered porches so they could enjoy the courtyard during inclement weather. A definite mistake. The thick white trunks of two ancient bent sycamores, their branches running parallel, four feet off the ground, the length of the patio, disappeared in dense foliage; once they went vertical and rose above the foliage, they formed a seventy-five-foot canopy above the hacienda. Were their branches rustling with the breeze or because of a *concealed observer*? Now Lyndy felt like a hamster in one of those clear plastic cages.

Even though Lyndy wore Tod's car moccasins, her footfalls echoed on the time-polished Saultio tiles, emphasizing the solitariness of her chore. Both Max and the dog were upstairs sleeping, without remorse.

The house alarm gave her no comfort. The police and the police-reject-security-service's armed response never arrived in under fifteen minutes. That was enough time for an intruder to commit unspeakable acts.

Gone were the days when a soul could sleep peacefully—thanks to Marion Zane. She'd ruined it for everybody when she'd posted round-the-clock private security guards at the Zane compound.

Lyndy had always considered her neighborhood safe until she saw those guards and started wondering what had compelled Marion to hire them. Did Marion have inside information from law enforcement? (The Zanes always gave a ridiculously excessive contribution to the policemen's fund.) Were there maniacs on the loose, whose existence the real-estate lobby suppressed from public disclosure? Maniacs whose existence was divulged only to those who paid for special treatment and insider tips?

Max wouldn't spring for round-the-clock private security guards, Lyndy knew, he'd merely suggest she just keep wearing her green night cream to bed, saying, "One look at you and that burglar'll crap his pants."

Left utterly vulnerable, Lyndy had been forced to alter her lifestyle, locking away the silver and Wedgwood collections she once proudly displayed. She stopped wearing her statement jewelry, checked the crime Web site three times a day, and changed gate codes every other week, refusing to give them to the staff.

California sunsets used to be a source of solace. Now, thanks to Marion Zane, nightfall made her feel like prey.

Lyndy stored these slights the way Joseph had stored grain in Egypt. She knew she should not waste her vital life force on the doomed, but with every click of a lock and every snick of a latch, all of the sins of Marion Zane came flooding back.

Click! Marion rubbing salt in Lyndy's wounds by casually mentioning that she planned to *miss* the White House screening of the latest offering from Zane-owned Century Studios. So what if she wasn't a Republican? It was the *White House!*

For years, Lyndy had lusted after a White House invitation. She'd slaved away, coordinating countless campaign fund-raisers and ladies' teas and attending tedious Ranger think-tanks and yet her dance card remained, thanklessly, empty. Meanwhile Marion turned down that golden ticket as if it were a coupon for free teeth bleaching.

Snick! W interviewing Marion instead of her about Hollywood hostess etiquette.

Lyndera Montgomery Wallert had been *the* reigning hostess of Tinsel Town when Marion Zane was still peddling waste dumps in Costa Mesa. The Zanes had owned Century Studios for *barely two years* at the time of the interview. The woman was a newcomer! Lyndy was sure the Zanes must have hired a publicist or found some other vulgar means of promoting themselves in order to barge Marion into print.

That *W* article was responsible for Sunday Night Spaghetti Screenings at the Wallerts' fading from A-list status. Lyndy knew Marion and her publicist were targeting her.

Click! Marion buying that grotesquely humongous boat and inviting every A-list body for a "girl party" at Cannes.

Lyndy had *always* hosted the girl party at Cannes. Her dusk-until-midnight soiree was famous throughout the festival as the only "No Boys Allowed" event. Every wife in the business attended. (Well, not Marion, but back then, she was a nobody and didn't merit an invite.)

And Lyndy had *always* offered a suite at Hotel du Cap in Cannes as the high-stakes centerpiece of the Beverly Hills Central Gala live auction. The suite had *always* instigated tooth-and-claw competition among designing Trophies who longed to be close to Lyndy and her girl party. The year of Marion's boat bash, Lyndy had been forced to practically give the suite away at only fifty dollars above rate.

Marion shamelessly spoiled her boatload of traitors and *her* girl party became an annual event, forcing the Gala to give up the suite as a money-maker. And Lyndy to forever scratch Cannes off her calendar.

It didn't take a detective to figure out Marion's goal was to undermine Lyndy's influence and spoil her traditions.

Snick! That horrible fitting at Chanel.

Lyndy had specifically made her fitting appointment for a late Monday afternoon in order to have both the good seamstress and the Rodeo Drive store manager at her disposal without silly interference from tourists and pretenders. Then, surprise! Marion Zane dropped in "unannounced" and the entire store's personnel practically left footprints on Lyndy's back in their rush to fawn.

She remembered the simpering manager producing a garment bag with a ridiculous flourish and withdrawing that gorgeous chiffon couture gown. Lyndy had tried to order the gown at the trunk show but had been informed that it was "no longer in the collection."

Porfidio tequila had magically appeared for Marion, complete with chips and fresh salsa. Lyndy was left a human pincushion, begging for a Diet Coke and the return of her seamstress. If that wasn't bad enough, Marion then announced that she was headed to Saint-Tropez and needed to practice her French, so everyone instantly started chattering away like frogs. Lyndy spent the rest of her fitting having her ears bruised by god-awful pronunciation.

Surely, Marion had bribed those shopgirls. They probably came cheap.

Finished with downstairs security, Lyndy trudged up to the second level, checking behind herself every few steps. The long upstairs photo gallery, commemorating happier pre-Zane days, provided no uplifting nostalgia since her beloved chow dog, Prince Matthew, had claimed it as his sleeping quarters and farted the air green. And what was that noise?

Three streets below, some rap artist's party was continuing way past civilized hours. Lyndy drew a hassock to the stair landing, climbed upon it, and peered out an octagon-shaped casement-window opening. Through the foliage beneath, she could just make out the half-clad silhouettes cavorting against an oval of gaudy pool light that morphed from turquoise to emerald to indigo.

She used to dance by the light of a pool . . .

The original grounds of the home she'd just fortified used to encompass the entire mountain and the flatlands below. The rap artist's house occupied the former location of the kitchen garden. The street immediately below hers used to host the stables, servants' quarters, and a gentleman's gaming cottage.

Then came the Depression and Great Fire. Bit by bit, Nedio del Sol's kingdom was forever lost. It was only fitting, Lyndy thought, that she should reside here.

"I too have lost my kingdom, Prince Matthew. But take heart. It shall be avenged and regained!"

At the sound of his name, the aged chow painstakingly rose up on his feet and pissed on the carpet.

18

Secrets of the Stars

Maya and Tom's Gothic crib lay in the leafy lowlands along the border of either Bel Air or Holmby Hills, depending on the real-estate agent you spoke to and which neighborhood was more desirable at the moment. Six acres of private grounds wrapped an almost century-old three-story stone manor, straight out of a Scottish fairy tale, built by silent-screen stars and occupied by stars ever since. The whole property was walled off and hidden from prying eyes by towering specimens of ficus, pine, costal oak, sycamore, horse chestnut, and palm. Masses of bougainvillea the size of buses entwined the trees and almost obscured the iron-spike-tipped entrance gates

The romantic manse had experienced few changes over the years, save for minor technological updates like Tom's well-hidden giant plasma-TV screens and sound systems. Few changes, until Maya got a look at the electric bill.

"Aaiieeee! Tom! This is nightmare! We have to change fucking everything! We are PIGS!"

For three days, Tom thought his wife was upset about their waistlines. On the fourth, when the contractors and heavy machinery arrived, he discovered Maya had meant "*ENERGY* PIGS."

All thirty-six rooms of the manor were currently undergoing conversion to solar power, low-flow toilets, energy-saving appliances, energy-saving heating and cooling systems, energy-saving lightbulbs, tankless water heaters, microradiation-free phones and computers, electromagnetic deflectors, and balancing magnetic gyroscopes to help their bodies oscillate at the same megahertz as the earth. The only areas left somewhat inhabitable during the ecotransformation were the palatial master suite, the huge medieval-style kitchen, and the guest cottage.

With bowers of pink climbing roses, a whimsical kitchen garden, and dainty window boxes of ivy geraniums, the stone guest cottage on the estate could have been the inspiration for a Thomas Kinkade painting. Its occupants, Vlad and the gardeners Dudayev and Sasha, could have been the inspiration for Siberian gulags. The three men were Maya's homies from the old country, where, as war orphans, they'd bonded inseparably. Tom had inherited them as part of the marriage package and readily accepted his wife's rough-looking entourage since the men provided security, groundskeeping, and had excellent organization skills. Vlad alone worked harder than ten personal secretaries. The fact that the only compensation the homies required for their services was room and board made Tom especially accepting of them and their ways.

Vlad was happy that his employers were confined to two rooms in the manse. Since Maya allowed rooms to be lit only when they were occupied, he could easily keep track of her and Tom's whereabouts without missing any of the *American Idol* he'd TiVo'd. Dudayev and Sasha's bookmaking operation had taken in over a hundred thousand dollars in action on *Idol* alone tonight, and at the moment he was eager to see if it was because the fat kid had gotten cut. From the upstairs cottage window, Vlad focused his Russian-army-issue field binoculars and noted that the kitchen of the manse was still glowing.

Good. That meant Tom couldn't see Sasha driving in the second "borrowed" truckload of bootleg computer software. After Maya and Tom went to bed, his roommates would drive the trucks alongside the cottage and unload their contents into its spacious root cellar. A scene Thomas Kinkade never dreamed of painting.

Vlad knocked back a third shot of iced Stoli and turned his focus back to the plasma screen, where the fat kid was making a mess out of "Yesterday."

Two acres away, Vlad's employers sat atop the age-warped butcher block, swinging their feet like delighted children as they ravaged the Bel-Air Hotel take-out tins. Vlad had picked up a late supper of field greens, truffle risotto, lamb chops, and bistro fries knowing that the guests at political receptions tended to be so enthusiastic that they never allowed celebrities the time to stop talking and eat.

He was good that way.

"So, did we give any money to Powell?" asked Tom.

"No. I think I must talk with Marion first. I see her look at him and she looked pissed. Tch! Don't manhandle the *frites*!"

"Nobody says 'manhandle' anymore."

"I do," said Maya, piling a greedy handful onto her plate. "And I am Queen of the Manhandlers."

"Politicians suck. They're all agents for transnational corporations."

"But creatures of greed can be tempted. So we must play devil and seduce them to our side with equal support. The world is burning her children."

"I wonder what our child would look like," Tom suddenly said.

For a nanosecond, Maya's forkful of risotto hesitated in its path toward her mouth. But only for a nanosecond. Tom wasn't the only Hanson who possessed well-honed acting skills. As she chewed, Maya caressed her beloved with an appraising gaze and languidly replied, "A monkey's behind."

(More forkfuls.)

"Should I do Victoria's Secret show when we're in Cannes?" she asked. "Or do you need the spotlight to yourself? They want my answer."

Tom had stopped eating. "He'd probably have your eyes and mouth," he answered, still thinking of their child.

"And we have to give answer to that ecotour in Suriname."

"Hopefully, not your temper. He'd be athletic, like me. Big hands . . ."

"And a tiny little penis."

"No way. My son's gonna have a log, like this," he bragged, grabbing his groin for illustration.

"And tell terrible jokes."

"Only if he takes after you. So, when do we start?"

"Start what?"

"Having a baby!"

"A baby what? Are you going to have any more salad?"

"Seriously, girl. I want a child. Outta *you*."

Avoiding his eyes, Maya picked out a brown lettuce leaf and flicked it into the trough-size sink. "I'm not sure what my booking rate is for that job. You'll have to call my agent."

Tom grabbed her arm and, with a growl, pulled her to him. "I've got your rate right here, lady."

With one sweep, two hundred dollars' worth of leftovers fell to the floor and Tom took her there, on the butcher block.

An hour later, they dragged themselves through the maze of plastic sheeting to their other habitable space. Tom was asleep before his head hit the pillow, but Maya lay beside him for another fifteen minutes, just to be sure. Satisfied, she slipped out of bed, went downstairs, unlatched the tall, stained-glass doors of the ballroom, and walked into the garden.

Tom had said the garden would smell like underpants when she put in the gray water irrigation, but it didn't, thanks to charcoal filters. Bionutrients, plus regular additions of worm castings, compost, bone- and blood meal, turned the formerly barren soil of the old estate rich, moist, and fertile. The garden smelled of life force.

Maya negotiated the boxwood maze by the ghostly glowing solar lights, turned off on a narrow path that cut through a thickly planted cedar grove, and walked out onto a long black acre of lawn. The lawn was an old croquet-course-turned-overflow-parking-lot, but Maya had walled it off with fast-growing cedars, keeping the secret of the space for herself. It was like having her own mountain meadow or field.

The moon was dark but unseasonable gusts revealed a canopy of stars seldom seen in Los Angeles. There was the Dipper and Cassiopeia, the three sisters. There was Venus, huge and round.

Maya tasted the wind without shivering. She would not sleep tonight.

She was remembering a time when she'd stood under different constellations.

19

Welcome Home

"Mrs. Zane. We're here. Do you need assistance?"

Marion tried to work her mouth but it was drool-glued to the seat and carpeted with sandpaper. She snatched up the thermos and drained the last of the melted ice. "No Carl, I'm fine. I just have to figure out where my feet are. And thanks for not screaming when Xio told us Carita's life story for the third time."

In truth, Xiocena had repeated Carita's history *five* times during the ride to her home. Thanks to Ivan's margaritas, Marion knew more about Xiocena's niece than she knew about her own blood relatives.

"No problem, Mrs. Zane. She's in grief."

"Well, then, good night and good grief, Carl. Thanks for staying awake."

Marion walked in the front door, half expecting to find Ivan waiting. He would always rouse himself from the deepest sleep on Thursday nights. Richard always conked out after his Thursday massage and it was household policy that Marion never arrived home ungreeted.

She doubted that Ivan's temporary replacement, Evelyn, would perform the same service since she'd already tried dickering for a higher overtime fee. The woman was obviously a local.

Marion left the lights off. Not because of Maya's lecture on "dirty fucking electricity" but because she couldn't remember the last time she'd been alone in the dark downstairs.

It felt like a luxury.

And the perfect opportunity for encountering Gilda.

Since Ivan came on board, Marion had confined her ghost hunting to the servants' staircase. Yes, it was the most likely place but it was also somewhere she could be alone without an intercom interrupting her with five thousand requests, reminders, questions, and phone calls.

Of course she'd set that level of service up for herself.

Or had Richard?

No matter. At least she had this moment. Who knew when she'd get another? And even then, she might not be drunk enough to try. Marion positioned herself in the center of the foyer and tried to focus her tipsy thoughts on her memory of an old photograph from Gilda's obituary.

It had to be the husband. Marion felt it in her bones. She was sure he'd either pushed Gilda off the parapet or driven her to jump.

Out of the corner of her eye, Marion saw shadowy movement but didn't dare turn for fear that she'd spook the spirit.

That's right, Gilda, she thought, *just show yourself and say what happened. Why get written off as a suicide when you were shoved in the name of Italian capital?* Less than four months after Gilda's death, Rutherford Wilson had married Sophia Marcotti, an heiress from Genoa. Her hefty dowry saved his ailing import business. Marion's research had uncovered Wilson's business ledgers and travel records. In the year leading up to Gilda's death, Rutherford had traveled to Italy on two occasions, supposedly negotiating contracts with marble quarries. Specifically, the *Marcotti* quarry.

As the new Mrs. Wilson, Sophia had commissioned a marble statue of Venus and Apollo, carved in hers and Rutherford's likenesses, and placed it in the center of the conservatory. Marion relocated the thing outside the parking garage, under a ficus tree, condemning the cheaters to an eternal barrage of bird poop.

To be honest, considering all the freakin' time and energy she'd put into researching Gilda and running her former home, Gilda's ghost really owed her an apparition.

One glimpse, Gilda, and I swear I'll give the story to Vanity Fair. *This is right up Dominick Dunne's alley. He and I are very close. You'd be immortalized and I'd get six months of dinner-party conversational mileage. Come on, come on . . .*

No longer able to stand the suspense, Marion whirled around.

Nothing. No movement. No sound, except that of her own tired-ass breath. Only dark, enormous spaces filled with dark, enormous stuff.

If she were to die tonight, would she too be erased from memory while another woman filled her place?

The notion overwhelmed Marion with a sudden desire for the shelter of Richard's warm arms. Why was she wasting time on drunken ghost fantasies when there was a live husband upstairs? Who cared if he was still angry about the hospital? Richard never cheated. He'd never throw her off a parapet. How lucky she was! How *bulletproof*!

She hiked up the grand staircase and scooted down the corridor. Passing the Picasso, which remained, sadly, unadjusted, she entered the master suite, squished across the sitting room, and flung open the bedroom door to behold her husband naked in slumber.

On top of the naked masseuse.

20

Sucker-Punched

They didn't awaken as she stepped inside the room, and Marion felt her adrenals kick in with a jolt, causing hundreds of chemical reactions to course through her body, giving birth to a gamut of thoughts—ranging from despair to murder. These newborn thoughts presented themselves in a frantic water ballet around her tequila-bathed brain. The first one that came to the surface was:

Well, this ruins my buzz.

The second thought was:

Whoa, haven't heard that since the eighties.

The third was:

Wait a minute. They aren't moving.

Marion clapped her hands once, then twice, but got no reaction. Not even a twitch. Richard was a light sleeper. Her eyes moved to their torsos.

Were they breathing?

She couldn't tell because she was frozen across the room. From twelve feet away, she could detect no visible rise and fall of respiration. Marion thought about the time she took that meditation class with Patti and peeked at the teacher to see if she was doing it right (and because she was bored out of her skull) and he didn't seem to be breathing either. But he was a yogi dude and she couldn't tell if these two motherfuckers were meditating or if they'd met with foul play and now she was beginning to feel like she was trapped in an episode of *Law & Order. Think. Think. Think.*

What did the detectives do?

Could she do it from twelve feet away? She was friendly with Dick Wolf and wanted to call and ask, but he probably used a service after 1 A.M.

Feeling as if her liver had been relocated to her mouth, Marion crept closer to the bed until she was one foot away, then realized she was too close to tell jackshit without her reading glasses and backed up until the bodies were in focus.

They still weren't moving.

What now?

She started to think about *CSI* but that was too gross (and really Richard's show), so she went back to *Law & Order* and remembered the signature camera pans over bodies. Bodies?! Marion did her own pan, scanning Richard and the masseuse for signs of bleeding or bruises. (Okay, she scanned the masseuse for cellulite as well, but only for a second.) She didn't see anything. But what if she flipped them over? Ew.

And they still weren't moving.

Trembling, she forced herself to reach out and feel Richard's neck for a pulse. It was at that moment that he emitted a deep, drawn-out snore. In reply, the masseuse curled her free hand around the small of his back and let loose a fart.

This wasn't the first shock-horror moment in Marion's life. It wasn't the first time she'd been burned by a man or had her heart broken. And she knew this shit went down in France all the time, where wives of a certain age accepted mistresses without so much as batting an eyelash, but this was *America,* dammit! And she was an *American wife* who didn't have centuries of emotional disassociation from centuries of doormat treatment bred into her blood! Hell, she was a friggin' Stage III Trophy!

So Marion reacted emotionally. And did what any red-blooded, American Stage III Trophy wife would do:

She whipped out her cell phone and took about forty digital photographs, from all possible angles, for court documentation.

The rest happened pretty quickly. She wasn't sure what woke them up, the flash, the exploding glass, or the water.

The mantel in the master bedroom held an eclectic array of fine art. There was a Robert Graham torso sculpture, a translucent, lapis lazuli Egyptian bowl, six Art Nouveau hand-carved, blue-and-green glass fish, a trio of silver-framed family photos, a delicate, life-size magnolia blossom fashioned from pink jade, and a bouquet of parrot tulips in an exquisitely paper-thin Tiffany vase.

Richard's mother had given them that vase on their wedding day. It was inscribed with the advice *Always forgive, always forget. But never forget, you'll always be my baby.*

Marion threw that first.

There were screams, more projectiles, spectacular bursts, and scrambling flesh. Somewhere in the storm of bedclothes, Richard bellowed, "What the fuck is going on?!"

Following the sound of his voice, Marion began hurling glass fish like Ninja fighting stars.

"The destruction of fifty percent"—(hurl!)—"of YOUR COMMU-NITY PROPERTY, ASSHOLE!" Hurl! "THAT'S WHAT'S GOING ON!"

The masseuse, no less than Richard, was acting as if she had no idea how she came to be naked under Marion's naked husband. She scrambled to hide her (bad-boob-job) body with a pillow and make bullshit expressions of astonished terror. She had a scratchy, annoying voice.

"Ahhhh! Quit it, crazy bitch! Whatthefuck . . ."

That's when Marion caught her in the mouth with the Egyptian bowl and sent her sprawling over the edge of the bed.

Despite two framed photographs and a well-placed magnolia, Richard managed to stand and take a step toward her. The Robert Graham missed him completely. (But fortuitously destroyed that awful bust of Abe Lincoln he'd brought home from his office!)

"Honey, what's happening? I feel drugged!"

Then, as if to illustrate his pronouncement, Richard's eyes fluttered, his knees buckled, and he fell face-first onto the carpet like he'd been KO'd in a prizefight. This gave Marion pause as she realized that none of her ammo had connected with his head.

She'd been targeting his crotch.

Marion turned toward the fleeing masseuse, who'd placed a large bed sham on her back and was speed-crawling away like a silk jacquard turtle on meth. But unlike a turtle, the masseuse didn't look where she was going and smacked headfirst into the marble fireplace. A moment later, she flattened out like a turtle roadkill.

Satisfied that the masseuse wasn't going anywhere, Marion turned back to Richard.

Did he say *drugged*?

A new scenario bubbled to the surface of Marion's brain. This masseuse was new. They were rich. What if the masseuse slipped him something and was staging what she would call a rape in order to blackmail them? She'd heard about those date-rape drugs, where the victim didn't remember anything. Maybe they were being set up.

Nailing Richard with the last fish (in case her hypothesis was wrong), Marion then bent down and checked his pulse, respiration, and pupils (in case her hypothesis was right). He was definitely high but his heart was beating and he was breathing normally. After covering him with a robe from her dressing rooms, she lunged for the bedside and slapped at the panic button.

B y the time Carter and Gary burst in, Marion had already phoned her doctor and lawyer and checked the masseuse's bag and the master suite's trash receptacles for evidence. The still-naked masseuse was just staggering to her feet and the guards tackled her with gusto. Marion wasn't too drunk to note that Carter was taking his sweet time covering the girl with his jacket, so she swatted away his hands and tossed a blanket over her. Suspended between security guards, the masseuse, Marion noticed, also appeared groggy and drugged.

"Le-lemme goo, mutherfucks!" she blurted, slurring her words.

"Gary, call Roger," Marion said. "I need to know what Richard drank."

Her guards looked at each other for a second. What was this about?

"Roger had a date tonight," said Gary.

"And he really couldn't miss it," added Carter.

Great. Two ex–Navy Seals were terrified of a guy who rolled pastry for a living.

"Okay, so you covered for Roger. Didn't you think it was strange that the masseuse was still here after midnight? A massage lasts two hours, tops."

Gary looked at Carter. Carter stared at his shoes. Then Gary spoke.

"I—we thought maybe he . . . had a lot of knots?"

Even better. They were covering for Richard.

"Say no more."

"Yoo-hoo! Psssycho!" squalled the masseuse. "I de-*mand* you call the policcce! I've been like, dosssed or ssssomething by your hussssbanddd!"

By the sound of her accent, the masseuse was San Fernando Valley born and bred. She did seem woozy, but catching a lapis lazuli Frisbee in the mouth, followed by a head conk on solid marble, could probably produce the same effect.

Staring the masseuse down, Marion picked up a fireplace poker and advanced. This elicited moans and squeaks, but instead of braining her, Marion used the poker to collect the woman's clothes and offer them to her like diseased linens as she said, "And I de-*mand* that you get dressed. These gentlemen are licensed security officers who will detain your person in our guardhouse until the authorities arrive."

(After she'd covered all the bases with the doctor and lawyer.)

"I'm not a perssson!" the masseuse returned. "My name is *Tawnee*! Tawnee Dymns!"

Lovely.

Carter and Gary released her and she wriggled into her G-string, jeans, push-up bra, and tank top with the words NATURAL BLONDE emblazoned across the front. She wasn't. Marion did a quick appraisal and put her age to be around twenty-four. A slightly chunky, unremarkable twenty-four. Marion felt insulted. If Richard was going to cheat on her, he could at least do better than this.

But the masseuse wasn't done yet. "Ya hear me, psssycho violent lady? You're making a big fuckin' missstake!"

"And you were making naked farts under my husband in my bed. But your biggest 'missstake' is assuming I want to hear your annoying voice." This said, Marion turned her back. "Get her out of here."

Carter and Gary wrangled the struggling masseuse out like two cowboys in a bulldogging event while Marion knelt down to check Richard. He was shaking his head as if trying to clear it.

"Ugh! So foggy! I need coffee. Do you know how to—"

"I wasn't always married to you, Richard. I know how to do a shit ton of things. But you're not drinking anything until Dr. Purdue gets a urine and blood sample."

"It was the masseuse. She did it!"

"Funny, she said the same thing about you."

Richard looked alarmed. Or as alarmed as a groggy guy can look. "Good God, you don't think I would . . . Marion! I didn't touch her . . . This is crazy. Honey, ya gotta believe me!"

Marion really wanted to. She wanted to tell him she wanted to. Instead, she helped him to an armchair with as little physical contact as possible. Richard strained to look at the folded massage table against the wall.

"I started out there." Then, pointing to the bed, "How'd I end up there? I need to know how this happened!"

Marion nodded. "My sentiments exactly."

Then he put his arms around her hips and held on. She didn't pull away. Not just because she'd peppered him with bruises and cuts, or because he was drugged and confused (maybe), or even because he looked so forlorn in her pink satin robe with the marabou trim. Marion let her husband hold on to her because it just felt so damn good.

Richard sighed and let his head rest against her tummy. "Oh, Marion! I wanna sober up."

"Not me. I want to stay tanked for a month."

"You call Barry Shapiro?" he asked.

"Yep."

"And Dr. Purdue is on his way?"

"Yep."

"So now we just wait?"

Marion looked around the room. The mementos she and Richard collected over twenty years of marriage had been reduced to shards in seconds.

"Yep."

"Mmm."

At this point Richard started nuzzling her tummy. It felt nice. A little too nice. Like being pulled into warm-husband riptide. Pulling her down toward his lap . . .

(Oh, no you don't.)

Ten minutes earlier, this riptide was lying on top of a naked twenty-four-year-old.

Marion pulled away and headed for her closet. It was way too early for such tender affections. Not without seeing some drug-test results. Yes, she and Richard shared a twenty-year bond so close they knew each other on a freakin' cellular level, and up until this horror show she would have bet her life that he could be trusted as a faithful, loving husband. But she'd seen too many trusting casualties of twenty-plus-year unions. Life had shown her "faithful" can turn into "bored" in the blink of an eye.

When push came to shove, Marion's instinct for protecting her heart was stronger than the instinct that made her risk losing it to a man.

Extracting her *Black Book* from the safe, she flipped past the vast numbers of listings under the categories of Babies, Baggage, Ballet, Ballrooms, Banks, Bankers, Beach, Beachclubs, Biographers, and Biologists and stopped at the category titled Body Workers. Marion ran her finger past the international listings and the state listings, arriving at the Los Angeles listings, then, specifically, the House Calls section. She practically tore a hole in the page, drawing a thick black line through a newly entered service agency named Total Satisfaction. She added a cautionary skull and crossbones next to the cross-out, emphasized by three exclamation points—the strongest warning possible. And who had recommended this junk-show service, again? She had to erase half her cross-out line to see the name.

Marion returned the *Black Book* to the safe, moved back into the bedroom, and grabbed her purse from the hearth. She fished her cell phone out and flipped it open.

"What are you doing, now?" Richard complained.

"Texting Lyndy. I'm letting her know the massage agency she so highly recommended sucks."

Unfortunately, the first thing that popped up on Marion's screen was a close-up of Richard and Tawnee-of-the-Valley.

"Big-time," she added.

21

A Fresh New Start

"This waffle smells like ass."

"Manners, Brooke," said Billy, without looking up from the fax he was reading.

That's it? thought Claire. *Manners?*

In spite of last week's torturous first night as a stepmom, she'd risen at five and painstakingly prepared strawberry-and-whipped-cream-topped Belgian waffles from scratch, fresh-squeezed orange juice, French coffee, and hot cocoa with teensy tiny marshmallows, also from scratch. It took half an hour to locate the waffle iron in Billy's huge white-with-genuine-marble-countertops kitchen and she'd torn off a fingernail trying to open the evil European monster. Running late, she rushed on the nutmeg and grated the skin off a knuckle, burned her thumb, slopped orange pulp on her Ralph Lauren slippers, and ruined her new Hermès top with chocolate blobs and strawberry juice. The top cost more than her last car, back in Winamac. All in the name of getting a fresh new start with the girls.

The feast she'd laid out in the baby-pale yellow breakfast room was nicer than anything she'd ever seen in *Redbook* or *InStyle,* but when the three girls came in, they walked past her and her table without so much as a "Good morning" and started looking for cereal in the pantry. The only greeting she received was from Katia.

"We eat in the car, so we're on time for school," the nanny announced.

If you could call venom a greeting.

Luckily, Billy came in and coaxed the girls into joining them at the table. But as soon as he sat down, he buried his nose in his fax papers, leaving Brooke and Haley free to poke the waffles on their plates as if they were biology frogs for dissecting. Now they were openly insulting Claire! Why wasn't Billy defending her? Where was her prince?

"Maybe they like that smell in Belgium." Haley giggled. "Booty waffles!"

"It's vanilla and fresh nutmeg," clipped Claire, who'd had just about enough. "See? Here's the knuckle I scraped off on the grater because I was rushing to make everything perfect for all of you."

Brooke dropped her fork. "You bled in the food? That is *so* unsanitary!"

This wasn't going well. They were baiting her and she was taking the bait. *Kill 'em with kindness, remember? Just rise above.*

"Nooo. Don't be a silly! The only things in these waffles are organic farm-fresh ingredients and I think you'll find they're delicious if you'd stop poking and take a nice big bite."

"I love this breakfast! It's delicious!" yelled Eva.

She was the only one eating. Billy had barely sipped his French coffee. Judging from the six-year-old's wildly smiling, sticky face and hyper-bouncing knees, Claire could tell that Eva was coming on to the hot chocolate and syrup.

"Well, thank you, Eva! Why don't you show your sisters what they're missing?"

"I'm going to take the biggest bite in the world!" Eva shrieked. "First a plump, juicy strawberry, then a crispy golden waffle, then some syrup and a big blob of whipped cream!"

Correction: Eva was experiencing a full-spectrum sugar rush.

"Atta girl," cheered Claire.

It was working. The big girls weren't about to let their sister be the only one to get a treat. Brooke actually took a bite and Haley sipped her hot chocolate. Nobody could resist this breakfast. Soon they'd be digging in. Claire clapped her hands in delight as Eva strained to get her jaws around the bite she'd speared. Everything was going to be fine.

"Eva, that is too big a bite."

Katia entered and put her hands on her hips in disapproval. Claire wondered if the nanny came equipped with a pleasure detector that sounded an alarm for her when any opportunity arose to crush some joy in the vicinity. Well, she wasn't about to let a sourpuss ruin a Secret Rainbow

Princess Breakfast Party Moment. (Claire had revised her promise to incorporate marriage and stepchildren.)

"That's the only way to eat Belgian waffles, Katia! Go, Eva, go!"

Eva's sisters joined in. "Go, Eva! Go, Eva! Go, Eva!" they chanted.

Even Billy looked up from his reading. "Whoa, that is some bite!" He chuckled.

(Take that, sourpuss.)

Eva did her best imitation of a boa constrictor unhinging its jaws and stuffed the forkful in her mouth. She bit down, squirting strawberry juice, syrup, and cream goo all over herself. Everyone cheered. Everyone except Katia.

"Now look what you've done. You've ruined your sweater," she snipped.

"Well, we'll get her another one," countered Claire. "Dig in, everybody. Let's see if we can beat Eva's record."

"We won't get another sweater like that one. Her *grandmother* knitted that sweater."

"Well, she'll just have to knit another one, because it's waffle time!" Claire sang out, with glee.

Then she noticed everybody had stopped eating. And smiling.

"Our grandmother died last month," said Haley.

"Oh, I'm so sorry . . ." Claire gasped as the whirlpool took hold of her.

"She knitted that sweater for me," said Brooke. "I handed it down to Haley and she gave it to Eva. It was the last thing she knitted before the stroke took away the use of her hands."

Correction: not just any old whirlpool, a giant toilet. Katia pointed out the handle and her stepdaughters gave it a six-handed flush.

"Go upstairs, Eva," commanded Katia as she lifted the girl from her seat. "We need to get you clean clothes and wash that nasty syrup out of your hair."

"I loved my grandma!" Eva yelled at Claire, without removing her thumb from her mouth. Then she burst into tears and ran upstairs.

"I didn't know," Claire said helplessly, wondering if it would kill Billy to step in on her behalf. He was back in his papers!

"Now you do," spat Katia, and followed Eva out.

Making a quick mental estimate, Claire figured the nanny's head was just thin enough to fit between the jaws of the waffle iron.

"Now we'll be late," mumbled Haley.

"Oh, God, I've got a test!" gasped Brooke. "I knew we shouldn't have sat down!"

"Daddy to the rescue," said Billy, rising. "My chariot awaits."

He was rescuing the wrong princess. And Claire was the wrong dragon.

"Can I make anyone a to-go package for the road?" she offered in desperation.

Haley and Brooke looked at her like she'd offered to stab them, while Billy shook his head for her to back off.

"Grab your stuff, girls."

Claire simply couldn't compute what was going down. How was it happening? How, in this baby-pale-yellow breakfast room with the tasteful crown-and-baseboard moldings, with the best breakfast ever served? She'd always been the most popular—always crowned, never runner-up. And never, ever, a *loser*! How the hell did Belgian waffles turn her 'Breakfast Moment' into a shit sandwich? No. No, this wasn't a disaster, just a *tiny bump* in her Promise. Claire was a Rainbow Princess and Billy's wife, and Eva, Haley, and Brooke's *stepmom*. *She'd act like a stepmom and she'd be one, goddammit!* Claire threw back her shoulders and flashed her best pageant smile at the girls.

"Bye, Brooke. Bye, Haley. Have a nice day at school! I'll have chocolate chip cookies for homework, this afternoon!" she said, with dazzling enthusiasm.

They snatched up their backpacks and ran past her for the car without saying good-bye. Billy looked at his watch and drained his coffee. Thinking fast, Claire took his hand. If they could use tears, so could she.

"Oh, Billy, I tried so hard to make a nice breakfast for them. I didn't know the grandma died." She sniffed.

"Of course you didn't, Cookie. Don't worry, they're just fussy in the morning. I'll see ya tonight."

Fussy? Claire had another adjective in mind. He'd called her Cookie again too. "But you didn't even get to try the waffles."

"Got a breakfast meeting at the studio. I know, you can make new ones tonight. We'll eat waffle supper."

Claire almost told Billy that she would rather eat off her arm, but he was looking at her with such love, she just smiled and tipped her head back so they could melt into a kiss.

Then Katia reappeared. "Your homosexual friend is here with more of your expensive purchases," she announced, and Craig-the-stylist burst in with an armload of designer bags.

"It's a good thing you're rich!" he trilled.

Instead of a kiss, Claire got an arm squeeze and a quick exit.

"Good thing, indeed," huffed Katia, judgmentally.

"Billy is so *progressive*," said Craig, quite loudly, as if Katia were invisible, "allowing a *transvestite* to care for his girls."

Enraged and insulted beyond words, the nanny could only hiss and make the sign of the evil eye at Claire, before she ducked out.

"Great, you call her names and I get the scary hissing noise. She's probably upstairs putting depilatory in my shampoo bottle." said Claire as she collected the silverware and tried not to cry for real.

"There's no staff problem a good blow job won't fix. Tell Billy to dump her." Craig looked at Claire's bandaged fingers. "Don't tell me you're *cutting* over her. You look like Edward Scissorhands on a bad day!"

Claire finally broke down and Craig encircled her with his heavily cologned arms. "Weeping? Girl, this can't all be about the tranny."

"My stepchildren hate me."

"Uh-huh, that's their job. What else?"

"And Billy won't defend me against them."

"Uh-huh. He's a divorced dad. They don't."

"And he's so busy I hardly see him."

"That's *good*, Edward Scissorhands. He's making money for you to spend. You've got to start thinking like a Trophy and see past the small shit to the big picture."

Craig released her and started digging through the bags, like an excited child. "Speaking of money and scissors, go shower and put this on."

He withdrew a tiny lime-colored dress that looked like it was made out of skinny Ace bandages and tossed it to her.

"Her-vé Lé-ger," he cooed, and dove back into the bags. "And this cashmere day coat and where are the shoes? Ugh, we've got less than an hour to meet Rhone!"

"Craig, I can't meet anybody. I have to clean up the kitchen because I don't speak Spanish and I don't want the maid to hate me too. My hair needs to be washed, set, and dried. I'll have to miss Patti's birthday party if I don't shop for a gift."

"You'll do nothing of the sort! Patti's parties are insane and the swag is extreme. You're giving her this." Craig pulled out an elaborate box and opened it. Inside was something that looked like a large cow patty. "A petrified dinosaur heart. She'll be the first on her block and go batshit. Leave the mess for the tranny, and don't think about your hair. Just scrub your face and bod. We'll do the rest at the salon. *Rhone* is your new hairdresser. It's makeover day!"

Makeover? In Claire's mind, that was something for homely people. "But I like my hair . . ." she began.

"You are so *cute* when you're traumatized. Now we have less than fifty minutes. Aha! Here's your kicks."

Craig produced a pair of five-inch pumps and added them to the pile in Claire's arms. They had complicated straps and buckles that reminded her of a straitjacket, especially since they were white. *White?* Was Craig out of his mind? Even she knew better than to commit such a serious fashion "don't."

"Craig, it's way before Memorial Day," she said, offering the shoes back.

Craig drew himself up but made no move to accept them. "*So cute!* Eddie, you're in L.A. now. Your husband is in 'The Business.' Ladies in 'The Business' don't subscribe to provincial guidelines for the ignorant masses. They wear couture *before* it's in on the runway or copied by discount houses and offered on the Web, because they are *connected*. This causes them to be photographed and emulated, which causes juice, which causes exclusivity and garners male attention. Those pumps happen to be the only pair of spring made-to-order D-squared on the West Coast. But if you'd feel more secure wearing something with a pork-'n-beans sensibility, I know of at least three actresses who would kill for a chance to wear these to their premieres . . ."

Claire yanked back the shoes and clutched them to her breast like holy relics. "Give me ten minutes," she said, and dashed past Katia and Eva on the stairs.

Without saying good-bye.

22

A Gift from Greece

The sight of Pepper nursing his infant son was a beautiful thing to behold. That is, unless your lap is suddenly filled with Fruit Loops and iced milk.

"I make Daddy wet!" two-year-old Chevelle proudly squealed.

"You make Daddy cry," gasped Ari, too stunned to move.

"Chevelle, *no*. We don't pour food on Daddy," Pepper scolded as she tossed Ari her spit-up cloth. "Sorry, hon. Wipe it off before it soaks in."

"Yes, I will do that, as soon as my testicles descend from behind my spleen."

Cooter laughed like a donkey until Chevelle bounced her bowl across the table, nailing him right between the eyes.

"You're gonna pay for that!" Cooter yelled as he leaped to his feet and reached for his sister.

"I'm telling!" screamed four-year-old Maybelle.

"Don't you *dare* hit the baby!" yelled Pepper. "And you don't need to tell, Maybelle. Mom and Dad are right here. We can see what he did."

No MIT for that one, thought Ari, mopping his painfully thawing lap. They'd have to arrange a rich marriage or support Maybelle until their graves.

"Everybody's the baby, 'cept me," grumbled Cooter. He was pouring an obscene amount of jelly into his grits, followed by the drippings from the plate that had once held Canadian bacon.

"What am I, knucklehead?" asked Jerry, beaning his brother with a biscuit chunk, which banked into Ari's coffee cup and ominously dissolved.

"I'm telling!" screamed Maybelle.

"Next one to throw food gets m' bad side," warned Pepper as she removed Ari's biscuit coffee and poured him a fresh cup, poked Maybelle to sit in her seat, snatched up Chevelle's cereal bowl, refilled it, and whapped Jed for taking butter with his fingers. All this with a baby latched on like a limpet. It seemed to Ari his wife sometimes had more arms than a Hindu goddess.

"Hon, lemme fix you some oatmeal," she offered.

As she stood, Baby Jed's full-diaper aroma wafted over the table, sending his father's appetite into hibernation.

"PU!" screamed the kids.

"Nuclear butt fallout!" wailed Jerry.

"I think I'll get something at the office, my baby," Ari fibbed. "I set up a meeting with a tax fellow and I need to prepare. And maybe we could raise the temperature on the refrigerator."

"With the way these monkeys leave the doors open? We'll all croak from botulism. Sure you don't want oatmeal?"

"Quite sure."

Ari stood and went around the table, kissing heads. When he came to Jerry, the boy shrank away.

"Jerry?" asked Pepper.

"I ain't no fag."

"You ain't gonna draw no breath if you don't kiss Daddy good-bye!" she snarled. "An' deprogram the gay-bashin' before I bash yer playdates off yer schedule for a month."

Jerry obeyed like a soldier, laying a jelly skid mark across his father's cheek. Ari turned to his wife, but she waved him off, pointing to the toxic diaper.

"Wouldn't come any closer if you wanna keep what's left of your nose hairs. Have a good day and don't agree to any structure reorganization. You know what happened the last time!"

How could he forget?

Five years ago, Ari had just finished laying out a proposed multicompany consolidation plan for seven of his three companies' executives when his enormously pregnant wife swept in to announce that she was near labor. Ari sprang into action, grabbing his coat and directing his assistant to find a new date to reconvene the meeting. But before he could hustle his balloon of a wife out the door, she caught sight of his business plan on the display screen. With one cursory look, Pepper pointed out three flaws and a deferment proposal that would have, at best, landed the accountants in jail. Next, she proceeded to revise the plan completely. Ari begged her to stop and go with him for the sake of the baby, but she'd locked onto his plan like a pit bull. In front of everyone. Worst of all, she'd been right. The third time he asked her to quit and make haste for the delivery room, six of the seven executives actually shushed him! (The seventh had fainted when her water broke.) It was the most humiliating and hysterical half hour in his life. He could still see her hovering over the conference table in that zeppelin-size minidress. Sure, she saved them all $400 million, but Paris/Cooter ended up being delivered in the secretaries' pantry.

That plan had still been in the *development stage*. He would have caught those mistakes. Him or the accountant. Probably.

In the end, Ari had saved face by explaining about Pepper's former profession and the fact that she was a mathematics savant, but ever since that day, any plans he made involving figures were always met with the question "Did you check this out with your wife?"

Yes, Pepper only did it out of love. She couldn't help it if she had a gift with numbers. He certainly had no reason to whine. Most men would trade their teeth for a wife who saved their companies money. Wives who would risk everything for them, the way Pepper had done back in D.C. Plus, the girl still stopped traffic even after five kids. Come to think of it, he was the luckiest man on earth.

And with that thought, Ari loped back to the dining room, back through the kiddie circus and the baby stink, and planted a big French kiss on his magnificent wife.

"Why is everybody kissing good-bye? Daddy's still here," Maybelle puzzled.

Ari smiled at the tot, silently praying the girl would grow up to be pretty.

Ten minutes later, as he headed west on Santa Monica Boulevard, Ari's appetite reappeared with a vengeance and he found himself turning in to the Peninsula. The Belvedere's pastel garden-view ambience guaranteed it would be one of the few restaurants in town that could be packed with breakfast-meeting crowds and still offer padded peace. But ambience wasn't the reason he'd come. Ari was answering the siren call of Belvedere's coffee cake. Coffee cake was Ari's cocaine. When he was a child, his Austrian governess, Heidel, had expressed her affection through baking, her specialty being a moist, rich pound-cake-style wonder with butter-brown sugar crumble on top. Heidel must have loved Ari better than Jesus because Ari didn't lose his baby fat until boarding school, where ridicule forced him to swear off all baked goods. As an adult, his high blood pressure compelled Pepper to impose further diet restrictions, which he readily accepted in the name of longevity. But left alone with a coffee cake, especially the Heidel-style beauty calling his name from the table of breakfast goodies next to the maître d' station, he lost all control.

Because of the coffee cake, Ari might never have noticed the petite young woman behind him in line had she not been speaking Greek. And even then, she never would have distracted his focus from the coffee cake's seduction had she not started to cry. Eavesdropping in earnest, he learned that the raven-haired girl had tried to eat breakfast in the park along Santa Monica Boulevard but was harassed by two panhandling veterans and a man in torn leotards on roller skates who kept trying to make her dance with him. When she asked a policeman for advice as to where she could dine undisturbed, he demanded identification, as if she were a suspected terrorist. Throughout her interrogation, the man on the skates kept circling them screaming, "Kiss me dirty!" but the policeman paid him no heed. The veterans had eaten her food while she spoke to the policeman, and now the girl was wailing to her mother in Athens and trying to get fed.

Poor thing, thought Ari. The skating guy had been a local fixture for years. The black-swathed fruitcake was Cooter's answered profession when people asked him what he wanted to be when he grew up. Even Beverly Hills cops, who mercilessly rousted nonlocals, tolerated the skating guy like a goofy pet.

"Just cleared a table, Mr. Papadopoulos," said the maître d'.

"Excuse me," said the young woman, "How long for table for one?"

"Do you have a reservation?" the maître d' sniffed.

"No."

"Are you a guest of the hotel?"

She shook her head.

"I'm sorry, we're totally booked at the moment. I could serve you a continental breakfast at the bar, but you'd have better luck somewhere else, ma'am."

"I cannot sit alone at a bar," she said, then muttering a Greek curse, she turned to go.

"I'm going to eat fast; you could join me, then have the table to yourself after I leave," said Ari, taking pity on her. And he added in Greek, *"Don't curse the poor man, it's his job to be snobbish."*

The young woman was taken aback but pleased. "Are you sure I won't disturb you?"

Ari thought of his morning at home. "I'm sure your idea of disturbance is quite different from mine. Though you might lose a finger if you come between me and my cake."

The young woman broke into a smile that was like sunlight piercing storm clouds and sparkling the top of the sea. "My name is Mariah," she said as they walked to the table.

"I'm Ari Papadopoulos and I only roller-skate with six-year-olds."

After coffee and a bit of coaxing, Mariah finally confessed that it wasn't just the park episode that had reduced her to calling her mother in tears. She'd relocated to America, taking a position as a translator and researcher with a prestigious firm that sold rare antiquities. She enjoyed her new job but she could not stay in the apartment the company had secured for her because it was in a dangerous neighborhood. After weeks of searching, she'd finally found a security building in Century City, but the owner refused to rent to her unless the lease was cosigned by an American. Mariah was still a newcomer at her firm and could hardly expect any of her coworkers to take such a risk and she couldn't approach her boss. He was already losing patience at having to pay for the hotel at Santa Monica and Doheny.

"It would be, how you say, *flaky* to ask him."

"I'll do it," offered Ari, finishing the last bite of his second piece of coffee cake without a raindrop of guilt.

"But you don't even know my last name!" she gasped.

"I'll learn it when you send over the lease," he said, tossing her a business card, grabbing the check, and looking at his watch. "I just committed a deadly sin, you'll be my good deed to balance it out. We Greeks need to stick together."

"You've just gone from sinner to saint. Thank you. Bless you! But how do you know I'm not a charlatan?"

Ari stood and looked at Mariah. The pale, bird-boned girl, with her prim dress and corkscrew hair tied back with a scarlet ribbon, reminded him of a shy young housekeeper who had tended his gay uncle's summerhouse on Mikonos. That housekeeper was so pious she ended up joining a convent.

"I cannot imagine in my wildest dreams that that is possible," he said.

Mariah's dark eyes sparked, making Ari think of flint spark, fire, and caves.

As he pulled out of the parking lot, Ari knew he was taking a ridiculous risk. Maybe it was the schoolboy giddiness of playing hooky from the family and sneaking off for cake that had made him so impetuous. And what of it? He'd check the lease papers when he got them, and if the girl ended up stiffing him, big deal. He was rich. And he could always give the apartment to Patti Fink, who'd use it to stash stepchildren or Hondurans. But he couldn't imagine this Mariah cheating him. His own children possessed more guile. Every inch of her looked like a convent candidate.

Only her eyes were bewitching.

23

Two-Piece Karma

Patti Fink's BlackBerry rang as she speed-clicked across Shutters's parking lot toward the hotel's less populated boardwalk entrance. During morning hours, Shutters's front entrance was too bustling for comfort. Unsnapping the BlackBerry's Hermès orange alligator cover, she recognized Maya's phone number on the screen and came to an abrupt and gritty halt on the edge of the boardwalk.

"Don't you dare back out of my party!" Patti squealed, nearly causing a bicyclist to wipe out.

By insisting on giving her a morning "birthday bang," Ricky, her paramour, had totally thrown her off schedule. Party cancellations would be too much to bear. Patti took a deep breath of ocean air (with low notes of garbage, urine, and cotton candy) and kept her fingers crossed.

"Do I sound like I want my ass kicked?" Maya replied. "Listen, are you in the middle of something?"

"No, but something's about to be in the middle of me."

Continuing toward the hotel, Patti stepped around a huge pile of filthy clothing and garbage that later in the day would transform into a person. A seagull tentatively picked at the edges.

"*Don't want to know!*" insisted Maya. "I'm calling to ask what you like for swimwear this summer. I hold back on my commitment to *Sports Illustrated* so they send over ten thousand bikinis and cover-up shit to bribe me."

"Ooh, I haven't thought about it yet," Patti crooned, instantly visualizing an extensive bikini look-book of herself and flipping through it.

Patterns or solids? Jewel tones or pastels? Were metallics still in? How could she decide?

"Are you still there?" Maya asked.

"Uh-huh."

Scanning the beach and boardwalk for inspiration, Patti locked onto an old homeless woman. She was about fifty yards in from the tide line, beachcombing along the polluted lake formed by Pico Avenue storm-drain runoff. Lacking a jacket, the crone had wrapped a striped purple rug around herself, secured with belts and pieces of twine.

"And . . . ah, one other thing." Maya's voice was strained, almost whispering.

"Uh-huh," Patti said, raising her forearm to check her skin tone against the alternating aubergine and lavender of the rug jacket. Good thing she'd had Lasik.

"Did any of your husbands ever . . . insist you bear them children?"

Patti found that the stripes looked disruptive against the blue expanse of the sea. Worse, her skin took on a grayish tone against the purples. Not good at all! "Uh-huh . . . not stripes. And *definitely* not purple."

Patti lowered her arm and held it against the concrete-and-bronze trash receptacle, which held the still-smoldering ashes of a fire someone had lit against last night's cold.

"Really? Which one?" Maya asked.

"Any of them. Even wide stripes aren't good. Let's say earth tones for pool and hot colors for beach. And no cutout styles that give weird tan lines."

Patti did a double take as she noticed her new birthday bracelet from Lou. The biggest emerald looked like it had a crack, but she realized it was just some ash from the trash can. Phew!

"No," Maya barked, exasperated. "Which *husband*?"

"Mmmph."

Now the bracelet was snagged in her Chloé sweater sleeve! Patti carefully struggled to disentangle the yarn so it wouldn't make a pull and resumed power-clicking toward the hotel's glass doors.

"Did he insist?" Maya continued. "How did you change his mind?"

"I'm married to *Lou* now. He never insists on any particular suit, as long as it comes off easy. Honey, if I don't get going with Ricky, I'll miss the Sri Baba's annual Meditation to Banish the Sufferings of the Poor. The temple's clear across town!"

"Huh?"

"Lou! Is there anything else before I go inside?"

"Um, no. Never mind. I'll see you at one. Happy birthday."

"Thanks, bye!"

Patti tucked the Hermès-clad BlackBerry into her giant orange alligator Hermès tote and scooted around a blue-suited Shutters hotel assistant manager who was giving the bum's rush to a young shoeless girl who'd been trying to enter the Pedals restaurant. The girl's hollowed eyes, dirty clothes, and scarecrow frame were consistent with what Patti knew of the drug-addicted runaways who congregated at the nearby pier—a location that provided survival through panhandling, petty theft, and if things got bleak, prostitution. Local businesses regarded the scruffy minors as profit-deterring public nuisances. Patti felt herself fortunate that the assistant manager was occupied and took no notice of her. She also liked the cut of his suit.

Once inside Shutters's boardwalk entrance, Patti whipped off her Paco Rabanne pumps and sprinted for the rear elevators. She'd have to throw Ricky down on the bed and climax as fast as possible. If she missed the Meditation to Banish the Sufferings of the Poor on her birthday, it might throw her karma off for a year.

24

A Night to Forget

*A*t the sound of her name, Marion rose from her seat while the ball-room exploded in thunderous applause and cheers. A spotlight iso-lated her in a pool of blinding whiteness, making it difficult for her to navigate between the tables of adoring friends and luminaries on her way to the stage. Being blinded, she couldn't see which adoring friends or luminaries had leaped to their feet in wild applause until she was practically on top of them. They just popped out of the dark.

Here was Crystal, who'd surprised everyone by getting up off her self-centered ass and flying out for the occasion. Of course she was too preoc-cupied with chatting on her cell and reading a magazine to get up off her self-centered ass and applaud right now, but that was a good thing, since she was naked from the waist down.

Dickie Jr. had flown out as well and was sitting back at her own table with Zephyr. He looked so slick in his tux. Not the good kind of slick. The kind that made her want to kick herself for leaving her purse on the chair next to his light fingers.

Marion wasn't sure why Patti Fink had chosen to wear three outfits on top of one another. Wasn't she hot? Patti was trying to tell her something, but Marion couldn't make it out because Patti's mouth was obscured by a turtle-neck of at least thirty necklaces. Pepper too was trying to give her advice, but her kids had lit the tablecloth on fire and Marion had to back away from the billowing smoke. She tried to say hi when she spotted Maya, but her glamorous pal was in the process of choking an oil industry lobbyist. Why spoil her fun?

"*Marion, you look tired. Do you want me to accept the award for you?*" Lyndy asked, popping out of the darkness. In a Dior gown (that camouflaged her butt panties), Cartier panther bracelets, and twenty carats of Harry Winston diamond teardrops, Lyndy looked ten years younger and more glamorous than Marion had ever witnessed. Even her hairstyle and makeup were fresh and alluring. Marion couldn't believe the makeover. Lyndy had finally achieved, without a doubt, pure Trophy perfection. Except for the long red forked tongue that flicked in and out of her mouth.

"*I'm fine, darling. I can do it. And you should see a specialist about that,*" Marion whispered. Maybe Patti knew somebody.

"*About what?*"

Lyndy's forked tongue flicked silently in and out, as if tasting Marion's essence. Well, if she didn't want to discuss it . . .

"*Don't go up there,*" a voice said.

It was Xiocena's niece Carita. She was sitting with her aunt, who was completely absorbed in scratching off lottery tickets. Thank God the whole death thing had been a mistake and how dear of them to come, but why didn't Carita want her to accept her award?

"*Of course I'm going up there silly! I can't go back now.*" Marion patted Carita's hand and noticed it was alarmingly cold. "*They always keep these damn ballrooms like meat lockers, Xio. I have a wrap over at my table. Why don't you grab it for Carita? She feels like an icicle and there's at least another half hour to go.*"

But Xiocena just kept scratching, as if she were deaf.

"*Xio?*"

"*Shhh!*" said Carita. "*She's praying.*"

Now, where was that stage?

Camera flashes started erupting like fireworks, so Marion figured she had to be close. Close and completely blind. How did celebrities do this? Luckily, Richard was there to help guide her up the stairs and hand her off to the host, who led her to the podium.

And who was the host again? Shit! She'd read his name in the program but was now drawing a blank. She recognized him but couldn't place the face. Actor? Comedian? Sports figure? This was going to make for one awkward acceptance speech. And speaking of awkward, who wears a paisley smoking jacket and a fez in public? It was Ralph Lauren gone terribly wrong. And *those things over his shoes. What were they called, "spats"? Another colossally poor choice. Was he a writer?*

Marion reached the podium, but before she could speak, a reporter from the mosh pit interrupted her.

"Marion, now that the hospital's built, what are you going to do with your life?"

Naturally, she ignored him with a smile but the host encouraged her to answer.

"Yes, Marion, what shall we do with your life?"

She didn't like the way he was smiling. It was practically wolflike. Why did he say "we"? "I hadn't really thought about—"

"Marion, why don't you start a religion? Then you'll really be immortal!" another reporter yelled.

"What? That's not why I built Carita Memorial!" She turned to the host for help, but he was smiling even more broadly and started calling on reporters, like he was presiding over a freakin' press conference.

"Why don't you donate a kidney, Marion? That's truly 'giving of yourself'!"

"Why haven't you cured cancer? Or AIDS? You've got enough money to cure either one!"

"That's hardly the case, but Richard and I are major contributors to medical research aimed toward developing a cure for both," she blurted, amazed that she'd actually been forced to defend herself. Well, she'd be damned if she'd ever give another penny to this fucked-up organization. Allowing the honoree to be grilled by the press.

"That's not enough!" This wasn't from a reporter; it was from Lyndy. Marion could tell by the forked tongue catching the light. Why on earth was Lyndy treating her this way?

"Not enough!" Lyndy yelled again.

The host was laughing. What kind of awards ceremony was this? A Candid Camera show? Was she being punked? She was pretty sure this host wasn't on a television show, though.

"Not enough! Not enough!" chanted the audience.

This was getting ugly. Marion looked across the dark ballroom, but she could no longer see her friends. Even her stepkids were gone, not that they'd be any help. The pools of light revealed only reporters and hecklers. And enemies. There was Jack Powell, shaking a fistful of political donor lists at her, and Craig-the-stylist, brandishing a Manolo Blahnik five-inch stiletto pump. They looked hostile, like those villagers with torches in the Frankenstein movies.

And where was her husband? Normally, he wouldn't stand for this. Why didn't he save her?

"Richard?" Marion called into the mike. "I want to go home now."

"He's in the men's room," chortled the host. "You know how he likes to dawdle."

It was Marion's pet peeve. What was it with men spending so much time upon toilets? And what if he had the trades or Sunday papers with him in there? She couldn't wait that long. She needed to leave now!

Fortunately, there was a monk next to the stage. He wore a brown-hooded robe and pulled down on an enormous rope that rang a bell so loud it shook the entire ballroom. Surely a man of the cloth would show compassion.

"Father," Marion yelled, "or Brother or whatever you are. I'm lapsed but I'd give you first crack at confession if you call for my car! The ticket is in my purse at that table. On the chair. Yes, that's right. Not the black one, the Vivier. If you'd just take the blue ticket to valet . . ."

But the monk was shaking his head. He held up her purse and showed her that it was empty. Damn you, Dickie Jr.!

"Okay, maybe you could describe the car to the valet. It's a midnight-black Maybach . . ."

Then the monk's hood fell back. Holy shit, it was Ivan! What had he done?

"Ivan, noooo!" Marion pleaded. "Not going into events season! I'll double your health care!"

"Not enough!" chanted the audience.

Ivan gave the rope a final yank and faded away into darkness. Would no one take her away?

"Why did you leave me in Cleveland?" Zephyr was standing in the mosh pit with the reporters. At least she hadn't left, like everyone else was doing.

"I didn't want to! I loved you!"

"Not enough!" Zephyr roared.

"Not enough!" echoed the ballroom.

The reporters mobbed Zephyr with questions until all Marion could see was a tuft of nonstraightened hair. Then Marion saw her squirt out of the crush and run for the door. At least ten reporters gave chase.

"Leave her alone! Zephyr, wait! I can explain on the ride home!"

"You can't leave now, Marion. You haven't told us about Cleveland." Even though she hadn't heard it in years, Marion recognized the voice that had once sent her screaming for designer sedatives and hair-loss-prevention salves. It belonged to that horrible gossip ghoul, Verna Hale! She was standing in the center of the mosh pit, tape recorder poised and ready. Verna was still wearing her signature nineties look: monochromatic black, with her slick black dominatrix hair and sparse makeup. Didn't she update? She even wore that awful wolf-eating-a-rabbit bracelet. Wait a minute. Hadn't she destroyed Verna back in the nineties? How did she get a press pass?

"I don't have to talk to you. You're out of the business," Marion replied triumphantly.

"Oh, yes you do," purred Verna. "What was it they called you back then in Cleveland? 'Blood sausage'?"

"Don't you dare call me that nickname! That's why I destroyed you!"

"Yes, it wasn't to protect your friends, was it? That's also why you don't gossip. It's all about you, isn't it, Marion?"

"Go fuck yourself, Verna."

Okay, that wasn't the most ladylike utterance, but this was no tea party. Marion was afraid that if she stayed onstage any longer, the whole agonizing truth about her would come wriggling out like a tapeworm. Her only hope was to run as fast and as far as she could, but just then, the host clamped down on her shoulders with an iron grip. Her naked shoulders! She was completely nude! And she hadn't done her Power Plate this week (or gotten waxed!). And now Verna was holding a camera!

"Richard! Help! Aren't you finished yet?" Marion yelped.

She received no reply. Not even the sound of a hopeful "flush."

Marion tried to rip away from the stage, but the host turned her around. Instead of the back of the stage, she saw trees and sky. When she looked down, she saw the reflecting pond in her backyard. But she'd torn that thing out years ago. What asshole had restored it? And then she saw her toes and realized she was standing on the edge of the tower parapet!

Now Marion suddenly remembered the host's name.

"RUTHERFORD, NOOOO!"

Rutherford Wilson, now sporting the head of a wolf, gave her a vicious shove and she was falling headfirst—algae and water lilies rushing up at her! And that dreadful little boy statue peeing! Rutherford's laughter rang in her ears like a deafening buzz saw; louder and louder and . . .

25

Rolling Over

ZZZZ! Not quite out of her dream, Marion whipped around to accuse Richard of . . . but he wasn't in the men's room. He was right beside her, and snoring to beat the band. Holy saints in a school bus! She hadn't had a nightmare that bad since the aftermath of Patti's "Taste of New Delhi" dinner party! Marion wished she could tell him about it and see if he had any interpretations, but only his penis seemed to be awake.

She and Richard had just started sleeping together again. But no sex. Not yet. Not since that night. Although the sight of her husband's only waking part made Marion almost forget both her nightmare and the reasons she'd imposed the nookie embargo. Sure, the loose ends of *l'affaire masseuse* were troubling, but so was "pelvic congestion." (Especially with Richard's great big "decongestant" staring her in the face.)

Marion rolled out from under Richard's arm and onto her back, deciding to allow herself a mental backtrack before passion got the best of her.

Dr. Purdue had put a rush on the blood and urine samples, and yes, Richard had been drugged with Rohypnol, the famous "roofie" date-rape drug but it turned out that Tawnee-of-the-Valley had the same date-rape drug in her own system. There was no evidence whatsoever of a sexual encounter. But then, why were they naked in bed together? Their bodies weren't puppeteered by Frank Oz! Neither of them claimed to remember jackshit. How convenient.

They both said they remembered drinking from separate bottles of Hildon water, but the empties were nowhere to be found even though the instant-response private forensic team Marion had selected from her *Black Book* combed the grounds until 3 A.M. What was up with that?

Then there was the sideshow with the staff. Roger had rushed over so fast he was still sporting buffalo bedhead when he lunged through the door. He swore on his mother's soul in heaven that he'd personally inspected every water bottle that had come into the house for tampering and personally set the ice bucket and Hildon water out before he'd left for his date. All the bottles had been sealed. Then there was the problem of Roger's deserting them for a booty call and the cover-up. Richard was so furious to learn he'd been alone with the masseuse that for a second Marion thought she'd be headed back to Paris to poach another five-star chef, becoming persona non grata at another five-star hotel. (And there were only so many places to stay!) Luckily, whoever held the position of chef at the compound was historically always Richard's favorite employee, so he just suspended Roger for one week without pay, then decided that this was punishing himself, so he suspended the suspension until "further notice."

Gary and Carter were almost fired as well, until Marion pointed out they'd been coerced by the chef, who wasn't getting fired, so they too were put on suspended suspension. Still, there was a millisecond of a moment when Marion spotted Roger exchanging a look with Gary and Carter. Were they hiding something?

As always, the legalities had been most pressing that night. Barry Shapiro wasn't called "the Dustbuster" for nothing. People joked that he cleaned up so many ugly messes on the Westside, his offices had been raided by immigration. Barry understood that even the smallest crumb of a scandal could be turned into a feast by the press.

The Zanes had made the lawyer's acquaintance on the occasion of Dickie Jr.'s first escapade with a high-priced call girl. Of course it wasn't Dickie's deflowering that called for Barry's services; he was eleven at the time. Dickie Jr.'s mess had been the result of his appropriating the call girl's client book and launching a lucrative blackmailing operation. (The kid had had two full-time employees just to handle the drop-offs.) For a mere astronomical fee, Barry Shapiro dustbusted the blackmailing mess and got Dickie Jr. a movie deal with Showtime to boot. Throughout Dickie Jr.'s childhood, Barry maintained a second office in the Zanes' guesthouse (when he wasn't working for Patti Fink), and even though Marion's stepson was now at an age when he required the services of lawyers more specialized in federal cases, Barry Shapiro remained on permanent Zane retainer.

That night, Barry arrived in record speed and scoped out the situation in a heartbeat. It took him less than ten minutes behind closed doors with Tawnee before he rejoined them in the kitchen with a signed confidentiality agreement and a covenant not to sue.

"Confidentiality's gonna cost you two U2 tickets. They're playing the Hollywood Bowl this fall," Barry added, grabbing his jacket and an apple for the road.

Reminder: She needed to hit Bono up for the hospital.

"How do we know she won't press charges?" Richard had asked.

"You'll know when you get my bill," Barry replied.

"How do we know she won't say she signed under duress or under the influence of a drug?" asked Marion.

"Jimmy Purdue gave her the same stuff as Richard. She's as sober as the heart attack I almost gave her with my 'What Happens When You Piss Off Very Private Billionaires' lecture. Doc said she could drive herself home."

"Well, we'll need confidentiality agreements from the staff too," Richard added, trying hard to make a contribution to the proceedings.

"Already got 'em." Barry headed for the front door with Marion and Richard trailing him.

"How do we get the tickets to the masseuse?" Marion asked.

"What masseuse? As far as you're concerned, they're for me. Just messenger 'em to my office when you get 'em."

Barry then opened the front door and momentarily shocked them with a flash of predawn light.

"So it's as if it never happened?" Marion had asked.

"Yep. See ya, Zanes."

Then they were alone in the shadows of the foyer.

"As if it never happened," Richard had echoed, amazed at the dustbusting he'd just witnessed.

"Not where we're concerned," Marion said balefully.

And then she went up to bed in Crystal's old room and locked the door.

And that was that. There was no dustbusting the image of Richard mounted on Tawnee from her mind. Marion couldn't stop wondering which one of them had initiated the birthday-suit action in bed. She didn't care if they were drugged. Somebody started it. Somebody hid the empty water bottles. She hated unsolved mysteries and she wasn't sleeping with Richard until this one was solved.

That week, Marion deleted (archived) the pictures of Richard and Tawnee, burned the sheets she'd discovered them on, and went about her daily activities with various upkeep specialists, stylists, decorators, foundation advisers, publicists, friends, and prospective hospital donors as though nothing were wrong. But the mystery had eaten away at her with every breath. For at least the first two days.

The mystery occupied less of her consciousness the third day, and Richard's contrition gift of a ten-carat heart-shaped ruby ring from Bulgari really kicked it onto the back burner on the fourth. By the fifth day, Marion was seeing phallic images in her bowl of cereal and spending a little too much time on the Power Plate.

On the sixth night, Richard stood outside her door and sang "I Wanna Dance with Somebody" by Whitney Houston. It was the tune that had been playing in the elevator the first time she and Richard "accidentally" (she was stalking him) met, so even though it was lame, it was technically "their song" and no small challenge for Richard's vocal abilities. Marion was so touched she finally gave in and returned to their bed and the comfort of spooning, but she drew the line at sex since she hadn't solved the friggin' mystery.

And where did that get her? No closer to any answers and disturbed by pelvic congestion to the point of having intricately torturous nightmares! She could either move on or purchase something with batteries. Choosing the former, Marion dove underneath the sheets.

She took her time. Patti Fink's party wasn't until one.

26

Preparty

The second she saw the glint of the gorgeous little pink-jeweled ring, Claire gasped and frantically tried to rewrap the jewelry box she'd just opened. "Oh, my gosh, Patti! I think I just accidentally unwrapped one of your presents! I am so sorry!" she cried.

"That's your party favor, goofaloo!" said Patti, tilting her head down a just a fraction in order to maximize the size of her eyes for four fashion photographers jostling below her on the sidewalk.

Naturally, Patti's birthday lunch was taking place at the Ivy. It sat at the epicenter of the Robertson Boulevard paparazzi perp walk, a stretch of chic boutiques between Burton Way and Melrose Avenue where celebrities went to be photographed in "casual dress" doing "normal shopping errands" whenever they felt publicity-deprived. The restaurant patio sat five feet above street level and Patti, Pepper, Claire, and Lyndy were all smashed into the pillows of table P-31, like kids in a cool, exclusive tree house.

"One more, Patti! Can we see the necklace?" asked a graying photographer, angling for a marketable picture.

Patti leaned over the white picket fence that surrounded the patio and opened her Alexander McQueen jacket, exposing her big-ass Cartier diamond garland and the top of one perfect (and natural) areola.

"Whoops!" She giggled and stuffed herself back into the matching McQueen bustier while the flashes went staccato.

"A pink pinkie ring. And it spells my name," Pepper exclaimed, slipping on her party favor. "This feels so strange. New jewelry an' I'm not even on m' knees." She leaned over to give Patti a thank-you kiss and ended up squashed in for a two-shot.

"The day isn't over yet," joked Patti, assuming her favorite head angle.

"That's one big-ass sparkler, Patti," noted Pepper, disentangling her hair from Patti's necklace. "Lou's kids gettin' hostile again?"

"Three depositions this month. If I make another emergency trip to the Caymans, I'm going to change my last name to Offshore Account."

"Oh, you *earned* that big-girl honker," agreed Pepper.

Lyndy got out of her chair and bounced (literally) across the banquette so she could air-kiss Patti and admire her own ring in the sunlight. "Cute, P. Goes with my nails."

Claire re-unwrapped her box, studied the contents, and scooted over to Lyndy. "I feel so stupid. At first I thought this was real." She giggled.

Lyndy smiled and giggled back. Then Claire leaned in close.

"I think there's a mix-up. This ring says *baby*," she whispered. "The box it came in says *jar*. If you could give me directions to that novelty store, I can go there and exchange it for another rhinestone ring with my name."

Lyndy returned the conspiratorial lean-in. "You'll want to get on Sepulveda going south. Take that all the way down to LAX, get on a plane to Charles de Gaulle Airport, and when you arrive in Paris, take a cab to Place Vendôme. JAR is on the left side of the Ritz Hotel. You can't miss it. Just tell them you want another custom ring in pink pavé *diamonds*. With any luck, it'll only take about nine months."

"Pink diamonds?" Claire croaked.

"The good kind. Incidentally, if memory serves, Patti's dearly departed mother used to call her 'baby' as a pet name, so she most likely fashioned that ring for herself with some sentimental significance in mind. Patti would only sacrifice such a personalized treasure for someone she really liked and would want to honor with a gift of friendship. Someone *new*. As a rule, I tend to avoid stating the obvious, but now that you've made it so blaringly apparent, that's *you*, dear. 'Course, if you've got your heart set on exchanging it . . ."

Claire slowly shook her head and wilted back in shock. She stared at her party-favor box for a few seconds, then ripping off the top like a grizzly, shoved the ring on her pinkie and threw her arms around the birthday girl, getting introduced to the photographers in the process, with special emphasis on her "fashion forward" white shoes from Craig-the-stylist.

"Patti, this is the prettiest ring I've ever seen in my life!" she squealed. "Thank you! It's so generous! I can't believe it's mine!"

"Okay, that's a little over-the-top," muttered Lyndy to no one in particular as she snatched one of the restaurant's famous gimlets from a waiter's tray.

"Lyndy, are you talking to yourself again?" called out Marion as she mounted the steps, leaving a phalanx of begging photographers in her wake. Turning and giving them a final money shot of her Versace ensemble and Bottega Veneta bag, she skipped up the steps to their table and smack into Lyndy's standing double air-kiss and embrace. "Quick, say something bitchy or I'm calling an ambulance," Marion said, in a seriously concerned voice.

"Oh, birthday luncheons always make me buoyant," Lyndy trilled.

"No, they don't," said Pepper.

"*Yes, they do!*" Lyndy snarled. "By the way, Marion, there's something I've been meaning to ask you—"

"How wonderful to see you again, Mrs. Zane!" exclaimed the young and adorable restaurant manager as he leaped in front of Lyndy and drew a chair out so Marion could sit down.

"Same here, Kevin. I've been jonesing for crab cakes all week," Marion replied.

Saved by the boyish!

Kevin's arm shot out, practically clotheslining a waiter, and returned holding a freshly mixed gimlet. "I hope the photo commotion doesn't disturb you," he apologized, briskly presenting the drink.

"Disturb her? She arranged it!" barked Lyndy.

"Shush!" said Marion, unwrapping her ring. "Everyone should be in *W* and *Harper's* on their birthday. But first let's talk about this party favor! Home run, birthday girl!"

With that, she was swept away into Patti's vortex.

"*W* and *Harper's*? Are those the local papers?" asked Claire.

"Yep," said Pepper, simultaneously unbuttoning her blouse and hauling a bundle out from under the table. She practically jumped out of her seat when she discovered she was holding a cloth dog purse containing a King Charles spaniel puppy to her breast. "Patti, these gimlets almost made me nurse yer dog instead a' my son," she chortled.

Pepper let the puppy out and he waddled around the table, picking at

Caesar salads and calamari. Everyone gave a collective "awwww" except Lyndy, who was appalled.

Pepper disappeared under the table and came back up with Jed, who gave an eardrum-piercing squall before latching onto mom's amazingly firm booby.

"That's Mr. Peepers number six," Patti cooed, stroking the puppy. In a more somber voice, she added, "We lost number five last month when he OD'd on Wanda's back medicine."

Amid a chorus of sympathetic offerings, Lyndy leaned close to Claire and whispered, "Tip of the day: never leave pets or husbands with Patti. She's got the same luck with both."

She might as well have been speaking Swahili.

"Don't let me drink too much or your son will go home in my purse," Patti chirped, stroking Jed's hungry body.

Making a subtle gesture for Claire's benefit (and further bafflement), Lyndy rolled her eyes and ominously shook her head.

"We could all go home in *that* purse," said Marion, referring to the gigantic Chanel crocodile tote that Maya extracted with her from the Escalade at the curb. The photographers spastically switched focus and scrambled over one another for a shot while the entire street exploded with an invading motorcade of *real* paparazzi, descending from all directions and stopping traffic dead in its tracks. The photographers poured out of the vehicles as if they were clown cars and stampeded toward Maya, who climbed the steps without turning. (She only posed for free on Tom's arm.)

Claire screamed as a long lens was shoved in across her plate while Pepper calmly whacked a fence climber with a wooden bread paddle.

"And the circus continues," groused Lyndy, frowning and shooing the puppy away from her plate.

Vlad, Sasha, and Dudayev shot out of the Escalade and, armed with cans of spray paint, dispersed the photographers like crows. The paparazzi then regrouped, opting for safer positions on their car roofs or across the street.

"Hey, thanks for getting rid of my press." Patti pouted.

"Well, fuck-you-happy-birthday," said Maya, handing Patti the gigantic bag.

Patti opened it and pulled out a huge tangle of bathing suits. "Hot colors and earth tones! And the bag! Forgiven!" Then she jumped in Maya's lap as Vlad, Dudayev, and Sasha arrived at their table to wish her a happy birthday.

"Who are they?" Claire asked Pepper. "I'm not up with all the rock stars these days."

"Bald one's a personal secretary. Brunette with the goatee and the big blond with the diamond in the front tooth are gardeners," Pepper said, chomping a burger.

"So this dog is gift or guest?" asked Maya, picking up the puppy.

"He's your entrée. Do us all a favor and eat him," grumbled Lyndy, and suddenly disappeared behind the ass of a woman wearing aggressive Prada and scary orange lipstick. The woman curled herself around Marion, making a show of the fact that they were "friendly."

"Okay, guess who's lunching together in the back room on the same side of the table, almost sucking each other's face off," she said, practically frothing at the mouth.

"I have no idea, Chloe. How's Doug?" Marion answered, coming up for air.

"John Byers and Lily Horowitz! Didn't know she was alive until Trisha's divorce lawyers left him broke and Lily's mother conveniently passed away. Lily has that soap-opera empire to herself now."

"*Had*. We just bought it," said Marion.

That took the wind right out of Chloe's Prada sails.

"Chloe, did you know it's Patti Fink's birthday? Patti, look who's here," Marion said, and she handed Chloe off.

Pepper leaned over to Marion. "I swear, that woman must've been an Injun scout inna past life."

"Pointiest fingers west of the Pecos," Marion mused.

Unfortunately, Chloe's assault had emboldened scads of other diners to pay homage to Marion, as well as the rest of the Trophies, forcing them to focus on names and relationships rather than on their meals.

While Patti air-kissed Chloe and ordered the puppy a salt-free steamed-salmon fillet, Claire felt a hand on her elbow and discovered Craig-the-stylist squatting next to her.

"This is the part where everybody kisses ass," he said to her. "They either need a favor for their husbands or charities or they're former 'it' girls who didn't live up to their press. Your pals are masters at this. Watch and learn."

Claire followed Craig's look and saw an Etro-clad Chinese woman who headed straight for their table, passed it, and then backed up until she was alongside Pepper.

"Pepper," the woman cried, "I was *just* going to call you!"

"Hey!" said Pepper, air-kissing the woman and simultaneously clinking her fork against Marion's gimlet glass to get her attention.

"Pepper has no idea who that is," whispered Craig for Claire's benefit.

"*Lucy Wai!*" Marion interrupted. "I can't thank you enough for your Carita Memorial pledge last week. You're a saint. And did you get our table order and ad for your AFREAD event next month? I read that those boarding schools are the last hope for girls who refuse genital mutilation in Somalia. Is it black tie?"

"Um, yes and yes. You're totally set up, Marion. You and Richard are always so generous to us. And *you're* the one who's a saint, for jumping in like that and turning a tragedy into action."

As Lucy spoke, Marion traced the letter *B* in a pool of ketchup on Pepper's plate.

"*B* for board member," whispered Craig.

"You got our AFREAD table order too, right? I figure bein' a *board member*, you might know," Pepper said.

"Wow. I was just about to ask if you got the packet—" Lucy returned.

Now Marion traced the letters *D* and *C* in the salad dressing on her own plate.

"*DC* means dinner chairman." Craig giggled.

"Good Lord, Lucy, you think I forgot that was your charity?" Pepper exclaimed. "You told me all about it when we sat together at that thing. You're the *dinner chairman* of the event, right?"

"Well, now I feel silly . . ."

"You should! Have you met Lyndy Wallert?" asked Pepper, ending the subject.

"She's an anti-genital-mutilation champion," Marion offered.

Pepper pointed Lucy in Lyndy's direction and low-fived Marion under the table as the next diner approached.

"Totally seamless," said Craig to Claire.

"Aren't some of them just friends?" she asked.

"Hon, if they were friends, they'd let them eat. Or wave or say hi on their way in and out. Table rushers are all about usage. Just wait until your picture shows up on WireImage in those shoes! They'll be mobbing you too. Now let me see your first JAR bling."

"First?" she asked.

"Are you kidding? JAR is Trophy cocaine. Every piece leaves you craving for more. Check out Patti Fink's bracelet. She could injure people with those rocks!"

"What's WireImage?" asked Claire.

But Craig was gone. Ten seconds later, Claire spied him across the patio pouncing on Kirsten Dunst.

Marion had just finished introducing Pepper to the ex-wife of the Zane Internet marketing CEO when the dreaded question came.

"Sooo, Marion," Lyndy called out, above the fray. "What happened with my massage service? Didn't Richard like the bodyworker they sent over?"

Okay, here we go, thought Marion.

"Not so much," she said, with practiced vagueness. "But it was sweet of you to recommend them. He's trying Maya's person this week."

"But you said it sucked," Lyndy persisted. "You texted me at *two* A.M. What on earth happened?"

Now Marion launched herself into practiced stomach relaxation. Sending Lyndy that text had been as bad as making a drunk call, but she hadn't realized it until after they spoke to Barry. It was the only loose end of their legal "never happened." "Really?" she said. "It was that late?"

"Yes." Lyndy's intensely expectant look reminded Marion of a cat watching its owner peel the top off a Fancy Feast can. What did she know?

"I was just restless and amped from the whole thing with Xiocena and the hospital, so I got out of bed and cleaned out my e-mails. It always makes me sleepy."

"But what happened that made the massage 'suck'?"

I suck, for sending that dorky text!

"Oh, you know what it's like when you get the wrong masseuse."

"Like sex that stops just before you're 'bout to come," Pepper interjected.

"I wouldn't know about that!" Patti giggled. "This morning took *forever*."

"*Don't want to know*," yelled Maya, Pepper, Lyndy, and Marion in unison as the well-wishers crowded back in.

And so the texting episode was handled. For now. Marion downed her gimlet and skipped off to the ladies' room to loosen her bra strap a notch.

Almost an hour later, Patti was unwrapping her gifts. Lyndy gave her two sweater sets from Malo, Marion gave her a spa stay in Switzerland, and Pepper gave her spectacle in the form of a muscle car. Using her cell phone like a big-budget film director, Pepper cued the valets and they pulled the '68 327 turbo Camaro in front of the restaurant. It was classic flaming orange with two white racing stripes down the middle, tied up with a gigantic leopard-skin bow. The entire restaurant and street scene went berserk. Everyone except Claire.

She was too busy agonizing over the square white box with the morbid-looking black ribbon left for last on the table. The one whose card Patti was now tearing open.

"From Claire!" Patti announced. Then she opened the box and just stared.

"Whatcha get?" asked Pepper.

"Is it dirty?" asked Maya.

Having just had a manicure, Claire lacked a hangnail and so bit down on her swizzle stick. Patti was still staring into the box. Marion leaned over, touched her hand, and whispered, "Should I call the bomb squad? Because you look like it's about to explode."

"My gift is weird," Claire moaned, through a bite so tense it snapped off the tip of the swizzle stick.

"Okay, I don't know where you've been lunching for the past hour and a half, but the rest of us have been sitting with Patti Fink," Marion answered, gently extracting the remaining piece of plastic wand from Claire's mouth.

"Then why isn't she saying anything? My first lunch and I've grossed out the birthday girl! She's too grossed out for words!" babbled Claire.

"Nah, she's just scanning and processing," replied Marion. "After three gimlets, she needs more time to boot up."

"Huh?"

"Come on, P. While we're semi-young," said Lyndy.

A look of recognition finally washed over Patti's face. "It's . . . it's . . . aaaaahhhhhhhhhh! PETRIFIED DINOSAUR HEAAARRRT! HOW DID YOU KNOW?" she screamed, and snatched Claire up in a headlock of joy. Past the swells of bustiered breasts, Claire saw Marion wink and Craig-the-stylist smugly salute her with a french fry.

"I knew you were one of us!" Pepper chirped.

"Hey, save that stuff for the beach," said Maya.

"Good thing you all brought coats," Patti added. "The nights are still cold out there."

"We better get going with the cake," said Pepper, signaling a waiter. "The bus will be here at two-thirty."

Claire looked completely lost in the woods.

"You didn't think this was it, did you?" Patti laughed. "This is the pre-party! The BJ party's in Malibu!"

"I thought blow-job Tupperware parties went out with the nineties," Lyndy whined.

As the remains of her gimlet shot out of her nose, Claire recoiled from the burn.

"No, no. They evolve like fashion. New dicks, new tricks, and you're not bunting out," said Maya.

"No, thank you. I'm quite adept at the practice," Lyndy firmly sniffed.

"Not me, I love Tupperware an' there's always room for new technique. Besides, I need a new sports car," Pepper said as a nanny materialized at her side to take Jed. "Ari trashed the Porsche again."

"I'm always up for education," Marion added.

"So you're in?" Patti asked Claire.

Craig-the-stylist's head popped up over the picket fence like an apple-cheeked jack-o'-lantern and barked, "You have to go! It's a rite of passage!"

"Which he knows *nothing* about," added Marion. "Craig, what shall I put down for your hospital pledge—ten thousand?"

She might as well have said "Boo!"

"I already have a new car," mumbled Claire, but the Trophies' attention flitted off to who was driving their cars home for them.

Then everyone screamed as Patti's cake arrived. It was in the shape of a giant syringe with the word *Botox* across it in piped pink frosting.

"And they thought we were trashy *before* this lunch," said Pepper.

"Speak for yourself," said Maya, then added, "They think I give head to the pope."

"Well, thank God we've got each other and we're not trashy alone," said Marion. "Now let's eat cake before we blow."

As the restaurant broke into "Happy Birthday," five pinkie rings and one honking big-ass diamond necklace twinkled in agreement.

27

Cats and Canaries

Vespers were over, and after the last of the congregation emptied out of the little Baroque jewel-box chapel, Ivan helped the aged monsignor with the bolts on the heavy wooden doors. Rainy winters alternating with bone-dry summers had warped them into an almost unmanageable state and he made a mental note that before painting them in the morning, he'd file the left bolt latch, in order to accommodate the changing shape of the tortured wood.

Nodding good night, he started off across the crushed-stone path through the courtyard that led out behind the monastery and down the hill. He wasn't staying in the east cloister rooms of the monastery among the other guests. Ivan required certain accommodations not available within those walls.

Ivan's quarters were at the bottom of an arroyo that formed a wooded gash between the monastery grounds and fields of tomatoes and safflower. The ancient caretaker's terreras was a low wood-and-stone hut, once the traditional Canary Island dwelling. It was nestled under a long-neglected olive grove, overtaken by towering laurels, barbusanos, canary pines, and invasive orchids, making its tiled roof and dirt-colored walls quite invisible from both hilltop and fields.

In other words, it was perfect.

Negotiating the hillside of volcanic rock in sandals fashioned from old tires and leather and a monk's habit was treacherous enough during the day. At night, without a flashlight, it was an invitation for a broken leg or neck, yet Ivan picked his way down like a leopard, guided by starlight and smell. Reaching the bottom of the arroyo, he listened for any extraordinary sounds apart from roosting finches and feral pigs.

Satisfied he was alone, he stepped around boulders and broken bits of mangled oxcarts until he reached the terreras, and going inside the vaulted entrance niche, discovered he had received three coded locational printouts, a video-conference response to his inquiries, and an intoxicating black-haired beauty who was cooking paella in the nude.

He hadn't exactly lied to the Zanes. Ivan's sabbatical destination *was* the Castillo de la Conquista, a fifteenth-century monastery, famous for its code of devotional silence. He'd simply omitted the facts that he would *not be participating* in the devotional-silence guest program or *dwelling within the monastery's walls*. Or that it was his *only* destination. Allowing them to believe otherwise prevented the Zanes from trying to establish contact with him, which might blow his cover, or worse, endanger them—a tiny yet completely unacceptable risk.

The truth was that the terreras hut had concealed a NATO intelligence listening post since the height of the Cold War. The same NATO intelligence agency that had employed him and two fellow assassins to "tie up" some East German "loose ends" in Central America fifteen years ago. Later, Ivan revealed himself to a few select and trustworthy friends within that intelligence agency and maintained contact with them over the years, resulting in his receiving clearance to use the terreras hut. Its technical capabilities were consistently updated and state-of-the-art, despite the infrequency of its use.

Since the time of Columbus, the seven Canary Islands, off the Moroccan coast, had been an important sea-traffic and communications hub between Europe, Africa, and America. The hut gave Ivan NATO intelligence at his fingertips without his having to set foot in a European airport. He couldn't approach Europe directly because he didn't know how many loyal friends and contacts within world intelligence networks his old partners still retained. No use spooking his prey to go back into hiding. Ivan planned to succeed where NATO had failed.

Ravishing Rhodessa, however, came first. Removing his habit, Ivan caught up his lover with one arm and carried her to the bed while she bit into his newly grown beard. He had waited fifteen years to deal with the men who'd double-crossed him in South America. Time enough for them to grow lazy, forgetful, and unsuspecting. And he now knew their locations. He could wait a few more hours to begin his manhunt.

28

Blowing It

Pepper let loose a triumphant rebel yell and screamed, "I win!" The bare-chested young man in jodhpurs and riding boots let go and she fell backward into the impossibly squashy pillows of the pale blue ten-by-twenty-by-ten wraparound chaise.

"Not a fair match! Your guy was younger!" Maya screamed seconds later as her young man spun and released her onto the other end of the chaise. Both women fell into fits of giggles as they struggled to upright themselves, with Pepper finally flopping off onto the carpet.

"Everythin's so goddamn light in here, I can't tell the walls from the floor!" she squealed.

Patti's Caribbean colonial beach house had been newly reincarnated in "Carolina Pales," meaning all formerly espresso hardwood floors were now covered in spotless white Norwegian goat-hair shag, so the male strippers Patti had hired were forced to meet the women in the driveway, pluck them from the party bus, remove their shoes, and piggyback them into the living room lest their shoes sully the decor.

"Ugh! This reminds me of Girl Scouts when they forced us to tour the Grand Canyon," said Lyndy as she crested the foyer. She was perched upon a very slight but enthusiastic stripper, whose sharp, narrow strides, combined with her ass-panty gel, resulted in an extremely bouncy ride down the ramp into the living room. "Why on earth would you carpet in white, P? Broad Beach is peppered with tar."

"I've got a thirty-gallon barrel of acetone with a pump top at the bottom of the walkway. Everyone cleans before they come in," said Patti as her stripper beat Lyndy's to the living room and released her onto a huge white silk ottoman that faced the chaise.

"So that toxin runs into the ocean?" asked Maya, starting to stand and look outside.

"No, it goes down in the sand," Patti nonchalantly replied.

"Keep yer hair on, she's got a catch basin under the thing," said Pepper, finally surfacing from under the chaise. "Yer gettin' too easy ta tease."

"And speaking of tease," Lyndy mused as she picked up a harness with a feather-tufted wand. There were fifty or so impressive sex toys laid out on the pink shell mosaic coffee table. "How does one operate this contraption?" she wondered.

"I *told* you new tricks," said Maya as she accepted a colorless white-chocolate martini from a stripper's tray.

"That's for the advanced class," said Marion, arriving on the back of a beautiful Hawaiian boy and sliding off into the cushions. "Whoo!" She rolled up and accepted her drink. Your bus cookies gave me the munchies."

"Munchies?" asked Claire, dumping off and attempting to sprawl in a ladylike way. "That cookie was so filling, I could barely eat the whole thing."

"You ate a *whole cookie*?" Pepper gaped as Lyndy rolled her eyes and Maya stifled a laugh. "I did that *once,* over in Amsterdam. Ari found me in front a' Anne Frank's house peelin' six giant chocolate bars. He says I was fixin' ta sculpt the damn thing."

"We tag-team the babysitting," decided Maya as the waiters brought in plates of salad and white truffle risotto.

"What do you mean?" asked Claire.

"It will all become apparent soon enough," said Lyndy, then turned to regard an aging dominatrix in a tight black Gaultier suit saunter barefoot down the ramp. She carried a briefcase and a riding crop, which she switched across a waiter's fanny, almost causing him to lose half his drinks. "Eleanor, the years have been good to you."

"She's the instructor," whispered Marion to Claire as Eleanor air-kissed her way around the chaise.

"Eleanor's *everybody's* instructor," said Lyndy, playing with a whip. "She's taught this town fellatio since my husband Wang-Chunged."

"Thank you for the carbon dating, Lyndera, and unlike your spouse, these instruments of pleasure are completely new, unused, and available," said the dominatrix in a low whiskey voice. "But we'll get to that after instruction. Good evening, ladies. Ready for class?"

Dramatically backlit by the pollution-enhanced sunset, Eleanor sat at the center of the chaise and gave directions to dim the living-room sconces and chandeliers until only a pin spot lit the glistening pink coffee table and toys.

Claire nervously eyed the strippers, who were passing out drinks and pink Sherman cigarettes. "D-do we choose one or does the instructor pair us off?" she asked, giving rise to an instant round of guffaws

"You're not blowing them! They're the waiters!" Maya howled.

"At least not at their current pay rate." Marion chuckled.

"The *practice sticks* are in here," Eleanor said, indicating her briefcase.

"Oh, oh! I'm so sorry!" Claire apologized to a blond stripper as she accepted her plate.

"It's not the first time I've been scratched," he reassured her in a voice more feminine than her own.

Eleanor gathered the sex toys into a fur-lined basket as a waiter placed a silver tray in the center of the table.

"I don't s'pose you got drapes that drop down from the ceilin' or that Hal Conrad suddenly up an' moved?" asked Pepper, scanning the beach.

"No and no. Hal's still in that ugly eighties modern, two doors down," answered Patti, taking a drag from her cigarette and waving the smoke away from Mr. Peepers Number Six.

"Then I gotta change places with Claire," Pepper declared, springing from her seat and hauling Claire up by the armpits. "Sorry, hon, but Patti's neighbor's the director of Wallis Academy. The school's not too keen on m' three kids they got now an' I need ta get two more in."

"I hope he sees me," said Patti. "Hal dumped me for a bowlegged cheerleader back in high school and I want him to eat his heart out."

"As long as he doesn't seize up an' die! I am not spendin' the next twelve years crossin' town for two schools," Pepper said, checking the sight lines from her new location.

"The man lives on Broad Beach on a *school director's* pay?" Lyndy wondered.

"No, we bought 'im the house last year, 'cuz of Cooter an' all the stitches. Boy bites like a gator," Pepper confessed, shaking her head.

"But we're not blowing waiters!" Claire exclaimed, through a mouthful of risotto. "Hey, I rhymed! 'Gator, waiter.' Get it?"

Even the strippers nodded and winked.

"Well, we're not playing bridge," Lyndy said, reaching for one of the six assorted dildos Eleanor had placed on the silver tray.

When Claire saw the dildos, she gave a small scream, then joined in the group tug-of-war over the largest black one. Using an expert twist, Maya wrenched the dildo away for herself.

"Sorry, I'm playing race card," said Maya with a smirk.

"If that's the case, then you also qualify for that high-mileage Asian model on the left," Lyndy griped, attempting a final snatch.

"Don't be sore loser. You're not going to be sitting on them," said Maya, waggling the dildo at Lyndy.

"Have they been sat on before?" asked Claire, dropping hers.

"These are all *virgin* practice sticks. I guarantee," said Eleanor.

"Ladies, ladies," Marion cautioned as she selected a sparkly purple one. "These are hypothetical rather than realistic. Although there was a boy back in Berkeley who was almost this—"

"That was just the acid, Marion!" Patti called out.

"I have a body paint that's close to that purple," offered Eleanor.

"I like this stubby red one," Pepper said, twirling hers. "It reminds me a m' brother."

After a few seconds of dead silence, everyone burst out laughing.

"Kidding!" Pepper yelled at a stripper who'd gone white. She looked at the dildo again and added, "It actually looks more like m' cousin."

"Kidding!" everyone yelled at the poor stripper.

"Mine has balls." Claire marveled as she petted her small but anatomically correct yellow model, eliciting even more nods and winks.

"At least it's not green." Lyndy winced and tossed a Granny Smith–colored model toward a curious Mr. Peepers before settling for a long thin blue one.

"And this is for the birthday girl," said Eleanor, handing Patti a big multicolored one with balls and an extra head. Patti gave it a tentative sniff.

"Mmm. Tutti-frutti," she purred.

Everyone screamed as Patti made both heads disappear into her mouth.

"Ah, ah, ah! Lubrication first!" scolded Eleanor, and passed out lip gloss while a movie screen descended from the ceiling in front of the picture window. "We wouldn't want to wreck that lovely smile."

"Patti Fink, you *can* cover that window!" hissed Pepper.

"You asked for drapes." Patti winked.

As an eight-foot-tall penis filled the screen, Eleanor launched into her lesson. "Now let's get down to the basics . . ."

Hours later, the beach house was all out of lip gloss and chocolate liqueur. Righteously looped, the Trophies were all kneeling around the coffee table, sipping espresso and examining the sex toys for sale.

"Two hundred dollars for this little mask?" complained Lyndy.

"It's velvet, leather, and lace," reasoned Eleanor.

"I am in the wrong business!" Lyndy declared.

"But we *are* in the same business as Eleanor," Marion said with a sigh. "We're just upper management."

"We sell naughty and nice," offered Patti. "Too much of either results in termination."

"Don't you dare get profound over a table fulla dildos!" warned Pepper.

"Nobody's firing me," Claire singsonged, grabbing a long strand of pearls and draping them around her neck and head. "I'm a Secret Rainbow Princess!"

Eleanor smiled. "I see you've found the anal pearls."

"Yeah, they go up the bum and you pull them out as he comes," Patti piped up.

Claire clawed off the pearls as if they were a viper.

"Easy girl, they haven't been used yet," said Pepper, picking them up.

"And they'll never be by me!" Claire exclaimed. "I am not one of those Trophy wives!"

Everyone gave a collective low "oooh."

"Careful, them's fightin' words," Pepper drawled.

"Trophy is pet name we use for each other," said Maya.

"And you *are* a Trophy, dear, in all senses of the word," Lyndy corrected as she accepted another espresso and aspirin from a woman in a white catering jacket.

It took Marion a second to recognize the woman as the arm-hair-raising waitress from the week before. "You worked the Jack Powell event at my home last week," she said suddenly, almost making the waitress jump.

"Yes, ma'am," replied the waitress in a voice so hoarse it was down to a whisper. She continued to serve around the table and collect empty plates.

"I know this sounds silly, but . . . do we know each other from anywhere else?" Marion asked.

"Probably. I float with three or four companies," the waitress whispered over her shoulder.

Why won't she look at me?

"Maybe somewhere other than catering?" Marion persisted.

But the waitress just shrugged and kept serving. "Don't think so," she said, gingerly lifting a dildo off the edge of a plate.

Marion wanted to stare at her face, but she could tell she was making the woman uncomfortable. That meant they'd definitely met before in a social capacity. Probably as the wife of some guy who divorced her without much support. Her skin and hair were too good for someone who'd spent her life serving. Well, no sense shaming the poor thing. Even though her arms were doing the raw-chicken thing.

"What happened to our lovely boys?" asked Eleanor, adding "No offense" to the waitress, who didn't even appear to notice.

"They were due back at the strip club at nine," said Patti, motioning for Lyndy to drink her espresso over the coffee table. "We weren't supposed to go this long. Anyway, they were mostly for floor protection and you'll be barefoot on the way out."

"I don't blame you for wanting to protect this floor. This goat hair in white is *beyond*," Marion put in, draining her cup and lying back on the floor.

"And we still have the caterers here, to serve," added Lyndy, watching the waitress exit then whispering, "Wasn't she married to Walter Hertz?"

"No, that was that little bitch Missy," hissed Patti. "The one who kicked me out of the Riviera Women's Golfing Tournament."

"But you don't play," said Pepper.

"I wanted to meet Tiger Woods!" Patti whined.

"Choosing to meet him in the men's locker room is why you got kicked out," offered Marion.

"What do you mean I'm a Trophy?" Claire suddenly asked Lyndy. "Billy was divorced when he met me."

"First we were pearl pullers and now we are predators," muttered Maya, reconstructing two harnesses into a pair of garter belts, much to Eleanor's fascination.

"I think you've got your terms confused," Lyndy added

"Then what's the right one?" asked Claire, jumping down from the back of the chaise.

"Let me take a crack at this," said Marion, rising up on an elbow. "Okay, first of all, don't take it personally, but when men marry for a second—"

"Or third or fourth," interjected Patti.

"—time," Marion continued, "they tend to have more of a concrete idea what they want in a wife and partner. Especially men of a certain age and of certain financial means—"

"Those men have reached a *connoisseurial* level," added Lyndy.

"Is that even a word?" asked Pepper.

"—where they can attract," Marion went on, "what they personally believe to be the most emotionally, mentally, and let's cut the crap, *physically* attractive women—"

"You forgot *socially* attractive," Lyndy interrupted.

"Yeah, when I wear jeans, guys're always checkin' out *my social*," muttered Pepper.

Claire's eyes, if possible, were becoming more glazed over than ever.

"You're losing her," said Patti, crossing the room and tossing her cigarette out onto the sand. "Claire, how many guys under thirty, on food stamps, have you ever seen driving Ferraris?"

"Um, none," Claire answered.

"Exactly. And why do those older, wealthier guys buy Ferraris?" Patti continued, crossing back.

"Because they drive the best?" Claire guessed.

"And?" asked Pepper.

"Because they can afford them," said Claire.

"And?" asked Lyndy.

"Because they're beautiful and the most fun?" Claire was running out of answers.

"And?" asked the Trophies in unison.

"They make them . . . look cool?" she said finally.

"*Yes!*" they all replied.

"They don't call it Trophy for nothing," Patti said.

"And don't take it too seriously. We don't," said Marion. "We call our-selves Trophies as an in-joke because we're all good-looking second wives with wealthy husbands. And I'm dizzy." Thus saying, she melted back into the floor

"Second-marriage Ferraris." Claire sighed and played with her wedding band. "You know, I had my own job. Before Billy."

"We all did," said Patti. "We all had dreams or directions that didn't work out."

And the room fell silent.

"I work a lot less now," offered Maya.

"But that only jacks up your fees. 'Not available' is hot," said Patti.

"Yes, but I'm old for model. How hot would I be without my marriage?" Maya mused.

"Well, one door shuts and another one opens. All we can do is walk on," said Lyndy.

And the silence resumed. Even Eleanor had a faraway look in her eyes. Then Pepper let out a huge horse laugh.

"Now, I warned y'all 'bout profunty. No, profundy. I mean, *profundity,*" said Pepper, ducking just in time to avoid the pair of crotchless leather panties Maya slingshotted at her. "Y'all'r gorgeous, happily married ta men who poop dollar bills, loved by yer friends, able to party like wicked bitches, an' armed with new skills that can only grab you more a' the pie. An' now yer gettin' maudlin 'cuz y'all quit yer shitty jobs ta get here? Let's see a raise a hands. Who'd like ta go back to the way they were before they were married?"

Nobody moved.

"I oughta take that purple pecker and slap y'all upside yer heads. We didn't *settle* for shit. We wanted this," Pepper sneered.

"As they say in France, Pepper, 'fffucking-A!'" Marion said from the floor. "I like my lifestyle and I intend to hang on to it."

"And I can't feel my legs," added Claire, hopping over to the patio door.

"I have six bedrooms prepared," Patti announced.

"That sounds lovely," said Lyndy, rising. "But I've got a BH Central board meeting at eight-thirty A.M. and that coffee has replaced all the booze in my bloodstream. Besides, my new Vanden Plas practically drives itself. Happy Birthday, P. Lovely party." She tucked her new dildo into her Birkin bag and air-kissed around the coffee table. "Eleanor, I'd say good-bye but I live on the Westside, so I'll just say I'll need a bigger one, next time," Lyndy said, waving to the dominatrix. Then, looking at the floor, she added, "Oh, dear."

Patti gasped and took the green dildo away from Mr. Peepers Number Six. The puppy had gnawed half the head away.

"Puppy or husband? I'm seeing the future of *someone's* demise," Lyndy remarked.

"Seriously, Patti Fink, don't let that thing near Lou when 'e's sleepin'," Pepper said with a shudder.

Lyndy rolled her eyes at Claire then turned and walked toward the kitchen.

"The front door is that way!" shouted Maya.

"I'm going out the kitchen," Lyndy said, without stopping. "I want to ask my caterers why they never make that risotto for me. Toodles!"

"That was Lyndy's people catering? And no baked Alaska?" Maya teased as she settled up with Eleanor and tucked her new garter belt into her bag.

"She comped them for me as a birthday gift," said Patti. "I think it was sweet."

"So is this wonnn-derful air," singsonged Claire, who was twirling around on the patio.

"There'll be a price," assured Pepper, rising. "You'll just pay it later."

"She'll be back," Maya said, doing her best Terminator imitation. She took one baleful look at Claire and walked over to the patio door.

"Dibs on the green room," called Pepper.

"Hey, that's my favorite!" said Maya, yanking Claire back inside, where she flopped facedown into the chaise.

"It's not green anymore," said Patti. "And the memory-foam bed was moved to a different room too."

Pepper and Maya looked at each other then started racing for the back hallway.

"'Night!" Pepper shouted.

"Lock that door!" yelled Maya, pointing at the patio.

Patti gave Eleanor a kiss and, after the dominatrix sashayed out, knelt down to Marion, who was still spread-eagled on the goatskin. "I lied," she told her. "The memory-foam bed's in the guesthouse and it's all yours."

"Can't, birthday girl," said Marion, wobbling up and reaching for her bag. "I have a full morning and I want to sleep with my guy."

"Okay, but call Carl. He's parked on the new lot and there are no lights out there."

"So Mrs. Calley finally passed," said Marion, digging through her purse.

"Yes, probate was endless. We're extending the kids' wing next week. Now, if only Hal Conrad would die. I still want that yoga studio," said Patti, scooping up her puppy.

"You don't do yoga anymore," said Marion, still searching.

"Yeah, but Lenny Kravitz does and he's in escrow up the street," Patti replied with a leer.

"Shit, I think I lost my phone," said Marion, giving up her search. "I can make it to the car as long as you have a flashlight."

"Um, maybe in the kitchen," said Patti.

"We'll walk her to her car," the waitress whispered hoarsely.

She was standing just inside the living room. Behind her was a large man wearing the same white catering jacket that she wore.

When did they come in? wondered Marion.

"I've got a flashlight on my car keys," the man offered, and went to take Marion's elbow.

"Great, but I'm not paraplegic," said Marion, keeping her elbow to herself, then turning to Patti and hugging her. "Perfect party, as usual. Remember to lock that door."

"I will," Patti said, rolling Claire over so she could breathe. "Your shoes are in the basket by the door and let him take your elbow out there. That lot is full of gopher holes."

Marion walked up the ramp and fished her Alaia shoes out of the basket while the waitress and waiter stood by patiently.

"Thanks, both of you," she said as she slipped on the shoes.

Neither one said a word.

Negotiating a gravel path in stilettos was trickier than Marion had anticipated, and more than once she almost wobbled into a row of hydrangeas. On the turn onto the new lot, she actually lost her balance and fell against a bush. "Ow!" she squeaked, feeling a sharp prick in her thigh.

"Careful, those things have thorns," said the man, pulling her out.

"Hydrangeas? I don't think so," said Marion, rubbing her leg. "I hope it wasn't a rusty old stake or a spider."

As she stepped onto the soft dirt where Patti's next-door neighbor's house had once stood, she became disoriented in the darkness and a warm wave of dizziness forced her to stop. Maybe it *was* a spider. "Great," she said, breathing deeply. "I'm looking for a black car in blackness."

"All the cars are parked on the old driveway, over there," said the man, taking a firm grip on her elbow.

Marion didn't resist. She was getting woozier by the second and couldn't see for shit.

"How was the party?" he asked.

The man's hand and huge forearm were firm, yet gentle and supportive.

"Oh, sssilly and fun, whoops!" Marion blurted. The ground seemed to be sliding out from under her knees, like she was walking on the deck of a boat. She felt someone grab her other elbow and welcomed the bracing.

"Bet your husband will be happy. Did you buy him anything?" asked a hoarse voice that must've belonged to the waitress.

"No, no. Richard doesn't even like blow jobs that much. And when he wants one, he likes it only one particular way." Marion laughed, marveling that her voice now sounded like an echo chamber.

"Really? Poor you. That leaves you no room for creativity," said the voice. It didn't sound as hoarse now.

"Tell me about it. Two barks and a whine and he's done. Then again, what woman complains about fast fellatio? Not me!" She was babbling now. "And he's really free and generous with all the rest, which is really fantastic—"

"Go back to the '*two barks and a whine*'! What's *that* about?" asked the voice. It was definitely familiar now. Or was that the man's voice?

"Oh, you know how first sexual experiences imprint," she said. "Richard's mom had this poodle. She used to dye the poor thing pink . . ." Marion said, gazing at the stars, which looked so very, very close.

"Did he fuck it?" asked the voice. Harsh and fast. Like a snakebite.

"Heavens, no! What a question! He was a just a kid changing his clothes and the poodle got, you know, friendly. How could you think that? By the way, I know who you are!"

They came to an abrupt halt. Well, part of her kept walking, but most of her was standing still. Both the waiter and the waitress were holding her elbows so tight, it almost hurt. And why didn't they turn on the flashlight?

"You do?" asked the voice.

"Yes, your son used to go to Harvard Westlake with Dickie Zane. Lots of curly brown hair? I didn't want to embarrass you."

"You have an amazing memory, Marion. And here's your car. One more question and then you take ten big mother-may-I steps forward: What was the name of the poodle?"

"Pinky," answered Marion, and lurched ten steps forward on her own. She was relieved to see Carl snap awake and blast out of the driver's seat to open the door for her. Melting into the backseat, she removed her ruined shoes.

"How big is this lot, anyway? We were walking forever," she said, looking up from her feet to find her guides.

But no one was there.

Just pitch black and the distant sounds of the coast highway and surf, which, oddly, sounded similar.

"Are you all right, Mrs. Zane?" Carl asked.

"Yeah, where's the waiter and waitress who walked me here? I wanted to thank them."

"You didn't walk here by yourself?" asked Carl as he pulled out of the driveway and turned right, toward the coast highway.

"Not in these shoes. We were walking and talking about . . . something. That's right. Her boy went to school with Dickie Jr. Did you know he got caught insider-trading?"

"No, Mrs. Zane."

Fortunately, Carl had signed a confidentiality agreement.

29

Richard

Richard finished tying his Windsor knot, slipped on his suit jacket, exited his richly-appointed-but-manly closet, and went back into the darkened bedroom. He bent down to kiss his slumbering wife good-bye, but just before his lips touched her cheek, she emitted a pitiful hound-dog-like moan.

"Aaahoooo! *No breathing!* It hurts the inside of my head!"

Whew! Talk about breath, Marion's smelled like a distillery. Naughty girl. Richard figured he knew of five other naughty girls who were probably hurting the same way. That's what you get for celebrating without keeping track of your intake. A whole new world of hurt. If she hadn't been writhing in pain, Marion's prone, naked form under the sheets would've resembled that of a corpse. Make that a really sexy corpse, like the dead ladies in detective movies. He sat on the bed and patted her bottom.

"Want me to call the doctor, honey?" he asked. "One of those guys in your little book? What can I do to make you feel better?"

"C'mere," croaked the corpse.

Richard held his breath and bent back down.

"Go down to the guardhouse. Get Gary's gun and put it right here and pull the trigger."

Marion was pointing to her temple.

"Too messy. Want some water?"

He removed the top from her bedside carafe and filled a glass full. It was distilled water and didn't taste half as good as Hildon, but Marion had declared a one-month Hildon moratorium because of the "never happened" night. He held the glass to her lips, but she could barely take a sip.

"How about starting with an ice pack?" he suggested.

More moaning and writhing.

Richard went into his bathroom, rummaged around in the cabinets, and finding nothing, checked the minifridge. He'd had a rotator-cuff thing last year and used a cold-pack wrap, but it must've got tossed. It was time to venture where no heterosexual man had gone before.

Richard walked back through the bedroom and headed for Marion's bathroom.

Holy smokes! How many clothes did she have? He couldn't remember the last time he'd gone farther than her *first* dressing room. And here was another one! And another of wall-to-wall purses and shoes! When did she wear all this stuff? She'd have to change six times a day. Maybe she did. He didn't want to know. And what was this room? A mirror-and-chair setup for war paint. No bathroom, yet. He should've dropped bread crumbs so he wouldn't get lost on the way back.

Okay, here was the bathroom. When did all this pink marble go in? And why did women always get the bigger tub? Richard chuckled at the framed old photo she'd set on the marble surround alongside a basket of big pink rocks. What were those, crystals? They looked sharp.

The photo was starting to fade. He'd take it into that camera place and get it restored. And make a copy for himself. It showed Marion and him on what had to be their first trip to Portofino. Man, Marion was smokin' hot in that bikini. And he had a lot more hair. And muscles. But Marion had barely aged, God love her. He remembered how she'd squealed when he bought her that brooch. They weren't even married yet. (No wonder the photo was faded.) But he'd decided on that trip that he was going to make her his wife. Good times. Back when the dollar had balls. Okay, where would his wife keep an ice pack?

Richard squatted and checked the minifridge. Vitamins, serums, scary-looking needles . . . what was this box? There were vials inside. Human growth hormone? He didn't want to know. Aha! A Lone Ranger mask made out of pink cold-pack stuff. He leaned in to grab it. Then he froze.

Lying on their sides in the back of the top rack were two empty bottles of Hildon water.

One of the bottles had a peeled label. Richard habitually peeled the Hildon labels with his thumb while he drank.

Were these the ones that had been spiked? he found himself wondering. And if so, what were they doing in Marion's fridge? When they were searching, she'd said she'd checked every inch of her rooms. Could she possibly have missed them?

Or *stashed* them?

Nah. That was crazy thinking. Marion could bullshit but even she couldn't fake the meltdown she'd had on the "never happened" night. And why on earth would she do such a thing? They were still the same kids they'd been in the Portofino picture. Solid in love, then and now.

Right?

Still staring inside the minifridge, Richard picked up the phone next to the sink.

"Yes, Mrs. Zane?" a voice answered.

What was the name of Ivan's temp? Who cared?

"It's Richard. Could you get Dr. James Purdue—"

"Is Mrs. Zane sick?"

"No. Just . . ."

There was an unwrapped bottle of Visine next to the empty Hildon bottles.

Marion didn't use Visine.

She had a dry-eye condition and used prescription drops. He knew this because they'd had to wait three hours for the fucking things to arrive at a post office in Morocco one year. He picked up the Visine bottle. The dropper top was off. The stuff inside didn't look like Visine. Richard replaced the cap and snatched out the two Hildon bottles.

"Hello?" said the temporary assistant. She was still on the line. "There's Alka-Seltzer, B vitamins, Excedrin, and tons of prescriptions in the cabinet up there. Or I could go to the store—"

"It's not about her goddamn hangover! Just connect me with Dr. Purdue—no! You call him and tell him I'm bringing something over to his office for testing. Right now!"

"Yes, Mr. Zane."

Richard caught himself peeling the Hildon label with his thumb at the exact place where he'd surely left off. If this was his bottle from "never happened" night, he needed some answers.

Richard went back into Marion's closet and grabbed the first big purse he saw. He stuffed the Hildon and Visine bottles into it and stormed out.

A half hour later, Xiocena came into the darkened master bedroom and yanked open the curtains, causing Marion to do another hound-dog imitation. "You have a ten o'clock meeting with Warren Buffett and you look like hammered shit," the housekeeper said.

"Can you go to it for me?" Marion pleaded.

"No."

"I have a wig left over from that party. You could put on my clothes—"

"No." Xiocena slapped a damp, iced washcloth on Marion's forehead, tipped her head back, and shoved three aspirin into her mouth. Marion made a face but chewed them up and chased them down with a glass of water.

"Come into the dressing rooms. We have that Mr. Fink tank," said Xiocena, pulling Marion's legs over the edge of the bed.

"*Erhardt,*" Marion sighed. "Good idea."

Nervous about Patti's matrimonial track record, Marion had long insisted on keeping a spare oxygen tank for Lou on the premises. Maybe pure O-two would clear her head.

Xiocena stood her employer up, threw a robe over her, and walked her to the dressing rooms.

"Where's Richard?" Marion muttered.

"He left for work. And he was carrying your crocodile Marc Jacobs purse."

Marion shuffled forward for a few seconds, then turned to her housekeeper. "Did it go with his tie?" she demanded.

30

Strings Attached

"This is the greatest kindness anyone has ever done for me," Mariah said reverently, accepting her lease papers back. Wearing a red-embroidered black peasant dress, ballet flats, and another red ribbon tied up in her hair, she was sitting demurely in the black leather club chair in front of Ari's sleek glass and brushed-steel desk.

"Don't say that in front of your mother," warned Ari.

Mariah laughed and Ari again thought of sunlight and dark sea. "She will bless you as a saint."

Ari glanced at the messages on his computer screen. This morning, he'd bought out two independent labels he'd been purposely starving and had been called many names in the process, none remotely related to "saint." Doing this poor kid a good deed made him feel less monstrous. In fact, it lightened his day. "Nonsense. My wife spends more on hairdressers each month."

"Well, it is the greatest kindness anyone *in America* has shown me," Mariah said, rising. Ari rose as well, to say good-bye, but Mariah was moving to the office window facing southwest. Nineteen floors up, the window afforded a view clear to the Pacific on even nonclear days.

"*It is just there, on Beverly Glen. In one week, I will wave up at you,*" Mariah said, switching to Greek and pointing.

"*And I will watch over you. The patron saint of cosigners,*" Ari replied, also in Greek, wondering if he'd used the right tense.

"*Your view is good. The ocean brings many Greeks luck,*" Mariah said.

"*I wear Poseidon's medal,*" Ari confessed. This was starting to get goofy, he thought. He needed to wind it up with this mouse and prepare for his next business.

"Oh! May I see it?" she asked, suddenly switching back to English and approaching the desk.

For some reason, Ari suddenly wanted to keep his desk between them. He reached up, quickly unfastened his medal, and tossed it to her. "It hasn't left my body in years but since we are cosigners—"

Mariah snatched it out of the air with one hand. Placing it in the center of her palm, she covered it with her other hand and closed her eyes, giving Ari the impression she was attempting to commune with the jewelry piece.

"It is old," she announced.

What? She could tell that by "vibing" it? Was that the way she authenticated antiquities? This was turning weird and Ari was feeling unnerved. "Yes, well, it was my great-uncle's and he was old. And I'm kind of old now too," he replied. He wanted the medal back. He wanted Mariah to go.

But Mariah was walking over to him. She was holding the necklace open in her hands, intending to refasten it around his neck. She had that fire-flint thing in her eyes. Ari knew it was foolish but she made him sort of afraid.

"Your two o'clock is here," said Carley's voice, over the phone speaker. "Do you need help finding the file?"

Normally, Ari thought of his secretary as a pushy brat, always whining for concert tickets and introductions to eligible music executives, but at this moment she'd risen to the stature of savior.

He didn't want Mariah's hands anywhere near his neck.

"Yes!" he barked (frantically) at the phone. "You need to come in."

Carley banged into his office and Mariah instantly lowered her hands and the necklace.

"You've met Miss Fine," said Ari, quickly pulling his confused assistant around in front of him and pointing to the computer.

"Yes. Outside," replied Mariah. She was staring evenly at him.

Ari made what he believed to be a frustrated-looking face at the computer. "I'm sorry to cut our visit short, but many, many lawyers are about to walk in here and these files are so elusive!"

"Here we go," said Carley unhelpfully, bringing the files up with one touch. She wedged away from Ari and trotted out the door. "I'll go get their drinks."

"And I need to *study* these files," Ari stammered. "So good luck with your relocation and—"

Mariah moved so swiftly he could have sworn she teleported.

Click. The necklace was clasped round his neck. Her hands felt cool and dry and she smelled like the earth. Then Mariah stepped back and smiled. She had beautiful lips.

"Your assistant has my phone number, if you ever need an antiquity. Or want to talk to a Greek. I will wave at you soon."

And Mariah swept out. Ari felt like an ass. Why the fuck had he ever been afraid of a beautiful woman putting her arms around his neck? He was watching too many shows on the Science Fiction Channel. From now on, he would read. Maybe a book about Poseidon, he decided, tucking his medal back into his shirt.

He didn't see the tiny red string Mariah had tied into the chain, by the clasp.

It was dipped in menstrual blood.

31

The Deadliest Word

Marcy grimaced as if she were having a seizure then slumped across the desk while Patti picked at her eye makeup, then at the glitter on the disturbing birthday card she was incapable of putting down. She wished the medium would get on with her spiel. There was a preferred-clients sale of one-of-a-kind items at Dolce & Gabbana and she wanted to catch Katsume's first pep rally before the Dior retrospective at the Getty. She had thought that doing a session at the Beverly Park house would save time, but Marcy-the-medium had been at it twenty minutes so far and the spirit had yet to show.

At the moment, the medium was grinding her head back and forth, gibbering like a rhesus monkey and making Patti glad she'd replaced her white suede-topped desk with the glossy blond Biedermeier antique. Marcy-the-medium's hair looked like it had a lot of product in it. Patti decided on the spot to do her entire office in blond Biedermeier to match the desk, as long as she had the crew redoing the bedroom and, hopefully, the closets (which still needed that variance to go through before they could put in the third-story cold-storage unit; everything had fur on it nowadays).

Marcy suddenly jerked upright, reminding Patti of a skydiver deploying a parachute, and opened her eyes. Only the whites were showing.

Patti looked left and saw Lizzy-the-decorator crab-walk in with a swatch book and she motioned for the woman to quietly come over and squat down alongside her, behind the desk. While Marcy hyperventilated, they flipped through the swatches, arriving at a tie between "Peacock" and "Mediterranean."

An operatic voice warbled out of the medium. *"I am with you,"* it announced.

"Finally!" Patti exhaled. "Malachite, there must be some way we could put you on speed dial or get a high-speed line!"

"Passing between the kingdoms takes time," the spirit replied.

Marcy-the-medium channeled "Malachite," a green-agate-type female entity from the mineral kingdom who vibrated at the same level as the heart chakra, making her an excellent consultant on matters of romance and dreams (as opposed to Murray-the-medium, who channeled "Cog-knarle," a thirteenth-century wizard; or Lucy-the-medium, who channeled "Bentbough," some guy made out of trees).

"Well, time's almost up, so let's get going with the marriage outlook for, say, the next nine months—make it a year," Patti said briskly.

"Ahhhh," began Malachite, *"love is the shield against life's most fearsome—"*

"I'm asking about *marriage*," Patti corrected. "Mine. Do you see any harm coming to my marriage with Lou?"

"I see no harm. Your bond is a boat which will float above—"

"No obstacles, challenges, or bumps in the road?" interrupted Patti.

"No, gentle traveler, Louis is yet strong and his body shall remain healthy for—"

"*Marriage*, Malachite. Focus. Is anything or anybody going to fuck up my marriage this year?" Patti asked, flipping over the birthday card to the white side and placing the two swatches upon it for comparison.

"Nothing shall come between partners on the road to—"

"No outside relationship developing and messing it up?"

"Yours is a bond that can withstand—"

"No threatening e-mails, confessional letters, or other communication stuff?" Patti pushed.

"My sight tells me none shall damage—"

"How about photos, schemes, stuff that's going to develop or grow into a problem?"

"No. Nothing. Nada. Nilch."

"Any men who—"

"Your marriage is totally safe, for Christ's sake!" Malachite snapped.

"Well, there's no need to get testy," sniffed Patti.

It took three minutes of rhesus-monkey shrieking before Malachite regained her composure.

"You must have faith, gentle traveler. Mine is a sight that sees beyond planes of existence and time. What other knowledge of the ages are you wishing to seek?" the spirit asked, now apparently calmed down.

"Um, well, the marriage thing was pretty much it," Patti answered, checking her watch.

"No questions of the heart?"

"Nah."

"No loved ones you wish to contact?"

"Not today," Patti replied as her attention switched back to the swatches.

She okayed a picture of a stool that the Lizzy-the-decorator held up for approval and gestured to show how high she wanted it built.

"There must be some questing left in you," Malachite coaxed. *"Look inside. Look deeply and name that which burns for an answer."*

Patti closed her eyes and took a moment. "I have to make a decision," she said. "About something that will affect my life for better or for worse. And frankly, I'm torn, Malachite. Should I go with the Peacock ultrasuede or Mediterranean for this office?"

"Did you know *Halston* invented ultrasuede?" asked Lizzy.

"Get out!" squealed Patti. "It's the greatest stuff in the world. I spilled chili all over the divan and Wanda washed it off *completely* with Ivory soap. Good as new!"

Marcy-the-medium's eyeballs were back in their right position. She reached down and groped for her satchel.

"So, what color is best, Malachite?" Patti continued. "I'm leaning toward the Peacock, myself—"

"Malachite has left the building," said Marcy, stomping out of the room.

"If only she'd show up that fast," said Patti, decisively handing Lizzy the Peacock swatch. "Anyway, I can't use her anymore. She's lost her sight."

"How do you know?" asked Lizzy.

Patti tapped the birthday card on her desktop. "She was way off on a question."

"Oh. Okay," said Lizzy, turning away to roll her eyes. "I'm going to go look for that carpenter."

Lizzy-the-decorator left Patti staring down at her card. Inside it, the sender had scrawled a message that, without a doubt, spelled danger ahead. She'd experienced enough of this cruel life to recognize the tick-tock of a time bomb. If she didn't act to dismantle this, it could blow up in her face. And blow away her marriage.

Slowly, as if it contained firecrackers, she opened the card and reread the terrible sentiment inside. Patti Fink couldn't think of a deadlier word in the English language. Yet there it was, staring up at her. She had to act carefully. And she had to act fast. Because the birthday card was signed: *Love, Ricky.*

32

Weeds in the Garden

"Fucking pollution!" Maya exclaimed, rubbing a jasmine leaf with her thumb then offering the thumb for her gardeners' examination. It looked like she'd dipped it in graphite.

"Is soot?" Sasha asked, taking a guess.

"It's mold! The same stuff is growing all over town. It grows inside houses and makes people sick," she declared, rubbing more leaves. "Tch! All of it fucked! Why you let it get so bad? The tour is in . . ."

"Six weeks," finished Dudayev.

Maya had surprised her gardeners by returning early that morning to do a walk-through inspection of the grounds. They were currently standing on the east side of the estate, next to the tennis court. All four chain-link "walls" surrounding the court were completely enveloped by voluptuously thick jasmine vines, which normally were a feast for the eyes and nose. Today, the vines looked blackish and droopy.

"It looks like soot," Dudayev remarked, squinting at the thumb. "You say pollution—"

"Pollution is *brown* not black," corrected Maya. "And it goes in the air. Like line over ocean."

"Are you sure? Maybe neighbors burn coal?" Dudayev suggested.

"They burn only dollars," she said, growing irritated. "This mold is from all the cars, all the diesel ships at San Pedro, oil refineries, Chinese factories, and the rest of the fucked-up planet."

Maya threw her hands up in exasperation and headed down the path, pulling the two confused men in her wake. "Pollution make global warming and acid air," she said over her shoulder as she walked. "I go to lecture with tree scientists. This was desert until they steal water. The air was dry. But polar caps melt and now air is wet and mold loves wet. This was clean air and now it is polluted. Pollution make air and rain acidic. Mold loves acidic. Soon we grow nothing but fucking mold."

"That is fucked up," agreed Dudayev.

Sasha just followed, smoking a cigarette. He'd given up after "soot."

"Are we looking at other side because whole thing is the same," whined Dudayev.

"We are getting Serenade spray to kill that shit. You should have done two weeks ago!" Maya announced, and added, "We have in shed."

Behind Maya's back, Sasha swatted Dudayev and pantomimed the internationally recognized sign for "gun."

Dudayev shook his head and said, "Moved it."

"You move spray?" Maya asked, stopping.

"No. I moved, ah, car," Dudayev lied, prompting Sasha to look disgusted.

Maya continued leading them through the orchard, checking the lemon-, grapefruit-, and orange-tree leaves with her thumb. Sasha plucked a scarlet-blushed orb off a blood-orange tree and threw it, nailing Dudayev in the middle of his back. When he had his friend's attention, Sasha put his finger over one nostril, making the internationally recognized sign for "cocaine."

Again, Dudayev shook his head. "All gone."

"The Serenade is all gone?" asked Maya.

"No my *cigarettes* are all gone," Dudayev lied.

"Sasha has," said Maya, as if she were speaking to an idiot, then turned to Sasha. "You have enough for me too?"

"You quit!" cried Dudayev, pointing his finger in her face.

"So did you," Maya coolly replied.

Sasha gave them both cigarettes and, as he lit them both up, broke into a wicked grin that exposed the diamond stud in his front tooth.

A moment later, as they neared the gardening shed, Dudayev, who'd sincerely quit for six months, doubled over in a coughing fit. Between coughs, he threw the cigarette he was smoking into the bushes.

Sasha bent down to him and pantomimed the not-so-internationally-recognized sign for "cordless drill." It took Dudayev a few seconds to decipher the meaning, but when he finally got it, his face registered panic, then relaxed into a cunning expression.

"Better I get spray," he said evenly, swiftly slipping in front of Maya so that he reached the shed first. "I spilled stuff for slug."

Maya eyed him suspiciously. "You spill diatomaceous earth? *Indoors?*" she asked.

"I know," Dudayev muttered, lowering his eyes like a naughty child and tugging on the gold hoop in his ear. "You say keep in *outside* cabinet, but I forget." He opened the shed door, holding it very close to his body so that it was impossible for Maya to see the three hundred "recently emancipated" new cordless drills stacked in the back.

"He forget everything!" complained Sasha, getting into the charade. He flicked his cigarette butt at Dudayev to emphasize disgust.

Dudayev whipped around, his eyes flashing murderously at his coconspirator. Maya reached out and grabbed his sleeve and he turned to her, recomposing his face into that of a sheepish boy.

"You can't go in either," she cautioned. "That stuff is tiny razor blades. It will fuck your lungs!"

Dudayev looked down at the cigarette in the hand that trapped his sleeve.

"Fuck it. Don't breathe," Maya said, releasing him and standing back.

Dudayev made a show of taking a deep breath and, still blocking Maya's view, leaned awkwardly into the shed and extracted a bucket of Serenade powder. Sasha's hand shot out and slammed the shed door shut.

"We don't want to breathe your mistake," he scolded Dudayev. Unseen by Maya, his ice-colored eyes danced with merriment.

Maya studied the label on the Serenade bucket. "Two tablespoons per gallon," she read. "Do you have—"

"We have spoons," interrupted Sasha, who was now leaning up against the shed door.

Dudayev took advantage of his partner's position and whacked him across the chest (as hard as he could, for revenge), saying, "And you forgot to fix hunter head on backyard grass."

The rawboned giant barely felt the blow. But Maya grew alarmed and held out her hand.

"I do it. Give me wrench."

Sasha pulled the sprinkler wrench from his back pocket and Maya grabbed it away from him.

"I wait for you, I have brown yard for the tour!" she barked. "Spray the entire court at sunset then power-wash off in morning. And clean that shit up inside. And wear masks."

Maya headed for the backyard.

"And hold my broken balls!" Dudayev called out.

Maya turned, flashing the smile that compelled consumers worldwide to reach for their wallets (or Vaseline) and sweetly said, "Please, thank you."

She kept grinning as she sauntered to the backyard, past mounds of azaleas, hydrangeas, pittosporum, and lilies. She knew the boys had stashed drills in the shed. And they'd all been a tribe long enough for her to know they'd never get arrested. She just didn't want them getting sloppy around Tom. That's why she'd instituted the "no boosted goods at the house" rule. Maya also knew they were bullshitting her about the hunter-head sprinkler. But they needed to save face and she hadn't been out to her meadow all week.

She walked past the maze, through the wall of cedars, and emerged onto her secret lawn, feeling suddenly wider and calmed. Spotting a sprouting cluster of chickweed, she squatted down to pull it out, using the wrench as a weeding tool. Because of her world-famous behind, journalists always requested the secret of Maya's exercise regimen and she always told them, "Get a garden. Your manicurist will hate you, but your boyfriend will love."

Pulling weeds always made her feel better. Sometimes it was nice to have something to attack.

She ripped out a few more clusters then tucked the seed heads in her pocket and headed across the lawn to dump the weed bodies in the compost bucket behind the huge Monterey pine.

Maya swung her arms as she crossed the emerald acre, feeling the freedom of its space. It brought back memories of walking around the family farm with her father as a girl. That was how she'd developed her jaw-dropping gait. His legs were so long she had to take leaps instead of steps to keep up with even his narrowest stride. They'd both unfairly called her mother "the snail." Maya closed her eyes and remembered the comical sound of her mother calling out for them to slow down. She had nothing left of her parents but memories. Memories that this small meadow of lawn somehow never failed to evoke.

When the Russians arrived, the whole country of Chechnya had become extremely nationalistic and racially prejudiced toward their own *"teips,"* as the clans were called. Even the morsel of tolerance that had been spared for the African-Chinese basketball player who defected Yugoslavia to farm and raise a family with his Chechan wife was consumed in the bonfire of racism.

Maya's uncles had sold every single photo and keepsake to rag peddlers when they claimed the farm as their own.

And then they had sold Maya.

"Maya! Are you out there?" called Tom, breaking her bittersweet memory.

"Yah! Wait a minute!" she hollered back.

Maya jogged back across the lawn and emerged on the other side of the cedars. Tom was hanging out the upstairs music-room window.

"Bob and I are flying to Vegas for the day. The technology show is going on. Wanna come?"

Maya raised an eyebrow in disapproval. "Three people on a G-5?"

"We'll carbon-offset," Tom retorted. "I heard this year's show is *sick*. Hologram communications and computer sunglasses! Like stepping into the future. They'll customize anything we want."

"I'm not in mood to nerd today, baby. And I've got fitting at three," she apologized.

"Yeah, we might not be back by then. Is there anything I can pick out for you?"

Yeah, I want memory blocker to forget I was forced to fuck Russian soldiers at fourteen.

But she'd told only Marion about that part of her history.

Instead, Maya smiled up at her husband and answered, "Anything you think I like."

"How about a video vibrator so I can watch you from location?" Tom asked, with a leer.

"How do you know I don't have one already?" she replied with a sultry wink.

"We could have the plane fly you home early and come back for us later," he suggested.

Maya shook her head in disbelief. "Then I be one person flying back on G-5 that make one more round-trip for you two persons? Tch! That's really fucked!"

"Fuck is the *idea*," Tom whispered loudly, appraising his wife. "Think about it: screwing in one of those 'virtual' booths? Make a baby while exploring the moon?"

"I don't want a moon baby."

He's not giving up.

"Well, text me if you think of anything." Tom chuckled.

"Just make it black," she replied.

"The baby? That's a given," he teased.

Tom ducked as Maya threw her handful of weeds and dirt through the window. "We've got homework tonight," he warned. "I'm not giving up on this!"

No shit, thought Maya, heading inside to kiss him good-bye.

33

Un-Easy Lessons

"Dad, I think Claire farted," said Haley, from the backseat.

"I did not!" said Claire. "Besides: he who smelt it dealt it."

Just then Eva started giggling. Claire was grateful. At least her littlest stepdaughter was acting neutral that afternoon. She'd given up hoping for an ally among them. Haley wasn't swift with the comebacks, so she was safe for a few minutes. They were all returning from Brooke's hip-hop recital at the Wallis Academy Upper School, where Claire had actually been looking forward to getting a glimpse of the *former* Mrs. Price. And letting the former Mrs. Price get a glimpse of her.

It was clear that everyone in the family was terrified of upsetting the woman. Even Billy. Whenever his ex-wife called, he acted as though the Pentagon was on the hotline and followed her orders—no questions asked. If she wanted the girls to stay with them an extra day, he obliged. If she wanted the girls to come over a day early and cut Billy's time with them short, he obliged—delivering them personally at any hour of the day or night. Then there was that eleven o'clock "emergency" call about Brooke leaving her favorite sandals at his and Claire's house and refusing to go to bed without them. It had been *winter*, for goodness' sake. And the woman lived three streets away!

One night, when Billy was having a production meeting at the house, his ex-wife had called and demanded he drop everything and bring over Haley's thermos for school. Claire, who'd been trying to make sure he wasn't disturbed, answered his cell phone.

She was met with silence and almost hung up when she heard a small distressed voice say: "Billy."

"Who's calling?" she asked, thinking it was a weirdo.

"I need Billy. Tell him it's *me*."

"Who are *you*?" Claire persisted.

More silence.

At that point Billy came into the kitchen, overheard her, and flew across the room to take over the phone. Claire noted that her husband never used that servant voice when *they* were talking together. Why with her ex-wife? Claire knew it was silly, since Billy and the woman had been divorced for three years, but she was beginning to feel jealous.

Hanging up, Billy had started tearing the kitchen apart. When he told Claire what his ex requested, she'd laughed and offered to buy Haley a brand-new thermos at the drugstore and drive it over.

"Oh, no, honey," he'd said, digging through the dishwasher. "That'd freak her out. And it's best you not answer my cell either."

Claire was a newlywed. She wanted Billy to be joyful about having married her. She didn't want to be a nag. So she shut up.

Then he drove off and left Claire to entertain eight strangers in the den for forty-five minutes. At least they were friendly and relaxed. It turned out to be her first non-eggshell-walking experience in the house.

The ex had the same effect on her daughters as she had on Billy. All Katia had to say was, "Your mother wants you to . . ." or, "Your mother would be upset if you don't . . ." and Brooke, Haley, and Eva instantly behaved like neurotic robots.

Doesn't leave the house. Doesn't lift a finger. Very fragile. She was beginning to think Billy's ex was an agoraphobic paralyzed person with glass bones and nitroglycerin in her veins. (Or that she was a graduate of the best friggin' motivational leadership seminar on planet Earth.) Either way, the ex-wife obviously didn't want to face the fact that Claire even existed.

Well, it was high time she did.

And Brooke's recital, she'd decided, would be the perfect place to give the woman a reality check.

Craig had helped her pick out an I'm-his-new-wife-and-I'm-not-a-cheap-whore outfit. He'd decided on a camel cashmere suit ensemble by a new German designer, Walter Hessen. The suit jacket had Hessen's signature eagle sitting on top of the world logo embroidered in black thread just between the shoulder blades. Conservative but cool. He accessorized Claire's ensemble with brown croc Manolo Blahnik pumps, ropes of Chanel signature pearls and chains, Chanel pearl earrings, a Cartier chunky gold watch, three diamond bangles from Fred (to fall over the watch), topped off with a "fuck you" brown croc Hermès Birkin bag. Claire added the crowning touch with sleek, upswept hair. This was her favorite look. Conservative, classic, and rich. Like a well-kept wife.

Big mistake.

It was bad enough that she'd wasted all that energy on a woman who turned out to be out of town and thus unable to attend the recital, but when they arrived at the Wallis Academy auditorium, Claire was horrified to discover she was overdressed.

Really overdressed.

Most of the other parents were wearing jeans and T-shirts. Most of the mothers had no purses at all or cloth bags imprinted with environmental slogans. Like the ones you took to the grocery store. Some of them looked like they hadn't brushed their hair in a week. Oh well, thought Claire, it's never too late to set a good example. But during the program, she noticed some of the parents looking over at her and frowning. Some were staring and whispering. Were they mean friends of Billy's ex?

After the recital, Brooke pretty much disowned her. The thirteen-year-old had never been particularly friendly to begin with, but she'd never appeared to be *ashamed* of Claire. Every time Claire tried to congratulate her, she'd fled across the room. Brooke refused to take family pictures if it meant posing with Claire, and when Billy tried to coax her into it, she whispered, "I'm embarrassed! Don't do this to me, Daddy, Please!"

Mortified, Claire headed for the girls' bathroom rather than stick around and risk witnessing her husband back down. If it came down to either her or the girls, she'd rather not find out whom Billy would choose.

Inside the bathroom, Claire tried not to cry and instead concentrated on revising her Secret Rainbow Princess Promise with the "Married with Kids" addendum. What could she have done to Brooke to make the girl hate her so much? Then again, maybe it wasn't hate. Maybe it was just acting out, a reaction to her mother's being away and wanting to feel some sort of connection through loyalty. (That psych paperback ruled!) Maybe Billy's ex-wife had coached her children to give their stepmother a hard time. Claire shook out her dismay. She was silly to take it so personally. She smoothed her hair and prepared to go back outside.

That was when the tall, lemon-faced woman in an ugly monochromatic gray pantsuit, gray hair, and black-framed glasses strode into the bathroom and looked her over with a sigh.

"We really can't have you doing this," the woman said.

"Doing what?" Claire asked, unnerved by the surprise assault. "Oh, are adults not supposed to use the children's bathrooms? I completely understand. With all the perverts hanging around schools these days, you can't be too careful." She flashed her best pageant smile and offered her hand. "I'm Claire Price, Brooke's new stepmother."

The woman wasn't shaking her hand. "I know," she said, drawing herself up even taller. "Since you haven't been by the school yet, I'll have to introduce myself. I'm Doris Whiting, director of Wallis Academy family relations, and this display is a clear violation of the parental covenant."

"Huh?" asked Claire, checking her rear view in the mirror to see if she'd accidentally tucked the back of her dress into her panty hose. "What are you talking about?"

"Wallis Academy," Doris continued, "prides itself on being one of the most progressive and non-background-biased private schools in the nation. We admit families purely on a basis of merit, without regard to socioeconomic status, sexual orientation, religious orientation, political orientation, physical limitation—"

"I get the picture," Claire cut in indignantly. "What does that have to do with me? What display?" This was getting insane.

"You're wearing a Walter Hessen outfit," the director of family relations declared, pointing at her.

Jeez, these private school people knew their stuff.

"As a matter of fact, I am. Well, the bag is Hermès—"

"And it didn't occur to you that Herr Hessen's behavior last week made him a poster child for everything Wallis Academy stands against?" she asked, incredulous.

"I don't know what he did, but I'm wearing his *suit*, not him," Claire replied, grasping for reason.

"Last week," said Doris, growing exasperated, "Walter Hessen declared himself a member of the Aryan Supremacist Society. The one that believes that whites are the true intended masters of the world and should reclaim their birthright."

Oops.

"Your dress is a walking hate crime against our Jewish-descent families, our same-sex-parent families, our families of non-Caucasian descent, and our families of Polish, Russian, Belgian, Dutch, and French descent. Plus, the ridiculously extravagant price tag of your garment is an affront to our scholarship and nonunion families."

"Nonunion?"

"Hessen employs scabs," spat Doris.

Really, really knew their stuff.

"I am so sorry," stammered Claire. "And embarrassed. But I had no idea—"

"You're a parent of a Wallis Academy student and you don't read the newspaper?" the director asked.

"I've been really busy lately, what with the move and—"

"Yes, I've seen your priorities on WireImage," Doris sneered. "I'm going to have to put the Price family on probation. It's procedure in the family covenants to which your husband is a signatory," said the director, handing Claire her card. "Please don't miss your new parent orientation appointment, next week. You've broken two appointments already."

"Wait a minute, nobody told me I had an appointment!"

"The notice came home in Brooke's backpack, as did your personal copy of the family covenant," said the director.

Claire smelled a rat. "She never gave it to me," said the rat's stepmother.

"Maybe if you invested more time communicating with your stepdaughter instead of preening in front of cameras, you'd be better informed."

Doris Whiting turned to leave.

"Hold on," Claire cried. "Where do you get off being so judgmental? You're supposed to be a school about tolerance. I just wanted to look nice. It was an honest mistake."

The director eyed her gravely and said, "Even at Wallis Academy, that excuse won't cut it."

And she was gone.

When Claire had removed her jacket and exited the bathroom, she found no family waiting for her and had to catch up in the parking lot. When she complained to Billy about her tongue-lashing in the john, he said, "Relax, Cookie. It's no biggie, just clothes."

"She said the family is on probation." Claire whispered, desperately hoping the girls wouldn't hear.

"With the money I've sunk in?" Billy laughed. "Being on probation means nothing. Don't worry!"

"Oh, my God!" cried Brooke. "We're on probation? Claire's going to get us kicked out of school!"

The ride home had been less than jolly. Billy was preoccupied on the phone, Brooke fumed dramatically, and Haley took potshots at Claire.

As they turned into the driveway, Haley said, "I know it's her fart, Dad. I've smelled that in your bathroom after she was in there."

"Haley, that's enough," said Claire, wearily getting out of the car. "It's rude and unladylike."

"So is a Hitler dress!" hissed Brooke as she stomped inside with Eva in tow.

Lacking a good comeback, as usual, Haley punted by crying and throwing herself into her father's arms. "She's always picking on me!" the nine-year-old dramatically sobbed.

Luckily, Billy was still on his earpiece and only absentmindedly patted Claire's back, totally uninformed about his offsprings' callousness.

Eager to discard her heels, Claire entered through the side door and skipped up the back stairs, intending to cross through the children's wing. As she passed Brooke's room, she looked inside and saw her oldest step-daughter sobbing in the nanny's arms.

"I hate her so much! I wish she'd just get out of our lives! I hate her! I hate her!" the girl wailed.

"I know, I know," Katia soothed.

And now I know too, thought Claire as she trudged to her room.

34

Pinky

"There's enough Rohypnol in that Visine bottle to rape Santa Monica," said Jimmy Purdue over the Ferrari's Bluetooth speaker. Not wanting to lose the doctor's call, Richard pulled up short of the Zane Building's parking entrance, almost causing the Mack truck behind him to put him out of his misery by crushing him like a grape. The doctor's next words were blasted away by the trucker's outraged air horn.

"What?" Richard yelled at the dashboard, hoping the microphone was there somewhere. "What about the water bottles?"

"Positive," said Jimmy. "Both of 'em. What do you want me to do with this stuff?"

Good question.

"Richard?"

"Ass wipe!" screamed the trucker as the big rig roared around the vulnerable Ferrari.

"What was that?" asked the doctor.

"Give me a minute," Richard mumbled.

"Sure. I'm going to put you on hold. I've got a two o'clock patient and I have to review his files," Jimmy answered, clicking the line over to Muzak.

How far did he want to go with this?

Richard wanted to dust the three bottles for prints, but he couldn't go to the police. He considered take-out pizza orders private information. Just thinking about asking a detective to keep the naked-date-rape juice-doped-masseuse part "confidential" gave him the willies. Anyway, no police *communications* were truly confidential. And this was *fucking confidential*!

He didn't know where to begin to look for someone who would dust for prints on the sly. Marion was the spook in the family. Only *she* had access to all the secret contacts and private services in that *Black Book* and she kept the thing locked up God knows where. That's where she'd found those private forensic guys. He couldn't very well ask her outright for their number. She'd ask why. And she could always tell when he was lying. Ever since she and crazy Patti took that body-language course. Something about pupils expanding . . .

Then Richard's thoughts came to a screeching halt and threw themselves into reverse. Back to "never happened" night.

Oh, shit. That's right. It was Marion's *forensic team!*

Richard closed his eyes as the wave of paranoia swept over him. Then he ransacked the car's compartments for a leftover stash of beta-blockers. No luck. He resorted to rolling his shoulders and trying to slow his breathing, coaxing his thoughts back to what he hoped was the "male side" of his brain. He'd grown up in the forests of Michigan, in the company of men. He'd never witnessed a grown man becoming hysterical until he came to California.

His discovery that the forensic team had failed to notice the bottles in Marion's minifridge didn't *prove* anything except that the team sucked. The bottles weren't in plain sight. He only found them after removing ten items. No. Not his Marion. It was stupid to suspect her of setting him up. He'd analyzed it to death already. The smart money was on that masseuse and they'd already settled with her, so who gave a goddamn?

"Richard?" said Dr. Purdue, coming back on the line. "Have you reached a decision?"

Richard put the Ferrari in gear and rolled into the driveway of the Zane Building's parking garage. "Destroy 'em."

He couldn't help chuckling at his near hysteria in the speed elevator going up to his penthouse offices. He'd been hanging out with too many girls. Maybe he should jack up his testosterone by getting back in that senior rugby league. Ah, who was he kidding? Those guys were dropping like flies. He couldn't risk blowing his knee out again. He'd lost a whole ski, tennis, and polo season that year.

That hunt bunch was male only. But they were all about wine and food. And the actual hunting was on those private reserves that practically shot the elk for you. So much for Iron John. He couldn't think of any other sport for men his age that wasn't infiltrated by women. Even his sailing team had a gal now. She was a beast.

Richard stepped out of the elevator, still contemplating hormone-enhancing opportunities. Maybe a fishing trip. And he still had the number for that guide in Scotland. Or was Belize better this time of year?

He was about to use the private entrance to his office suite when Estelle, the receptionist, flagged him down with a message slip.

"This guy came by while you were out and didn't want to wait. A Mr. Watson. Claims to be a private detective on referral from Barry Shapiro."

Richard jammed the slip in his pocket and quickly excused himself. Barry must have thought they wanted more follow-up on "never happened" night. Good thing he hadn't called Watson *before* he used his male brain, when he was flipping out. He might have requested something ridiculous like surveillance on his wife. He could only imagine how that would've gone over with Marion.

After entering his mahogany-paneled power nest, he crossed the antique scarlet-and-cobalt Persian carpet—wrangled by Marion from the family castle of a cash-poor Welsh viscount—to the Edwardian green-marble-and-brass bar cart in the corner. Twisting the top off an antique cut-crystal Waterford decanter, he proceeded to pour himself a generous dose of scotch.

Richard looked up at the mounted ibex and water-buffalo trophy heads, the various contact sports and sailing cups, and the enormous painting depicting Wellington's victory at Waterloo that covered the wall in front of him. At least his offices were manly and solid.

He didn't see the pink stuffed poodle sitting on his desk with the attached note:

Greetings from Your Old Flame. Love, Pinky.

The carpet hadn't tasted such good scotch in over one hundred years.

By two-thirty, Richard was so stricken with grief, rage, and panic he didn't notice that he'd double-dosed on his beta-blockers. There was only one human on earth besides himself who knew about the Pinky experience. He'd confessed it in utter loving trust. And he hadn't confessed it until they were ten years into their marriage, and even then, he never would have uttered a word if they'd hadn't been prisoners in Patti's Austrian ski chalet and trying Ecstasy for their first and only time. It was Marion's idea to try the Pinky thing out. It was *their* thing now. Why the fuck would she taunt him so cruelly? Was this her idea of a joke?

He picked up a framed photo of his beautiful (and formerly loving) wife. He'd marched into this office thinking about testosterone and now tears were plopping down on the desktop. When he'd tried to get ahold of Marion, the temp taking Ivan's place said she was in transit to a meeting and had lost her cell. Marion never lost anything. She was up to something.

By three o'clock, Richard was beginning to remember and sympathize with every girl he'd ever known in junior high and high school who'd been sexually harassed. The stuffed poodle was bad enough, but the e-mails were disgusting. The *mildest* one had an attachment of a poodle licking a Big Stick Popsicle. Then there was that message from the phone-sex worker who'd offered to "bark" the words to "Love to Love You Baby." This wasn't funny. This was cruel. How could he have married cruel? This wasn't a setup. Marion had half no matter what. No. This was revenge.

"Who is Pinky?" Richard's assistant, Miriam, queried after the tenth crank call.

"Oh, it's an in-joke with a group of my old paintball buddies," Richard lied. "Do you have the projections for—"

"*You* play paintball?" she interrupted.

"Somebody got me pretty bad with a pink one and I wore it the rest of the game."

"I thought if you got hit, you were out," she skeptically asked.

"Yeah, well, that's *one* way to play. At the *beginning* level. Now, about those projections . . ." Richard babbled, trying to change the subject for the second time.

"Hold on. You've got a call . . . It's Mr. Pinkerton. Do you want to take—"

"I told you no more cranks!" Richard bellowed.

"Harry Pinkerton is the director of marketing at Sanji. Are you all right, Mr. Zane?"

Sanji was a Zane Enterprises television network. It was the chief outlet for Korean powerhouse Sanji Animation, supplemented with product made in the United States. There was SanjiGames, a teen channel of game shows and outdoor survival challenges; Sanjitoons, a cartoon channel featuring two of the top cartoon series in the world; and WeeSanji, a channel for the baby-to-toddler demographic that featured cutting-edge reading-readiness programs for parents trying to create Harvard grads.

"Right. Sorry. Right. Got mixed up," said Richard, hoping Miriam wasn't looking too hard for logic. "Put him through."

"And why are you so upset if the cranks are your friends?"

"Oh, long story. I better take the call," he said, checking his pulse.

"And after you're done with Harry, could you tell me which are the safest paintball parks? My fourteen-year-old is dying to play, but I just don't know anything about—"

"Yeah," he said, cutting her off. "Sure." Richard was Googling paintball parks when Harry's voice boomed over the speaker.

"Richard, you madman!"

"Trust me, today is not the day to call me a madman," Richard bitterly replied.

"Can it be the day to discuss why I've locked the door and canceled all phone and wireless service to the marketing division? Can it be the day to discuss why I'm holed up at Runyon's, where I plan to get so shit-faced I'll wake up beside my fat mustachioed waitress if I don't jump out the fuckin' window first?" wailed Harry, evidently well on his way to inebriation. "Your fun factoid in the trades has emptied the advertising slate before hitting the street! Even the local companies have pulled their ads!"

"Pulled ads? From Sanji?" asked Richard, reaching for the beta-blockers then throwing them back in the drawer. Maybe the things were making him hallucinate.

"Every single channel. Every single company. Even the local ones that barely pay spit. If there's one thing that'll make kiddie products run, it's bestiality! Yessiree!" Harry made a laughing sound that ended in a sob.

"Bestiality?" Richard asked, in a voice a million miles away.

"Oh, and the president of Sanji Animation was my *first* call, this after-noon. I can barely understand those guys. When he started screaming about a dog, I thought he didn't like his lunch. You're still keeping me in the Zane Enterprises family, right? I'd kick ass with the music channel—"

"*Bestiality?*" asked Richard again, developing a slight twitch in his eye.

"Half the country's heard about the poodle piece by now. It's up on the preview Web site. So why'd ya blow your network up? Was there some sort of hostile takeover in the works, Richard? Or should I call you *Pinky*?"

Riiiiiiiiiiiiiiiiiiiipppppppppppppppppppp · · ·

Richard cracked a crown tearing the stuffed poodle in half.

"Harry, I can't tell you what's going on, but just know this: if there's one thing for certain, it's that there'll be *no hostile takeover*! I'll get back to you ASAP."

"You *are* keeping me on, right, Richard? Richard?"

Richard jabbed the computer keys and brought up the trade preview site that featured the next day's trade-paper articles as they came in. Only six to ten people in the industry had been given access to the site, mostly lawyers for huge transnationals or power players like himself. At least it wasn't in *Variety* or the *Hollywood Reporter,* but in that stupid industry cheat sheet that featured little-known info about the players around town. The column was on the front page, entitled "First Nookie." He was listed third, underneath a pair of actors and an exhibitionist director who claimed his first sexual experience had been with a legendary, and conve-niently dead, screen goddess. Under "Richard Zane," it listed "Pinky, Richard's mother's poodle" as the partner with whom he'd had his first sexual encounter.

That was when one water-buffalo head and eight Waterford cut-crystal rocks glasses lost their lives.

It fucking-A was a setup! Marion wanted more than half! And she was willing to publicly paint him as a deprived pervert to do it. Well, he wasn't going down without a struggle. As long as they were telling secrets, he had a few tales of his own to tell.

"Miriam!" Richard called into his desk phone, trying not to screech.

"Are you all right in there? Did you think of a safe paintball—"

"I'm going to need to talk to the lawyers. *All of them.* Now."

"I'll make the calls. Is there anything else?"

It took Richard about three seething seconds to remember. He grabbed his suit jacket and located the message slip in the pocket. "Yeah, I want you to put me on with a Mr. D. Watson, ASAP. Here's the number . . ."

By seven o'clock, Richard had moved into the guest wing of the Zane compound and installed new locks on the doors. The lawyers had contacted no fewer than thirty-five news and gossip-purveying entities threatening a lawsuit. They actually filed one against a porn site with luridly creative photoshopping and another against that piece-of-shit blog that called him "Pinky the Beast Boy."

They also drew up formal separation papers against his wife of twenty-one years. But they hadn't been filed as of yet. Just in case.

Forget teenage girls. Richard Zane's sympathies had traded up for Richard Gere.

35

Hitting an Iceberg

After forty-five minutes of meditation, a workout with her personal trainer, home sessions with her healer, homeopath, and colonic irrigation technician, consultations with two detectives (one had found the source of Richard's crank calls and one the source that gave the Pinky-pairing to the industry cheat-sheet columnist), another session with her healer (after learning all the crank calls had been placed from her missing cell phone), home visits from her dermatologist and makeup artist and hairstylist, Marion, still in a dressing gown, dove into the Biographies section of her *Black Book* to look up information for her lunch meeting.

It was better than rolling back into a yip.

LEONARD GRIFFON—58
$1.8 billion
Hedge funds—flagship Kentway fund up 18% as of '08
Divorced x 2 remarried '06—Evelyn Marks—37
No longer active in trading. Wife manages Fletcher-
Hastings fund, up 9%
Primary residence—Rhode Island

Because of the Pinky scandal, Marion had decided that it was best to mine another end of the country until things cooled off. They *would* cool off, right?

>   Secondaries—Hawaii, Antigua
>   Lutheran—both

Uh-oh.

Marion went back into the bathroom and toned down the eyeliner. Robyn-the-makeup-artist had layered a gray-green powder to distract from her tear-reddened eyes. Maybe they'd clear up in time.

Back in the *Black Book,* she continued on the Griffons.

>   No mitigating incidents
>   [Marion's nice way of saying they had no skeletons.]
>   Survived prostate cancer
>   Donations—Urban education and Health Services

Bingo.

>   Registered Republican in last election
>   Wife registered Democrat
>   Enjoys sailing, water sports, fishing

Okay, they were eastern, sporty, and probably conservative.

With Xiocena's help, she quickly threw on a Loro Piana sweater set, Chloé skirt, medium-heeled Tod's pumps, her single-strand pearl choker, pearl earrings, and a quiet quilted Valentino bag. Marion decided to add an eastern-sporty-conservative finish of a clipped ponytail and her favorite brooch.

She had to repair her eye makeup when she realized the brooch was the one Richard'd bought her in Portofino.

Xiocena thought Marion's costume made her look like she was celibate.

"Trust me, I am celibate these days. Don't worry, Zephyr's going. Next to her, I'll look like an Italian whore."

Crossing to the guest wing, she slipped another note under Richard's door that read:

>   *Darling, it wasn't me. Swear on my life.*
>   *M*

He'd left the last fourteen balled up in hall, including the "Are we still booked for the cruise?" one. That one was returned with a huge iceberg drawn over it in red marker. She hadn't known Richard could draw so well.

Then she added another note that read:

> *Take your enzymes! Not the prescription antacid! And don't increase the beta-blockers. It's unsafe!"*
> M

She was worried about his health. And hers. Heartache and stress definitely caused water retention, she'd discovered.

Marion knew this was going to blow over. Just as soon as they found the *real* perpetrators of the Pinky scandal. She'd spent two sleepless nights racking her brain, but she was absolutely positive she'd never told a soul.

It wasn't exactly something to crow about.

The only suspects she'd come up with were Richard's old psychiatrist and the five people who'd joined them in a "vision vine" ceremony up in Napa. Its purpose was to connect with your spirit animal and learn how to heal. This was accomplished by ingesting a hallucinatory rain-forest vine that made LSD look like cooking sherry. (Patti's recommendation, of course.) The shaman who'd conducted the ceremony was back in Colombia now. She directed the detectives to track down the other four participants and see if any had been in the L.A. area last week. Maybe Richard's spirit animal was a poodle who told tales.

She had shot down the ridiculous accusations about the Rohypnol with Carl and Xio, who testified outside Richard's locked door as alibi witnesses. He *had* to believe them. Right?

Even though the Zanes' lawyers had squelched the Pinky items from every corner of the print world, airwaves, and Internet, nothing could stop people from talking, and the damage was done. Richard now had a permanent scandal footnote. Which meant *they* now had a permanent scandal footnote.

Patti Fink, in an effort to comfort, told Marion that only interesting people had permanent scandal footnotes. Marion didn't think that would cheer her husband up.

He was still her husband. And this was going to blow over. And as her healer kept reminding her, she was bulletproof.

In the meantime, she had her Trophy friends.

And her work. She had a hospital to finance. So far the total fund-raising was around $400 million. Not bad for a bunch of "poodles" with "no real power." *Screw you too, Craig.*

Fund-raising always helped her keep it together and she *had* to keep it together.

Otherwise, whoever was out to get her and Richard might just succeed, because whoever they were, they were very very good at exhuming secrets.

Marion's yips weren't strictly about Richard.

36

Movin' On Up

*I*t was working! It was working! Marion Zane was now associated with something absolutely sick!

Lyndy was blasting vintage Debbie Gibson songs and doing a victory dance around her living room, taking care not to shake her fake fanny too vigorously (lest the weight of the gel seat carry her into the baby grand piano. She didn't want to knock over the precious collection of silver-framed Montgomery family portraits).

How she wished her mystery partner had been notified in time to view the trades preview online! Richard must have had a conniption fit. He must have screamed at his blindsided wife. Lyndy could just imagine the look on Marion's face. It was only a matter of time before their marriage permanently disintegrated and Marion became an ex!

And took a nosedive from the TOP.

"Shake your love, shake your love!"

Who knew the Zanes had such an obnoxious, disgusting skeleton? Who knew the rat-fuck plan would actually work this time? Lyndy had to confess to herself that after hearing Marion blithely shrug off the massage incident, she'd assumed yet another dud had been shot off.

But "Pinky" had hit dead center in the gossip grinder.

Pinky!

Lyndy decided that her next dog would be a big fluffy standard poodle!

———

Already there were signs of a shift in the social hierarchy. Reservations were starting to pour in about the BHC Winter Gala. The most in ten years. Lyndy knew how quick the tide could turn. She hoped that Marion would be drowning by the time of the event. So she could tie a cement block to her ankles.

"And what shall *our* theme be for the Winter Gala, Prince Matthew?" she asked her aged chow. "Let's see, it should be a winter one. How about 'The Frozen Future of Marion Zane'? Or 'Giving Cold Shoulders to Marion Zane'? Or 'Marion's Descent Snowballs'?"

The dog bobbed his huge cloudy-eyed head, trying to follow the trajectory of his mistress's monologue as she danced up to a Ramos Martinez portrait of a somber Latina holding an artichoke.

"Do I remember Marion Zane? Hmm. Oh, yes, the Zanes used to be 'in the business,'" Lyndy chattered at the painting, practicing for future rosy conversations. "Yes, they garnered quite a bit of attention for themselves for a while there. Honestly, I haven't seen hide nor hair of her since she split up with Richard . . . Yes, that scandal was simply nauseating! Turned them into virtual social lepers. I think she's selling industrial space now somewhere in the Midwest . . . My Girl Party in Cannes? Well, the waiting list is rather long, this year but I'll see what I can do."

"Shake your love, shake your love!"

Lyndy tossed her hair and boogied back to the center of the living room. These were the moves she'd make on the dance floor of the Winter Gala! Ta-da! Lyndy imagined herself dancing with George Clooney and her face took on a look of restrained sultry sophistication. Poor George would spend the rest of the night wondering whether or not she had been flirting with him—

"Whatsa matter? We got roach infestation again?" asked Max, who'd returned home unexpectedly in order to retrieve a FedEx envelope containing brochures of five-star Brazilian resorts. (He had big plans for the annual Zippy Cleaners company retreat.)

"I refuse to allow you to diminish my joy," Lyndy snipped, continuing her victory dance. "Not today!"

"What's there to be joyful about? The Lakers lost last night," muttered Max, shaking his head and walking out of the room.

"Shake your love, shake your love!"

Lyndy laughed maniacally and shimmied (carefully) on the downbeats.

It was high time she made that plastic-surgery appointment. There'd be a lull after the Winter Gala, providing the perfect opportunity for a buttock-augmentation procedure to heal.

Poor Marion Zane! Where would she be wounded next? Lyndy couldn't wait to find out!

37

Gnarly News

"Pass me on to Deloris?" cried Ricky, springing upright on the mattress as if he was catching a wave. "No fuckin' way! I'm balls-to-the-wall majorly sick in love with you, Patti! You're like, my universe!"

Eat me, Malachite.

Patti and her golden boy had just finished another steamy early-morning session at Shutters hotel. After they fell apart and after she let her eyes take one last, luxurious stroll over the caramel landscape of Ricky's hard-muscled (every muscle!), long (every muscle!), flawless physique, Patti had made a command decision to farm her paramour out before things progressed any further.

Deloris Crane was a beautiful blonde with a darling figure and a tolerant sense of humor. And she'd just been shock-dumped by her husband of eight years. Since she was still in the process of negotiating a financial settlement, Deloris couldn't risk dating in public. Ricky was perfect for her. Plus, Deloris loved the beach and was the heiress to a comic-book publishing fortune. She'd be perfect for Ricky.

Patti figured the time was ripe since Ricky was most receptive to change after he'd "blasted out an ungodly amount of super-swimmers." But instead of even considering discussing her proposition, he reacted as if she'd shoved a cattle prod up his heartbreakingly perfect ass.

"But Deloris has been through such a rough time. She's rich, she loves water sports, and has a charming Victorian ranch on Oahu. Plus, she's younger than me. By maybe a year or two. I think she's thirty." Patti continued with her pitch.

(Patti was forty-six.)

"You can't just pass me on to a girlfriend like a doob!" Ricky protested.

"But that's *how I got you*," Patti gently reasoned, admiring her view from below and getting a sudden inspiration to plant banana trees around the Beverly Park house cabana. "Greta Switzer was moving to Europe and knew I was in the market for—"

"Patti, that was back when I was the bone-for-coin dude," Ricky said.

"And you're *not* the bone-for-coin dude now?" asked Patti, thinking about Ricky-the-surfer's North Shore Christmas-vacation bills.

"No," he said, flipping his buttery pale bangs to reveal the serious stokage in his sea-glass-colored eyes. "I am your *man*, Patti Fink. And guess what my bounteous love drove to go down? I made a deal with Grunt for sponsorship! Man, I was so smart to get rid of that Barney agent."

Patti had been known to spend as much as an hour describing Ricky-the-surfer to trusted girlfriends. *Smart* was not one of the adjectives she usually chose.

"All I have to do is dominate at Micro and I'm signed. Which will be total future, the way I shred."

"Micro" was a surfing contest in Micronesia at which Ricky was favored to win. Patti began silently praying for tsunamis.

Now Ricky bounced down on his knees. "Then I'll be making enough to support us both!"

This notion struck Patti as so hysterically hilarious that she almost swallowed her tongue.

Ricky looked slighted. "Don't laugh. They're starting me at *one million a year*."

Now Patti laughed even harder.

"Grunt is a monster brand," he argued. "I mean think about it: everything snow and water! Snowboards, skis, surfboards, boogie boards . . ."

Patti's sides were beginning to ache.

". . . skateboards, kite kits, wakeboards, water skis, and all the gear that goes with them. And sunglasses, school supplies, decals . . . backpacks, fins, wax. They even have a GirlGrunt line of clothes for splits. The contract includes free products. We'll have anything we need *and* travel the world, for free!"

Now Patti was practicing her Kegels out of fear she'd pee the bed.

"I want you to leave the old dude so we can get married. And if you don't tell him about our love, I'll do it myself!"

Now Patti stopped laughing and started wondering if Marion had a *Black Book* listing for a good hit man.

"Well, what do you think?" Ricky asked, climbing on top of her and nibbling her face.

That you'd probably manage to yank away before I could bite cleanly through your jugular vein!

"C'mon, Mama, want to be Mrs. Grunt guy?" Ricky murmured.

Warning! Hazard Area Ahead! Proceed with Extreme Caution!

Patti's brain was pixelating into a million disastrous scenarios all based on her next response. Because of her paramour's rash nature, she had to handle this situation with kid gloves! No, those really soft cashmere ones from TSE. No, Harrington House used to make those gloves that were deerskin lined with rabbit fur. She got a dark olive pair in Edinburgh, on that fishing trip with Henrik (number three), or was that Mitsu (number four)? Wearing them was like feeling up Thumper. But Ricky wasn't a bunny! (All puns aside.) Ricky was a nuclear rod! Where were her tongs?!

"Oh, Ricky," Patti choked out. "This is just so sudden."

"That's the kinda dude I am," he said, rolling Patti on her side to get a handful of her butt.

That's what I get for boinking a nineteen-year-old, thought Patti.

The lovers' bodies entwined and they commenced a second round of what Ricky termed "touching tailbone," completely unaware of the photos they were providing for the detective's long-lens camera.

38

Spooky

And the king returns from battle triumphant.

Ari rolled up the driveway to his castle in the sky, expertly avoiding bikes, scooters, Barbie cars, and balls. With every obstacle, the weighty mantle of his day slipped away like a snake's skin as he remembered the loving souls who awaited his return.

Most people romanticized the recording industry as a collaborative and glamorous journey of creativity. Today his journey had been tedious at best.

It began with a grueling four-hour phoner rearguing previously agreed-upon negotiating points for the tenth time with amnesia-feigning Chinese government officials. The translation process drove him nuts. How did these people become so globally connected and successful with a language that sounded like cats fucking?

He'd lost his lunch hour settling an in-house argument between executives who didn't want to share credit with each other for landing the Pharma advertising accounts. Those guys should have been dancing topless on tabletops instead of squabbling like greedy children. When did life become all about press announcements?

His afternoon consisted of arm-twisting managers in search of a replacement artist for the Parisian venue of their Internet World Saves Africa simulcast because the original headliner had arrived early and gobbled his way into gout.

The day came to a lovely crescendo when he had to beg building management not to evict him from his corporate offices because of a custo-

dian's complaint. Evidently, America's sweetheart and teenage pop sensation Lacey Ray had helped herself to some badly cut cocaine in the parking
garage. The effects of the cheap blow inspired her to take an emergency
poop behind her Hummer. Fortunately, the custodian who'd witnessed
the act was a lonely sixty-two-year-old Croatian who'd never heard of
camera phones or YouTube, which made destroying the security tape and
buying his silence relatively easy. Although Ari decided it was best to wait
until Friday to inform Carley that she'd just been affianced to an older
man she'd never met.

Romantic, indeed!

But now he was safely behind gates in his kingdom, looking forward to
sticky kisses, fine wine, and a play-off game on a big screen, safely insu-
lated from the insane asylum of the city below.

And yet, Ari somehow felt that his property's grounds of endless lawns
and austerely, controlled plantings didn't seem as refreshing as usual. In
fact, they almost struck him as barren and he found himself wondering
why he ever let Pepper talk him into buying a modern home. This green
moonscape with its lone oak and geometrically patterned succulents was
the opposite of his brother's abundant gardens in Athens with their sentinel
cypress, meandering gravel paths, fountains, and classical statues. There
was nothing on this property that even whispered of Greece. Nothing that
said "a Greek man lives here." Maybe he'd have Carley contact that Mariah
and ask her to send over some tear sheets of her company's statuary inventory. Adding a few select pieces might make him feel more at home.

As he pulled up to the house, it too felt curiously foreign. The brushed
steel, exotic woods, and glass spoke of a people without tradition or roots. A
people unlike his own. Where were the columns and porticos? Where were
the arches or niches for sculpted mythological figures? He remembered how
he had always superstitiously touched the timeworn face of Bacchus on the
cistern outside his grandfather's blue wooden front door before entering to
summer dining and stories under a pergola of gold-and-purple grapes. No
ancestral ghosts would ever abide in this sterile strange-angled configura-
tion before him. No Olympian deity would ever grace this home with protection or luck.

With a sigh, he got out of his Rolls and trudged past the huge steel
front doors that hung wide open. Why were outside doors the only ones
his children refrained from slamming? Ari shut the doors and turned to

behold two scruffy-looking brown-skinned men wrestling one of his twelve-thousand-dollar custom Swiss toilets down the front staircase. He'd special-ordered the state-of-the-art his-and-hers toilets from a manufacturer in Geneva. They'd arrived along with two Swiss technicians who'd overseen their complicated installation. The one these men were currently holding, however, had tangled wiring hanging from its base as if it had been ripped out of the floor by its roots.

Burglars! Ari immediately thought. And ones who appreciated fine technology!

That battle-ax Lyndy Wallert had been right!

What had they done with Pepper and the kids?!

The men didn't flee. They just kept coming down the stairs.

So be it. He, Aristotle Papadopoulos, would teach them the price of stealing from a Greek!

As a teen, Ari had done a brief (and hellish) stint at a military-style camp and now he tore over his memories to recall the self-defense techniques the sadistic sergeant at the place had drilled into his mind that summer (before his mother answered his pleas for release and spirited him away to Cap Ferrat).

First, balance. Then raise left arm in defensive position . . . or was it right arm? Punch straight out, then retract. Repeat? And when did the death kick come in? Shit!

He needed a weapon. Keeping his eye on the advancing burglars, Ari bent down and frantically felt around for one of the dozen toys scattered at his feet. Unfortunately, he came up with a bald, naked Barbie. At least he could inflict some damage with the doll's feet, which Maybelle had gnawed into dangerously sharp points. Ari assumed a balanced position, held the doll like a dagger ready to strike, and made an intimidating face.

"What have you done with my wife?" he demanded, in what he hoped was a terrifying baritone.

As if in answer to his query, Pepper popped her head over the upstairs landing. "Hey, Ari. Where's your latest hidin' place for the TV clicker? Maybelle wants to watch *Kim Possible.*"

Ari was still in his fighting stance as the men heaved the toilet past him.

"Do you remember?" Pepper continued. "'Cuz her punishment's over today, and I wanted her to watch her half hour early so she could get to bed on time—"

"Who are these men, Pepper?!" Ari yowled. "What are they doing with that toilet?" He looked at the doll in his hand and dropped it like it was made of molten lava.

"Oh, that's Jesús and Manuel," she replied nonchalantly. "They're movin' that thing to your office. Don't worry, it's the one from *my side*."

"That 'thing' cost twelve thousand dollars!" he sputtered. "I spent eight months on a waiting list!"

Pepper was unable to contain her guffaw. "Boy, they saw you comin'! Twelve thou' apiece?"

"They are precision Swiss instruments!"

"Yeah, well, that 'precision Swiss instrument' makes me jump outta my skin every time it comes alive."

"It only raises its lid, my baby!" Ari watched helplessly as the brown-skinned men settled the Swiss toilet into the back of Pepper's hybrid Lexus SUV. "It has a movement sensor to recognize when someone intends to use it—"

"It looks like it's gonna bite off my bum! Chencha feels the same way. Makes the evil eye every time she's in the bathroom. Refuses ta clean either one a' the damn things."

"They're self-cleaning," he said feebly.

Pepper smiled down in pity. "It was a sweet gesture, hon, sharin' your potty fetish with me, but personally, I wanna be euthanized if I ever get to the point where I can't wipe m' own ass an' I definitely don't want no spooky crapper doin' it for me—even if it does squirt warm water. I put in a nice American Standard john an' bidet in my bathroom. Ones that don't squirt or salute without my say-so. Yours is still in your bath. An' you'll love the spooky crapper at your office. You'll have the cleanest bum in showbiz. 'Course I wouldn't hold m' breath for the janitor ta clean it—"

"It's *self-cleaning*!" Ari thundered. "You should have *told me* you wanted to replace it! That instrument has to be installed by a company technician! I flew two of them out from Switzerland just to—"

"Those guys were Swiss? The ones who messed up m' drywall an' spliced inta the light-switch wirin'? Hell, they really saw you comin'!"

"You cannot allow just any common plumber to disconnect—"

"Oh, Jesús an' Manuel aren't plumbers. I picked 'em up on the corner in front a' Home Depot." Pepper checked her watch. "An' I better get goin' on yer office so they can make their bus."

Aghast, Ari stared out at the men. He looked up to let loose on his wife but she'd disappeared, and now Cooter's head replaced hers over the upstairs landing.

"I always forget to wash my bum, Daddy," he called. "Can I have a twelve-thousand-dollar toilet?"

"You can have a twelve-thousand-dollar whuppin' if you don't find the clicker for your sister," said Pepper, appearing on the stairs with her purse and sunglasses. Cooter took off like a shot.

"Those men are day laborers!" Ari shouted. "Illegals! You've been alone with them and the children? This is madness, Pepper! Haven't you been paying attention to Lyndy Wallert? The Bel Air burglaries? You could have been killed!"

Pepper chuckled and kissed him on the nose. "Don't be silly, hon; I outweigh 'em both. Woulda done the job m'self but I just got a manicure. An' Lyndy's a paranoid freak. Now, we'll take good care of your spooky crapper an' we won't make the same mess as the Swiss rip-offs. Take a nice hot shower, have some wine, and cuddle up with the boys an' a play-off game on the big-screen. I'll be back before eight."

And she was gone. Jerry popped his head over the upstairs landing, and yelled, "If Cooter's getting a twelve-thousand-dollar toilet, I want one too!"

"Too late. Mommy killed it," whispered Ari as he slunk off to the living room.

Ari felt like a fool. In fact, he couldn't recall a time when he hadn't felt ridiculous and incompetent around his wife. Was he like that around all women? Ari fingered his Poseidon medal and began reviewing a lifetime of relationships: his mother, his nanny, his teachers, girlfriends, and his titanic first wife. All of them had made him their bitch. Even his secretary was a ballbuster, but . . .

He didn't feel like a fool around Mariah.

The brief moments he'd spent with that enchanting girl had made him feel like a prince.

Like a man.

Everything about her was traditionally feminine: yielding, helpless, and impressed by his wisdom and wealth. Soft and round as a ripened fruit. Mysterious and gracious. Even her size was coquettishly petite.

Pepper had hands as big as a man.

Ari caught himself and felt ashamed. Pepper was his wife, for God's sake. The mother of his children! He loved her. And as annoying as her love was, it was real. The woman had risked a lifetime in jail for high treason when she erased the U.S. government's evidence against him. Ari doubted his own brothers would have considered doing him such a dangerous favor.

But perhaps that was just it. Perhaps he was so *beholden* to Pepper he'd let go of control. Let go of his manhood.

Maybe that was why he was the only one of the Papadopoulos brothers without a mistress. He used to think that it was because his brothers' wives resembled bad-tempered camels compared to Pepper's perfection or that one woman was pain in the ass enough, but maybe *he just hadn't met the right woman* . . .

Most parts of Ari hated these musings. Most of his being worshipped Pepper and considered the mere notion of infidelity stupidly traitorous and wicked. But a tiny part of him reasoned that there was little harm in daydreaming. It wasn't as if he was going to *act* on a fantasy.

Then again, maybe it wasn't so tiny a part.

Ari's erection was enormous.

As his children upstairs argued over whose turn it was to pee in "Daddy's expensive butt-washer," Ari looked outside his wall of glass at the endless lawn merging into the coral embers of clouds above the sea.

He'd place the statue where it could bask in that burning pink.

39

The Luckiest Girl on Earth

"No, this is not for her," said the Italian representative for Lystrada couture, unzipping the back of the yellow-and-white corseted puff dress.

Claire no longer felt self-conscious when she was buck naked in front of strange men as she was now in the dressing room of the new Melrose Place flagship store. By now, her body was so personally trained, waxed, mud-packed, exfoliated, lasered, and fake-tanned that it looked more like a mannequin than something she recognized as her own. Besides, all that mattered was whether or not it pleased Billy and he seemed to like it fine, although lately he only saw her body in the dark.

She'd spent the past eight minutes struggling into the dress, but the Lystrada rep gave three rough tugs and it crunched down around her ankles.

"She makes it look like a boiled egg," he pronounced.

Claire also no longer took the catty comments personally. She could wipe out almost any feeling with the champagne these fancy stores kept on hand.

"I'd lay off the bread and pasta for a while, Eddie," said Craig, holding out a hand for her to balance as she stepped out of the dress. "I thought we'd have to grease your hips to get that off."

"Can I get another glass of Cristal?"

"Certainly, Mrs. Price."

Claire's days with Craig had become routine.

First was morning maintenance, which meant hair, face, body, nails, or workout. Craig was always there to keep her company, usually getting a facial or massage for himself.

Second was shopping in increasingly new and obscure design houses or stores. Wearing clothes that no one had ever seen or heard of was a surefire way of getting your picture in party recap sections of local magazines, and Claire's name was now preceded by the epithet "fashionista" in all the captions. How fortunate it was that Craig just happened to have publicity deals with almost every new designer they chose!

Third was a lunch at a see-and-be-seen restaurant where Craig always happened to run into a woman who wanted to sign Claire up for the "exclusive" dinner committee of a pet charity event. Being on a dinner committee meant she was responsible for raising ten thousand dollars through inviting her list of Los Angeles contacts to an event. Claire never understood why these women had recruited her since she was friendly only with Marion, Patti, Pepper, Maya, and Lyndy and they were already invited to everything in town. Luckily, the women always reassured her that she could *personally donate* the ten thousand dollars instead, if she didn't want to keep pestering the same folks time after time.

Custody-on weeks, she went home in the afternoons to greet her stepchildren after school, and once or twice they had even greeted her back—if you could call "Don't come in my room!" a greeting. Baby steps, she told herself. Even her own family back in Winomac had taken two years to accept her cousin's Unitarian husband. And Claire wasn't giving up on becoming accepted as a member of the Price family. Three six-hour orientation sessions had canceled the family probation at the girls' school and she'd even remembered to wear jeans and one of Billy's dirty T-shirts to Eva's spelling bee. Claire felt so lucky that Billy's ex-wife never seemed to be available for any of her daughters' events. Neither was Billy, for that matter. Soon the girls would come to welcome and rely on Claire's face as an island of loving support in a sea of nonfamily members.

Custody-off weeks, Claire either had more "maintenance" or went to private estate sales of vintage jewelry or clothes. Her latest purchase was an eight-pound gold-plated tortoiseshell that hung on a necklace made out of an old plastic jump rope. It hurt her neck like the dickens, but the photographers loved it and Anna Sui was rumored to be copying it for next year's spring collection.

Around five, Claire would get ready for night action. She spent weekday cocktail hours being photographed at charity or designer-honoring events that her publicist, Walton, arranged for her to attend (with Craig) until dinner was served, because that was the hour Claire had to rush home to Billy. (Craig always stayed.) The only soul Claire ever knew at these events was Patti Fink, who had an even busier social schedule than her own, except Patti managed to eat when and where she wanted because she always had her husband, Lou, in tow. Claire promised herself that if anything ever happened to Billy, her next husband would be available at night and on wheels.

Back home, she was usually too tired to cook. If she had dinner at all, it was cold no-salt chicken broth (from the can) and an extra apple, snack bar, or a juice from the sack lunches Katia allowed her to prepare for the girls.

And she always dined alone. Billy was currently engaged in both "prep" and "postproduction" on two different projects. As his deadlines grew nearer, he started grabbing take-out dinners in the editing room or office, coming home later and later each night. There was little time left over for Claire. Even their sex seemed squeezed in. She'd tried to counteract this phenomenon by greeting him at the door in fantastically expensive lingerie, but so far it hadn't worked. After Billy fell asleep, she'd spend a few minutes on the phone with Craig to get her schedule for the next day and then about an hour on nighttime applications of all her new mysterious skin remedies before she dumped into bed.

But was she complaining? Heck no! If it wasn't for Billy, Claire would still be in Winamac, ridiculously pleased and confident about her dowdy-nobody little fashion-ignorant self. To think, she used to wear J.Crew! And took pleasure in attending Lions Club dances or harvest festivals! That sitting on the little dock of her uncle's fishing lodge with a football player and a fresh-roasted wienie, dipping her toes and watching the summer sunset turn the lake into gold, used to be the height of her day!

Thank goodness she'd been whisked away from that life. She had to be the luckiest girl on earth!

At that moment the Lystrada representative broke her reverie as he returned to the dressing room carrying a fresh glass of champagne, pointy pumps, white gloves, and what looked to be a classic navy shift with some ostrich plumes tacked onto the back, just below the curve of the ass.

"She can't possibly, possibly fuck this up," he sneered, holding the frock for her to wriggle into. "See?"

He threw down the shoes and Claire stepped into them while Craig forced the gloves onto her hands.

"See?" said the rep.

Craig gathered a fistful of Claire's now-blondish hair and held it on top of her head for "the look." Claire thought she looked like a Princess Grace impersonator farting feathers, but knew that her opinion was better left unsaid. And the champagne was cold.

"We'll take it," said Craig. "Oh, by the way, Eddie, Billy left a message when I was using your phone. You're giving a dinner party next Friday for Aubrey."

The Lystrada representative didn't appreciate getting an impromptu Cristal facial, but Claire couldn't help spraying the champagne she was drinking. "Aubrey? Aubrey Dutton?" she asked.

"Uh-huh. Are we sure about the shoes with that toe cleavage?"

"*Lord* Aubrey Dutton?" Claire cried, realizing the gravity of her situation. "Oh, this is terrible! Billy *needs* Aubrey Dutton for his new movie. The studio is insisting my husband include him in the cast because he's an auto-Oscar and they want lots of Oscars to impress their stockholders."

"*If* Dutton lives until the ceremony. He's like a hundred years old," Craig said, frowning and studying Claire's feet.

"I thought he was *already* dead," interjected the Lystrada representative. He eyed Claire sympathetically. "I don't blame you for being upset. I too am repulsed by the old."

"No, you don't understand! Billy said Dutton is like the classiest actor in the world. He runs around with Prince Andrew and Elton John. The Queen made him one of her knights! He probably eats at her house all the time with William and Harry and the Spice soccer wife! I'm not *ready* for that level of entertaining!"

Claire wanted to kick herself. She'd spent all her energy on her looks without a thought to the fact that as Billy's new wife, she'd have A-list hostess duties. A-list people were accustomed to gourmet meals and elegant table settings. They used fish knives! And then there was dinner-table conversation, which would surely be about fine art or European history with lots of ironic quips. A-list people expected their hostesses to be witty. Now she had less than a week to learn and prepare!

Claire ripped off her new feather-farting dress and clawed for the clothes she'd arrived in. She had to get to work! She needed to locate the nearest supermarket and get her hands on an *In Style*!

"Calm down, Eddie! I pulled a few strings, and at this moment Lamare le Quinne is pulling into your driveway."

"Who's Lamar Lay-kin?" she asked, wincing as she caught her rib skin in her zipper.

"Le *Quinne*. Only the hottest personal-dwelling makeover artist of the moment. Careful with that zipper, girl. People will think you're cutting again."

"I've seen Lamar remake entire homes in one television episode," said the Lystrada representative, impressed.

"Six days to transform your dining tragedy will be child's play," Craig concluded.

"What's wrong with my dining room?" asked Claire, who thought the pearl-gray walls, hand-painted murals, crystal light fixtures, and walnut coffered ceiling made it the loveliest room in the house. Her dining set was Chippendale!

Craig only chuckled and handed her the remains of her champagne. "And before you hightail it to Hickory Farms, I booked you Geoffre-the-chef. You won't greet your guests wearing a dirty apron and a shiny red face."

"Did someone say they needed help with a dinner party?"

All three heads turned in unison as Patti Fink pulled the curtain back from the adjoining dressing room and Claire grew tearful with relief. She didn't even care that the boiled-egg dress actually looked chic on Patti. A fairy godmother was rescuing the Rainbow Princess!

"Oh, Patti, would you?" Claire supplicated.

Patti rubbed her hands together with project-embarking pleasure. "We'll start with a theme: I'm envisioning English colonial exotic," she began.

40

Poison Pics

"Y ou know, from your face, I can tell you're about to call this whole thing off," said Watson-the-private-detective, fiddling with the locks on a shabby briefcase that to Richard's dismay, he'd tossed on the bed. There was something thuggish about him that cut through the haze of Richard's nightly Ambien, setting off his inner alarms and making him glad that Gary and Carter were on the property. Even though the hand-woven Italian linen curtains were drawn in the guesthouse living room, it had felt too exposed for such company.

Richard knew he was taking a risk meeting the private detective in the Zane compound guesthouse, but Watson had called from within the neighborhood and Marion's bedroom windows had been dark for at least an hour.

"Then you're a good judge of faces," Richard replied.

His self-imposed solitude had allowed him to begin thinking with the male side of his brain again, and Marion's adamant denial compounded with her doggedly unwavering devotion was changing his mind about his wife's culpability. What guilty party would spend hours sequestered with detectives? She was actually taking the time to track down every single kook from that voodoo ceremony they'd done up north. And Marion was almost as private and public-opinion-conscious as he was. The Pinky thing had made her look like a freak too. A direct hit to her social gut.

Now that he'd had time to contemplate things rationally, Richard knew that there could be several people who might have found out about their sexual secret. There was that shrink he saw when the nineties real-estate crash caused those anxiety attacks. And he had no idea what he said in those hypnosis sessions to quit smoking. Over the years, they'd fired dozens of unfit employees before arriving at the top-notch staff they had now. Maybe one of them was a Peeping Tom and needed a quick buck. And of course there was the "voodoo vine" bunch.

It just didn't work logically. Marion was too freaked out about the death of her poor maid's niece to mastermind a drugging. Plus, she couldn't have been on the premises when the bottles were spiked. Carl and Xio were witnesses. Even though they were loyal to her, Richard knew that when a paycheck was at stake, staff would always narc out the wife to her husband. And Gary and Carter were *his* boys. He had gotten them through that admiral when he gave the guy's daughter a studio job.

And Marion had always been his sweetheart. The cute little notes she'd been leaving every morning and night, in which she fussed over his health and pledged her undying love, weren't the scribblings of someone who wanted him hurt. They were softening his heart to the point where he felt like a heel for sticking a detective on her tail. She was the girl who'd held his hand through that prostate scare and Dickie's arrests. The one who used to make him comforting toasted cheese sandwiches and tomato-soup-with-a-big-blob-of-cream when the environmental regulations stopped his Humboldt County developments. The one who used to help his kids with their homework even though they hated her guts. The one who never left his side during the knee surgery because she didn't trust the hospital's sanitary standards. Hell, he knew he was going to apologize eventually, which was why he needed to cut the cord with the tailing nonsense. Richard wanted to be back with his girl.

"Some developments have come to light this week that led me to a change of heart. I love my wife. It's an insult not to trust her," Richard began, rubbing his eyes and wondering how much Watson was going to spin him to keep quiet.

"Well, I just need to give you this," said the private detective, pulling a manila envelope from the briefcase and opening it.

"No, seriously, I don't even want to know what she does with her day," Richard protested as the detective pulled out an eight-by-ten photograph. "It's wrong and invasive. Marion's my wife. My beloved, in fact. She's . . . she's . . . she's a *lying, evil WHORE!*"

The photograph showed Marion getting her lights fucked out by a blond Adonis clearly less than half her age.

"Your wife's into chicken, Mr. Zane. Or chicken's into *her,* as the case may be."

Richard flung the photograph across the room and balled his fists, ready to strike out, until he looked Watson-the-detective in the eye and realized the man was the size of a refrigerator and not even flinching.

"I always hate this part of my job, Mr. Zane. I just wanna say I'm sorry 'cause you seem like a really nice guy and don't deserve this. Ah, that was taken two days ago, at Shutters hotel in Santa Monica. I got more photos of 'em—"

Suppressing a sob, Richard held up his hand and shook his head.

"Yeah," said the detective. "That pretty much says it all. I can get more info on the guy. And if you think it might be appropriate for him or her to succumb to an 'unfortunate accident,' I know people who can make it happen for you—"

"Get out," Richard whispered, crossing the guesthouse in three lurches and flinging the door open. He couldn't bear to share his grief with this man who profited from pain.

"Yeah, they always wanna kill the messenger, at first," Watson said, tossing the envelope in his case and snapping it shut. He had huge forearms. "Gimme a call when you get it together."

He took his time crossing the guesthouse, eyeing the rooms in a way that struck Richard as that of a criminal casing a potential hit. He had no doubt that when Watson said he knew people who could make accidents happen, the detective was referring to himself.

"Send your bill to the office," said Richard as Watson-the-detective brushed past him at the door. Then the giant turned, speaking so close, Richard felt his breath being sucked from his lips.

"She was smilin' and laughin' the whole time she was gettin' porked. I'd wanna wipe that smile off her face."

Richard recoiled back into the guesthouse, slammed the door, and locked it.

He spent the next ten minutes injuring his fists on the walls.

She'd played him for a fool! A stupid, trusting, egotistical fool! Goddamn male brain! Thinking he was the center of her universe! That his billions would protect him! That a Trophy would never do anything to jeopardize her marriage! Falling madly in love and believing Marion felt the same way! She'd probably faked everything, biding her time for the big payday when she'd frame him as a louse!

When his body finally stopped striking out, Richard grabbed the eight-by-ten off the floor and flipped it over on the bed. He could only stand to look at it for a second. But a second was enough to see that the blond kid on top of his wife had a bigger dick than his own. And a physique to back it up. Marion never curled her toes that way for him. She never smiled like that either. Like she was laughing at some joke.

That thug Watson had the right idea.

Richard too wanted to wipe that smile off her face.

But he wasn't going to use violence to do it. He had much more painful ways of erasing Marion's smile. Resisting the urge to burn it, Richard balled up the eight-by-ten and threw it into an empty bottom drawer of a built-in dresser in the closet. It might be needed later.

He kicked the drawer shut and slammed the closet door. Going into the living room, he sat down at the seventeenth-century Italian inlaid desk, donned his reading glasses, and thumbed through his wallet until he located Barry Shapiro's phone number.

Obviously yanked out of slumber but still able to read the number on his cell phone, Barry answered, saying, "Okay, Richard, I'll be there in ten. What's going on?"

"I don't need you to come," Richard said quickly. "There's nothing going on. Well, actually, there's a shit ton of wrong shit that's been going on, but I don't need *you*. I need a phone number."

"Richard, this is my *emergency* line."

"This is an emergency. I need the number of that masseuse who got drugged. Tawnee something."

"*Never happened*, Richard," the lawyer replied.

"No, seriously, Barry. I need it."

"Seriously, Richard. If you need a happy-ending massage, I can give you ten services—"

"No, I need *her*," Richard insisted. "Just give me the number."

"You know, as your lawyer, I can't let you do that. It's opening you up for—"

"You've always been *Marion's* lawyer!" Richard bellowed into the phone. "Don't test me, Barry. Not tonight."

"Okay, I'm going to hang up now, and in the morning, you'll understand why—"

"Give me the fucking number *now* or I'll have your license yanked! You know I can do it! I'll call every judge and every politician in this state who owes me and I'll destroy your practice!"

Richard heard Barry sigh and make shuffling noises. Then the lawyer came back on the line.

"I'm giving you this number, Richard, on the condition you lose mine. Tawnee Dymns's cell is 818-663-2927. Good-bye, Richard, and heaven help you when you sober up."

"By the way," Richard said, "your private dick was an asshole."

"Huh?"

Richard hung up and dialed the number.

"Hel-loo?"

Every single syllable she uttered was San Fernando Valley. Richard thought of the images from *American Graffiti* and *Fast Times at Ridgemont High*. Marion had always advised him against venturing into development in that area of the Southland. Probably because she was a snob. Or a psychic.

"Tawnee, this is Richard Zane."

"Oh my God! How'd you get my number?"

"I, ah, have ways."

"Well, don't call it ever a-gain!" she hissed.

"Don't hang up, Tawnee! Please! Just hear me out, okay?"

"I'm not, like, giving back the concert ticketsss—"

"Keep them! And there's more where they came from. I'm calling because—"

"Are you friggin' high?" Tawnee asked.

"My wife was the one who drugged us."

"Like no ssshit, SSSherlock!"

"And I know we treated you pretty rough and unfair, and I just wanted to, um, apologize."

"Apologize to yoursssself, for being married to that psssycho!"

Richard, surprisingly, found himself laughing for the first time in a week.

He never guessed Tawnee would be funny.

"Yeah, I finally caught on. And I've moved into the guesthouse."

"Sssmart move. Ssso, what the fuck do you want? More sssignaturesss for your mean and ssscary lawyer?"

"No. Nothing like that. Look, I know this is awkward, but I have a proposal for you. Could you come over to my house? I'll make it worth your while."

Silence.

"Hello?"

"Can I call you back in five?" she asked.

"Sure, Tawnee. Use this line . . ."

She took more than twenty minutes. Richard had dozed off at the desk and the ring made him jerk his neck out of whack.

"Hello? Tawnee?"

"You know, before we passsed out that night," Tawnee said in a surprisingly sultry singsong. "When I wasss giving you a masssage? I wasss, like, thinking to myssself that you were pretty hot. Jussst thinking about you now, all alone on that big Beverly Hillsss essstate, makesss me hot all over again."

Richard smiled and slipped off his wedding ring. All women were the same.

After he hung up with Tawnee, Richard turned on the shower and buzzed the guardhouse.

"Yes, Mr. Zane?"

"Gary, I'm getting a massage in twenty minutes and I'd like you to escort the young lady to the guesthouse."

"Certainly. How long will your treatment last?"

"All night."

"Oh."

"That a problem?"

"No, sir."

Good little soldiers.

"I also need you to leave a note for Mrs. Zane to find in the morning. Could you swing by right now and pick it up?"

"Right away, Mr. Zane."

Richard took out a sheet of stationery and grabbed a pen.

> *Dearest Marion,*
>
> *Please join me for breakfast in the guesthouse. I'm ready to cruise.*
>
> *Love,*
> *Richard*

41

Sucker-Punched Redux

"**B**ut Jamie Turan is *your* friend, not mine!" Zephyr protested. "He's an actor!"

"An actor who, if you read the fax I sent you, *accidentally inherited a CDMA patent*, giving him money to burn," Marion said into the wall speaker in her third dressing room as she held up a pair of black-seamed silk stockings for inspection. "Jamie's little brother learned code division in the military then headed for Silicon and developed a multiple-access design that's used in every cell phone on the planet. The poor thing was out celebrating his first option when his Segway was hit by a bus. Jamie only has that series on FX because he pays three-quarters of the licensing fees himself."

"He's still an actor."

"Who is *damn* lucky to be able to meet a brilliant young woman who's offering him the privilege of contributing to a noble cause. You've been slam-dunking pledges at every lunch, Zephyr. You could do this in your sleep. Why are you getting insecure now?"

"I just wish I wasn't going alone. Jamie was in my class at Harvard Westlake."

"Really?" Marion asked.

"He was named James, then. James Klemmer."

"James Klemmer, the little fat boy who sang show tunes at choral cabaret, is Jamie Turan the ladykiller?" Marion tossed the black-seamed stockings back in the white enameled drawer in favor of a nude seamless pair. (After all, it was day.) "Boy, were we wrong about—"

"No, James Klemmer, the gorgeous football player who didn't know I was alive, is Jamie Turan."

"Well, its high time he learned." Marion shimmied into a green lace bustier corset. "Zeph, you're a darling girl! All you need is some hair product . . . and lip gloss . . . a skirt would be nice."

"Marion!"

"And you're witty and fun . . . when you're not pulling the wings off of flies."

"You don't understand!" Zephyr wailed.

"Yes, I do," Marion assured her, nixing the corset for a hot-pink see-through G-string, bra, and garter belt. "High school's awful for everybody. I'd show you my yearbooks if I didn't have them burned. Take my word, I was target practice . . . but look at me now. And you've got to think of Jamie as a potential donor instead of your first crush. You're Zephyr Mintz, head counsel for Zane Enterprises Realty Development. If not for his brother, Jamie would be going on cattle calls in Studio City."

"You really think I need makeup?"

"I think you're hiding behind the hair."

Marion smiled as she slipped into a pearlescent beige Donna Karan sheath. She found it heartwarming when Zephyr got like this. Like a vulnerable little thirteen-year-old. It made her seem almost human.

"You did and still do *a lot more* than just makeup to every inch of yourself," Zephyr fired back.

(Okay, not so heartwarming.)

"I'm not as young and lovely as you, Miss Cheap Shot."

"Sorry, sis."

"Go to the lunch. You need to exorcise those high school ghosts. Not everybody gets that chance. And remember to get some money in the process."

"I'll go. But I'll still feel abandoned."

"Don't you say that! Don't you *ever* say that! I love you and I will never, ever, abandon you!"

"Okay, okay! It was a figure of speech. Do everyone a favor and dial back on the hormone treatments. I'll think about the skirt."

"Atta girl."

"Have fun at your making-up breakfast."

"I will. I'm canceling everything on the books until three o'clock."

"Too much information. Bye."

Marion hung up and looked at her reflection in the dressing-room mirror. The sheath she had on was just sheer and clingy enough to hint at the goodies she wore underneath. She went into the shoe closet and added satin Jimmy Choo fuck-me strappy stiletto sandals with five-inch heels.

In her makeup room, she styled her hair tousled and sexy, added clear Dior lip gloss with just a hint of shimmer (to *both* upper and lower lip), and skipped the jewelry entirely. Richard would probably gift her with something new and she didn't want any competition. After spraying the air with Tom Ford's Black Orchid, Marion walked through mist.

She stopped by her nightstand and popped a butterscotch Life Saver (Richard's favorite) in her mouth and shivered with anticipation. Maybe it was a good thing, these bouts of abstention. Last time, she and Richard had coupled like tigers. This morning, she was raring to go.

She took one last look at the note from her darling husband. *Ready to cruise.* What a cutie! She'd known all along that they were solid, but this reassurance made her feel extra safe and warm. Come to think of it, Richard was the only "safe and warm" she'd ever known in her entire life.

Enough gush.

Right now she was safe, warm, and *horny*!

Picking her feet up like a horse at the starting gate lest her shoes catch in the pile of clothes at her feet, Marion negotiated the plush master-bedroom and sitting-room carpets, clicked down the colonnaded corridor and the grand staircase, then crossed the constellations of the foyer and marched out the front door.

The stone-and-tile steps had just been hosed off by the gardeners, so Marion was paying more attention to the wet spots than the forgotten machete her gardeners had left leaning against the wall of the second landing. It caught on her heel, flipped, and clattered into the flower bed below.

Damn! Those guys were always leaving their tools around! And what did they expect to encounter on her steps? Gorillas? She was lucky the blade didn't slice open her foot. She'd have Ivan remind them. Oh yeah, two more months . . .

Halfway down the gravel path to the guesthouse, she took a peek at her shoes and noticed that the left heel was just starting to fray. Oh well, the presentation was worth it!

She smiled when she saw that all the curtains in the guesthouse were drawn. Mmm! Richard was prepared. Marion stepped onto the porch and knocked.

Shave-and-a-haircut!

The steps advancing to the door sounded quick and stompy. Not like Richard's at all. And the person who answered the door was not Richard at all.

(!!!)

Tawnee-of-the-Valley stood before her wearing Richard's rumpled Lanvin shirt (over the tackiest, pill-balled, nylon slip Marion had ever seen in her life).

Alternate universe?

Marion blinked. The masseuse was still there.

"Morning, Mrsss. Zane. Nice dresss. My mom hasss one just like it."

This time, Marion had no alcohol in her system to buffer the shock-horror-heartbreak and the first yip bent her in half. She stared at Tawnee's (shapely, tight-skinned) knees and fought it, managing to whisper, "Donna Karan doesn't make sizes for hyenas. What have you done with my husband?"

"Oh, he'sss ssstill wiped out in bed. We were at it until three. He knowsss all about you and your boyfriend."

"What *boyfriend*?"

"The bedroom out here isss ssso cute. Did you get that curtain fabric from Diamond Foam on La Bre-a? They have the *bessst* dissscountsss!"

"Richard!" Marion yelled through her pain. "Richard!"

She started to push past Tawnee into the guesthouse, but the masseuse shot out the heel of her hand, hard, catching Marion square in the chest and sending her stumbling backward, almost off the porch.

"No can do, psssycho," Tawnee singsonged. "Richie'sss only talking to you through his lawyer. Oh, here'sss the ressst of my ssstuff!"

Marion turned to see that Charlie, the daytime security guard, was trudging up the path to the guesthouse lugging three mismatched suitcases and a Wet Seal shopping bag full of stuffed animals.

That's when the second yip hit.

Marion forced herself upright and stared incredulously at her guard as he stepped onto the porch.

"Charlie?! What the fuck?!"

"'Scuse me, Mrs. Zane."

Charlie kept his head down and maneuvered the luggage past Marion, into the guesthouse.

"RI-CHARD!" Marion screamed into the guesthouse. "RICHARD, IT'S A LIE! THERE'S NO BOYFRIEND! RI-CHARD!"

The bedroom door remained closed.

"Shhh! Keep it down, psssycho!" Tawnee winced at the decibel level of Marion's shouting. "Like, go ssscream in your quiet room, or sssomething. SSSome of usss haven't lost our hearing yet."

"Fuck off!" Marion grated, cracking a vicious backhand across the hypersibilant's mouth.

Tawnee rocked back but she was braced in the doorway and stayed on her feet. She leveled her gaze at Marion, licked her lips, and broke into a cruelly triumphant smile. "Eat me, Mrsss. Zane. Whoopsss! I forgot! Your *husssband* already did!"

Marion managed to come away with two handfuls of brown-rooted, overprocessed bronze hair and a Lanvin sleeve before Charlie separated them and barred the door himself.

There was a reason why there was only one security guard to watch over the Zane compound in daytime. Charlie was taller than the guesthouse door and now, with his arms outstretched, looked like a crucified Paul Bunyan. Under one of his tree-trunk arms, Marion had a full view of Tawnee, standing upright and clutching her now-patchy scalp. And just where was Richard-the-coward-hearted?

"I told you ssshe'd go psssycho! Oh, my God! I'm bleed-ing!" Tawnee squealed.

"Why don't you go back into the house, Mrs. Zane," said Charlie, in an utterly calm monotone, characteristic of behemoths. (Although, from the look on his face, Marion could see he was secretly digging the catfight.)

"Why don't you throw that piece of shit out in the gutter where she belongs!" Marion yelled back.

"Ow-oww! Ow-oww!" Tawnee howled.

Charlie stared at his shoes. "Sorry. I, um, ride for the brand. Mr. Zane gave instructions that any messages you have for him should go through his divorce lawyer . . ."

That's when the third yip hit, with predictable results.

The result in question was the same as it was the time she'd had to give that speech back in high school. When she found out that the boy to whom she'd given her virginity had only boinked her on a bet.

So forceful was the trajectory of the vomit Marion emitted that it shot cleanly under Charlie's arm and landed in Tawnee's gaping mouth.

Marion didn't stick around to savor the aftermath.

42

Giving Up the Ghost

Marion's legs and feet were doing the thinking now. Unfortunately, they couldn't see and she fled blindly, almost out onto Foothill, before she turned around. By the time she reached the service driveway, both heels of her Jimmy Choos had broken off and she tumbled across the gravel and banged her head into the kitchen door. She sat there, on the sharp little stones, thinking about the sharp little dents they were putting on the backs of her thighs but not wanting to get up because she had no idea where she was running to. So she dazedly reviewed her morning while removing her ruined fuck-me shoes:

Worked out. Found Richard's note. Cleared the books until three. Arranged for Zephyr to take hospital donor lunch by herself. Got gussied up. Met Richard's slut. Learned he's got a divorce lawyer. Yipped. Ran like hell.

Oh yeah. Now she remembered where she was running.

Marion got to her feet, kicked open the kitchen door, and laid rubber across the marble checkerboard floor, then took the tower's spiral service stairs in a leap.

As she neared the second-floor landing, Marion launched into an impromptu tête-à-tête with Gilda-the-ghost:

Okay, I get it! I get it! You weren't pushed! You walked in on Rutherford and the Italian! And you made them pay for it with a swan dive! You could have at least WARNED MY ASS that the same thing was about to happen to me! You could have at least said something: look out . . . watch your back. If we were sharing the same fate, you could have at least told me what to do . . .

Nothing. It figured. Marion reached the second floor but kept climbing. *Don't bother now. I know the routine.*

Marion tore off her Donna Karan sheath and watched it fall down the center of the tower.

Easy revenge, right? It'll fuck them up for the rest of their lives.

And then she climbed higher.

Richard will be racked with crippling guilt and everyone will suspect him of murder.

Marion tore off her stockings and let them fall.

The invitations will dry up. (Not at first, because an infamous guest is a dinner-table stimulant.) Maybe it'll start with Richard's name getting "accidentally dropped" from the list for Vanity Fair's Oscar Night at Morton's. (Graydon is my friend!)

Marion tore off her garter belt and let it fall.

David Geffen's boat will be "accidentally" full. (My friend, again!)

And then she climbed higher.

Marion tore off her bra and let it fall.

Maya and Tom will be "too busy" to make Zane premieres. (Totally, absolutely, mine!)

And then she climbed higher still.

The left side tables at Chow's will be "pre-reserved." (My turf!) Crustacean will be completely full. And Georgio's in the canyon won't even take your call.

Marion, after a quick check at her wax job, stepped out of her G-string and let it fall.

And then she climbed even higher.

Then the politicians won't join him for photographs, his business contacts will stop doing public meal meetings, his tennis foursome will switch courts, and one by one his friends will drop away because he's turned into a boorish, maudlin, sloppy alcoholic! Eventually, the only people left on this earth who will welcome Richard Zane's sorry carcass will be O. J. Simpson and the state of Idaho!

Marion opened the cupola hatch window.

And at last, when his calendar has cobwebs and his liver's the size of an Olsen-twin tote, he'll croak. Just like Rutherford!

Marion climbed out onto the tiny balcony.

She'd never been out here before. It felt invigorating. And she could get a look at the neighbors' remodeling of the back of their house, at last. Looking down, she was glad she'd torn out the reflecting pond and replaced it with sod. No algae-covered corpses in *her* backyard.

From her high-altitude vantage point, the guesthouse looked to be quiet. Richard and Tawnee-of-the-Valley were probably inside, fucking and bleeding. She didn't want to imagine.

And Charlie was back in the guardhouse. Marion could only see his hands through the guardhouse window, but they were the size of Birkin bags and unmistakable.

Hmm. The guardhouse had *no view* of the guesthouse or cupola. All the cameras were focused on the compound perimeters.

All she had to do was wait a few minutes. Until enough time had passed for Richard and/or Tawnee to sneak into the house, push her off the roof, and sneak back.

Even a mediocre prosecutor would force Charlie to testify that he'd had no idea what Richard and the slut did after he left them alone.

Marion felt a tickle on her hand and found that a wad of Tawnee's hair and a shirt button with thread from Richard's shirt were caught in her eleven-carat cushion-cut D-color flawless Key to the Kingdom. She laughed as she pulled the wad off and stripped bits around the little cupola-balcony floor.

Oh, this is too easy, Gilda! A little DNA here, a little incriminating evidence there!

Marion stepped up onto the low, fat balcony wall. Exactly where the no-doubt-distraught Gilda had once stood.

AAAND JUMP!

Marion felt a sudden rushing of wind around her body and the weirdest feeling of someone holding her hand and she knew that Gilda was with her. Just behind the veil . . .

But she stayed on the balcony wall.

Marion eased the pounding of her heart with several shallow gulps of air. Then she wiped away the mascara runs under her eyes and refluffed her hair. With one hand on her hip, she assumed a self-possessed stance and addressed the vibrating air in front of her.

"Gilda, Gilda, Gilda. There's only one problem with our fate-sharing scenario. Unlike you, I'm not a first wife. Richard *left* his first wife for *me!* I didn't have a period of dating, then courtship, then wedding bells with stars in my eyes. Love didn't come knocking at *my* door. I had to *cheat* and *scheme* and *steal* my way into love! And I used my wits to keep it! Because *I am a* STAGE III TROPHY! *I am a* SURVIVOR! AND *I have no* PRENUPTIAL! So you can keep your little brokenhearted suicide and kiss my bulletproof ass! *I've* got options."

Marion stepped down onto the balcony, opened the cupola hatch, and climbed inside.

Moments later, Xiocena was hysterically rushing up the spiral staircase. Marion padded down and flung herself into her arms.

"*Madre de Dios!*" the housekeeper cried. "*Madre de Dios!* I see the whore at the guesthouse! I look for you and I see the clothes! And the window is open! And the ghost of that girl!"

Marion jerked back. "You *saw* Gilda?"

"Many times," Xiocena said through her tears. "All of us see . . . Jeff, Mr. Ivan, Carl—"

"Surely not Roger! He doesn't even believe . . ."

Xiocena shrugged apologetically, then took Marion's face in her hands. "I so scared! I thought you join her!"

Marion smiled at her friend. "No fucking way. I've got a hospital to build . . . and a husband to rescue."

After they'd cried and hugged a bit longer, they linked arms and headed back down toward the second floor.

"You need clothes," Xiocena observed.

Marion looked down at herself and nodded. Then she looked up at the cupola window. "And the Louis Vuitton luggage set. I can't stay here."

43

War Is Hell

Night fell on the grim figure of Marion-at-War and she turned on the light in her war room (the living room of a two-bedroom private-entrance bungalow at the Beverly Hills Hotel) then called room service for a pitcher of margaritas before reviewing her theaters of operation.

On the Legal Front:

Richard had made his first crucial mistake when he contacted the legendary legal legion of Newberg, Fligstein, Sacks & a-million-other-partners-names-and-associates at the time that the Pinky scandal broke. What kind of Trophy did he think she was?

Marion already had NFS & etc. on retainer before "Never-Happened Night."

She'd had them on retainer—and their Los Angeles, New York, Chicago, and Dallas offices on speed dial—since the day she and Richard were married.

Over the years, her payments to NFS & etc. had been funneled through Patti Fink, who forwarded the payments to NFS & etc. in untraceable cash. Richard's accountants thought they were paybacks for lousy luck on Girl Poker Night. Trophies all over the Westside had been known to suffer similar losing streaks in Girl Poker. You'd think the guys would catch on.

Up until today, Richard thought NFS & etc. was merely "too overextended to represent him in a divorce."

He had settled on Frank Greene and a-million-other-partners-and-associates for representation. He had confidence in his lawyer and was

relieved to learn that Marion hadn't hired Frank first. Zane corporate lawyers were meeting tomorrow with Frank to begin to compile an assessment of Richard's net worth.

Frank's firm's nickname around the Westside was "The Tough Guys."

NFS & etc.'s nickname around the world was "The Keyser Sozes."

One button on the speed dial and all three senior partners sprang into
action, as co-generals in Marion's war, deploying a battalion of etcetera
partners and associates from four different offices in rapid response. Three
of the etceteras took the NFS & etc. G-5 to Switzerland.

Seven took the other to the Caymans.

At noon, Horton Newberg showed up on her war-room doorstep and
handed her a sack containing a Diet Coke, a chopped salad from the Palm,
and a red velvet cupcake from Sprinkles.

"It's best you eat now," he said.

At twelve-fifteen, Simon Sacks and Bucky (really!) Fligstein arrived
with an armed guard handcuffed to a titanium-lined briefcase containing
a forty-gigabyte Jaz drive with listings of every single asset that bore the
Zane name and thousands of pages of supporting documents and Excel
files.

Horton, Bucky, and Simon never left Marion's side the entire time she
reviewed the information on her Tulip E-Go Diamond laptop. NFS & etc.
had been following the intricacies of Zane income for twenty years. Hope
that the Zane marriage might still hit the rocks had caused Simon Sacks to
postpone his retirement. This was the firm's mother-lode day. They were
prepared.

At one-fifteen, while they were going over the file on stocks and bonds,
Marion detected a tiny joyful tear in Simon Sacks's eye.

At one-thirty, she stopped checking eyes because she was too busy becoming acquainted with her Chinese profit-sharing deal.

By two, she learned she had stock in Google, and at four, she found out
she actually owned swampland in Florida. (Maya would be horrified!)

At 4:20, they were nearly finished, leaving Marion breathlessly aware of
thirty-two Zane-owned accounts, investments, and properties she never
knew existed. (But her lawyers did. They'd known all along.)

Then they reviewed the final Jaz file. It contained three estimated
Excel-based projections of Richard's future earnings—ten, fifteen, and
twenty years into the future. (At this point she saw Bucky part his lips in

sublime bliss and discreetly move a legal pad over his lap; she knew he had a boner.)

At five, they finished and the three senior partners of NFS & etc. packed up the briefcase, reattached it to the armed guard, and left. Marion-at-War stood up in wonder. She now realized that she had awesome power, power beyond her wildest imaginings.

She could go almost five hours without taking a pee.

She also realized she was even richer than she'd thought.

And she also realized Richard didn't have a prayer.

On the Who's *"Fucking Us Over?" Front:*

Marion-at-War's covert intelligence operatives (planted Zane-office secretaries and a few other strategically placed folks on her take) were able to secure the phone number of a private detective Richard had contacted the previous week. The number had been disconnected. No great surprise, considering the phony name "D. [as in Dr.] Watson!" He had to be the one pulling the "boyfriend" ruse; Tawnee herself wasn't smart enough to pull toilet paper off the bottom of her shoe. Marion prayed that her private detectives would track him down soon.

Historically, journalists would rather face jail time than reveal their sources, but Marion doubted that the ethic was as strong with gossip columnists. Her five-thousand-dollar-a-day private detectives were trying to get some dirt on Joey Stern, the editor of the industry cheat sheet, to trade for the Pinky source. If that didn't work, they'd set him up with a girl. If that didn't work, they'd try bribing a different employee of the rag. And if that didn't work, Marion planned to start dating one of the investigative team in order to recoup her investment.

On the Assistant *Front:*

Marion knew it was cruel and selfish and demanding to ask her most valued employee—who hadn't had a break for friggin' fifteen years—to cut short his much-needed dream vacation on shut-up island, but this was a friggin' crisis and she was a Stage III Trophy. Self-preservation was not only in her blood, at times like this it was a primal reflex. And she was, after all, at war. She wanted her Ivan and she wanted him now. The problem was that when she tried to call, Ivan's cell wasn't picking up. Marion pictured the cell phone locked away in a monastery strongbox. Well, she reasoned, the monastery had to have a phone of its own. What if they needed medical attention for one of their guests? Or a pizza? She hated to pull a detective off the Who's Fucking Us Over? Front, but if she still got no answer tomorrow . . . Now that she thought about it, she was surprised to realize that Ivan had been gone so long without giving in to the urge to check in on them. Surely, he still had that urge. Right? Right? Surely he wouldn't go native! . . . Where was that pitcher of margaritas?

On the Public Front:

There was an old saying that living well was the best revenge. Marion believed that living well was also the best defense. Nothing would piss Richard and his lawyers off more than if she continued to roll merrily along, attending social functions as if nothing had happened. After all, this was L.A. Even half the Zane fortune dwarfed most of those in town. Her invitations were secure.

On the Friend Front:

It was only a matter of breaking selected news to a selected few. She'd do that tomorrow at their hospital fund-raising strategy lunch. Somehow.

On the Hospital Front:

As she feared, Richard had changed his mind about using their downtown property for a hospital, and a zoning hearing before the city council had been scheduled in six weeks. And now that Jack Powell was a senator, she was sure he'd make an appearance to lend her husband federal muscle. So far there was no sign that Powell would even get close to the appropriations committee, but she wasn't going to underestimate her husband's reach.

But Marion held an ace: her friendship with UCLA's dean of medicine, its chancellor, and a majority of the University of California Board of Regents.

After three weeks of negotiating and voting, she finally got the call saying that UCLA would be delighted to take over a hospital and much-needed trauma center in downtown Los Angeles—as long as all funds were ready to go. That meant she needed all of $500 million in the bank before the city-council meeting.

Up until today, it would have been no problem for Marion to make up the remaining funds with Zane money. But now she couldn't risk waiting for a settlement to get her hands on that large a sum. Her and Richard's separation would probably eliminate some of the donors on her list. She needed to light a fire under everyone's fund-raising butt, including her own.

A UCLA-partnered hospital would eliminate any arguments Richard could make about poorly run trauma centers being doomed to fail. Surely a hospital and low-income housing trumped hotel and office space. Surely. (Oh, please, let it be true!)

On the Marion Front:

Despite learning that her husband had dumped her for a dipshit, having her world shatter, resisting suicide, viewing the fruits of a twenty-year-union about to be squashed, not gathering enough info about her mystery adversary, being unable to reach the one human being she needed most in a crisis, Marion-at-War thought she was holding up pretty well. She hadn't cried in almost an hour. And she was prepared.

She had copied all the sources and records she needed from her *Black Book* before retreating from the compound. But the *Black Book* stayed put. It was, by far, too precious to store anywhere outside of her dressing-room thumb-activated wall safe. Besides, the compound was only a couple of blocks away. According to the separation agreement, she could come and go to the compound as she pleased (and would probably be taking sole possession of it within the year, if Richard chose to progress).

But she hoped he wouldn't.

Marion-at-War's strategy was to capture the scoundrels behind their marriage's destruction and shock and awe Richard into realizing what he was about to give up. And she didn't just mean three-quarters of his assets and future fortune.

She figured two weeks with Tawnee-of-the-Valley would drive Richard *totally oh-my-God ssscreaming* back into her arms. Maybe one and a half.

Summation:

It was too early in the war to claim victory, but it was definitely happy hour.

The war room's doorbell rang and Marion-at-War checked the peep-hole. All she saw was a pitcher of margaritas and three frosted glasses.

"Room service with your cocktails, Mrs. Zane," said a hoarse, faintly familiar voice.

That was the password. She opened the door and then crossed the room to retrieve her purse and give the room-service person a tip. She didn't see the waitress who pulled the cart into the room until the door shut. When she did, Marion stopped dead in her tracks.

"Hello, Mrs. Zane."

She still had that hoarse voice. Poor thing probably had polyps.

"Wow," said Marion. "When you said you float three or four jobs, you weren't kidding."

"Girl's gotta eat."

"And drink. Could you pull that thing into the bedroom, please?"

"Sure, Mrs. Zane."

Marion plopped down on her bed, kicked off her shoes, and stretched as the waitress brought in her cart. "So. I never got a chance to thank you for walking me to my car the other night. I mean, I probably did get the chance, but I was so plowed I don't remember a thing. So, thanks. You work here as well?"

"I'm not here for the spa," said the waitress, expertly rimming the glass with a wedge of lime and dipping it in a plate of salt.

"Sorry I'm making a big deal out of it." Marion yawned. "It's just good to see someone who's completely not involved in my completely out-of-whack world. Today has been one of the most empowering and worst of my life."

"Well, a nice frozen margarita oughta take the edge off," whispered the waitress as she handed Marion her drink.

Marion handed her a tip.

"Thank you. Will there be anything else?"

"Nope. At least not until after this starts to kick in."

"It will."

And Marion-at-War was left alone with her drinks.

Twenty minutes later, she was out colder than a Yard-dog Roadshow fan on the third morning of Burning Man.

The waitress let herself back in with the key she'd stolen from the housekeeper. After checking Marion's eyes, she snatched up her Louis Vuitton tote and felt around inside. Then she looked around and snatched up Marion's caramel Bottega Veneta tote and felt around inside. Then she looked around and snatched up Marion's black-and-white Chanel tote and looked inside. Exasperated, she looked around and snatched up Marion's orange ostrich Hermès traveling tote and felt inside. Bingo. She pulled out Marion's orange ostrich Hermès wallet and opened it.

"Eenie, meenie, minie, mo."

The waitress pulled out three of Marion's black American Express cards. She then located the TV remote, turned on the plasma screen, selected the television feature, and scrolled up the channels.

Helping herself to a minibar Snickers, she shoved Marion over and sat down on the bed.

"Let's get creative . . ."

44

Tube-Top Memories

M arion gave thanks to Advil's hangover-banishing powers and waded into the sense-memory bath of Michael's Restaurant in Santa Monica. Her silk jersey Hermès dress and coat morphed into a pair of plier-zipped Lois London slims, a stretchy red tube top, and a Chemin de Fer lace-up jacket. Vivier pumps became Corkies six-inchers and her black Armani alligator clutch dissolved into something woven in Guatemala with a shoulder strap.

It was 1980. When nineteen-year-old Marion Mintz first set foot on the airy, high-canopied patio, surrounded by raised gardens with a splendid modern sculpture fountain at the end, she wasn't worried about lawyers or commonly held assets or husbands. In 1980, all she was worried about was that she'd be spotted as a fake.

It all started when she'd moved into the condo.

Marion had come to a dead end. After leaving her hometown of Cleveland brokenhearted, she returned to her roach-infested studio apartment in Hollywood determined to become wildly successful. Problem was, she worked as a telemarketing operator selling industrial cleaning supplies. Paid by commission. No matter how hard she worked, no matter how late she stayed or how many weekends she put in, all alone at the phones, the market was weak, and her pay remained paltry. All she'd managed to gain was that she was trusted enough to receive a key to the office, so she could lock up after hours.

But her grindstone-ground nose was not overlooked. Impressed by her diligence and responsibility, the boss and owner of the telemarketing company asked Marion to perform a task that would forever change her life. He wanted her to house-sit his daughter's condo in Westwood. The daughter was a UCLA coed who would be "away on exchange in Paris" for two years. Marion's boss didn't trust his daughter's ditzy sorority friends to be responsible in a pricey Wilshire-corridor high-rise property. The building had security with maid service and Marion would have use of the daughter's MG.

It took Marion ten minutes to pack up and bid her roach roommates adieu.

The building was heaven on earth, with a doorman, parking attendants, and a concierge desk. And the eleventh-floor condo held the luxurious trappings of a life she'd never imagined: beautiful modern furniture, a stereo and entertainment system, and a wet bar full of exotic liqueurs like Kahlúa and wines like Mateus Rosé. The daughter's clothes were youthful, fashionable, and in sizes that hadn't fit Marion since grade school. And the bed had scandalous black satin sheets! But the most luxurious items of all were the daughter's UCLA course books.

Marion had left school at sixteen and received her GED through a mail-order course. She'd grown up with no expectations greater than working for her parents in their Polish deli. College never entered her dreams. Yet here were books for courses in economics and political science. Architecture and art! Marion spent her first evenings in the condo poring over them, yearning for more. And yearning for the opportunities life offered the condo's true occupant.

And then the extension-course catalog came in the mail.

At first she thought she could cover the night courses in real estate with the money she was saving on rent. But the courses were more expensive than the price of the roach nest she'd been living inn in Hollywood.

And so Marion thrilled the building's parking attendants by removing her rusty Dodge Dart from their care. The car sale just covered the cost of the courses. And she was thrilled to be driving the daughter's MG! But then there was the price of the extension-course books. They used up her entire food budget, but Marion was young and delusional enough to believe she could subsist on supermarket samples. Soon her stomach grumbles started disturbing people at work and her clothes began to hang off her frame. When she started falling asleep in class, Marion realized she needed more nutrition than crackers and spray cheese.

She never meant to assume the daughter's identity. She only wanted to survive. When Marion overheard some fellow students talking about the "serious spread" Monty's bar put on at happy hour, she became inspired. Monty's was a high-end steak house on the penthouse level of a Westwood professional building. The restaurant's bar catered to a professional clientele, weeding out the riffraff through strictly enforced carding and dress-code policies. They only made exceptions for pretty, well-dressed coeds.

Marion wasn't pretty but there was a shit ton of "well dressed" in the condo closet. She'd lost enough weight to fit into some of the daughter's things and there was a bag of makeup in the condo bathroom drawers. She brought the bag to Bullock's Wilshire, and after learning she had a mustache that could be removed with purchasing a simple depilatory, received lessons in the art of mask making. Although she was rarely lacking self-confidence, her hunger gave her some Dutch courage and she strolled up to the chafing dishes at Monty's bar like she owned them. Soon she was a happy-hour regular.

And that's where she met Josh. He was a wealthy full-time UCLA student with a frat brother's fake ID, his own sport coat and tie, and, unfortunately, an abnormally large head. He was also a budding alcoholic. He couldn't afford to be picky, so he decided to chat up the potato-nosed girl heaping her plate with a third helping of Swedish meatballs and chicken wings. Josh had grown up going to Beverly Hills schools with Beverly Hills girls. Thus Marion seemed to him to be the nicest girl he'd ever met in his life. And Josh was the only boy who'd ever offered to buy Marion a drink. Or pay for anything, for that matter. He naturally assumed Marion was a wealthy student like himself. She didn't correct his misperception and they soon became an item.

It was easy posing as rich, what with the car, condo, and clothes, and Josh was usually too sloshed to ever suspect that she wasn't a full-time UCLA coed or that her night classes were actually extension courses. He took Marion to formals and keggers and UCLA carnival, making up for all that she missed in high school and more. It wasn't hard for her to mix in with the rest of the coeds at these events, where everybody seemed to be loaded on something. All she had to do was giggle.

Since Marion drew a Maginot Line at her waist, Josh showered her with expensive gifts of jewelry and cologne. Those gifts were pawned to pay for course books with enough left over for sorority-style haircuts and the ultimate luxury: manicures. Nails were important for coeds with coin. She needed to look the part.

Every weekday, Marion drove like a demon from the telemarketing office in West Hollywood to join Josh at the north campus kiosk where she indulged on the salad bar and watched her big-headed boyfriend sneak hair-of-the-dog vodka into a glass of tomato juice. She got nutrition, stayed thin, and saved her paychecks. Josh got steady hands and blue balls. Weekends, there was always a frat activity that included pizza or sandwiches.

And Marion got the education she craved. Seven quarters into her masquerade, she'd earned her real-estate broker's license and mastered private and corporate property-tax structure. Once she finished her spring courses in investment property law, she'd be ready to switch jobs. That would mean abandoning the condo *and* big-headed Josh. But not yet. The books for her spring courses would be expensive. The money she'd saved from her telemarketing salary had enabled her to purchase her way into a promising hedge fund that couldn't be touched for two years. She needed more gifts. Even if it meant allowing Josh to "go to third."

Or meeting his family. Unfortunately, Josh was in love. He wanted to take their relationship to "the next level," which meant getting parental approval. She'd put him off for over a half a year and he was beginning to get a complex about it. Not wanting to lose her book budget, Marion finally agreed to meet Josh's family at an early Mother's Day lunch at a new superchic restaurant in Santa Monica. His parents were "in the business" and she had tried to tell herself that it might be interesting to meet them. The minute she entered Michael's Restaurant and got a look at the clientele, she knew she could kiss her free course books good-bye.

Her borrowed espadrilles, winged bangs, and giggles might have been enough to trick a bunch of fucked-up college kids into thinking that she was born sucking a silver spoon, but this was a roomful of sophisticated, wealthy, glamorous *adults*. Adults who looked like sleek, hungry cats (wearing small-size cruise wear) just waiting to rip apart a dumpy Cleveland mouse posing as one of their own. Marion had been so busy studying for finals that she'd forgotten to study the habits and lifestyle of the privileged rich. Adults asked questions. They made observations and connections and drew conclusions. The minute she opened her mouth, she'd be toast! She couldn't even remember what she'd told Josh her father did for a living. Where did her supposedly wealthy family supposedly spend their vacations? And which fork did she use first? She should have taken courses in etiquette instead of property taxes! She was starting to yip! And needed a White Russian! Marion grabbed a busboy by the sleeve and ordered the soothing milky drink before she knew the location of the table at which she'd be meeting the family.

Two steps onto Michael's patio and Marion knew that she was too dull, awkward, and ugly to ever pull off her charade. When she threaded her way between white pool-furniture-style plastic chairs, occupied by people with perfect everything, she knew that at nineteen, she was way too old to still have a lumpy nose. Her supposedly rich parents would have fixed it at fourteen. By the time she sat down with Josh's family, she was wishing she'd been born with an unusually large head. Anything to fit in!

Luckily, the family was too busy with their own masquerade to pay any attention to her. As he drunk-drove Marion to the restaurant, Josh had informed her that his mother had recently caught his father in bed with an Asian stewardess. Although Josh's parents had separated, they'd insisted on celebrating an early Mother's Day as one big still-cohesive family. The practice, she would learn in later years, was a common one among L.A. people with money.

Josh's soap-opera-star mother was a cloud of pink blond curls attached to cheekbones and a long linen-y pantsuit. Her perfect soap-opera-star smile gritted and ricocheted around Marion in disappointment before she quickly handed her off to Josh's distracted, too-open-shirted, enormous-headed dad. But not before Marion noticed Mom's nickel-size pupils. Dad was about as friendly as any producer in middle-age crisis with skittish financing and an Asian stewardess waiting for him back at the Marina City Club would have been. He sized Marion up for fuckability then turned away. Josh's siblings were so self-pitying and self-absorbed they didn't even say hello. As soon as Marion's White Russian arrived, she buried her lips in it.

While the family ignored her, Marion stole glances at the other tables. She recognized a famous composer and his wife, the movie star. There was a man who'd won an Oscar for something sitting with a woman who'd had several disco hits. There was a comedian from a sitcom with three men in nearly identical Armani suits. There was a man with a dog-in-a-purse and a woman who wore pounds of diamonds with purposely torn jeans and sneakers. They all kissed one another like they were mother and child and they all had perfect teeth. Marion couldn't hear what they were saying, but she imagined that conversation on this patio must be centered around lofty exclusive subjects. Were they discussing film noir? Quantum physics? Deconstruction?

Her own table answered that question.

"Dad, her clit is as big as my thumb!" Josh's brother informed his father (and the entire patio). "I can see it outlined in her bikini bottom!"

Josh's father was laughing lecherously—with a full mouth. "Don't complain, she's young. Young nipples and pussies are as pink as bubble gum." As he spoke, food bits were spraying all over the tablecloth.

(!)

Moments later, Josh's high-school-aged sister began to complain. "That Beemer is over *three years old*!" she lamented. "I'm the only girl in my class who drives a piece of shit! They all think I'm poor!"

Suddenly a red blur flew past Marion's ear.

"BREAST-FEEDING MAKES PINK NIPPLES TURN BROWN, MOTHERFUCKER!" This, from Josh's clearly irate mother.

(!)

Josh's mother wasn't giving a medical seminar. She had just broken family cohesion by flinging a shrimp cocktail at her husband. Marion's yips began to grow as strong as her embarrassment. Surely Josh's family was ruining the rest of the patrons' lunches as well as offending their ears.

She instinctively slid her chair closer to the sitcom comedian's table so she wouldn't be mistaken for a member of the bigheaded tribe.

That was when she overheard the sitcom comedian tell the Armani triplets that Josh's mother "gave the best rim jobs in the business."

"This shirt cost three hundred dollars, you fucking has-been!" moaned Josh's father, wiping cocktail sauce off his chest.

And the food fight was on.

As much as she felt for poor Josh, Marion was more interested in the reactions of the other patrons. Yes, they were looking, but it wasn't because they were shocked. They were looking at the squalling family and *they were enjoying what they saw*. Their eyes were feasting on the bighead family and they were laughing and whispering and gossiping like fishwives.

Marion's yips were replaced by a hot gush of confidence and a sudden sense of possibility. Los Angeles was a *new-money* town. It was doable. She leaned over the homeliest Armani triplet and introduced herself.

45

Who Ordered the Eggs?

"Marion! You look like the cat that swallowed the canary!"

"Among other unmentionable things. Good to see you, Michael," Marion replied.

Back in reality and fifteen thousand dollars' worth of wardrobe, Marion air-kissed Michael McCarty and allowed him to help her down the steps to the patio. In its center, the fateful bighead family's table was still standing. It was *her* table now. And her lifeboat sat around it.

Of all the thousands of people Marion Zane counted among her friends, there were only six who qualified for hypothetical lifeboat-sharing status. And with the exception of Ivan, Xiocena, and Lyndy, who was going to be late, they were all here. Okay, only half of them, but it was a start.

Patti, Pepper, and Maya thought they were joining her for lunch in order to strategize about hospital fund-raising. They had no idea what Marion was about to announce. Neither did Marion, for that matter. But she savored the sight of her wonderful friends:

Patti was using a fork to discreetly pull away the back neckline of the dress on the woman sitting behind her so she could read the label. Pepper was packing a cocktail napkin into the left cup of her bra, tantalizing the male population of the patio, and Maya was terrorizing them in a three-foot white Afro and silver face powder.

What was she going to say? How much was she going to say? How much were they going to hear from other people? How could she arm them and minimize the damage while still holding on to her status and dignity?

The only thing she was sure of was that she was definitely going to be spinning the truth. Sometimes lifeboats leaked.

After air-kisses and fashion petting and food ordering and kir royales all around, Maya looked at Patti's watch.

"Marion, can we start? I have to go back to my Lystrada shoot and wear more pieces of shit."

"Lystrada's *bad*?" Patti interrupted, quickly adding, "I haven't gone in yet."

"Piece of shit. One dress has feathers coming out of ass and that is 'good one.' The other looks like rotten egg."

"Ew. I won't bother."

"Don't."

"If you can just hang on until Lyndy gets here . . . ." Marion began.

"You sure you want her on board?" Patti asked.

"Ya know her BH Central Gala is in two weeks. I'd think she might be offended if we ask her ta raise for another hospital," Pepper warned.

"And she's an asshole," added Maya.

"Lyndy's my oldest friend in L.A. and as a matter of fact, she *demanded* to be allowed to help set up Carita Memorial," Marion corrected. "So maybe we can change the subject and hang on five minutes more."

She hated to shut them down when they were watching her back, but in truth Lyndy had been uncharacteristically supportive since the day after the Throw-Down. Marion knew it must have taken a huge effort for the woman she called her friend to suppress her natural personality and behave so kindly. And considering the cost of the hospital, Marion needed all the help she could get. Besides, she didn't want to make her announcement twice.

Luckily, changing the subject was something Patti Fink's brain function was capable of connecting with. "How's the weight training coming along?" she asked Pepper with an intriguing conspiratorial wink.

"Patti was worried for m' marriage, 'cuz I delivered five kids the ol'-fashioned way," Pepper explained to Maya and Marion. "So she gave me a set a' vaginal egg weights."

"Patti Fink!" Marion cried.

"Well, they've kept *me* in shape over the years," Patti reasoned. "Ever since Finnegan told me that making love with his ex was like screwing the Holland Tunnel."

"But you don't have any kids," Marion interrupted.

"But she's had a lot of . . ." said Maya, making a fist.

"Don't want to know!" said Marion and Pepper in unison.

"So which one are you up to?" Patti asked Pepper, lowering her voice. "That four-ounce is a killer!"

"The one I've got now is eight," answered Pepper. "How long do I keep it in, anyway?"

Maya and Marion screamed in their napkins.

"You're supposed to squeeze it for five minutes a day, not walk around town wearing it!" Patti cried. "Are you *sure* it's the eight-ounce?"

"Pretty sure . . . at least I think I am." Pepper was looking confused.

"Don't check it here!" Maya squealed.

"Maybe you should go check in the bathroom. The eight-ounce is *red,*" said Patti, clearly jealous.

What goes down on this patio hasn't changed a bit since I was here with the bigheads, thought Marion.

"That's the color of the one I got in," said Pepper, closing the subject and turning to Marion. "Your five minutes of waiting is up. I talked to Marcie Delanoth, in France. She owed me a hugie for gettin' her backstage at Justin Timberlake's Paris show. She's in for one million, goin' for two, if I do the same for Shakira."

"She should go in for ten million! Her fucking husband mines coal!" Maya groused.

"Good work, Pepper."

"How come you never hooked *me* up with Justin Timberlake in Paris?" Patti was still miffed about their reaction to the egg.

"Because I don't want Lou's tank ta blow over the Atlantic. Remember Spain?" Pepper replied.

"Who blew *who* over the Atlantic?" asked Lyndy as she clicked in, snatched a menu from a waiter, and sat. "I've half a mind to ask Michael to fire that valet!" She turned to the waiter, who'd been waiting to drape her napkin. "No, I don't want to hear the specials. G and T and Caesar as fast as you can, no anchovies." Lyndy turned her back on him and addressed the table again. "I wasted ten minutes teaching that midget about the Vanden Plas and then he peeled away like he was in the Tijuana Grand Prix!"

The waiter was still standing there. He was Latino. "The Caesar salad can come with grilled chicken," he said stiffly. "Would you like that?"

"No," said Lyndy, oblivious to the racial slur she'd casually made. "And put a rush on the drink."

"Very good, ma'am." The waiter stalked off.

"That's mighty white of you," said Pepper, while Maya made the internationally recognized sign for asshole behind Lyndy's back.

"Oh, grow up, Pepper Papadopoulos!" said Lyndy, removing her sunglasses. "You think they don't talk shit behind all of *our* backs? They're staff, not our friends. They hate the rich! Yours probably light candles each day in their churches, praying you come down with cancer and leave them jewelry in your will."

They all saw their waiter whispering to their busboy.

"They'll be leaving *us* spit and buggers in our meals if you don't quit brown-bashin'," whispered Pepper.

Lyndy dismissed her with a wave. "At least I don't adopt them in order to assuage some ridiculous unworthiness complex." She was looking at Patti Fink, but Patti was still obsessing about Pepper and didn't notice. Lyndy turned to Marion. "So tell me where you are and who I can help tag-team. I've got a two-thirty."

Now she had Patti's attention.

"With Dr. Ganes!" Patti announced the name of the plastic surgeon cheerfully.

Marion deftly slid Lyndy's knife out of reach.

"My gardener's niece cleans his office," said Patti sheepishly. "She knows I like to keep up. Don't worry. Ganes gave Jenette Armour beautiful eyes!"

"I'm not doing eyes," growled Lyndy. "Okay, Marion, I'm waiting."

Marion took a long pull of her kir royale.

"First of all, we've crossed the four-hundred-million mark, thanks to all of you and the Brodie Foundation . . . the board of regents gave the go-ahead for UCLA to partner if we make it to five hundred."

Everyone raised their drinks in salute.

"Zephyr didn't get to first base with Jamie Turan, but at least she got money. He's in for five million. Pepper needs to work on Marcie Delanoth," Marion continued. "Maya is working on Tom's producer, Mr. Sokolov. I need someone to help me steamroller Jeff Yarnell, preferably with alcohol and some not-so-veiled threats, and I'm living at the Beverly Hills Hotel because I've left my husband."

The deafening silence that followed was broken only when a red, egg-shaped vaginal weight dropped onto the terra-cotta floor underneath the center table and rolled out into the middle of Michael's patio.

"Oh, my God." Patti gasped. "It *is* the eight-ounce!"

46

Ship-to-Shore

The captain shook Ivan awake when the leviathan-size container ship entered the Ligurian Sea.

"Hour to port."

"*Grazie,* Gianni."

Ivan showered, changed into the baggy, worn clothes he'd bought off a crewman, and rechecked his gear. He'd met Gianni, the freighter captain, in Naples several years earlier while accompanying the Zanes on holiday and he was glad he'd kept up the contact. Although he possessed three excellent sets of passports, credit cards in various names, and other forged identification papers, he preferred to enter European Union countries "off the books." Airports had cameras and manifests and so did docks. Before staging his own death in Guatemala, Ivan had been a "known" on this continent. Considering the nature of this visit, it was best to leave no trail and no red flags.

Gianni, at seventy-five, had lived most of his life at sea. The captain was used to the intrigues of his trade and had agreed to help his enigmatic friend without hesitation, refusing compensation and offering him his sleeping quarters. Before coming on deck, Ivan tucked ten thousand euros and three Cuban Cohibas under his friend's pillow and hoped he would meet Gianni again someday in more positive circumstances.

When the freighter was halfway into the Golfo di Genova, Ivan climbed into a small dinghy containing an old Italian-made spinning rod and rudimentary night-fishing equipment and was silently lowered into the sea. Although commercial fishing fleets had diminished most of the restaurant-worthy species this near to the shore, locals still got lucky every now and then, especially at night. He'd blend right in.

The wine-dark bay was, thankfully, calm, and the moon full, ideal conditions for Ivan to reflect as he silently motored past Porto Vecchio's necklace of light:

How different his life would have been had he joined his old partners, if he had agreed to take over the drug-smuggling operation from the man they'd assassinated. He might be living like a king on the land off the starboard side of his boat.

Ivan and the other two NATO operatives had been as close as brothers, serving on scores of missions together, acting as a team and putting their lives in one another's hands. They even shared women from time to time, so close was their bond. As the mission in Colombia had progressed, Ivan never dreamed his brothers would want him dead. Even when he saw the way his partners gazed at the piles of cash and ardently sampled the cocaine. Even when he saw how greed had hardened their souls as he watched his partners torture their target into revealing the secret of his wealth, he never thought they'd turn on him.

Greasing borders to open new markets for coca lords was a business in which all three of them could excel, so Ivan's partners were astounded when he'd said he wanted no part in it, and they lobbied hard to change his mind. They told him it would be easy; they had connections, they had clearance; they'd never have to touch the drugs. They argued that here was tremendous money, untold riches, if they expanded their list of clientele. It was a chance to evolve beyond being mere hired guns. Such a chance they'd never have again.

Still, Ivan had refused. He told them they'd only be trading one kind of killing for another, and given the choice, he'd rather exterminate spies. By the time he'd finished making his case, he knew that the brotherhood that existed between them was broken. Later, when he saw his two partners speaking with the coca lord's men, he knew they'd put a price on his head.

How fortunate that he'd encountered the Zanes just at this time. He'd been on the lam, trying to lay low as he ran through three countries and managed to survive three attacks, but it was just a matter of time before the new partners of his old partners caught up with someone who was threatening their livelihood. And his old partners had put the word out in the intelligence community that Ivan was the one who was involved with cocaine, so he couldn't return home by normal means. A wealthy American family traveling with children was the perfect opportunity to erase himself for a while. That "while" turned out to be fifteen years.

Ivan had never dreamed he would actually enjoy his job. He certainly never considered making a switch from assassin to personal assistant when he'd embarked on his assignment in South America. But the precise agendas of the intelligence entities who contracted his services had become unclear to him, which meant he'd become unsure of his own agenda in working for them. Was he taking lives to benefit the greater good? Or to further the rise of an unscrupulous few? The line between good and evil was beginning to blur. The direction in which Marion Zane's moral compass was pointing, however, was something he was sure of, and he'd found more satisfaction in arranging donations to well-researched charities than in slitting the throats of men he was no longer able to clearly see as worthy of death.

It was only natural that cooped up as he was in a mansion, Ivan would begin to miss the adrenaline rush of his old profession, and so on his off days he began to keep his skills from getting rusty by doing some minor moonlighting for certain entities whose "hands were tied."

And if he'd never been betrayed? At thirty-seven, Ivan was too old for field operations in his old area of expertise. If he'd been lucky enough to have survived fifteen more years in his former job, he'd be working for some intelligence agency, making logistical decisions and working out detailed plans for operations he wouldn't participate in himself—which was, by no small irony, a good description of what he'd been doing for the Zanes.

And then there was Marion, the paradox. He'd never dreamed that a human being so caught up in trivialities could have so gigantic and positive an impact on mankind. Extravagant vanity and insecurities aside, Marion accomplished more social good than most governments or corporations—and did it without bloodshed. She'd never given Ivan a reason to question his loyalty.

So Ivan had waited fifteen years to avenge his betrayal, putting up with the nonsense of L.A. society life and enjoying his job and his relationship with his boss—even though his penchant for keeping his sex life private caused Marion to assume he was some kind of eunuch. How little she knew how much he enjoyed those "visual" perks she so blithely gave him.

Thinking about the Zanes, Ivan imagined that Marion was probably going crazy without him and he felt guilty for not checking in. But not guilty enough to risk her family's safety. She'd come a long way without him. She'd survive seven more weeks. Maybe longer.

Willing an end to these thoughts, Ivan beached the dinghy in Varazze, a few kilometers west of Genoa proper. He made his way up the beach, lugging the fishing gear and waterproof rucksack, clambered over a wall, and stepped onto a street. He was almost at a nearby rail station when a policeman in a Smart Car pulled alongside him and rolled down the window.

"Any luck?" the policeman asked in Italian, using the pretense of checking out Ivan's catch bucket to shine a light in his eyes.

Ivan kept his composure and tilted the bucket toward the Smart Car. Inside it was a bronzino large enough to feed a family of four. Captain Gianni had thought of everything.

"Funny," said the policeman. "My brother goes out three times a week and he never catches shit."

As the Smart Car disappeared, Ivan ducked into a dark doorway and changed into a jogging suit and shoes. Ditching the fishing gear and rumpled clothes in a trash bin, he trimmed his beard down to stubble by penlight, gathered his hair into a small ponytail, shrugged on the rucksack, and started jogging east. The car rentals in Genoa were open late. He'd decided to drive himself across the Alps.

47

Chin and Bear It

Marion pulled apart the tangle of exercise tanks, swimsuits, running shorts, sports bras, leggings, yoga pants, bike shorts, low-cut sports socks, cuffed sports socks, sweatsuits, and assorted sweatbands from the protective bags of six different purses and garment bags in search of her ringing telephone. She really needed maid service more than three times a day, especially in the second bedroom of the bungalow—aka the war room—that served as her closet. She just wasn't used to so little space. As the phone kept ringing, she made a mental note to call house keeping and ask for more of those little paper please-make-up-the-room thingies to hang on her door because the last three had disappeared. Giving up, she climbed over mountains of suitcases, jewelry cases, makeup cases, and non-fur coats, stepped into the living room, and snatched the phone off her desk.

"Who's calling please?"

"I look like the Man in the Moon!" screamed a horrified voice at the other end.

"Patti?" Marion asked. (Who else could it be?)

"God knows what it's doing to the rest of my face! It could be stretching it out!"

"Patti, what's wrong? What happened?"

"Oh, Marion, I have a medical emergency!"

(!)

"Honey, you've gotta call an ambulance!" Marion shouted into the phone. "Quick! Hang up and dial 911!"

"I can't let anybody see me like this! Are you crazy? That's why I called you!"

"Patti! Patti, if you're hurt—"

"Oh, it doesn't hurt. It just looks like I belong in the cir-cir-circus! *Waaaahhh!!!!*"

Marion sighed and sat down. "Okay. There, there. Start from the beginning."

"It's all that fucking mudslide's fault!"

(!)

"There's a mudslide in Beverly Park?"

"No! In Honduras! It destroyed the village where my gardener's brother lives. That poor darling girl's mother was squashed!"

"This morning?"

"No! Two months back. You know all the villagers who are staying with me?"

"Honey, you've always got *dozens* of people—"

"You met two sisters, three nieces, and a grandmother when you came over to pick up those hospital checks last week."

"I thought they were some sort of civic preservation society. Those Latina women in Chanel suits?"

"Those suits were over *three seasons old*! And all the villagers' clothes were buried in mud. Anyway, that poor darling sixteen-year-old, Alejandra, lost her mother before she had a chance to acquire all the essential life skills that are passed down from mother to daughter, and you know I'm the motherly type and so—"

As Patti's monologue wandered off into dimly-associative gibberish, Marion put on her readers and started skimming the TV guide. "Yes, go on."

"We were down in the dish vault, where I was teaching her the difference between Rosenthal and Limoges salad-plate finishes before we moved on to the Villeroy and Bosch—"

"Patti, I wanted to sun by the pool and there's only about nine hours of daylight left—"

"It was six in the morning and Alejandra was shivering! I had to get her a wrap."

"What happened to her Chanel suit jacket?"

"So I went down to our wing and went upstairs to the sweater bar," Patti continued, ignoring her. "That's when the phone rang!"

Marion noted that on Thursday, at seven o'clock, on Channel 9, a *Facts of Life* retrospective marathon was going to begin and that she wanted to beat herself with a two-pound wooden mallet for being so moronic as to even *attempt* trying to follow the meandering explanations of her batty friend. "Did the phone explode?" she asked, taking the bait.

"*No!* But I had to get it! *Ricky-the-surfer's* been calling the house!"

"Patti Fink McKay de Beers Suzuki Erhardt! Shame on you! Don't you know better than to give your home phone number to—"

"I didn't! Ricky must have snuck it out of my BlackBerry while I was in the bathroom or while I was going down—"

"Don't want to know!"

"He's been calling the house day and night! And you know how clever Lou is. He can answer a phone!"

Marion put her head down on the desk.

"Anyway," continued Patti. "I ran to get it and tripped over the brace."

"What brace?"

"Wanda's brace! My upstairs maid? She has advanced spina bifida."

Marion tried bumping her head on the surface of the desk but it hurt, so she finally gave in, and resigned, asked, "Why would you employ a maid who has—"

"She doesn't do heavy lifting anymore! Now, all heavy lifting and vacuuming is the job of Lucia-the-*Thursday*-maid!"

Luckily, Marion had breakfasted at her desk and was able to grab a napkin and bite down on it instead of her tongue.

"My chin connected with the edge of cashmere bar, but I was so freaked out, I didn't feel it, so I answered the phone."

"Did you ask him to stop calling, especially at an impolitic hour?"

"Oh, that doesn't work. He's in love with me."

"Oh, Patti! That's terrible. I'm so sorry."

"I mean, *really* in love."

"Then there's all the more reason to keep you alive. Didn't Lou serve in World War Two?"

(Or was it World War I?)

"Ricky wants me to leave Lou and marry him because he can finally *support* me. He just got a surfing sponsorship from Grunt with a salary of one million a year."

"*Aaah, ha, ha, ha, ha, ha, ha, ha, ha, ha, ha, ha, ha—*"

"Don't laugh. He's serious."

"—ha, ha, ha, ha, ha, hee, hee, ho, ha! Sorry," Marion said, removing her readers and wiping her eyes. "Did you tell him the price of your weekly highlights? Ha ha ha! One million just might be enough to cover—"

"I told him Lou was dying."

"Now, that's not funny."

"But it bought me some time! And technically, all of us start dying from the moment we reach eighteen—"

"Patti, you said you have an *injury*."

"Okay! After I got rid of Ricky, I went back into the sweater bar to get Alejandra that yummy Fendi electric-blue turtleneck that'll just pop on her—"

"Patti!"

"—coloring and that's when I looked in the mirror and saw it! My . . . my . . . my—"

"What? Saw what?"

"My chin implant! It's been knocked to the side! Waaahhh!"

"I'm surprised you didn't call the fire department."

"Are you kidding? Firemen are hot!" Patti blubbered. "I can't have them seeing me looking like I have one of those dormant Siamese twins hanging off of my head! *Wah, hanh, hanh!*"

"I think those twins are a myth," Marion said, then softening, added: "I'm sure it's nothing Dr. Steven can't handle on Monday, honey."

"But I can't wait until *Monday,* Marion!" Patti squealed. "We have that dinner party *tonight*! I'm coaching Claire. She's depending on me and it might be my only chance in this lifetime to sit next to Aubrey Dutton! I can't slip my hand on his thigh and make him wish he was twenty-five again if the *FUCKING ALIEN IS ABOUT TO BURST OUT OF MY FACE ANY SECOND*!"

"Patti? Patti? You're spinning out. If you'll just calm down, I'll put a call in to Henry Grassman and—"

"Not Grassman," Patti replied, instantly sobering. "David Thayer is better with chins."

"I don't know if he'll drop everything on his Saturday to open up for a new patient."

"*You're* not a new patient. Say it's for you."

"Damn, Patti, you're good."

"Please!"

"Okay, I'll call David Thayer and ask—"

"I already did."

"Patti Fink!"

"I'm desperate, Marion! I can't get within six feet of my own husband or I'll come into focus!"

"Patti, you can't make an appointment for me and have me not show," Marion began.

"Right. That's why you're going to need to pick me up in two hours. No way can I drive and I can't use a service; they might use hidden cameras. You know how I'm photographed!"

Marion wasn't physically capable of making a sufficient number of eye rolls. She'd throw up or go blind. But Patti was unstoppable.

"You're the only person on this planet that I'll allow to see me this way! The only one I trust. And I need you to get in."

"You're lucky I love you, Patti Fink!"

"I give thanks every day to Shiva and Ganesha and Jesus and—"

Marion hung up and speed-dialed the house in order to speak to Carl. Shit! She'd given him the day off since she'd assumed she'd be spending the day at the hotel, using the pool and spa.

Marion thought of her new Lexus hybrid sitting in the parking garage at the compound.

Next to the guesthouse. Where, at that very moment, Richard and Tawnee were probably . . .

Fuck it!

It was her house too! She could come and go as she pleased, and besides, it was 8 A.M. She'd take a healthy morning walk up the street to the compound and retrieve her car with her communal-property-owning head held high. Besides, Richard didn't get up on Saturdays until noon . . .

. . . with his hair all sticking out funny on the sides. And if he wanted to make love, he'd do a breath spray and then take all this time smoothing his hair down before rolling his leg over her and nibbling her . . .

. . . and so what if Tawnee was there? It wasn't as if the little scuz were allowed in the house.

Marion peeled off her exercise clothes and started getting ready. But not before ordering a hair-of-the-dog Bloody Mary with tequila (was that a Bloody Sunrise?) from room service. The Advil needed assistance.

48

Bad Dreams and Streams

"*Show me you hands, mud girl. Show me!*"

Maya did her best to look confused and slowly unfurled one hand in front of Madame Dzhova's face. She'd been hiding her pregnancy successfully for over two months, eating only a little and chewing licorice roots to stave off her nausea. She'd thought she was safe, using the knife she'd stolen from the Russian captain to open a vein several times a day and soak the menses pads she was given with blood. Five days of pain and her secret was safe.

She kept her other hand behind her back.

Madame Dzhova opened Maya's hand, inspecting it for incriminating cuts. "Now the other!"

Maya hesitated and the huge henna-haired woman burst into low, phlegmy laughter.

"You think just because you are his favorite, the captain will let you have his baby? You think he will take you away to Moscow and make you his mud-colored wife and give his name to your mud-colored brat? Show me your other hand, girl!"

Slowly, Maya put her fist under the madame's face, where it was seized and forced open in the same fashion as its mate.

"Who do you think told me to check you, you fool? Because he felt your little belly getting harder! Who do you think pays for the doctor? The captain might enjoy the perversion of fucking you, but he doesn't want your pup."

Maya averted her eyes. Beatings had conditioned her to remaining docile and obedient and life had conditioned her not to react to the racial slurs and insults, but the rage in her eyes was the hardest thing to disguise. She needed a second to recover. Finding no cuts, Madame Dzhova released Maya's hands and busied herself lighting one of her dark, stinky cigarettes. Thinking she was safe for at least another month, safe to plot her escape from this hellhole of a brothel and from the occupied land that held no mercy for people of her skin color, Maya turned to go.

"Now push up your sleeves."

She turned around, trying to conceal her trembling as she touched the edge of her right sleeve and slowly inched it up. Madame leaned closer for a better view and Maya's right hand involuntarily clenched. She knew that the crook of her elbow was crisscrossed with a fine network of tiny pink scars that would surely doom the sleeping child inside of her.

"All of you think you are so special," said Madame Dzhova, squinting her kohl-rimmed eyes in the sputtering lantern light. "That you will have a life outside of these walls. You are a whore, mud girl. No one will come and take you away."

As the putrid old madame leaned forward, Maya pulled her arm back then slammed it forward like a sledgehammer into one of the madame's double chins. The woman fell back into her chair then slammed onto the floor with a wet crack. Maya fled up the stairs.

There was a painted-shut window in the brothel's attic that Maya had been working loose for more than a year. It led onto the roof and ultimately to a tangle of alleys where she could lose any pursuers. Maya took the long strides she'd learned at her father's side in the fields, leaping up the stairs three at a time until she reached the top. She raced into the attic and clawed away three fingernails in her first attempt to lift the window. On her second attempt, the cold air of freedom greeted her for a glorious moment before she felt a sting and a hypodermic plunged into her arm.

She was halfway out the window before she succumbed to the drug. All coordination and strength fled from her body and she was easily pulled back into the attic and laid on a pile of crumbling old quilts. She expected the madame to start in on her with her cattle prod and padded coat hanger, but instead she beheld a long-faced, long-nosed man with spectacles and a milky right eye. He was holding something shiny and hooked, like a dental tool. And he was spreading her legs!

"Shhh, little one. Just go to sleep. I'm going to fix you so we won't have this problem again."

M aya woke up flailing at the bedcovers as her body fended off the attack it was helpless to prevent in that attic some fifteen years before. When at last she was fully awake and aware of her surroundings, she fell back into the bed pillows and focused her eyes on the hand-painted 1920s scroll-work and stars on the bedroom ceiling beams until she'd banished the face of the doctor from her mind.

She'd gone for almost nine years without the nightmare. Nine years of freedom from that milky eye and shiny sharp hook that had damaged her womb just enough so she could never carry a child.

But she wasn't surprised that the nightmare was back.

Maya pulled off her soaking-wet silk nightslip and padded into her bathroom to pee.

Tom was waiting for her. He was sitting on her antique green marble tub, using the remote to increase the volume on the little plasma on the opposite wall. He'd installed it so he could follow sports whenever he and Maya shared a bath. Since he was the only one who ever watched it, the noise startled the shit out of his wife.

But it didn't startle her as much as what Tom was holding in his other hand.

It was a pregnancy test stick.

"I've been counting the days since you said your period ended," he said, looking proud of himself. "Girl, I can hear that egg callin' my name! Here. You're supposed to hold this end with the tip directly immersed in your morning urine stream."

49

Beating the Bushes

Marion was trucking up the street, lookin' good. She had on a jaunty camel-colored Michael Kors mini mohair sweaterdress that hugged her in all the right places, a cool Fendi belt sitting on the back of her waist, and hanging on her flat belly in front, a (fabulous!) Marc Jacobs tomato-red car coat over her shoulders, an insanely indulgent custom gold cuff festooned with chunky emeralds, red coral, and yellow diamonds (to let Tawnee know she had a long way to go), Dolce & Gabbana camel-colored lizard stiletto pumps with sexy pointy toes, Prada sunglasses, and a big chocolate croc fuck-you tote from Hermès (again, for Tawnee's benefit).

Put together. In control. With a smile on her lips for every other morning soul who was gettin' busy being alive and free!

Marion rarely walked the neighborhood streets at this time of day. Or any hour, for that matter (after all, this *was* L.A.). Who knew so many housekeepers were out walking dogs at this hour? Who knew so many housekeepers pretended they didn't notice the steaming piles of dog shit their charges left behind—sometimes in the middle of the friggin' sidewalk, for mercy's sake?! The pungent stench wafted up in Marion's face every ten steps until she figured she could forgo waxing her nose hair that month because it had undoubtedly all been burned away. When she passed the fourth housekeeper pretending to be scanning the skies for incoming missiles or the Second Coming of Christ while her doggy took a dump, Marion felt it was her civic duty to keep the Beverly Hills nose-hair waxers off food stamps, so she stopped to confront the woman.

"Ahem," she said, angling downwind of the (obviously ailing) Portuguese water spaniel the woman was walking. But before she could speak, the woman made a clucking sound and pointed to Marion's stilettos.

"Señora, you wear wrong shoes," said the housekeeper with a doleful smile.

That's when Marion became aware that her pinkie toes were beginning to protest. She probably should have broken in the stiletto pumps before hiking uphill on hard sidewalks. Oh well. It was only a little farther. Maybe a mile.

"Don't worry. These pumps are well made," she replied.

The housekeeper looked dubiously up at the steep grade of the street then pulled a cell phone out of her uniform pocket. "I call a cab."

"Don't be ridiculous, my house is only right around that corner," said Marion, starting back on her way. "Thanks, but I'm fine! Finer than I look! Really!"

(That didn't come out right.)

Besides, the day wasn't getting any younger and she had to hurry if she wanted to make her appointment with David Thayer for Patti-the-Moon-faced-liar. She crossed over to the less dog-populated side of the street and kept on (painfully) truckin'.

Because of zoning restrictions on the erection of thirty-foot walls and less than positive ordinances regarding razor-wire barricades, Beverly Hills residents wanting privacy and protection had had to resign themselves to surrounding their homes and outbuildings with hedge fortresses that could easily compete with those that concealed Sleeping Beauty's castle, as far as height was concerned.

Some areas had no height limit, allowing ambitiously paranoid residents to mingle the fast-growing bush varieties with fearsomely thorned vine varieties until they reached indefinite heights and widths. Marion's neighborhood was one of those areas.

One mile later when she was now in the home stretch, the morning sun was no longer glorious. It was hot. Marion figured that she probably could have left her fabulous coat back at the war room since it was now crammed awkwardly into her getting-heavier-by-the-second tote. She had removed her shoes and was staining her turtleneck sweater dress with makeup as she stretched it up to mop her sweaty face. The mohair from the turtleneck stuck to her mascara in clumps and filled her ears. Thus, visually and aurally impaired, she was caught unawares by the stout woman in a Winnie-the-Pooh smock who was coming up on her left. The nanny plowed by her, towing an overweight mastiff that accidentally hip-checked Marion, sending her careering into the Mother of All Hedges: thirty feet of ficus exterior with a solid bougainvillea core.

Finding herself enmeshed in the hedge was like being in the embrace of an iron maiden. The more Marion struggled, the deeper she became entangled and the more she was pierced. During her efforts at writhing free, she managed to get a glimpse through to the other side of the hedge and recognized her neighbors' back house by the awful construction. So near and yet so far! Within a moment, she was reduced to balancing on one heel and chirping pitifully like a lost baby bird. After ten minutes, she was delirious and envisioning archaeologists discovering her skeleton one thousand years in the future: "The Bushwoman of Beverly Hills," they'd no doubt call her. Her remains would become a traveling museum exhibit and experts would debate the purpose of her breast implants. Had they been of ceremonial use? For protection? They'd determine that the North American continent must have undergone a brief ice age after noting the heavy clothing she was wearing at the time of her death. They'd describe her tribal jewelry as—

Suddenly, providentially, two brown hands pierced the hedge and started pulling the vines away from her legs and dress. Was it a thousand years later so soon?

Then a familiar voice said, "I tried to call cab but you no listen."

It took the housekeeper fifteen minutes to extricate Marion from the hedge fortress. When she realized she was free and—aside from a tattered dress and scratched-up legs—no longer doomed to become an exhibit, she reached into her tote to give the woman compensation, but the housekeeper held up her hand.

"You better than that *puta* at your home, Mrs. Zane," she said. "You keep it. You might need later."

Then she and her Portuguese water spaniel turned and walked away. Marion thought she was having a mystical experience until the housekeeper turned in to the service entrance of her neighbor's property and she finally realized the woman was Xio's coffee-break buddy from next door. Everybody's staff knew everything about everybody. Is that what they thought? That she was better than Tawnee-the-*puta*?!

"Wait!" she cried after the housekeeper. "I don't *need* it! I'm going to be fine! And the hedge wasn't my fault; I was bumped!"

Shredded, bleeding, and leafy, Marion silenced Charlie's astonished tongue with a withering look, passed through the gates of the compound, and trudged up the steep driveway to the steps of her house. It was 9:25. Time enough for a shower and a quick change (and a Polysporin application) before she had to get Patti. Thank God Richard slept late.

But just as she reached the main steps of the mansion, the front door opened and she heard Richard's voice.

"I'm only doing four miles," he was saying. "Tell him I'll meet him at noon."

Then Richard emerged in a sweatsuit.

Back in the bushes!

Marion almost landed on the gardener's machete as she dove in. She grabbed it by the handle to keep it from rattling against the base of the stairs her husband was bouncing down.

Richard was awake before noon? And he'd taken up *jogging*?

He must be trying to rejuvenate himself. Marion's heart sank because that meant he still had Tawnee around. (And that he obviously didn't know about the dog poop lying in wait for him.)

Marion's suspicions were confirmed when she stood up and heard a bloodcurdling twenty-syllable scream. She looked up to see Tawnee-of-the-Valley wearing cutoff jeans and one of Richard's Turnbull & Asser shirts tied at the waist, standing just inside the open French doors of the mansion's left-side living room. Marion should have taken satisfaction in the sight of the masseuse's lopsided ponytails, which failed to fully cover the bandages on her scalp, but instead she was outraged.

That bitch was in her house!

And screaming outside of her house to boot. Richard was now bouncing back up the driveway. When he caught sight of his formerly perfect wife, he tripped and rubbed his eyes to make sure he wasn't seeing a mirage.

"*Marion?* What the fuck?!"

Marion looked down and saw that she was still holding the machete, so she thought fast and started whacking a few bits off the pittosporum bush to her left, muttering, "Never did like the way they prune these . . ."

"Don't lisssten to her tricksss!" Tawnee wailed. "Ssshe wasss trying to kill me, Richie!"

"And ruin a perfectly good gardening tool? Don't be absssurd, Rich-ie." Marion leaned the machete against the stairs, smoothed back her leaf-filled hair, and picking up her thousand-pound tote, did her best to swan up the stairs.

"What the hell is going on with you?" Richard bellowed after her. "First the dog collars and now covered with blood, sneaking around with a knife?"

"It's called a *machete*. And I wasn't *sneaking*. I was trying to avoid crossing paths with the main symptom of your midlife crisis." And just what did he mean by "dog collars?"

Marion continued up the stairs, refusing to turn around and let Richard see the tears that were currently forming in the corners of her eyes.

"Ssso, you're, like, denying you bought one thoussand dog collarsss on the Home Ssshopping Network and had them overnighted to thisss addresss?" Tawnee screeched from her post on the portico. We *know* it was you becaussse it wasss on your credit card!"

(?)

Mystery rat fucker again!

Marion wanted to ask for more information. She wanted to put her detectives on it so they could catch whoever was masterminding the meltdown of her marriage, but the tears were now streaming down her face and she wanted to hold on to the last three ounces of pride she had left. "Rich-ie, please tell that thing to stop talking at me," she begged, grabbing the handle of the front door.

"I'm calling Dr. Wymer!" Richard called up the stairs. "Do you hear me, Marion? You're out of control! And I don't deserve this treatment! What did I ever do to make you treat me like this! What did I do?"

That was it. Marion *had* to turn around.

"What did you do, Richard? *What did you do?* How about Ellie-May-with-the-mange, for starters!" she cried, gesturing with her thumb at the portico. "You suspect the one person in your life who's showed you nothing but twenty years of undying love and support and honesty rather than consider for one second the hundreds of others who you might have crushed during your half century of business dealings—any of whom might want to see you destroyed! Or the vision-vine people or assorted

shrinks you might have blabbed to in a freaking altered state! You bring
that insulting, brain-dead bottom-feeder into your bed and *into our home*
and then ask: 'What did I do?' I'd say don't make me sick, but it's too late
for that!"

"He-ey," Tawnee singsonged. "Are you, like, disssing me?"

"I know about the boy, Marion," Richard said quietly. "I've seen a picture."

(?)

These accusations were getting beyond weird. But Marion was through
defending herself to someone whom she'd implicitly trusted for decades.
She no longer had the strength. "Neither one of us knows shit, Richard. Or
we wouldn't be in this position."

And with that she slammed the door.

Xiocena was there to hustle her up the stairs, past Tawnee-of-the-Valley,
who ran back inside before her, and past her master bedroom, where, she
noted, the bed was thankfully made. Marion complied numbly as her
friend bathed, made up, and dressed her. She numbly complied as she was
led down the colonnaded corridor and grand staircase, past Richard, who
was on the phone in his office, and Tawnee, who was trying futilely to figure out how to work the remote in the media room. She was almost
numbly complying herself out the front door when she saw a cat in the act
of spraying the Rodin and froze in her tracks.

"It belongs to the *puta*," whispered Xiocena.

Marion had always been an animal lover. She'd nurtured a menagerie
of critters over the years, including an old lame thoroughbred she didn't
have the heart to put down who was currently residing in a Malibu
"assisted-living pasture" with round-the-clock veterinary care. The only
reason she didn't have a dog at the moment was that she was still mourn-
ing Wally, her seventeen-year-old Bouvier des Flandres who'd passed away
at the foot of her bed six months back. But the strain of the tragedy she was
undergoing and the sight of the wretched masseuse's pet invading the
sanctity of her home and defiling her possessions made her bloodthirsty
with rage, and she lunged to punt the cat across the room. Fortunately, the
cat was faster than she was and Xiocena had opened the front door. Marion could only look at her shaken friend in self-ashamed disbelief.

Maybe Richard's right. Maybe I am going crazy.

50

Gods with Goods

"Tell me about the one on page four," Aristotle Papadopoulos said into the phone, folding the catalog and scooting his glasses down to the tip of his aquiline nose to get a closer look at the photograph.

Most of the statues in the catalog that Mariah had sent to him looked pretty much the same. He wasn't married to any particular period, material, subject or artisan, relying instead on instinct to guide him in his choice of the perfect statue for his endless lawn. Forty minutes earlier, his instincts had led him to settle on a fairly large form on page five, but he wasn't quite ready to cease savoring the sound of Mariah's velvety voice—so he'd been stalling by asking for information on every statue in the catalog that still possessed its head.

"That one too is Archaic period, Mr. Papadopoulos . . ."

"Ah! What did I tell you to call me?"

"I mean *Aristotle*. Archaic period because of the rigid stance, blank stare, and it's another kouros. We approximate the date of its creation as late fifth century B.C. due to the type of garment and limestone material. It is two and a half meters tall—"

"So am I."

Mariah laughed and Ari felt as if birds' wings had suddenly grazed the back of his skull. *So soft. So musical. He could go on listening like this forever.*

"Note the mannequin-like quality of the limbs and how at this time the Greeks had not yet developed . . ."

Ari looked at a torn paper towel on his desk on which Pepper had scratched down an address for him, and frowned.

Why had he allowed his wife to commit him to doing *her* job of collecting their daughter from a playdate? He'd have to end this phone pleasure too soon.

And why had he allowed her to commit him to an evening of misery, trapped at a table with, and subjected to the pretentious babblings of, her girlfriends? She'd decided both playdate and dinner party without consulting him.

His wife had stolen his time.

Yes, he loved Maybelle, and yes, Billy Price, who was hosting the dinner party, was his friend, but he saw the child daily and he and Billy ran into each other twice a week, attending other activities arranged by their wives. Also, without consultation. From now on, Ari vowed, he would refuse such wastes of time.

A man must determine his fate!

"Do you want to know about any other statues with heads?" Mariah asked.

"I beg your pardon?"

"Heads, Aristotle. You only wish to hear descriptions of the pieces with intact heads. Is that your prerequisite or are you simply having some fun?"

"Both," Ari chuckled. "I'm enjoying your knowledge. And your voice."

Again Mariah laughed. An American woman might admonish him for his blatant flirting, but Mariah found his compliments flattering. "I apologize and will not waste your time anymore."

"You are *never* a waste of my time," Ari replied smoothly. "I am very interested in the piece on page five. In fact, it calls out to me. What is the price?"

"A price can never be quoted without a prior viewing. Shall we arrange to meet at my company's warehouse?"

Should he? Why not?

"Ah, yes. That would be good. But we shall have to wait until Monday, and make the arrangement through my secretary. She grows claws if I mess with her schedule."

"Of course; I understand. Since I cannot, ah, satisfy your desires at this moment, will you settle for a verbal description of the statue?"

"Oh, yes. Tell me more!"

"The statue represents a river god—a *potami*, as they are called. So you'll need to keep it wet."

"I can do that," Ari breathed. "A wet fountain would be nice."

"It is a statue of Baphyras, a god of Pieria in the north." Maria began to giggle.

Oh! Oh, my goodness!

Ari's head began to tingle.

He had to end the call too soon since Maybelle's pickup time was nearing. Ari crunched Pepper's scribbled address information into his pocket and took the catalog with him on his way to the car. He wanted to hold the picture up against his lawn to see if it belonged there.

Outside, in the driveway Ari tucked the footless Barbie he was carrying into his back pocket and wedged Maybelle's Disney Princesses car cup under his arm. He held up the catalog, and gazing upon it, he smiled. The little minx had left out a key feature in her description of the statue. It was a feature that reaffirmed his wish to place it in his fountain, a feature that would send a strong visual message to his wife when she happened to pass by the river god.

Not only was Baphyras's head fully intact, but he also possessed a fully intact and generously proportioned set of male genitals.

Ari got in the driver's seat of his car and smiled.

Things were going to change.

51

Hard on the Knees

Before she had a driver, Marion used to relish cruising along the stretch of Sunset Boulevard between South Mapleton and Baroda on days with light traffic. Here, the street opened up and banked like a racetrack, giving a rare opportunity to Angelinos who drove cars designed for autobahn use to drive them as they were intended to be driven. But even though the traffic was sparse, she blew through the turn without joy. She was too occupied being pissed off and contemplating her body and comparing it to Tawnee's.

Marion had awakened anticipating a spa day. What she got was a shit-smelling, bush-sticking, husband-and-slut-encountering, cubist-faced-psycho-friend-pissed-off-plastic-surgeon-threatening-to-never-treat-her-again day.

Patti had been a nightmare at David Thayer's. It was bad enough giving the poor doctor the ol' switcheroo, but then Patti'd had the nerve to try to hustle extra procedures (like ear-pierce-hole reductions and eyelash implants) before David even started in on her chin. When David caught Patti perusing his confidential patient files, Marion thought she wouldn't escape with her life. Instead, she escaped with twenty-four hours to either convince the Riviera Country Club to allow David to drill a well on his adjoining Pacific Palisades property that tapped into their aquifer . . . or face life without David's laser.

That meant she had to get hold of eight board members she barely knew whose maids wouldn't give out the number of their second homes in Montecito and Malibu because they wanted to spend their weekends undisturbed. That meant she'd need to twist the arms of linking contacts in her *Black Book*. That meant she had to go back to the compound.

And you-know-who-wears-short-shorts would be there.

In her house.

And that pissed Marion off.

She was almost as pissed off as she'd been when David Thayer agreed to drive Patti home. She'd wasted her entire awful spa-deprived day waiting for Patti in that office. She'd read every pamphlet on every procedure David Thayer was licensed to perform.

And it was that that had made her contemplate her body—and compare it to Tawnee's—which wasn't a good thing to do when she was pissed off and driving and blowing through turns without joy.

By the time Marion was waiting for the Benedict Canyon light to change, pissed off and contemplating her body and comparing it to Tawnee's, she'd decided the only physical area where Tawnee had her beat was the knees. Marion had always been sensitive about her knees. They'd been so chubby in her chubby youth that when she'd lost the weight in her early twenties, the skin on her knees had never snapped back.

They had a baby-fat fold. Just inside the thigh. It formed every time she sat on her heels.

As Marion turned up her street, pissed off and contemplating her body and comparing it to Tawnee's, she thought about a pamphlet she'd read while wasting her spa-deprived day waiting for Patti Fink. It described a procedure that would pull up her leg skin the same way as you pulled up a stocking. It was probably painful, but squatting as she was under David's fluorescent waiting-room lights, it looked absolutely necessary.

Now, as she drove through the Zane compound gates and up the driveway, the fading afternoon light seemed kinder and she straightened and tensed her left leg to take another look.

So as she pulled up to the Zane mansion, pissed off and contemplating her body and comparing it to Tawnee's and looking at the skin above the knee on her extended left leg, Marion didn't see Tawnee, directly in her path, squatting (without a baby-fat fold), trying to pull her cat out from under a bush.

And Tawnee never saw what hit her.

52

Mad Friends and Englishmen

Her guests were due any second and Claire was frozen in her foyer, trying to make a decision. She couldn't decide which looked worse, her dining room or her face.

After viewing her four-hundred-plus picture gallery on WireImage, Craig-the-stylist determined that Claire's only impediment in her campaign to make the cover of *Town & Country* was her mouth. Since she'd always felt just the tiniest bit thin-lipped (and was shelling out twenty thousand a month for supposedly the best magazine-cover-grabbing publicist west of the Rockies), Claire took this observation as valid and allowed Craig to call her dermatologist and make arrangements. Problem was, she'd never had lip augmentation before.

When the dermatologist called and asked if she'd mind if he pushed the follow-up appointment on her procedure to Saturday, she'd innocently agreed. Now she looked like a rubber ducky. Make that a *battered* rubber ducky, because the bruises were getting darker by the second. If she tried to cover them with concealer, it globbed up in the corners, turning her into something that resembled a battered rubber ducky *with rabies,* so she was forced to settle for looking like a *transvestite* rubber ducky because after twenty trial-and-error tests, her "electroshock crimson" lipstick turned out to be the only shade intense enough to cover the purple. And it really didn't go with the baby-blue jumpsuit Craig had selected for her hostess frock. She looked like a bad flavor of bubble gum. Oh, well. The important thing was that Billy didn't mind.

Claire thought he would be as appalled as she was with her appearance, but when she crept into his office to face the music and reveal her monstrous self, he just said, "Cute jumpsuit, Cookie, gimme a smooch." And then he ran off to see dailies.

The kiss really hurt her lips.

Billy also didn't mind that Lamare le Quinne had turned their dining room into something Björk might see if she took ten tabs of acid. Claire's Chippendale set had been replaced by silver-coated horn things called "antler thrones" and a table that was made out of giant crystals.

What was it with rich people and crystals, anyway?

And she could still smell the industrial glue used to stick the shattered mirror collage on the ceiling. The daggerlike shards frightened her. Billy never even commented on the change in decor. When he was on the phone as he walked into the dining room, he didn't even pull off his earpiece. He just gave her a thumbs-up and continued arguing about nonunion crews.

Thinking about it now, Claire realized Billy didn't mind what she did or how much she spent. He gave in to her every whim, including the crazy-expensive Luchese lapis lazuli plates Craig had purchased for the evening. Personally, Claire was worried about how Patti's English colonial-exotic menu of poi Yorkshire pudding and rare roast beef with pineapple relish would look against an electric-blue background that cost six thousand dollars a table setting. Wasn't that too much? She almost discussed it with Geoffre-the-chef, but when she peeked into her kitchen and saw him covering one nostril with a finger and blowing the other into the sink, she decided not to disturb him.

All the Billy-not-minding made Claire wonder if her husband was on drugs. And assuming he was, wonder where he kept them. Then she remembered that there were two things that always trumped her with Billy: work and his ex-wife. Claire remembered this at the moment because Billy was still viewing dailies at the studio, and even though her stepdaughters were on a school camp-out, Billy's ex was having a "stressful" week and "couldn't take the demands" of her bichon frise, so the dog was currently barfing on Claire's foyer floor. Tossing the dog into the kitchen, Claire ran back to the foyer to clean up its mess. She was taking Spanish lessons in the hope of being able to converse with her staff, but it turned out that her maid was Sri Lankan, so she still couldn't tell her what to do.

Claire was on her knees wiping up bichon barf when the unlocked front door opened and Lord and Lady Dutton entered her home.

"Good evening," said Lord Dutton. "Could you tell your mistress her company has arrived?"

One hour later, both Zanes and Wallerts had canceled and she and the Duttons were still a threesome in the living room. As she watched her guest of honor, who, having already wiped out the scotch, had now been inspired to entertain by reciting dirty poems at the top of his lungs, Claire made a mental note to remember to invite future wealthy guests to arrive an hour earlier than required. Lady Dutton was obliviously reading a coffee-table book since she'd exhausted all conversation with Claire, who neither rode nor played golf.

Meanwhile, Geoffre-the-chef was getting out-and-out nasty about stalling his dinner and sharing space with a small puking dog. When Claire had peeked into the kitchen to check on him, he'd let loose with a lecture about sanitation that was so demeaning it prompted Claire into a "pot and kettle" reply. Looking back, she realized she'd have to work on her timing, since the fourth round of hors d'oeuvres consisted of brown bone-shaped crunchy pieces of stuff bearing a striking resemblance to the bichon's kibble with the addition of a glutinous sauce that was too scary to think about. Good thing her guests of honor were bombed.

"Look what I found on the front porch!" she suddenly heard.

Thank goodness Billy was back! He was pushing Lou's wheelchair and was—oh, thank the Lord—followed by the rest of her guests. Now her first Secret Rainbow Princess (with step kids) Fancy Dinner party was back on track.

But instead of sitting down with Lord and Lady Dutton, Billy, Ari, Tom, and Lou rolled right through the living room and into the den to watch the playoffs with barely a "Hi, we'll just be a minute." At least her new girlfriends were picking up the slack.

"Your lordship," Patti purred to Lord Dutton as she curtsied deep enough to pop an areola edge out of her Zac Posen strapless sheath.

Instead of being seduced, the old actor was inspired to intone, "There once was a harlot from Stussy, who blew the trombone with her . . ."

Aubrey Dutton was an instant hit.

"That accent is familiar. Where are you from originally, my dear?" Lady Dutton asked Pepper.

"Kentucky, yer ladyship, just outside a' Louisville," Pepper replied.

"Marvelous! Racing or hounds?"

"Both! Half m' brothers were NASCAR pits an' we raised Cattahula leopards an' redbones."

"Excuse me?" Lady Dutton looked perplexed.

Maya, who already knew the Duttons, immediately raced to the bar to hide the rest of the booze.

Patti didn't give a shit about meeting Lady Dutton and, instead of chatting her up, dragged her hostess into the dining room to see where she'd be sitting. When Claire pointed out her place card, Patti gasped in horror and grabbed the heavy lapis lazuli charger so fast that both areolas raised their heads from her dress in protest.

"But I put you next to Aubrey!" Claire began, in confusion.

"You don't understand. These plates are *Luchese*!"

"Too blue?"

"Too *traumatic*," Patti said, knocking over a wineglass and reaching for another one. "Last summer Lady Dutton walked into her back house in Marbella and caught her son and Flavio Luchese in bed."

"Oh, my gosh, I didn't know!" squealed Claire, instantly joining Patti in plate pulling. "I didn't know Luchese seduced her son!"

"No, her *son* seduced Luchese . . . and convinced him to leave three kids and a wife. We're removing these because Lady Dutton loved her bichon more than heaven and earth!"

Now Claire stopped pulling. Something was wrong here.

"The bichon loved hanging out in that back house," Patti offered.

Now Claire started putting the plate back down where it had been.

"When Lady Dutton walked in on them, her son and Luchese rolled right off the bed and squashed her poor bichon flat. She had to be sedated for two weeks, so unless you have some Thorazine on hand . . ."

Claire rejoined Patti in hefting chargers.

By the time they'd yanked them all, Patti's dress was hiked up around her waist and Claire's jumpsuit was ripped at the pits. That's when Maya and Pepper sneaked in.

"Oh, Patti! Not a repeat of the Clinton table dance!" Pepper scolded. "I didn't get to eat for two hours that night!"

"The plates are *Luchese!*" Patti said, pushing into the kitchen with the entire stack of chargers.

"Oh, yes. The squashed dog," recalled Maya, over the shrieks of the chef.

"Who's with the Duttons?" asked Claire, growing panicky. "You guys didn't leave them alone?!"

"No, a' course not," said Pepper. "Lou's way ahead a' the point spread, so he came back in the livin' room. Everythin's fine."

"Which set do you use instead?" asked Maya, and was answered by tremendous crashing sounds in the kitchen.

Claire wanted to go to see what happened but was frightened that she'd only incite more scary food.

"We can't use the dishes in the kitchen cabinets," answered Patti, returning redressed. "They smashed too, when Geoffre got burned."

"I don't have any other sets!" cried Claire, on the verge of hysteria. "I've got nothing at all!"

"How 'bout finger food?" offered Pepper, who was starving. "First yer Yorkshire puddin', then some beef and the relish on top. He could fry the whole thing up, just like Taco Bell."

Now Claire was openly weeping and six hands with napkins reached out to catch the tears, to prevent mascara run.

"English colonial exotic!" trilled Patti. "Remember? Who needs plates in the tropics? We duck out in the garden and grab the biggest leaves we see. The Duttons will think you're clever and be absolutely charmed."

"The English are always charmed by wacky shit," offered Maya. "Come, we all help."

Billy, Ari, and Tom returned from the den because their team had lost and were able to prevent Lord Dutton from removing all his clothes while his wife forced poor Lou to digest her views on the "downfall of decency" in today's golfing world. It was then that Ari looked up to find his wife's naked rear end mashing up against the picture window behind Lady Dutton's head.

"I've always thought golf was a sport for folks who weren't good enough to play anything else," offered Lou, before dozing off.

Outside, as Pepper angled for more leaves, Claire felt a sting on her eye and flicked off a garden spider the size of a marble. It flicked onto Patti and all of them screamed.

It was then that the chef stomped into the living room, cradling his arm in an ice pack, and announced, "Come eat this swill before it congeals!"

Which was Geoffre's way of saying that he'd burned the beef and added a sauce. And that dinner was served.

At first Patti's assessment proved to be right—the Duttons were charmed by the leaf plates. But then Geoffre-the-chef's sauce started dripping like hot wax onto everyone's laps.

Just as Claire's eye was beginning to close from the sting and she was wondering if Billy would let her keep her shoes after the divorce, she noticed Lady Dutton lift up her blouse and give her stomach a good scratching. She'd never seen such bad table manners and her heart swelled with hope. Maybe the evening wasn't lost after all. Maybe the English weren't as stuffy as they were reputed to be.

"Maybe you're allergic to sycamore," Patti suggested as she watched the woman squirm.

Lady Dutton charged into the kitchen to "flush out her eyes" and came face-to-face with Billy's ex's bichon eating off a Luchese plate a meal that looked to be identical to the one she had just consumed. She fainted dead away on the spot.

Sometime later, as the ambulance howled away with their guest of honor safely stowed inside, Claire and Billy faced each other on the porch of their home.

"Oh, Billy," she blubbered as her Princess Promise crumbled and turned into dust. "I've ruined the evening, and worse, let you down! I'm just not cut out to be a wife of this caliber and I don't blame you if you want to—"

"What are you talking about, Cookie? It went perfect," he said, "Everything exactly as planned."

"*Planned?* But I thought Lord Dutton was very important to your movie. I thought the studio demanded that you cast him."

Then Billy put a finger over her lips, which nearly caused her to howl in pain, and explained. "Right, the studio wanted Dutton, not me. The old fart ate up one-third of my casting budget and didn't do squat for the box. Who cares about Oscars when I can cast a cheap popular guy from TV and add the savings to the budget to use for effects!"

"Could you go back to the 'planned' part, please?" Claire asked timidly.

"Ahh, Cookie! Everybody knows first dinner parties are nightmares. I was counting on your freaking them out. Nigel was the one who suggested it."

Claire frowned. "That nice man who's your production manager?"

"You served him corn pudding last week. C'mon in so we can get some ice on that shiner before I go back to dailies." Billy put his arm around her and walked her to the kitchen, but then his phone rang and Patti wandered in.

"Last-to-leave-or-asked-to-leave," Patti singsonged buoyantly as she put a cold washcloth over Claire's puffed-out eye. "Can I borrow your bride for a second?" she asked Billy.

"Sure, I don't mind."

"He never does," whispered Claire.

Patti pumped a fist in the air. "I just got off the phone with Marion and we both agree: your first official dinner party was a smashing success!"

Claire wanted to ask Patti Fink if she ever saw the White Rabbit and if she ever played croquet with the Queen of Hearts. She wanted to ask her if losing your opinions and your mind was mandatory to survival in this Looking-Glass world they seemed to be living in. But then Claire would have to ask herself if she really wanted to stay here. And she wasn't ready to do that.

So she just answered, "Really?"

"You bet your Gaultier it was!" Patti crowed. "You've given us all something to talk about for weeks!"

53

Bad Pussy!

"Human growth hormone? Well, Richard, first of all, it is pretty controversial, but there's no definitive proof that it has any adverse effects. There's all sorts of factors that have to be taken into consideration that can only be determined with a blood test. So you'd need a blood workup first. It might not be a bad idea if it turns out that your own level's progressively lowering and you're losing muscle mass. It can improve skin thickness but don't expect miracles. And muscle repair and production. You'd have to get a full-body MRI-type scan. Some alternative practitioners use it to stave off menopause, but it's mostly used with the elderly. I can send you the literature—"

"But can it cause changes in mood, or aggression? Like steroids?" Richard asked.

"Oh, no. Nothing like that. If anything, there's an endorphin link with the muscle-exercise—"

"Nothing like changing a person into a totally different person? Can it cause someone to act irrationally and do something they don't remember later?"

"Even steroids don't do *that*. No. It sounds like your friend has advanced schizophrenia. Or multiple-personality disorder. You'd have to talk to a psychiatrist and get your friend's chemistry changed with drugs I could list but I'm not authorized to prescribe. Would you like a recommendation?"

"No thanks. You've, um, unfortunately, answered my questions, thanks."

"Anytime, Richard. And I'm sorry for your friend."

"Me too. Bye, Patti."

Richard hung up and sat back at his desk but kept his hand on the phone. He wanted to involve as few doctors in this decision as possible.

Who needed doctors when his wife's friend was a walking PDR? And crazy enough not to make any connections.

"Ri-chie!" blasted Tawnee's whiny voice over the speaker. "It'sss time to change my ow-ie! Could you come up and hold my hand?"

And then there was the mess upstairs.

"Be there in a minute!" Richard rubbed his hands over his face.

He now knew why he'd always hated cats.

All Richard had wanted was to hurt Marion the same way she'd hurt him, and Tawnee had played her part perfectly (even though she was so annoying and unattractive he couldn't perform).

But the deal was that she was only supposed to play the part *one time*.

Without her fucking pet.

He'd known he was in trouble when Tawnee brought the cat carrier into his bedroom, Wednesday night. He should have made her keep it down at the gate. Then she'd let the creature out to shit in his bathroom on Thursday morning, which just happened to be the exact same time Marion was approaching the guesthouse. While Tawnee and his wife had a catfight, he was locked away in the bedroom fighting cat spray. He missed the entire exchange! He knew he shouldn't have thrown the damn cat out the window, but who the hell could blame him?

After that, Tawnee had an excuse to come back: she had to find her lost pet. And come back again and again. His fucking ears were ringing with her whiny "He-ere, pusssycaaat! Like, where are you, pusssycaaat? Baaad pusssycaaat!" When she showed up to search on Saturday morning, Richard had Charlie all prepared with a lie about seeing the cat get whisked off by an owl, when lo and behold, the fucking thing walked out of the bushes! Richard had tackled the cat like an Oakland Raiders lineman.

Then Marion showed up at the gate. Like a bag lady.

And he got the bright idea to hurt his wife all over again.

(Which was as bright as having one more drink for the road or one more jump even though the bungee cord looks frayed.)

When Charlie told him Marion was coming in, he'd thrown his shirt on Tawnee and hustled her and her cat into the house. The whole time she was changing, the little slut was busy trying to renegotiate a second rendezvous.

Then Marion let the cat out again.

And Tawnee started whining and searching again.

Then Frank Greene had called whimpering about NFS & etc. and Richard had had to spend the rest of the day trying to calm the lawyer down. With Tawnee whining and searching in the background.

Next thing he knew, Marion's car hit Tawnee in the driveway.

Because Tawnee was looking for her fucking cat.

She was lucky it was Marion who knocked her into the bushes and not him.

At least the cat got crushed.

And Marion wasn't hurt.

Also lucky: Tawnee only had a broken ankle, bruising, and a couple of patches of missing skin.

The last thing he wanted was more scandals.

It was bad enough that they'd run into Lyndy Wallert in the emergency room. Even though she'd helped get the beat-up masseuse hooked up with the ortho-guy and the plastic surgeon, he didn't trust her. When it came to gossip, that old bitch was a friggin' bullhorn. He wasn't sure she'd swallowed their story that Tawnee was an indoor-plant caretaker who'd had a fall.

He'd been naive enough to think that with the extra compensation and plastic, Tawnee'd be satisfied.

But when she'd heard her cat was now toast, she'd made a *huge* fuss about how much she "missed" her "poor pusssy" and "couldn't bear that it, like, died for a lie!" She started threatening to get a lawyer and go to the police. He couldn't complicate the nightmare with his wife. He needed to take care of that before anything else.

So he'd brought Tawnee back to his house.

Another bright idea.

He'd thought he was keeping her quiet by giving her good care while she was suffering.

But the minute she moved into his bedroom, she forgot all about the cat and started flirting. For God's sake, the girl was currently missing the underside of her chin!

And then she got a text message from her *sister wanting to know what Tawnee did with her cat and when she was going to bring him back.*

It was then that Richard realized that the pussy had been no more than a prop.

Tawnee didn't want compensation money. What she wanted was to play her part for real! She wanted to be his friggin' girlfriend, with all the perks that went with it! And he'd given her the tools to commit blackmail!

So here he was, stuck keeping the freaking scumbag on ice and keeping her happy until he could think of a way to get rid of her.

"Ri-chie! My ow-ie!" he heard her whine again.

Jesus, like fingernails on a blackboard!

"Yeah, yeah. Be right up!" he replied, trying not to moan.

First things first.

Richard punched the speed dial for Frank Greene's cell. At least the accident gave them the leverage they needed with Marion, thank the Lord. For a minute he'd thought those fucking NFS ninjas had him by the balls. Okay, they actually did. But at least he could stall.

"Yes, Richard?" Frank said.

"You were right. It's not the hormones. Go ahead with the judge and the shrink."

"Good. Now my ulcer can stop bleeding."

Richard hung up and took a look around the magnificent walnut-paneled room that his formerly magnificent wife had created for him. He imagined his Marion in better times, sitting on the edge of his desk peering at photos through a loupe and how she'd made him stop working to decide on a Christmas picture and how they'd laughed so hard together trying to find the least dorky photo on her proof sheet and how they'd ended up clearing the desk to make love.

He grieved for both of them.

"Ri-chie! The nurssse sssaid I really need to change the dresssing on thisss skin graft! It's oo-zing! I neeeed yooou!"

Ugh!

Richard dragged himself to his feet. He'd thought allowing Tawnee to redecorate the bedroom would keep her happy and out of his hair. He needed to tie up her tiny mind while she was laid up or he was liable to put a pillow over her face. Maybe he'd tell her to redecorate the bedroom suite.

That always kept women busy. All he needed was a couple of more days . . .

As he trudged across the conservatory and up the grand staircase, two thoughts played over and over in the mind of Richard Zane.

One: *Barry Shapiro had been right, he should never have called Tawnee.*

Two: *Tawnee's cat was black.*

54

Who's Crazy Now?

A s Carl pulled the hybrid Lexus up to Fox Plaza on Avenue of the Stars, Marion knocked back a couple more Advil (to stamp out her now-daily happy-hour hangover) and checked her makeup for the hundredth time. And for the hundredth time, she sighed like a schoolgirl.

Richard wanted to reconcile!

There could be no other reason for the meeting at Frank Greene's. Horton Newberg had told her Richard had an offer for her. And he'd told her it was "good news."

Marion knew it was abominable to gloat over another human being's physical harm and she really was horrified she'd injured the little moron and killed her spraying cat, but just the same, if the Lexus had had more headroom, she'd be Cabbage-Patching right now.

The accident accidentally called Richard's bluff.

After she'd banked off of squatting Tawnee-of-the-Valley and knocked over a perfectly good yew, Richard had come running to *her* side first, yelling, "Marion! Oh, my God! Honey, are you okay?"

Not exactly the words of a guy who wanted a divorce. Seeing his wife smooshed behind an air bag must have shaken some sense into him.

The whole time Tawnee was lying in the garden bed, yowling about her ankle, Richard was tenderly reaching into the Lexus, checking Marion's neck and looking into her pupils to see if she had a concussion. He never once looked back at his banged-up slut. Not until her seal-like keening started to aggravate his ears. Then he'd promptly told Charlie to put

Tawnee in the extra Prius for her ride to the emergency room. He didn't even try to lift that heavy torso and hips. And he obviously didn't want her blood on his Ferrari.

That meant there was more than hope.

As she watched her bust jiggle—the right-side Lexus backseat was fully extended and the massage controls were set on shiatsu—Marion wondered if the low-cut emerald stretch-satin Dolce back-lacing dress under her black felt Celine swing coat was too tarty for an attorney's office. Then again, who cared? The lawyers were so focused on the money, they probably wouldn't even notice, and, more important, the dress drove Richard wild. She was even wearing the little ankle bracelet with the emerald four-leaf clover he gave her after she'd given him a particularly hard orgasm. An orgasm that made him wax so expansive he leveraged the Irvine development and bought two blocks of depressed downtown Palm Canyon Drive in Palm Springs just before the Gay Renaissance that eventually turned it into square-footage gold.

If that memory didn't seduce him, nothing would.

Carl opened her door, wished her good luck, and Marion started strutting toward the South Tower and her reconciled marriage.

"We are the champions, we are the champions! No time for losers 'cause we are the champions of the worrrrld!"

At first, Marion didn't recognize the song Pepper had programmed into her BlackBerry (after she'd learned that Marion was bulletproof, thanks to long-retained attorneys contracted at 5 percent of her monetary award). When she did recognize it, she snapped open her Fendi clutch and saw that it was Patti Fink on the line.

Patti'd been so sweet to send all the apology and thank-you notes and chocolates and roses and CDs and bracelets and purses and furs to the bungalow this morning to make up for the deprived-spa day. But seventeen calls were enough. Marion loved her loony friend but she had to set limits.

"Honey, I can't talk. I'm entering a war zone to commence for peace talks."

"Then you really need to hear what I say!"

Patti sounded frantic. More frantic than usual.

"Okay, tell. But make it quick."

Aaaaand over the falls!

"Okay, I got this phone call yesterday, and at first, I didn't think anything of it and the hectic around here was off the map with my closet plans being stalled and Kyle's arrest—"

"There's Barry Shapiro!" Marion interrupted. "I gotta go."

"I know, and then there was a big row because Alexandra, the gardener's niece, had her bas mitzvah scheduled for the same day as Berta's horse show and—"

"I thought you said the family was Honduran."

"I took her to Kabala," continued Patti seamlessly, "and she made friends and went to some of her new friends' bas mitzvahs and decided to convert and since she was the right age to have a—"

"I thought you said she was sixteen."

And I thought I was setting limits.

"No, that was *Alejandra,* the poor girl who lost her mother under thousands of tons of—"

"—mudslide. Right. Patti, I mean it. I'm fifty steps from the building—"

"I'm talking about *Alexandra,*" continued Patti. "She's thirteen, her mother is the *other* gardener's sister, and this morning, when Lou's mother wanted lamb chops for breakfast—"

"Not Lou's *real* mother! She'd have to be a hundred and two!"

"Five, actually. She's staying with us overnight before her flight to Hawaii, and talk about demanding! Anyway, so I didn't have time to really think about the phone call. But then I did have time to think about it, and when I thought about it, I thought I should tell you that Richard called me."

"He did? What was the call about?" Marion asked, slowing down.

"Oh, at first it was hormones and then steroids and then aggression and then advanced schizophrenia, where somebody changes—"

Marion sped up again. "Patti, I'm entering the building. Last chance: Why are you telling me about Richard's call?"

"Because he said he was calling for a friend, but when things died down and I got a chance to think about it, I realized he never calls for friends. *You* always make those kind of calls even for *his* friends, so maybe it wasn't a friend, maybe it was somebody else. Maybe all this stuff he was asking about for a friend was really for—"

The line suddenly cut off. "Patti?"

At least the South Tower had set limits for her.

As Marion headed happily for the bank of high-speed elevators, she was glad to have been cut off from her crazy friend's call.

And she wondered why her arm was shaking.

55

Skeleton Warfare

When Marion walked into the conference room and beheld all three senior NFS & etc. partners, a stenographer, Frank Greene, Frank Greene's associate, and her husband, her heart grew wide and warm and ripe. It sprouted out of her back and formed feathery coral-gold wings to carry her across the conference table into Richard's arms.

When she turned and saw Judge Elijah Volker and a man who looked like a Mr.-Rogers-may-his-better-than-ours-soul-rest-in-peace wannabe, her heart retracted back through her spine, flopped out of her mouth, and crumpled uselessly at her feet like a pair of old panty hose with runs.

Marion knew the added attendants would never be present at a reconciliation and her first thought was:

I could have worn H&M.

Her second was:

I am totally and utterly betrayed, and perhaps not so bulletproof either.

Her third was:

I am on my own.

And her fourth thought was:

Frank Greene had his neck done.

Marion thought this last thought because she'd entered a kind of limbo-like non-feeling state. Switching gears from basking-in-love to shock-horror to fighting-for-survival required several chemical changes and brain lobe leaps that took a few nanoseconds to complete. Fortunately, the yip hit during the transition from shock-horror to fighting, so she barely felt it—right about the time Richard said:

"Lying was the only way we could get you in here."

Almost all of the men in the room leaped to their feet to offer Marion a chair. Simon Sacks didn't. After fifty years of being in similar circumstances, he preferred to make sure he kept the use of his limbs and remained in his seat, a safe seven feet away.

"Marion, I want to extend my deepest apologies for the unexpected nature of our gathering," the senior-est NFS & etc. partner began. "But I want to assure you that we only have your best interests at heart—"

"Save the bullshit fawning for the next wife you sell out, old man," Marion replied, efficiently kicking two chairs away and jerking a third into the vacated space so she could sit alone. Dodging the chairs, Horton Newberg lost a cuff link and Frank Greene incurred a nasty coffee burn when he knocked over his own cup.

Marion had switched gears.

She'd become the most dangerous beast in the animal kingdom: a wounded, Stage III Trophy. When cornered, Stage IIIs experience heightened long-term memory—for every single *skeleton* they've ever read, heard, overheard, intuited, suspected, or stolen from the brains of other humans by means of alien mind melding.

In this state, there were no yips.

Around the table there rose a ruffling of "No!"s and "Ow!"s and one "We would never!" But Richard's voice spoke loudest.

"No Marion," it said. "We're not selling you out. It's an *intervention*."

"Intervention?" she asked evenly, removing her coat and licking the tip of an eyetooth. "To hear that coming from a man who can't miss a bowel movement without diving into a bucket of beta-blockers, Xanax, and scotch—"

"Not that kind of intervention, Mrs. Zane," said Frank Greene, taking over. "An intervention for your mental health."

After several more chemical changes, lobe leapings, and gear grindings—plus a brief self-promise to always let Patti Fink finish a story no matter how twisted and tortured her thought path—Marion turned to Frank Greene. The smell of his fear caused her nostrils to flare. "Pray, Frank, Go on."

"Well," said Frank Greene, who'd instinctively braced himself for a blow. "At this point, we thought Dr. Levinson should speak."

Levinson? As in "David Levinson, the Shrink to the Stars"? As in "the Levinson Clinic"?

Marion's left lobe seized the name and flung it into the fangs of her heightened long-term memory, which responded with voracious tearing and cutting until it was fully digested and ready to be expelled. In this state of mind, she had no need of her *Black Book*.

"Hello, Marion," said the man who looked like a Mr.-Rogers-may-his-better-than-ours-soul-rest-in-peace wannabe but was really Dr. Levinson. "I imagine you're feeling pretty bad about your husband's infidelity."

Marion turned toward Dr. Levinson and cocked her head like a raptor. "Almost as bad as you should have felt when you defaulted on the mortgage for your second facility and left your investors in the lurch," she replied with preternatural calmness.

The doctor was good. He dropped his pen to cover his shock. "Let it show in the record," he said, sitting up, "that Mrs. Zane has confused me with somebody else—"

"Are you saying you're *not* Dr. David Levinson, the psychiatrist who's treated three wives, one mistress, seven children, and assorted in-laws of the people in this room and, of course, the people in this room themselves? Are you ready to cut the crap, clinic boy, or shall I get more specific?"

Marion's brief monologue instigated a general outraged group uproar aimed at both her and the aghast psychiatrist along with an "I warned you she gets like this!" disclaimer from Richard.

During the fray, Marion locked eyes with Dr. Levinson. (To this day, Bucky Fligstein swears he saw her shoulder muscles bunch.)

"You wanna dance?" she growled. "Let's see whatcha got."

When Dr. Levinson blinked, Marion knew she could take him.

"Hostile sexual harassment through printed libel—" he began.

"And the cheat sheet confirmed it?" Marion riposted.

"Sexual harassment over the phone—"

"Lost the phone. At least one witness to the loss."

"Attempted suicide—"

"I love nudity when admiring a view. Who saw me?" she asked archly.

"Your north-side neighbor."

"The OxyContin abuser? Assuming motivation is hearsay, and you know it."

Then Marion turned to the NFS & etc. senior partners. "Feel free to cut in, boys, if you're getting bored."

"Stalking with a deadly weapon—" Dr. Levinson was reading from a document now and looking increasing insecure.

"Pruning bushes, not stalking. Again, hearsay from a hostile spouse and a possible prostitute. She was on her own property," sang out Horton Newberg.

"—with a bleeding, disheveled appearance. Would you please let me finish?" Dr. Levinson sputtered.

"Injuries incurred during an altercation with a mastiff and extraction from noncompliant vegetation," countered Bucky Fligstein.

"Documented witnessed events. Did you think I wouldn't fill my guys in?" Marion snapped at his heels.

"Vehicular assault—" resumed Dr. Levinson.

"A prostrate prostitute—" began Simon Sacks.

"*Alleged* prostitute," interjected Frank Greene's associate.

"—who deliberately placed herself on a blind curve of the victim's own driveway in order to fabricate an accident. Piffling accusations at best!" Simon Sacks gleefully shouted him down.

"You didn't even mention her affair with—" cried Richard, before Frank Greene promptly clapped a hand over his mouth.

"Careful, Richard. You wouldn't want to open yourself for harassment with a phony-baloney private detective. 'Dr. Watson'? How original!" snorted Marion, without breaking eye contact with Dr. Levinson.

"Strike that from the record," Frank Greene said to the stenographer.

"Yes, by all means, *invent* what we say," added Marion.

"Excuse me!" shouted Dr. Levinson, eager to finish his reading. "The overall conclusion these recent behaviors have led this psychiatrist to draw is that Marion Zane has become a danger to herself and others and requires immediate commitment to three months of rest and observation at the Levinson Clinic." When he was finished, Dr. Levinson laid the document down without breaking eye contact with Marion. "Marion, we're all in agreement on this—"

"Except Judge Volker, over there. Otherwise, the coward with the unfortunate selection of neckwear (because I wasn't there to check) across the table and his partners-in-bluff would have had me straitjacketed away by the men in white coats by now."

"Oh, yes. We shot that attempt down in a heartbeat," chirped Horton Newberg.

Marion leaped to her feet, simultaneously turning to face her attorneys and slamming her fists down on the tabletop. The jungle-cat velocity and force of this movement knocked everyone's beverages into their laps and propelled her chair to the side, where it shattered both Frank Greene's associate's class ring and the bones of his middle finger. (He'd foolishly relaxed an appendage on his unprotected armrest.)

"THEN WHY THE FUCK ARE YOU HERE?!" she roared.

"We were hoping you'd agree to a voluntary commitment," Simon Sacks said calmly, from his safe seven-foot-away seat.

No one noticed Frank Greene's associate yelp and stagger out of the conference room. They were too busy bracing for Marion's next reaction, which was aborted by Dr. Levinson's final attempt at rendering her docile.

"It's your highly irrational expenditures, Marion. One hundred thousand to the Home Shopping Network for dog collars, ten million pledged in scholarships to a certain 'Number One Bartending School,' twenty-five million to Keep a Kid—"

"A foundation with a notoriously fraudulent history! The guy who runs it just bought himself a hundred-thousand-acre ranch in Uruguay next door to Reverend Moon's and both ranches sit on top of the largest natural gas deposit in the whole of South America," Bucky Fligstein managed to babble, before Dr. Levinson silenced him with a look.

". . . Fifteen million pledged to prophet Sri Baba Dreyfus, one thousand scholarships pledged to Larry Hurla's How-to-Win-After-the-Bubble Real Estate Course—at three hundred dollars apiece—and a total of seven million dollars in various purchases ranging from weight-loss products to Add-a-Sparkle rhinestone inlaying kits."

"All over the past four nights. Made from your hotel room on your credit cards!" cried Horton Newberg.

"It's a clear psychic break with reality!" added Bucky Fligstein.

Old Simon Sacks was on his feet wringing his hands. "You're hemorrhaging money, woman! Over sixty million in four nights! We can cover your kooky behavior, but this spending is *crazy*! For God's sake, take a rest or there'll be nothing left!"

"Oh, sit down before you stroke out, Simon," snapped Marion, grabbing her purse.

"My diagnosis here would be a consumption addiction brought on by the discovery of her husband's affair—" began Dr. Levinson.

"And you shut up too!" Marion growled at the doctor as she picked up her coat. "I have no idea who made those calls in my name, but I know a frame when I see one, and even if I did have a problem, which I don't, I certainly wouldn't seek treatment in a—"

"Marion," said Richard quietly. "The Levinson Clinic is the most confidential—"

"—fishbowl of a nuthouse—"

"Delusional accusations. Stay with it, Richard, like we planned," Dr. Levinson nervously coached.

"Oh, yeah?" snarled Marion. "Then how come I know you're currently harboring two substance-abusing rock stars and an anorexic actress?"

Dr. Levinson froze for a half second in horror, then managed to produce a patronizing, dismissive shake of his head. "Let's stop talking of fantasy, Marion—"

"Derek Grimes, Kid Mars, and Melinda—"

"Stop!" Levinson looked like he might cry. "That's confidential information! How did you—"

"As I was saying, a fishbowl of a nuthouse with a man who's about to be charged with his third malpractice suit, this time stemming from Annette Resor's overdose—"

"How dare you. That's groundless . . ." Dr. Levinson, breaking into a blush that would put RuPaul to shame, leaped to his feet.

"Are the two suicides and mysterious underage pregnancy of—"

"Shut up! Shut her up!" the now red-faced doctor roared.

"Great choice, Frank," said Richard, now on *his* feet and restraining the irate psychiatrist before roughly handing him off to Frank Greene to be guided out. Once he was gone, Richard turned and faced his wife. "We'll find you a better place, Marion. But you've got to get help."

"Any fakakta clinic! Three little months. Lots of rest and relaxation. We'll be back on track, skinning Richard alive before you know it," cooed Simon Sacks, inciting a murderous look from Richard.

Marion-the-wounded-beast surveyed her wounded attacker and deemed its carcass unfit for consumption. "You're right Richard, I do need help . . ." she said quietly as she slipped on her coat. "Which is why I'm not going to spend another minute in this traitors' nest, taking crap. Good day, *gentle-men*."

"Then you leave me no choice," replied Richard as he crossed to the door. Before leaving, he looked at the judge. "She's all yours."

Marion whipped around to face the judge. In her fury, she'd momentarily forgotten he was there. "You must be joking."

"Unfortunately not," said Judge Volker, signing off on a document that he passed to Frank Greene, who pressed a button that summoned his secretary.

"You can't send me to a nuthouse. I'll hire new lawyers who'll fight it!"

"Nobody's sending you to a nuthouse, Marion." Volker sighed. "By the way, thanks for the help with Princeton."

"And *I'm* the one who indebted myself to half the eastern seaboard for your granddaughter, Eli. Richard didn't lift a finger."

Eli Volker was one of the finest, most honorable jurists in the state of California, and one of the finest men Marion knew. Even though it felt cheap, the college thing was the best ammunition she had and she'd had to use it.

"Believe me, I know. But until you stop your self-sabotaging, I'm going to rule you 'unfit to be in charge of your finances.' Just stay on a budget, get a shrink, and I'll rescind the order."

"B-budget?" The word caught in Marion's throat as the first yip hit her. "You're putting me on a budget?!"

"I'm not, your *trustee* is," said the judge quietly.

"Which one of these snakes did you pick?" whispered Marion, steadying herself against the table. "Don't tell me the trustee is Simon! His wife hasn't had new clothes since Reagan left office."

"No, *I'm* the trustee, Marion," announced Zephyr, entering the room like the deus ex machina in an old Greek play and delivering the death-blow to Marion-the-beast when she added: "Or, considering we're in a legal arena, shall I be more precise and call you 'Mom'?"

56

Regurgitating the Truth

Marion-the-dying-beast staggered back against the conference room's frosted-glass wall. Twenty-nine years before, she had staggered back in much the same way when her drunken father had slapped her upon learning that his sixteen-year-old daughter had been knocked up.

Mike was the first boy who'd ever kissed her. He was the first person who'd shown Marion *any* affection in as long as she could remember. Her father's drinking had driven her mother deeper into the Catholic Church and ever-growing criticism and judgments of her daughter. Marion never blamed her affection-starved teenage self for going all the way that night in Mike's backseat.

But her parents did. When Marion found out that her first crush had "screwed the blood-sausage-cootie-girl on a bet," she didn't know where else to turn, finally throwing herself on her parents' mercy. And they had thrown her out.

At least her mother had shown a small shred of humanity. As Marion numbly packed her meager belongings, Mrs. Mintz had pressed the address of a Catholic-run home for "girls in trouble" in Los Angeles, California, and eighty dollars into her hand. Marion could stay there and then give the baby up for adoption, returning home in time to help with the deli's holiday rush.

"Just say you're at a religious retreat," she whispered, literally keeping her distance.

Eighty dollars didn't even cover the bus ticket to Los Angeles, so Marion hitchhiked her way to the safe place of the gestating-girls-in-trouble home. The nuns were more progressive than the ones back in Cleveland; they only made her feel guilty for living a couple of times a day. So Marion felt a little sorry for slipping out the window that night and not staying until the morning, when they planned to give her week-old baby to their "fine Catholic" adoption candidates. But only a little and "a little" never stopped love.

The second she was born, Zephyr had taken Marion's needy heart prisoner. Nature had been merciful and she suffered no postpartum feelings of rejection, only a new kind of euphoric purpose and hope. She now had a reason for living far more uplifting than being future staff for her parents' deli.

She'd chosen the name "Zephyr" the night she'd snuck her out of the girls-in-trouble home during one of L.A.'s periodic Santa Anas or "devil winds"—the hot dry air that blew in off the desert periodically throughout the year. Though Santa Anas broiled the city oppressively during the day, at night they became warm zephyrs, making the normally chilly L.A. evenings delightful—a perfect metaphor for the effect the baby had had on Marion Mintz's heart.

Marion ran away to the apartment of a girl who'd left some months before. Michelle was a twenty-four-year-old adjuster for a large insurance company, having to travel often for her work and lonely for friends. Although Michelle didn't have room for a child in her personal life, she had room on her couch, and she allowed Marion and baby Zephyr to stay as long as it took to "get their shit together." (She had no idea that Marion Mintz was underage.)

Alone as she was in the tiny apartment, the first few months had been heaven for Marion, especially the morning she woke to be greeted by her baby's first smile of the day. She made a pittance running errands for the artist who lived downstairs, but it was enough to pay for the nursing baby's diapers and clothes, and Marion had few needs aside from the food she needed for healthy breast-feeding. Zephyr was so tiny and portable back then, Marion could speed-walk for miles with nine pounds strapped to her chest. They were 24/7 inseparable back then.

But babies grow bigger. Zephyr's father was a six-foot-five linebacker, and soon the baby, practically bursting out of her clothes a month after Marion had bought them, was too heavy for even a young woman to carry long distances. So, lacking a car, and needing both money and fleetness of foot, Marion didn't think twice the day she let Michelle mind the baby while she ran four miles to pick up supplies for the artist. Tired from a late flight, Michelle wasn't going to work that day anyway. Neither of them could have predicted that "tired" would turn out to be influenza.

Not even a library of medical books or the most saintly pediatrician can prepare a new mother for what she'll feel the first time her first child becomes ill. A baby with full-blown flu presents symptoms that are capable of frightening the most seasoned of nurses, let alone a panicky kid. When Zephyr's fever rose above 104, Marion didn't know it wasn't unusual for a baby, and with her heart in her mouth, she rushed her Zephyr to the local emergency room. She never paused to consider that the girls-in-trouble home and her parents might have filed missing-persons reports for both her and her baby. For once, the system worked to perfection.

The forced reunion with her parents was traumatic for seventeen-year-old Marion. And confusing. She had no idea people could change so much in under two years. The father and mother who showed up at Child Services bore little resemblance to the people who had raised her. A DUI had compelled her father to join Alcoholics Anonymous and her mother had been attending Al-Anon meetings regularly. They were both soft-spoken and eager to make "amends to those whom they may have harmed in the past." Marion was too confused and exhausted and naive to see that their "amends" would be extended only as far as baby Zephyr.

In their hotel room that night, her parents used their new soft-spoken voices to convince Marion that for the next several years she'd only be running from crisis to crisis and would never have sufficient resources to raise a young child. They used their new listening skills to understand that she had no desire to return to Cleveland. And they used their healthy new appearances and tenacity to convince her to allow them to "help" by taking Zephyr back with them until their daughter could afford a proper home for them both. They had successfully franchised the deli and her mother could now stay home with the baby. They "knew" young Marion would never want Zephyr to suffer again.

Jobs that paid enough money to cover L.A. apartments, and the expenses of motherhood, were scarce for seventeen-year-olds. Even bus tickets were too dear when one was saving for first and last. What Marion thought would take a few months turned out to be two years of separation, a separation made all the more torturous because she couldn't talk to her daughter. Marion sent photographs of herself with little hand-drawn hearts on the back. Her mother promised to show them each night to baby Zephyr and say, "Mommy loves you." In return, she received pictures with a child's crayoned scrawl. Marion could barely afford the monthly phone updates that always seemed to occur when Zephyr was napping. She guessed the deli franchise wasn't going so great because her folks were "unable" to accept collect calls.

But the separation served as a powerful incentive for young Marion Mintz. By the time two years had passed, she had her GED, a job, and a little studio in Hollywood that would work for a young mother and child.

When she finally showed up—full of pride and expectations—on her parents' new doorstep in the Shaker Heights suburb of Cleveland, Marion was more shocked than they were. They'd never told her how prosperous franchising had become. There were new cars in the driveway of the three-bedroom split level, a freshly dug swimming pool, and a pool house out back. It made her own childhood above the deli look like squalor. And it made Marion's present living conditions look worse.

Realizing her parents could easily have supported both her and Zephyr the entire time she was scraping and saving made nineteen-year-old Marion furious. When the precious little three-year-old girl opened the door and said, "Who are you?" Marion saw red through her tears. There had been no nightly mommy pictures, no "Mommy loves you." She'd had no connection with her daughter since the child had turned one, and there had been no reason to justify such indecency.

Her parents' pathetic explanations soon escalated into an old-fashioned Mintz scream fight. Marion's mother invoked Mary Mother of God fifteen times (detecting the devil in Marion's soul at least twice), and her father, proving a dry drunk can still be a drunk, punched two holes in the wall, during which he discovered that his daughter had learned how to duck. They said they'd never taken her desires to mother Zephyr seriously. They said she had failed them by being a no-show at the deli during the holiday crush. They said she would surely fail them again.

And finally they announced that they had "legally" adopted Zephyr, forging Marion's name for "the good of the child." They said they did so to give the child a chance to turn out better than her mother.

But Marion had been on her own for two years and was no longer a child. She knew she was within her legal rights when she marched into Zephyr's room and started packing her daughter's clothing.

Her parents switched tactics and begged to keep Zephyr. The child had renewed their lives, had given them a reason for living. Marion kicked the door shut in their faces.

And then little Zephyr walked out of her bathroom and asked, "Why are you stealing my stuff?"

When Marion told her that *she* was her real mommy and she'd come to take her home to California, she didn't get the reaction she'd dreamed of for two years. Her daughter shrank back in horror and beat on the bedroom door, screaming, "Don't let her take me away! Mommy! Daddy, Pleeeeease!"

As Zephyr cried in abject terror, Marion looked at the room around her and imagined her daughter's future in a Hollywood hellhole with cheap day care and the promise of ever-present crime. In less than two minutes, she made a heart-ripping decision.

Marion squatted down to Zephyr's level and said through her tears, "I'm kidding! I'm kidding! I'm really your *big sister*! Sometimes I don't know when to stop teasing."

"You're not going to take me away?" Zephyr asked as she wiped her nose in relief.

"No. Here, look, sweetie. Look, Zephyr, I'm putting it all back. I didn't mean to scare you. I never want to scare you again."

"That wasn't very nice," replied Zephyr, no longer alarmed. "Can I ask you a question?"

Marion returned, knelt down, and nodded, resisting the urge to hug the sweet little girl.

"Why are *you* crying?" Zephyr wanted to know.

But Marion couldn't tell the truth about that either. "Because I'm happy to see you," she said.

"You're really my sister?"

"Sure. Just go ask your mom."

So Marion Mintz struck a deal with her parents, promising swift legal action if they tried to waver from her rules. As much as losing Zephyr tore her up, she couldn't bear to hear the sound of her little girl's heart-breaking pain. And since she was used to settling for less, Marion actually took comfort in the knowledge that finally she'd have a connection with her child. She would have visits and vacations and thrice-weekly phone calls as the big sister Zephyr knew would "never scare her again."

For ten years they bonded as best as long-distance bonding allowed. Zephyr was always happy to see her big sister when she came out to stay. Meanwhile, Marion made a success of herself in the real-estate business, which led her to Orange County. She could have stayed there with Richard, but she was drawn back to L.A. because it was her and Zephyr's true home. When she convinced her husband to purchase a studio, Marion dreamed of convincing Zephyr to attend UCLA. And she dreamed of a tighter connection with her adult daughter, to whom she'd one day offer the Zane empire.

But she wasn't prepared for the big, surly grief-stricken thirteen-year-old who turned up after her "parents" kicked her out. Zephyr had been caught doing drugs at a boy's house, and just as they'd dropped her mother, her parents gave up on their granddaughter too. Knowing all too well how deeply her poor daughter was wounded, Marion didn't even attempt to tell her the truth.

There was a moment, during that time, though, when Marion almost told Zephyr the truth about herself.

Almost.

She never got beyond confessing that her parents had thrown her out as well because Zephyr flew into a rage over the fact that Marion hadn't told her sooner.

After all, they were *sisters*! Zephyr couldn't believe that Marion didn't tell her and warn her that Mom and Dad's forgiveness didn't extend past the cuddly and cute years. That their parents had no tolerance for behavior they perceived as "shameful" and "sinful." Mom and Dad had been one step away from "honor-killing" her like some fundamentalist wackos and Marion didn't even think to *warn her own sister*? Thanks a lot!

Marion didn't have the nerve to tell the rest. To tell Zephyr *the reason why* Marion had been cut away from the girl's life, like a cancer.

Zephyr had already had enough shock in her young life, Marion told herself. Normally extremely bright and motivated, the thirteen-year-old was now depressed and aimless. Marion told herself it would be dangerous to add any more psychic pain to the burden she already carried.

And the truth was, Marion was too terrified that she'd lose her again.

She couldn't trust her own parents to willingly collaborate if she risked telling her daughter that they'd basically *stolen* her as a baby from an insecure teen.

And why would her daughter believe her now, after being told lies for so many years?

Zephyr was fifteen before she finally got her shit together in school, and although she wasn't clinically depressed, the light never returned to her eyes in the way it used to shine.

Every time Marion wanted to tell Zephyr she was her mother, she'd think: Just wait until after she gets accepted to college.

Which became: until after she graduates.

Which became: until after she gets into law school.

And so on.

And all the years after that? Marion had been waiting until Zephyr became less sad, less surly, and more secure. The problem was she never did.

Marion thought that it was because her daughter had experienced a kinder beginning than she had, making the wound of her alleged parents' behavior harder to heal—and leaving deeper scars.

And maybe there were other, lesser reasons that might have hitched themselves to Marion's fears. But today, surrounded as she was by traitors, there was no time to think of such possibilities.

Looking at her adult daughter, all Marion Zane saw was a little girl pounding on her bedroom door, screaming in pain. And she wanted to make it go away.

"Don't worry," said Zephyr, still avoiding her mother's eyes. "Your maternal shame won't leave the confines of this room. You won't be embarrassed in front of your fans."

As Marion shook her head, dumbstruck, Zephyr opened her briefcase, removed some documents, cosigned the judge's order, and notarized it with the stenographer.

"I'm not about to claim you either, *Mom*. Okay, that should do it."

"It wasn't shame, honey!" Marion managed to get out past her churning guts. "Shame was never the reason. Never shame . . . it was love . . ."

Zephyr slammed her briefcase down on the table, silencing her mother. "Don't . . . you . . . dare!" she spat. Zephyr was a head taller than her mother. She had such venom in her eyes that again, the men in the room shrank back and covered up.

Zephyr tossed her stack of documents on the table. "Why don't you guys read her the rules?" she hissed. "You're getting paid to *deal with her.*"

And then she was gone, taking Marion's crumpled heart with her like a trophy. Gone with the same finality as the man who'd sworn to keep the secret of her parentage. But then Richard had sworn to "honor and cherish" as well.

Frank Greene cleared his throat and picked up Zephyr's documents.

"We were afraid you might have a delayed hostile reaction toward your husband for revealing certain, ah, secrets, which is why Judge Volker granted this restraining order against you."

"I know *I'd* want to kill Richard if I was in your shoes," said Judge Volker, rising to exit and revealing his ambivalence. "We'll talk in a couple of months, Marion. Good luck with your daughter. And your budget."

Marion stared at Eli Volker, utterly incapable of saying a word.

Frank Greene shuffled some papers. "Okay, well, let's get that budget over with . . ."

Upon hearing the dreaded B-word again, Marion swung her head in Greene's direction.

"You shall receive by way of your trustee, every month, a check for the total amount of . . ." Frank continued.

The third yip hit Marion-the-ghost with predictable results, flash-flooding the conference-room table and all those seated around it as well as the papers that officially granted her . . . only thirty thousand dollars a month.

She didn't stick around to enjoy the aftermath.

57

Burnout

As she lurched out of Fox Plaza, Marion was too stunned to be surprised to see her housekeeper leaning against the trunk of her Lexus hybrid. Xiocena was clutching a stack of suit bags and a large blackened sack. The day had turned chilly, and since she had no feeling left, Marion took off her black felt Celine car coat and put it around her housekeeper's shoulders. Then she went directly to the Lexus's backseat passenger door and stood in front of it. After a minute, Marion began to sense that something was off in the rhythms of the universe.

"Where's Carl?" she asked, staring at the car door, which hadn't opened.

Xiocena burst into tears. "He fired!" she sobbed, handing the Lexus's black key card to her employer. "Your sister say Mr. Zane no trust!"

"Don't worry, Xio," said Marion as she walked around to the front of the Lexus. "He'll keep you on as a spy."

Xiocena swiped at her tears. "I know."

There was an envelope under the Lexus's windshield wiper. Marion regarded it curiously.

"And Zephyr's not my sister. She's my daughter."

"*Madre de Dios!*" Xiocena crossed herself several times, trying to take in this news.

"Uh-huh," Marion said as she stared.

"She's *really* big girl."

"I know."

"It must have hurt."

"I was young." Marion slowly pulled the envelope out from under the rubber wiper blade.

"You help me, Mrs. Zane? I don't know open the trunk."

Marion walked to the back of the Lexus and opened the trunk with a wave of her card. She helped Xiocena put the suit bags and blackened sack inside and waved it shut. Then the two women got into the front seats.

"The backseat has massage," offered Marion, starting the car but not moving.

Xiocena started weeping again. "No, thank you."

Marion regarded the envelope without emotion, as if it were a long-forgotten algebra equation.

"Parking ticket," Xiocena informed her.

"Oh. Yes."

Marion put the ticket in her Fendi clutch and pulled out onto Avenue of the Stars, heading north. She rolled down her window and her hair began to whip around her face. Then she turned on the radio. It was set at Oldies 95.5, an FM station Carl liked, and Jimi Hendrix's "Purple Haze" blasted out of the speakers.

"Xio?" she asked, raising her voice.

"Yes, Mrs. Zane?" Xio yelled back

"What did we put in the trunk?"

Xiocena buried her face in her hands. "I'm so sorry, Mrs. Zane. It is all I can save! I curse that devil . . ."

The rest was all Spanish. Marion changed lanes and turned up Little Santa Monica, waiting for Xio to finish muttering curses before asking, "Which devil, Xio?"

"The *puta*!"

Marion rolled down the passenger window so her housekeeper could spit in disgust. "What did the devil *puta* do to you?" she asked.

More curses. Xiocena reached back, lifted the tray of backseat massage controls, and snatched a flask of Porfidio out of the ice in the cooler underneath. Settling back in the front seat, she took a two-gulp slug. Then she faced her employer.

"Not to me, Mrs. Zane! To you! Mr. Zane say is okay she redecorate." Marion snatched up the flask and took several gulps while Xiocena fingered her rosary beads before adding, "Then she wait till he gone an' take everything from all your closet into pile in parking garage . . . and set the pile on fire!"

It turned out to be fortunate that the day had turned chilly. That way most drivers on Little Santa Monica had their windows rolled up and were spared the sound of Marion's reaction.

58

Stacking the Dead

"Vlad! Vlaaad! Come now! Bring gun! Bring guuun! *Vlaaad!*"

Vlad was at the kitchen sink, filling a vase of budding Chinese dogwood branches he'd purchased at the farmers' market. At the sound of Maya's screaming he abandoned the vase without turning off the water and practically crashed through the French doors in the kitchen to the backyard. Hearing Maya scream his name and the word *gun* in the same screamed sentence could mean only one thing: a stalker had made it onto the estate.

"*Vlaaad!*"

Sprinting like a demon around the house, he yanked his Glock 9mm out of its shoulder holster and snapped off the safety. The stalker who'd managed to cut his way over the wall last month didn't have a knife and Maya hadn't screamed this hard. Sasha and Dudayev had immediately beaten the freak to a pulp. Knowing a stalker would have to kill both of them before being able to get within ten feet of Maya or Tom forced Vlad to ask himself an unspeakable question:

Were they dead?

"Bring guuun! Vlaad! Aieeeeee!"

Vlad dove into the bed behind the hibiscus and crawled on his belly like a commando toward the screaming. He couldn't allow himself to be taken by surprise if he was the last line of defense. As he belly-crawled through the freshly watered plantings, Vlad steeled himself for the sight of his comrades' bodies in the same state as the calla lilies that crushed and bled into his shirt underneath him.

Instead, he saw his comrades with their bodies very much intact, studying their fingernails and shifting their feet like guilty puppies while Maya hopped around them, freaking out.

Disgusted, he stood up, eliciting a conniption fit from his employer.

"What the fuck you do? The garden is fucked enough! Come out of there!" screeched Maya.

"You scream. I think there is stalker!" he puffed.

Maya rolled her eyes while his comrades smirked.

Vlad joined them in front of a row of old-growth camellias that had started out as bushes in the twenties and had matured into trees.

They were all dead. And the ground around them had sunk two feet.

Because two idiots had cut their taproots last night.

To make room for the body.

Fucking Sasha! He'd told him to wait to bury it until they had some new trees to replace the dead ones. But did he listen? No! He was too squeamish about the "basement smell"! Then they set the dead trees on top of their mess!

Did they think she wouldn't notice?

"Hand me gun," said Maya, studying the freshly dug ground around the dead trees.

"If you want to shoot them," Vlad said, keeping his weapon, "wait until they put new trees in."

"I want to shoot monster who did this!" squealed his employer.

Vlad shot a quick murderous look at Sasha and Dudayev, but they frantically made the internationally recognized sign for "we didn't blame you!" behind Maya's back.

"The gophers are back," Dudayev said, trying to keep a straight face.

"I find hole and shoot off their heads!" Maya had started to cry.

Vlad tried to comfort her while Sasha and Dudayev laid the dead trees down in the depressed soil and quickly shoveled dirt over them.

"See? It look better all ready!" said Sasha, admiring the now even-looking ground. It barely looked disturbed. "They live long life. Have nice burial."

But Maya only cried harder.

"*Nyet, nyet.* Don't cry," Vlad soothed. "They get new trees tomorrow. The old trees make compost and give new trees life. They fix. They fix."

But Maya wasn't crying about the trees anymore.

She was crying about their burial.

Because it reminded her of her flight out of Chechnya. Sasha, Dudayev, and Vlad had been alongside her back then and Maya was surprised that they didn't make the connection.

The madame had been right. Nobody took Maya away from the brothel.

A bomb hit it. Maya had been one of the few survivors. While the volunteer rescue crews were putting out the fires and searching for bodies, Maya managed to find the cache of money and valuables that the brothel had taken in trade for the flesh of its prisoners. It was under the half-crushed body of the madame, who'd been killed trying to run for safe cover.

Shortly after the bombing, as Maya had torn the rubble away from her captor's broken arms to see what she was carrying, the madame had looked into Maya's eyes.

But she'd made no pleas for mercy. She knew there'd be none. Maya pried the strongbox out of the woman's dying hands and then allowed her own body to do what it had been dreaming of doing every heinous second during the past two years:

She ran.

Maya didn't run for the border. Instead, she made her way back to the place where she was born. The Russians or the *teips* might have taken her parents. But her uncles were still there. She had unfinished business.

Along the way, Maya met the boys. The Russians had left a bloody legacy of their various attempts to tame the Chechnyans, and Vlad, Sasha, and Dudayev were living proof. As rape spawn, the three were considered outcasts in the code of the *teips* (much the same as Maya) and had been living a gypsy existence on the outskirts of her village. Since they were untethered teens like herself, their hearts were still partially intact. And their services were simple to buy. They agreed to escort her out of the country.

After they'd deposited the bodies of Maya's uncles in the foundations of the Russian bunker.

As they crossed the war-torn and racially torn countryside, they'd passed many horrors. The worst were the mass graves.

Looking at the camellia-tree burial, at the tangled limbs and graying blossoms, Maya couldn't help but recall what she'd witnessed during her exodus.

And she imagined her parents were buried the same way.

59

Stalling the Rapture

"And why is the most bulletproof woman in the Western Hemisphere staying cooped up in her hotel tonight? I would think you'd be out on the town celebrating by watching the most eligible bachelors in the Western Hemisphere drink champagne from your slippers!"

As she balefully watched Xiocena organize the remains of her wardrobe in the second bedroom, Marion thought that the last person she wanted to speak with at this pathetic and not-drunk-enough moment was Lyndy Wallert. (Even if she did feel bad that her friend hopelessly dated herself in some long-dead era. "Drink champagne from a slipper"? Who did that, Andy Rooney?)

"I'm actually, ah, recovering from the celebrating last night."

Good save.

"Smart thinking," said Lyndy. "You'll be well rested and irresistible to the four five-star bachelors I'm seating you with tomorrow night!"

Oh, shit. Lyndy's gala.

"Sweetheart, I was just going to call you about—"

"Oh, no, no, no, no, no! You can't cancel on me at this late a date, darling! Please! I have to have at least one Zane or the table seating will completely collapse, not to mention the prestige of the entire event! Richard has canceled, of course!"

"But I'm—"

"Nooo! You can't!" Lyndy brayed. "I took advantage of your failing to submit a guest list for your table, and when attendees heard there were openings, they actually upped their donations for a crack at sitting with you! I can't screw them now! Oh, please, you can't do this to me . . ."

In all the years she'd known Lyndy Wallert, Marion had never, *ever* heard her snobby friend beg. It was kind of frightening, like scenes of dark portent in those apocalypse movies where the heroine sees visions of four horsemen or the rivers run with blood. And it made her want to say yes because no matter how horribly fucked her life was at the moment, no matter that losing Richard, Zephyr, and her money in the same day was worse than anything the minions of hell could throw at her . . . Marion didn't want to be responsible for "The End of All Time."

But how was she going to attend the Beverly Hills Winter Gala on a budget?

It was bad enough that her new exquisite custom-couture Chanel gown had been barbecued. But after hitting up everybody in town for $250 million in Carita Memorial pledges, Marion was beholden.

She'd be expected to "give back."

Thirty thousand a month sounded like a king's ransom of a budget. But it didn't go very far when every woman on the Westside was demanding donations for *their own causes.* When every woman on the Westside knew Marion Zane to be a billionaire, and a bulletproof billionaire at that.

Marion had never bought a table at any event, ever, for under twenty-five thousand. And she knew what happened to Westside women who didn't reciprocate.

They received "instant detest."

It would be as bad as if she marched around Pacific Palisades with a sandwich board that read GLOBAL WARMING IS A HOAX!

You couldn't get into the game unless you were willing to give as much as you got.

At the moment, Marion was paid up for events through the Oscars.

But what would she do when next month rolled around?

To make matters worse, each event was preceded by a boozy silent auction, where every "Who-down-in-Whoville" noticed if you didn't bid high for hard-won donated items. She certainly didn't want to give a nonreciprocating scent to those hounds. Sometimes, there were even *live* auctions (which had evolved from Throw-Downs). The idea of being put on the public spot gave Marion chills.

And she couldn't bullshit everybody about how the divorce was "tying up her finances."

She wasn't ready to lose her friends.

Patti, Pepper, Maya, and even Lyndy were all she had left.

She knew she should give her lifeboat Trophies more credit. She should believe that they'd stick with her even if her money was gone. But fifteen years on the Westside had taught her differently.

Marion remembered back to her Stage I days, when everybody had dropped Patti Fink like a used Kleenex in the months following Barry Fink's death. Before Patti had "married up" and the adoration returned.

She'd been Patti's *only friend for nine months.*

She didn't want to risk finding out if the lifeboat Trophies would do the same for her.

"... might cause the BHC Winter Gala to drop down to a"—shudder—"B-level event!" Lyndy was saying. "I simply couldn't *live* with myself if that happened on my watch—"

Prepare for the Rapture!

But Marion couldn't screw over her friend. At least the invitation said there'd be no live auction at the gala.

"Of course I'm coming, Lyndy!" Marion interrupted. "I wouldn't dream of being a no-show. I've been trying to tell you I've got a late meeting with the lawyers, so I'll have to *miss the silent auction.*"

"Oh."

"What time are you serving dinner?"

"Nine o'clock sharp, darling. Thank you! You have no idea how relieved this has made me!"

"As much as the 2004 election?"

"Even more," Lyndy purred.

After she hung up with Lyndy, Marion went into the second bedroom to see what Xiocena was doing. For a minute, she thought her housekeeper had gone the way of the dodo, being absorbed by the piles of clothes. Following the sound of running water, however, she found her Xiocena in the bathroom, using shampoo to rinse out a handful of G-strings in the sink.

The end times are coming!

"Xio, I need you to make a call to the Canary Islands . . ."

She needed to get Ivan back before she was "Left Behind."

60

Berlin

Nowadays the sound of footfalls or car wheels crunching polished granite pea gravel is a particular sensory experience familiar only to the wealthy or those in their employ. Behind chin stubble and sunglasses, Ivan recognized this sound as he observed his old partner exit his front door and get into the backseat of a Mercedes 600 limousine.

Wealth had allowed his target to age well. In a tailored suit and with polished fingernails, he appeared far more sophisticated and trim than he'd been when Ivan last saw him in Colombia. The man's briefcase alone cost more than three months of their previous profession's pay. Even his former partner's entry into the backseat of the limousine possessed the graceful economy of movement developed only by those who are regularly chauffeured.

Again, the gravel crunched out privilege as the limo turned around in front of the Schloss Reinsdorff, his old partner's eighth-century castle, which lay north of Berlin in the idyllic *vorort* of Ruppinerand.

The fact that this castle was not his target's main or even secondary residence was not lost on Ivan. The Colombian venture had been as profitable as predicted. Cocaine had allowed him to literally live like a king.

As the German ambassador to Colombia, Ivan's former partner was well protected, even on this continent. A bodyguard watched from the doorway of the house and the limousine passed two more well-armed behemoths in a guardhouse as it rolled across the drawbridge.

Once the ambassador crossed over the castle moat, he was quite impossible to approach without being immediately detected by security cameras and well-armed guards. Intrusion upon the castle was out of the question.

For the past three days, Ivan's former partner had been in meetings at the Reichstag with three Bundestag legislators who wanted to explore a novel business opportunity in Santa Fe de Bogotá. Today he was headed for yet another meeting at the same central Berlin location twenty kilometers away. Ivan knew an attempted assassination in those high-security government offices would be suicide.

That meant his target was unapproachable at work as well as at home.

But the drivers who chauffeured him were not.

Ivan had gained valuable experience in the employ of the Zanes. On the occasion that Carl was ill and an outside limousine service was contracted to drive Marion until he returned to work, more attention was paid to the chauffeur *service's* credentials than to those of the individual drivers. The assumption being that the chauffeur service would clear its own employees.

Wealthy Germans shared the same assumptions.

It had been easy for Ivan to scoop up one of his target's contracted drivers. The one who matched his own height and build. The night before, Ivan had spent an extremely productive visit with the fellow, one that lasted until the wee hours of the morning.

He had plenty of time to study the intended route to Berlin and select the perfect spot to achieve his objective. Wooded and rarely traversed. Ivan pulled over and pressed the control to adjust the driver's seat backward.

"Why are you stopping?" asked the ambassador.

"I need more room," Ivan muttered, pretending to be adjusting his seatbelt.

"Fool! Why didn't you do this *before* you started driving?"

Ivan answered him by lunging backward and making a clean, professional slash across the man's jugular vein.

Not wanting to be confused with any of his former partner's other enemies, Ivan removed his sunglasses and looked into the eyes of the man he had once thought a brother.

At his moment of death, the light of recognition shone in the ambassador's eyes.

61

It Lives!

"And don't you dare consider squandering valuable seconds thanking Miriam Hoffman, *your secretary*," said Lyndy as she glowered over Dr. Frances Small, chief of surgery for Beverly Hills Central.

It was a half hour before gala showtime (and her own rapturous reassumption of the TOP!). A time that normally found her up in the VIP suite, fortifying herself with a protein shake and fielding compliments on her beauty from the room-service waiters, while hair and makeup fawned over her exquisite selection of jewels and finery. She should be enjoying the anticipation of regaining the glamorous power she was born to wield. And the Unforgivable Humiliation she was about to dole out to the Zanes.

But this was Frances's first year in the position of chief, so the Queen of the Evening was still stuck down here in the ballroom (with her hair still in rollers, for Christ's sake!), giving the nattering neophyte a remedial class in Gala 101!

Already she'd had to cross out three-quarters of the woman doctor's welcoming speech! Did she not tell her to "keep it under a minute at all costs"? Did Frances think this would be the same as her old job? The good patrons of Atlanta Presbyterian might be willing to be lulled to sleep by twenty minutes of Frances's meaningless acknowledgments, but this was Beverly Hills! This was the majors!

"But Miriam stayed until eleven o'clock the other night making your adjustments to the seating chart," argued Frances. "She's been working on this after hours for over three weeks."

"Then 'plaque' her! Preferably in a ceremony in the secretaries' lounge!" Lyndy snapped. "At this gala, we never thank anybody who isn't a *famous patron* or *celebrity* because nobody wants to pay fifty thousand dollars to listen to endless lists of people they neither know nor care about! They will only remain enthusiastic for *one* grisly hopeless scenario that turned out miraculously well. Then on to a thirty-second announcement of how much the night has raised and who it will serve. Then entertainment until eleven, when we kick their asses out, do-you-understand?"

"Yes, Lyndy," Frances sighed wearily. "Whatever you want."

"If you're aching to thank someone, then pick out a movie star, for 'their unwavering selfless support.' "

"But you comped all the actors, Lyndy."

Honestly, how did this woman ever get out of med school?

Before stalking out of the ballroom, Lyndy paused for a moment to savor her work. She had put the fear of God into that dinner committee this year, telling them that if they didn't step up their game, this would be BHC's *last* Winter Gala, and since the demise of this event would be on their heads, they would become permanently devalued as fund-raisers, causing all other philanthropic organizations to reject their services. For-ever.

The scare tactic worked.

The ballroom was perfect for her coronation. The blue bulbs in the crystal-flower-cluster ballroom chandelier cast an otherworldly light, setting the tone for Lyndy's wonderland, where white-suited magicians, jugglers, and acrobats would mingle with masked cigarette girls in fur-trimmed bustier minidresses toting fine cigars and brandy shots. All on a carpet of white fake fur!

Huge handblown glass candelabras woven with garlands of white peo-nies, tulips, and crystal chandelier drops, soon to be coupled with double-panned fantastical ice sculptures anchored each table as center-pieces. The gleaming silver and china were complemented by a wonderful table of Belgian chocolates, Cartier picture frames, hand mirrors, caviar, toast points, and iced vodka shots among strewn crystal beads. Her guests would surely be delighted and impressed.

And the goody bags were bursting with tantalizing party favors for a change, like Bulgari sunglasses, Ralph Lauren cashmere mufflers, Montblanc pen sets and Hermès notepads, and the grandest coup of all, a pre-programmed Google Phone with a CD of over sixteen thousand assorted ringtones.

All donated! When she'd blanketed the town with news of the Zane separation, RSVPs to her gala weren't the only thing that poured in. Every promotional representative in town flooded her phone lines at her gala office at BHC!

The silent auction alone was worth several million! Just like the old days!

People were beginning to realize where the power lay now. If not, they would learn as soon as they set foot in this ballroom dream.

It was the perfect setting in which to pound the stake into the heart of the Vampire Queen.

Lyndy envisioned her A-list guests, clad in elegant old-school black tie (not that "business attire" crap!). She envisioned the look on their faces as they beheld the Unforgivable Humiliation of Marion Zane.

Grandmother would be so proud!

Hitching up her (soon to be unemployed) custom ass-enhancing panties, Lyndy strode to the elevator.

Time to check on the wooden stake.

Riding up to the VIP suite, Lyndy thought of her fortuitous emergency-room encounter with Richard Zane and chortled until she feared she would damage her rhinestone lash spanglers. How thick *was* that man? Thinking she would believe his insulting and pathetic fabrications? A "plant caretaker" indeed! Tawnee's skin damage alone indicated she'd tangled with an entity more powerful than a pothos! And what about those claw marks surrounding the raw patches on her scalp? When Lyndy saw the manner in which Tawnee pawed at that fumbling buffoon and overheard the damaged creature calling him "Richie," every cell in her body went on high alert. And when she read the information card Tawnee had filled out that listed "masseuse" as her occupation, all the little Legos fell into one neat incriminating stack for Lyndera Montgomery Wallert.

This was the work of her partner in Marion hate!

When she received the first mysterious text, she thought it was too good to be true—not that others wouldn't want to seek revenge on the Vampire

Queen but that such a feat could be accomplished at all. She herself had been trying for over ten years and all attempts had been consistently foiled. (And as far as rat fucks go, Lyndy was good.)

And her partner had stolidly refused to reveal his or (surely!) her identity. Not even the most minuscule of clues. (Pity, since they shared such a noble agenda!) Just the same, Lyndy had agreed to join forces. She'd just assumed that she'd have to bear most of the burden.

First, she supplied a small bit of information about the whereabouts of that Teutonic automaton Ivan and the activities Marion had scheduled within the compound. After that, she'd received two assignments: Recommend this massage service. Hire this caterer.

Then she'd had nothing to do but hope.

The mystery partner had guaranteed a Zane marriage breakup and it appeared that the breakup had, in fact, occurred. But there had been nothing for poor Lyndy to personally sink her teeth into, no pound of flesh or firstborn to take. Her mystery partner had left her completely out of the action.

Then providence brought her the girl!

And a new plan presented itself.

She had taken no chances slipping three of her cards into Tawnee's bag. It wasn't two hours before her phone rang. She managed to lull the little lummox into friendship by playing sympathetic patron and offering ways to snag Richard as a beau. Her coaching would probably have worked had the size of Tawnee's brain been equal to her greed.

Of course Lyndy's own appetite for mischief had played a part in Tawnee's rejection, but that was before she fully grasped the vastness under that freshly plowed pate. When she'd told Tawnee to *damage* Marion's clothing, Lyndy had imagined furtive bleach spills or scissors, never fire. And not just a small fire. An entire wardrobe inferno!

The little bonfire set off smoke signals that could be seen from Sepulveda!

The blaze had spread across the Zanes' backyard, and had it not been for a neighbor's mature hedge refusing to burn, it would have taken out half of Beverly Hills and affected the gala attendance. Definitely a close one!

Thank God the pea-brained firebug had called her back. Evidently, avoiding arson charges took precedence over greed and Tawnee had allowed Richard's lawyers to turn her out on her ass. She was seeking refuge with Lyndy. Lyndy was seeking to salvage her plan. Good thing the Zanes were gullible. And the hairstylist had an amazing ability to make bald patches seem to vanish into thin air.

They'd been working on her for over six hours.

As Lyndy entered the VIP suite to behold her creation, she almost let out a mad scientist's laugh.

"Are you sssure thisss dresss looksss okay? I mean Marion and I aren't, like, exxxactly the sssame sssizzze. And I'm not sssure the patch isss going to hold."

"My dear, it's *Chanel*! It's the, uh, 'Big Gulp' of fashion. That gown will tell Richard you belong in his world. How's the walking cast holding up with one shoe?"

"It's kind of unbalancced."

"You'll get used to it."

The dress made Tawnee look like an overcooked hot dog and Dr. Frankenstein himself couldn't have made a worse back gusset. The girl's spray tan was so cheap she looked like an Oompa-Loompa. At least the wig covered the scabs, and if the whore kept her head down, the latex chin might not show in the dark.

"That's enough with her hair," said Lyndy, jumping into her silver Armani gown and pincering the stylist's elbow to redirect her. "Let's get going over here."

"Are you sure he won't bussst me for sssstealing the dresss?"

You mean Marion's custom-couture gown? Hee, hee!

Lyndy bent down and strapped on her sandals, fearing that if she looked the girl in the face, she might bray with laughter. "Trust me. He'll be too astounded for words."

62

Bidding Frenzy

Claire caught a glimpse of herself in the mirror as she and Billy descended the circular staircase to the Beverly Hills Hotel ballroom. She decided her grayish shredded dress looked more nuclear winter than winter wonderland. She couldn't remember the name of the designer, but she was sure it was something blasphemous. Her gloves were the color of blood. Outside on the red carpet, only one photographer had taken her picture with Billy. The rest had asked him to step back.

He didn't mind.

The second they finished taking their official Winter Gala photo with the disturbing white-feathered snowman on the landing, Craig shoved a cosmo in her hand and dragged her off toward the "Hermès Holiday!" table of silent-auction items, saying, "Sorry, Billy! She's mine for the next half hour!"

Billy didn't mind.

From over the tops of tote bags and riding boots, Claire saw him sneak out to the little smoking patio that was dressed up like Narnia during the Snow Queen's reign and whip out his cell. As she signed her name where Craig pointed, she saw an actress from one of Billy's movies prance out to join him in Narnia, like one of those fawns or whatever those tree girls were called, and throw her short, bare stubby arms around him in greeting. Then, attempting to look sultry, the actress leaned up against the fake lamppost as she babbled and almost knocked it over. She tried to cover by pawing Claire's husband some more.

Claire didn't mind.

In fact, she felt sorry for the actress who was hitting on her husband. That stubby-armed actress could set herself on fire and Billy wouldn't notice.

Not while he was on his phone.

Claire wondered if she might get a stronger drink if she got it herself from the bartender. And why was she buying size-twelve men's shoes? Billy was a nine and a half.

As much as Maya craned her head over the flash storm of paparazzi, she didn't see Marion anywhere. Pepper had texted her from the silent auction saying Marion hadn't arrived and Maya wanted to go to her friend's bungalow to see if she needed anything. But that might be hard with nine lunatics in a tangle around her ankles, taking pictures of her fucking-shit feet!

She'd been so distracted tonight that she'd accidentally put on two Louboutin pointy stiletto pumps in the same style but in different colors. One was gold and one was pink.

How could she pay attention to color when her husband had brought home that fur-lined leather harness thing? And then put a sack of flour inside and started wearing the fucking thing around the house. He was talking to the flour and patting it and she found it disturbing, and then he was jingling his keys! When she asked him if he had lost his fucking mind, he'd told her, "I'm nesting."

What were they now, fucking birds?

When she asked if the flour sack wanted to join her in a shot of Grey Goose, Tom said, "No, he'd rather have a bottle." That response made her back off and cry.

When Tom got out a disposable diaper and put it around the base of the sack, she figured out what he was doing and told him he'd have to switch to cloth ones.

She drew the line when he put the flour sack in a big Ziploc bag and asked her to take it with her in the shower. Sometime later, Tom came downstairs and found her cooking blinis.

And he'd asked her, "Where is he?"

And she'd told him that when she'd taken off the diaper and the wrapper, the flour turned out to be a girl—just before she'd FRIED IT ALIVE!

Then he'd called her an "abusive mother."

When Lou and Patti arrived on the red carpet, he'd taken over pushing Lou's wheelchair and left her all alone with the shoe-crazy assholes. Then he said he'd be right back. It had been over fucking five minutes! And Lou's wheelchair was fucking motorized!

He was punishing her for murdering flour!

She wanted her Marion.

She wanted Marion to slap her husband around.

And she wasn't taking these fuckers with her!

At the same time as Maya decided to find Marion, Lyndy was wedging her way through the paparazzi to get in on Maya's photo fest.

Maya mowed through the nine paparazzi like they were bowling pins.

And Lyndy made it a strike.

"Two thousand dollars? Are you joking? Who are these gorillas? Do they shit gold?"

"Shhh!" Pepper whispered to her husband as she read another silent-auction item. "Gorillaz, the *band,* Mr. Music Dude. It's for a walk-on in their next video. Jerry likes 'em an' his birthday's comin' up an' he's gone the whole year with no suspensions."

"Then we give him money, like Christmas, my baby," Ari argued. "One hundred dollars is enough."

"Enough ta buy another air rifle," Pepper reminded him, before moving down the table. He was getting on her nerves. The man was worth $3 billion. At last year's Winter Gala, he'd personally bought a Disney cruise, six pricey cases of Mouton Cadet, a custom Porsche cover, and a walk-in Dunhill humidor.

"You're bidding on *more* things?" Ari exclaimed, hovering over his wife's shoulder to read the item on the bidding sheet. "I don't need a ten-foot tool case and a shop vac!"

"*I* do," Pepper replied without stopping.

"But these prices are ridiculous! We could buy most of these things for wholesale and I can get that walk-on with one phone call! We've already given to Marion's hospital. Isn't that enough?"

Pepper whipped around and felt Ari's forehead. Sadly, there was no sign of fever, so she went back to bidding.

"I don't like wasting money!" Ari snapped at her back. "Do you hear me?"

Pepper turned around to face her husband. Slowly. She was wearing her "Mommy face."

"We Greeks are frugal, woman!" Ari sputtered, in a last-ditch effort at bravado.

"Ari Papadopoulos, take a time-out."

"But—"

"No buts. You heard me. March!" Pepper ordered, and pointed to the bar across the room.

Ari knew better than to persist and slunk off to join the rest of the banished husbands.

Sipping on iced vodka, Ari could hear his wife above the crowd as she called out to friends she'd probably been parted from for mere hours. Pepper was so *loud*. Unlike Mariah, who'd been as quiet as a breeze in a glade today. And the feeling when he brushed his hand against hers! He was definitely interested in buying more statues.

"So are you wondering what I'm wondering?" asked Patti as she sidled up and clamped onto Pepper's hand at the "Harry Winston Ice Delights!" jewelry table.

"Only if yer wonderin' if m' husband's lost 'is dang mind!"

"Take a look around," whispered Patti. "Who's missing?"

Pepper obliged. "Shit. Marion's not—"

"—here. Right. Should we go check on her?"

"Not yet," Pepper said, still surveying the crowd. "She might need a l'il more time ta get it up. It's her first time out, separated. Hoo-boy! Some chick just smacked Craig-the-stylist, over there!"

"That would be Keira Knightley," Patti said, distractedly checking out names on one of the jewelry bid sheets. "I'm wearing her Oscar dress. Did she hit him hard? I know I would, if I were her. Look how much better I fill it out. And I took a million photos."

"I thought you dumped Craig."

"I did. But Keira doesn't know that. Mr. Craig's last bill really pissed me off. The little shit charged a golf-club membership and two airplane tickets on my card without asking. He called it 'research.' So I decided to take over the car payments for every designer's personal assistant at every major fashion house in Paris, Rome, London, and New York in exchange for information about what Craig's actresses will be wearing."

"So you can show up in the same dresses first?"

"Let's just say this won't be the last time Craig will get smacked this season."

"They always underestimate us," Pepper sighed as she low-fived Patti. "You gonna bid on that?" she asked, pointing to a pair of emerald earrings. "I'm really pissed at m' husband."

"Oh, I've already got this shit at home. Go for it," said Patti, wedging away. "I'll check in about Marion in fifteen."

Continuing her search for Marion, Patti wandered back up the stairs into the hotel lobby, where the flashes coming from a small salon drew her like a moth to a flame. Inside, a line of adults and children were waiting to get their pictures taken with Matthew McConaughey.

(!)

Patti loved Matthew McConaughey. He was hunky even with his shirt on. Matthew was on her short list of "men worth stalking" and getting a photo-with would be a serious trophy! Patti beelined into the line and waited breathlessly for her turn to pose with the babalicious hunk.

Patti was so excited that she didn't notice that some of the people in line were in wheelchairs or walked with assistance. She had no idea that she was lined up with the "Success Patients" of Beverly Hills Central Hospital who'd been corralled in this room so they could be trotted out onstage as an "uplifter" in tonight's Winter Gala presentation. (As a *group,* so as not to waste valuable time.)

In fact, it wasn't until she heard Matthew ask the woman in front of her why she was hospitalized that Patti had an inkling that perhaps this was some sort of specialized group she was joining. She turned to the little girl in the wheelchair behind her and indicated the line. "Um, sweetie, does this group have a name?"

"We're the Success Patients! Duh!" the girl squeaked. "And *I'm* the one with the brain cancer! We have to come tonight or we won't get our free physical therapy. What did you recover from?"

Uh-oh.

"Yes, what *did* you recover from?" asked Matthew McConaughey.

Patti wanted to tell the truth but she was lost in Matthew's *extremely* sexy smile. And forearms. And eyes. And—

"Why don't we start with names. Hi. I'm Matthew. And you are . . ."

"Patricia," Patti answered in her best smolder.

"Great. Let's take a picture, Patricia."

Patti made it into his lap on the third shot. By the fifth, she had her hand on the inside of his thigh, much to the consternation of the others waiting in line:

"Hey, stop hogging Matthew! This crutch is killing me!"

"I need to put on another IV!"

Matthew looked deep into her eyes. "Natives are getting restless, Patricia. Last picture."

That was when Patti Frenched him.

She caught her breath and twisted around to dismount, but Matthew caught her by the wrist.

"You still didn't tell me what Beverly Hills Central did for you," he said.

"Where?" asked Patti dazedly.

"You know *the hospital that treated you*? You *are* a Success Patient, aren't you?"

All eyes were on Patti, so she really didn't stand a chance. "Um . . . spina bifida!" she blurted. "Beverly Hills Central stopped my spina bifida from progressing!"

"Whoa. That back must be fragile. Where's you brace, Patricia?"

"I'm, ah . . . flying without a parachute. That's an inside term we spina bifida sufferers use when we, you know, want a little freedom."

"Yeah, but you could injure yourself."

"Don't worry. I'm pretty tough," Patti said, dismounting.

"Come on! Get off already!"

Matthew actually picked her up and set her on the ground, which would have been majorly dreamy if it wasn't because he thought she was crippled.

Patti waved and was about to make a hasty exit, but a rather large hospital orderly stepped in front of her and blocked her way.

"Success Patients are to wait in this room until they're called onstage."

Uh-oh.

63

Tree Bumping

Sasha hauled ass back to the van and got in. "No fucking camellias. And you were wrong. They did have dog," he groused, examining his torn and slobbered-on pant leg.

Dudayev sighed and started up the van but kept the headlights off as they continued to prowl the street. He was beginning to believe that there were no old-growth camellia trees in all of Bel Air, which meant they might not be able to sleep in their beds that might since Vlad had told them not to come home without replacements for the ones they had killed. Maya's garden tour was next week.

Sasha retrieved a sack from the back of the van and peered into it.

"You bastard fuck!" he barked.

"What?" asked Dudayev, feigning innocence.

"You ate my chicken pieces!"

"There were no chicken pieces that bag."

"Oh? Then why is little paper house empty?" asked Sascha, shaking the empty cardboard carton that once held a children's fast-food meal.

"There were no chicken pieces in little paper house," said Dudayev, concentrating on navigating the van around a turn. "Only nugget."

"Nugget *is* chicken!" Sasha sputtered.

"Nooo," said Dudayev in disbelief.

"I tell you *is chicken!*"

"Is bread."

"*Chicken!* You eat so fast you no tell what you fucking eat!"

"Is maybe pork."

"I do not eat pig!" Sasha snapped back.

"No, you only eat little baby girl's food, like nugget . . . hoo, ha, hee, ha!"

Realizing he was being mocked, Sasha bashed Dudayev about the head with the cardboard container as his partner in crime howled with laughter. The two were so busy fussing that they almost missed the heavy, white double blossoms of old-growth camellia trees bordering the next property's turn-of-the-century river-rock wall. The wall stretched clear around the corner and so did the trees, which numbered over thirty.

Both men saw them at the same time. It was as if the universe had taken pity on them!

"We sleep at home tonight," said Dudayev reverently.

"You still owe me new nuggets," said Sasha.

"I buy you whole case of nugget."

The trees were right on the street and easily removable. Sasha and Dudayev clambered into the back of the van, then burst out the back, shovels in hand, and went to work, digging up the first tree (carefully, this time).

After stowing the fourth tree, Dudayev noticed an old wooden sign on the driveway gate. "What does 'Rancho del Sol' mean?" he asked Sasha.

"*Rancho* is cattle farm. *Sol* is sun," said Sasha, hefting the fifth tree and beckoning for Dudayev's help.

"*Sol* is also fish," said Dudayev, grabbing an end of the heavy root ball with one hand and barely lifting.

"That would be stupid. Nobody would live at 'Ranch of the Fish.'"

"*Rancho* is also stupid," said Dudayev, peeking over the old wall. "There are no cows. Just big house."

The sudden glare of headlights on the inside of the gate caused both men to dive into the back of the van and pull the doors shut.

"Is fish rancher!"

Dudayev (carefully) wriggled through the stacked trees and prepared to jump behind the wheel for a fast getaway as Sasha kept an eye on the opening gate to see if the driver would notice the missing trees or shovels.

But Max Wallert noticed nothing amiss as he pulled the Vanden Plas out of his driveway. In fact, he peeled rubber speeding away because he'd been watching the game too long. He knew he was going to catch hell from Lyndy for being late to her Winter Gala.

As the darkness safely reenveloped them, Sasha and Dudayev went back to work liberating the remaining fifteen trees.

64

Ultimate and Unforgivable

Maya stomped past the reception desk, made a left just before the Polo Lounge, slipped out a side door, and clicked along the garden path toward Marion's bungalow. It was outside, in the fresh air, amid banana trees and birds of paradise that she began to realize that she wasn't so much angry at her husband as she was scared at the prospect of disappointing him.

And maybe losing him.

Maya's stride broke into a jog as anger dissolved into fear, so she didn't notice Marion on the other side of a banana-tree clump, heading in the opposite direction for the ballroom. As Maya's fear began to couple with self-loathing, Tom caught up to her and spun her around.

"Aw, shit," he said, seeing the tears forming in his wife's eyes and enveloping her in a hug. "It was bad out there, wasn't it? I swear I told security to bring you in two seconds after I left, but there was a fight in the parking lot. When they told me, I freaked. I'm so sorry, girl! Forgive me?"

Her husband's embrace converted Maya's fear back into comfortable anger and she replied by stomping on Tom's left foot with her pink pump.

"Ow! You're right, I got chronic with the flour," Tom said, hopping and hoping to protect his other foot. "Sorry. Sorry. Sorry. And that was low; I know you'll be a *great* mother."

Not exactly what she was longing to hear.

"So where were you going?" he asked.

"Marion's bungalow. I want to talk to someone not insane."

"Oh. Yeah, Richard told me she wasn't coming, tonight."

"She tell me she go and *Richard* was not coming."

"No, Richard is *there*. The silent auction is over and he just sat down at the Zane table. We're sitting with him."

"Fuck!"

Tom waited while his wife pounded on the bungalow door.

"Fucking Lyndy!"

Maya kicked off her shoes and took off for the ballroom, leaving Tom bewildered as to why his wife would wear two colors of pumps.

"Back off, I got it," barked Lou Erhardt III, swatting away the busboy who was attempting to help him out of his wheelchair and into the seat at his table in the ballroom.

"Nah. Leave the chair. And gimme a scotch, neat, please." He liked the way everyone gasped as he stood up on his own steam and shifted into the folding chair. Truth was, his legs were getting stronger every day!

He wished he could say the same for his eyes, though. When that lady surgeon at the podium introduced those hospital "Success Patients," he could have sworn he saw an orderly push his wife onstage with the rest of the gimps. But by the time he had pulled his wheelchair away from the aisle and shifted his tank to the floor, Patti was sitting down, right next to him. She would have to have jumped off the damn stage in a sprint to make it there that fast.

He'd make an appointment with an optometrist on Monday.

Backstage, Queen-Bee-to-Be Lyndy Wallert, was pestering the lighting technician to review her crucial last-minute instructions. "Shall we go over it one more time?" she asked, rearranging his specially prepared instruction cards.

"Lady, I gotta do the rest of the program. Don't worry, I know what you want!" the technician moaned, trying to keep up with his cue sheet.

With a frown, Lyndy dug into the fortified bust support of her gown and tossed a hundred-dollar bill at his console. "Just don't fuck up."

She clicked over to the wings to take stock of the action onstage and, to her horror, watched as a girl with cerebral palsy slowly shimmied forward as her name was called. Frances was supposed to introduce them as a group, not *dwell* on every individual freak! Dinner wasn't even served yet and people were going to lose their appetites!

Lyndy practically pounced on the beleaguered stage manager. "Okay, we're moving on! Is that girl in place?"

"Yes, Mrs. Wallert, but I still don't know where she fits into the program—"

"—and that's none of your business, anyway. Just see that your assistant cues her when I say the words '*Throw-Down*,'" Lyndy said, "or I'll bust you back to community theater! What are the words?"

The stage manager had double-digit college debts to pay off; otherwise, she would have brained Lyndy with a light stand by now. Resigned to being the bitch of wealthy socialites for at least another year, she stared straight ahead and parroted: "Throw-Down."

Lyndy's ears pricked. She could tell from the lengthy round of applause that her poor guests were being forced to clap until that cerebral-palsy girl wobbled back to her place among the group. Ugh! Enough was enough!

Lyndy snatched up the lighting technician's pen and scratched off the Success Patients from his cue list. "Cut their lights."

"But they're not—"

"I said cut their lights or I'll do it myself. We're moving on!"

"Okay, okay!"

Dr. Frances Small and the Success Patients on stage left were suddenly plunged into darkness as a fully lit Lyndy sashayed in from stage right.

"Thank you, Dr. Small and Success Patients! Just a small sampling of the miracles performed every day at Beverly Hills Central, but now I want to talk about another miracle: the miracle of *you*! Drumroll, please!"

(Oh, God, don't let her be drunk!)

"Shelly! How much have we raised, tonight?" Lyndy declaimed.

The spotlight found a slightly tipsy blonde in a crooked updo and a slightly stained Valentino gown. A cigarette girl held a cordless mike to her slightly smeared lips.

"Nine thousand—no, um, *million*, eight hundred and fifty-two thousand!"

"Nine million eight hundred and fifty-two thousand dollars!" whooped Lyndy as the band broke into "Celebrate" and confetti guns shot off silver Mylar bits across the ballroom. "You're all heroes! Give yourselves a hand!"

---

*G*reat. *It's raining silver shit,* thought Marion, entering the ballroom. *Well, at least everyone's seated. I won't get noticed or have to make small talk I'm not up for yet. Now, where was table one?*

*A*s the confetti began to settle, Lyndy finally caught sight of her prey entering the ballroom. It was the moment she'd dreamed of for over ten torturous years!

That's right. Come closer, closer . . .

Incandescent with anticipation, she karate-chopped the air for the band to fade out.

It's payback time!

"That total is a record breaker!" she chirped into her mike. "Now, I know I promised everyone that I wasn't doing a live auction this year. But since we're just *dollars* away from fully funding the Montgomery Rapid Response Viral Detection and Containment Team, I find myself inspired to throw caution to the wind with a Throw-Down!"

*P*epper was the first to spot Marion heading toward table one. And she knew Marion had no idea that Richard was already seated there. At that moment she realized that this was no accident. It had been *planned*!

There was only one control freak who made out the seating chart for the Beverly Hills Central Hospital Winter Gala . . .

Pepper stood and tried to wedge toward her friend in the hope of heading off catastrophe, but to her dismay, she found that two fat guys at adjoining tables had pushed back their chairs so that she was literally being corralled into her seat.

Damn you, Lyndy Wallert!

*S*till recovering from her stint as a Success Patient, Patti was busy quaffing her second glass of Pinot when she was galvanized to attention by the sight of Marion entering the ballroom.

(!)

She's heading for table one. But that's where Richard was seated! Holy crap! Holy crap! Lyndy! You little . . .

Patti started to jump up and warn Marion, but when she turned, she found herself in the sight line of Matthew McConaughey, who had just entered the ballroom. If she had to walk like a Success Patient, she'd never make it to Marion in time!

Patti thought that waving her napkin might flag Marion down, but it only resulted in Matthew thinking he was being "waved over" to Patti's table and he took a seat next to Lou.

Fortunately, Michele Greer, the fast-food heiress who was sitting on Matthew's right, was a fan and immediately gushed all over the actor, which allowed Patti to make a last-ditch attempt to get her friend's attention.

Taking careful aim, she threw her bread roll in Marion's direction, but succeeded only in beaning poor George Clooney, who thought the roll had been hurled by Matthew McConaughey.

Ducking what soon turned into a reciprocal volley of rolls, Patti was helpless to prevent a train wreck.

"And the source of my inspiration . . ." continued Lyndy, feeling the wrath of the Furies coursing through her body, "is none other than the Throw-Down Queen herself! Ladies and gentlemen, Marion Zane! Can we get a spotlight? . . . *Now!*" she practically snarled.

But the spotlight didn't just fall on Marion Zane, who, upon hearing Lyndy call out her name, had frozen in mid-descent above the only seat at table one that was unoccupied by a coat, purse, or person. It fell upon Tawnee-of-the-Valley as well, who was *also* frozen in mid-descent above the *same seat.*

Aghast and aware that all eyes were upon her, Marion quickly sat down. It was then that she noticed Richard, and it took everything in her power to resist levitating away.

Now she was aware that everyone in the ballroom would think she'd mistakenly assumed possession of a seat that had been reserved for Richard's new girlfriend. It took less than a millisecond for her to realize that Lyndy had *planned* this humiliation for her. Screw that, this was an out-and-out rat fuck!

She wanted to leap up on the stage, grab her so-called friend by her scrawny throat, and ask why the fuck she would do such a thing. But the spotlight prevented her.

All she could do was make a pleasant face and maintain her position. Throughout the applause, Marion could hear more than a few people gasp and groan.

Tawnee was also aghast and aware that all eyes were upon her. But she didn't give a shit, and so, after lurching backward and knocking over a trolley full of entrées, she let loose with a bloodcurdling scream.

Up until this moment in time, Richard Zane had been completely unaware of what Lyndy was yammering about because he was happily adrift in the Wonderful World of Prescription Mood Elevators.

Now, looking at Marion and the screaming Tawnee, he felt like he'd fallen through Dante's Doorway to Hell.

Just then the spotlight went off and all three of them—Marion, Tawnee, and Richard—bolted in different directions. But like so many savage carnivores, Lyndy had plans to play with her food before she devoured it. Marion didn't get two steps before the spotlight recaptured her.

"There you are, Marion!" Lyndy cried, as if she'd just found a lost button. "Let's give her another hand, folks!"

Marion was trapped.

Which was exactly the way Lyndy wanted her when she delivered her message.

"Ladies and gentlemen, Marion Zane has recently dazzled us all by *suddenly seizing the baton of hospital philanthropy! Now I'd like to 'Throw-Down' right back at her!* Marion, we're only short ninety thousand dollars for the Rapid Response Viral Detection and Containment Team Unit. Can you cover the rest?"

Marion was a Stage III Trophy. She knew that Lyndy was turning the knife in her wounds and lingering over her humiliation. But even in her shock horror, she realized she'd hit up almost every person at every table for millions.

And so Marion drew herself up with regal grace. Her gracious smile revealed not a whisper of the first yip that had begun screaming into her stomach.

"Nothing would make me happier, Lyndy!" she called out.

Lyndy Wallert was also a Stage III Trophy. Her gracious smile revealed not a whisper of the glorious sense of vindication that was releasing more endorphins inside of her carcass than her last ten years of orgasms.

"Thank you, my darling! Ladies and gentlemen, the Montgomery Rapid Response Viral Detection and Containment Unit is a reality!"

And so was Marion Zane's Unforgivable Humiliation!

The audience applauded, relieved that the embarrassing accident was over and that everyone was smiling again.

"Thank you for joining our Winter Wonderland!" Lyndy proclaimed as the spotlight released Marion Zane to rush away in a flurry of chiffon. "Eat, dance and enjoy!"

Ari almost choked on his steak when he saw his wife plant one ass cheek on the shoulder of the fat man at the next table, swivel her legs over him, and sprint off out of the room.

Lou was too busy saying good-bye to the pushy fellow who'd sat down and flirted with Michele Greer to notice his wife jump into his motorized wheelchair and speed off at ten miles per hour, scattering waiters and guests like startled quail.

Tom wished *his* wife would go after Marion too. He and Maya had witnessed the whole thing from the back of the room and now she was smiling that scary smile and dragging him toward the crowded dance floor.

Maya never wanted to dance at these things. She was a club girl. This couldn't be good.

What Tom didn't see was Lyndy Wallert, who, at that moment, was engaged in dragging poor George Clooney onto the opposite side of the dance floor. He also didn't see his wife palm a fork from the closest table to the dance floor.

Tom was just trying to keep up as Maya used her powerful hips to bump her way through the crowd of dancers. The band was playing an old-school medley of eighties music and the dance floor had become a solid mass.

Luckily, Maya had put her shoes back on so he could see her over the sea of gyrating philanthropists.

And he could see that she that was headed straight for Lyndy. And what was that in her hand? A fork?

I'm Queen! It's my birthday! Get happy! With George Clooney!

Lyndy was too ecstatically busy attempting to hypnotize George Clooney with her "moves" to notice Maya come dancing up behind her. (Obviously, George was fearful of becoming too aroused because for some reason, he kept trying to dance away.)

Lyndy-the-seductress kept pulling him back.

Too bad, George! I'm going to torture you with pleasure!

When Tom saw Maya directly behind Lyndy, a chill rushed down his spine. When he saw her raise the fork, he dove through the dancers.

"No baby! She's not worth killing!"

But he was drowned out by the music and his hand grabbed only air.

Lyndy was too busy shimmying her bosom to notice the tines rapidly approaching the top of her spine.

George Clooney *did* notice the fork-wielding Maya and was secretly hoping she'd stab Lyndy right in the spinal cord before he lost his cookies.

A nanosecond later, Maya plunged the fork . . . into Lyndy's left fake-ass cheek, piercing the double silicone seal. When she withdrew it, four geysers of blue goo jetted forth, covering everyone within a four-foot radius.

It took Lyndy two more refrains of *"You can't touch this"* before she noticed that her left ass cheek was flat and that goo-covered guests were fleeing from her in all directions.

And that she was dancing alone.

And then she realized that she had just suffered an *Unforgivable Humiliation.*

65

Wheels That Spin

After kissing her husband good night, Patti Fink picked up his disconnected portable oxygen tank and carried it into his closets.

Carefully stepping around Genghis-the-mastiff, Matilda-the-Irish setter, Waldo-the-English-sheepdog, and Dingleberry-the-cat (who all liked to sleep in the oxygen-rich, sterile, and ionized piped-in air), she set the tank down in front of a wall of mahogany pullout storage trays. After giving thanks to Saint Francis that the rest of the twenty-three-pet menagerie that her stepchildren had managed to ensconce in her home hadn't discovered Lou's closets yet, she removed the custom black patent-leather oxygen-tank cover.

P. Diddy had *loved* seeing Lou wearing his design tonight at the gala!

Polishing it with her sleeve, she tucked it back into the "formal" section of the storage trays.

Her Lou had been such a great sport tonight! Patti had been so focused on comforting Marion that she'd forgotten she'd stranded her husband back in the ballroom.

She'd almost died of guilt when that busboy rolled Lou into the bungalow, sitting on top of the room-service cart, wired out of his mind, and talking a million miles a minute. No complaints, mind you. Away from her surveillance, the busboy had allowed the old man to down two cups of regular coffee over his limit.

Lou had been chattering away, trying to cheer Marion up with an animated comparison of Lyndy's ass leak to the big spitting thing in Waterworld. On a roll, he'd told her that Tawnee looked like "a bad sack of oysters" and that he'd "seen better heads on a mug of Budweiser."

What a sweetie! He just gave and gave!

Although he probably should have stopped before saying, "What's the big deal with screwing a different woman every night? Turned upside down, you all look the same: like a mashed cat!"

There was a reason for putting a limit on his coffee intake.

As she finished her business at the storage trays, her phone rang. Not used to the new earpiece phone she'd taken to wearing lately, Patti answered it on the first ring without checking to see who was calling.

"Guess who's the Supreme Raging Dominator at Micronesia and *your* new Grunt daddy?"

(!)

"Ahhh, you?" It was Ricky.

"You know it! Uh-huh! Is the old dude dead yet?"

Patti paused and helped herself to a generous hit of oxygen.

(Think!)

"Oh, Ricky! He's having a rough night and suffering terribly!"

"Oh, man."

"Listen for yourself."

Patti pulled off the tubing and opened the air valve on the oxygen, emitting a tortured hiss. Twisting sideways, she pinched poor Dingleberry's tail with the tip of her chinchilla mule until he yowled like the devil, then added a final brutal effect by squeezing a terrible wet raspberry out of Lou's tube of shoe polish.

"I just can't leave him like this," she whispered, yanking a bad plaid shirt (who the heck bought this?) off a hanger and wiping the polish off the top of the shoe storage case.

"Whoa! sounds like it won't be long now."

After she got off the phone and checked Dingleberry's tail for damage, Patti made a beeline to her Place of Supreme Solace:

Her evening-clutch closet.

She found that the light reflected from the mirrors, jewels, and shiny paillettes had a cleansing effect on her most feverish of mind states.

Sitting on the violet pin-tucked poof, alone among the glittering reflections, Patti thought about seeing Tawnee tonight and about how injured she looked with that prosthetic chin and walking cast.

And she thought about what terrible aim Marion had.

If only she'd centered the grille on the waistline, she decided, remembering how Marion had mowed the young woman down in the driveway of the Zane compound.

And she thought about what a really bad idea it is to be around a car when you've had a bad shock horror.

A really, really bad shock horror.

Like when the one and only passion—the one and only all-consuming, self-sacrificing love you've ever had in your life—tells you, out of the blue, he is leaving you, and that he "never loved you at all"!

Like when he tells you that you were "really a rebound thing" after his former wife ran off with the mold inspector.

Like when he announces now that the affair with the mold inspector is over, he's getting back together with her, and "doesn't want you to stand in his way"!

Like when he says you have to get out and that it doesn't matter that you put him through graduate school and sank every hard-earned penny from your stint on Star Trek into reviving his business that is now unbelievably profitable—and that he excluded from you in the prenuptial contract that you signed when he spiked your glass of Tab with two quaaludes.

Like when he doesn't give a crap that you are crumpling on the floor in devastation and informs you that he's going to go jogging now and wants you "gone" when he gets back!

It is a really, really, really bad idea to be around a car then.

Especially when you know his jogging route . . .

Then Patti, swaying ever so slightly, stared at the wall of evening clutches in front of her.

Mirrors, jewels, and shiny paillettes.

She focused on their reflections until these thoughts went away.

66

God Help Us

Baby Jed bit down hard on Pepper's nipple, as if he too were weighing in on his father's latest bit of lunatic behavior.

Ari had summoned the entire family to join him outside in the driveway to witness the unveiling of Daddy's "Big Surprise Delivery."

Pepper had tried telling her husband that "surprise" usually translates to a little kid as something that either fetches, gives rides, or plays Rabid Squirrel Monkey Smackdown and Barbie videos, but he wouldn't listen. In fact, he wasn't paying much heed to any of her ideas nowadays.

"Well, can't say I didn't warn 'im," she whispered to Jed as she watched the uncrating. Ari's buildup had gotten the kids so pumped they were practically spasming with anticipation around the gigantic crate, as if any second Santa Claus himself might pop out.

"Any second. Any second . . ." he teased, enjoying the torture.

"Tell us, Daddy! Is it a tank?"

"No."

"Is it a rocket?"

"No."

"Is it a hamster?" asked Maybelle, eliciting a slow, worried head shake from her father.

"Is it a disco?"

"Is it a pony?"

Or is it early-onset dementia? The whole thing reminded Pepper of those nature films where an unsuspecting goat is staked among Komodo dragons.

The children cheered as the delivery crew unscrewed the last of the lag bolts and let the front panel of the crate fall forward. With a huge whoosh of air, bland-faced Baphyrus was revealed, nestling in a bed of Styrofoam bits.

"Behold Baphyrus!" Ari blazoned gaily, reminding Pepper of a carnival freak-show barker.

Too bad Baphyrus doesn't have an extra leg or rattlesnake skin.

With the exception of a giggle from Maybelle, Ari's introduction fell upon a silent chorus of angry disappointment.

"Aww! It's just a gay man showing his weenie!" scowled Cooter. "Ow!"

Pepper decided that it was definitely time for shampoos.

Her cuffing palm came away greasy.

"No, noo! He is a *god*!" Ari sputtered. "A *Greek* god. A very, very *hetero* Greek god of a river named—"

"He's not he-ter-o if he's *Greek*," interrupted Jerry. "Nana took us to see statues at the Getty. She said Greek men liked men in those days."

"That's why Greek lady statues all have small boobies," Cooter added. "*Ow!*"

"Why are you always talking 'bout boobs?" Maybelle asked him, patting Jed's bottom as Pepper switched him over to her left breast. (Even the delivery crew rolled their eyes at that.)

"Your Nana thinks everybody's gay."

"I know *I'm* gay," Cooter announced. "I *hate* girls!"

"You don't know what you are!" Ari added quickly.

"Why don't you like families with two daddies, Daddy?" asked Maybelle. "Isabel Connor has two daddies. And she's my best friend."

"I *do* like two daddies, sweetheart. I mean I don't *like* two daddies—"

"Then why did you buy us a statue of a gay guy?" asked Jerry.

"The Greeks were not fags!" Ari's eyes were beginning to pop out of his head.

"And we *don't use that ugly word in this house*," Pepper reminded her husband.

"Our *decorator* uses it, Mama," said Cooter. "He says, 'This is too faggy and that is too faggy.'"

"That's diff'rent. He *is* gay. He's allowed to say it."

"But we're Greek," argued Jerry.

"And *I'm* gay," boasted Cooter. "Fag, fag, fag . . . *Ow!*"

The statue was enormous. Pepper knew that putting it out on the end-less lawn was as good as shoving the thing in their neighbors' faces.

"Hon," she said, quietly sidling up to her husband as the deliverymen removed the rest of the crate. "You're not askin' me ta put that thing out on the lawn."

"No, I'm *telling* you that I'm putting this fine antique fountain out on the lawn," huffed Ari, exercising his new dominance (until Pepper's "mommy face" sent him retreating two steps backward). "I mean it's time we started reclaiming our heritage, my baby."

"Like Mama's uncle, the 'human barfly'?" asked Cooter.

"Least he wasn't Greek," grumbled Jerry.

"The Greeks are not faggots and Greek Gods are not faggots!"

"I'm telling!" wailed Maybelle.

"I'm right here! You can't tell me on *me*!" her father bellowed back.

Nothing can make a father feel shittier than the sight of his children cowering and crying behind their mother. Pepper could have told him they were faking, but since her advice "wasn't needed" . . .

"Izzy's daddies are nicer than you!" Maybelle screeched. "I wanna be gay too, like Cooter!"

"Okay, okay. Don't be frightened, little one! I'm not mad," Ari said, lowering his voice and repentantly squatting down to kid level. "Daddy is sorry to lose his temper and say the ugly words, but I just want you chil-dren to appreciate and respect our heritage. Sometimes daddies get frus-trated and make bad decisions. I won't use the daddy voice again. Daddy is sorry. See? I am *nice* now."

The kids weren't about to let their father off the hook so easily and no-body moved.

Ari looked to Pepper for mercy, and hoping it would get her out of the driveway sooner, she decided to grant it.

"Kids, go on an' check out Daddy's statue. He's *nice* now," she mumbled, trying not to laugh.

Ari nodded enthusiastically and the children obeyed (but theatrically kept their distance, for extra guilt infliction).

Then Pepper remembered that Komodo dragons don't kill their prey right away. They take bites, then let gangrene do the rest. "So Baphyrus was the boss of *everything* in the river . . ." she said. "Can you see how he has the face of a boss?"

The children solemnly looked at the fountain.

"He has a big wiener," observed Chevelle.

"Yes, he does indeed."

"Ari!"

"Well, he does, but he also has huge muscles, and just look at those piercing eyes—"

"Does the water come out of his wiener?" interrupted Cooter. "Like Jerry's when he's sleeping?"

"Shut up, you scab!" Jerry socked his brother and a tussle ensued.

"Now, now, boys . . ."

"Wiener, wiener, wiener!" sang two-year-old Chevelle, pointing at her horrified father's crotch.

" 'Yes, he is indeed,' " mocked Pepper under her breath.

The boys started using Ari's legs for cover, causing him to knock up against the statue while Maybelle and Chevelle started a snowstorm of Styrofoam bits as Ari struggled to quell the growing chaos.

"Girls, girls! That can be messy . . . boys, settle down!"

Jed started squalling for a diaper change.

"Not yet, hon," his mother whispered to him. "The goat's still alive."

Lunging in an attempt to separate his sons, Ari ended up being temporarily blinded by a handful of Maybelle's Styrofoam while Chevelle, wanting in on the action, sank her teeth into Cooter's unprotected calf.

"My eyes!" screamed the Ari-the-goat.

"Owwww!" Cooter screamed. "You drew blood! That's it! I'm takin' you out!"

Happy to play chase, Chevelle squealed and ran behind the statue. Ari's vision cleared in time to see his son use Baphyrus's penis for a toehold as he climbed over the statue to cut his sister off.

"Don't step on that!"

"An' don't you touch that baby," Pepper added.

But Cooter was already over, leaving a blood smear across Baphyrus's mouth.

"Coot got blood on Daddy's naked gay man! I'm telling!" wailed Maybelle, hurling another handful of Styrofoam in her father's face for emphasis.

"I'm not done with you, Cooter!" Jerry followed his brother over the statue (using the same toehold).

Chevelle screamed. Cooter hollered. Maybelle screamed. Jerry hollered.

Hello, gangrene. Bye-bye, goat.

Ari felt his wife press Jed into his arms. She too stepped up on the statue's penis and vaulted over, letting her ruffled cashmere sweater fall off so that it landed across Baphyrus's shoulders.

Seconds later, Pepper emerged from behind Baphyrus with Chevelle under her arm and Jerry and Cooter by the ears.

"Naa-nies! It's baaath tiiime!" she hollered, hauling her brood toward the house.

Maybelle ran after them screaming, "Oooh! Can I unscrew all the bubble baths' heads now?"

"Yes, baby," her mother softly replied over her shoulder. "But only *after* you get in the tub."

Ari found himself alone in the driveway with wailing Jed. And feeling more than a little shell-shocked.

Hoping to draw forth some masculine strength and resolve, he turned to gaze upon his statue of the mighty river god.

Unfortunately, thanks to Cooter's lipstick-of-blood smear and Pepper's ruffled sweater, Baphyrus looked more like a Santa Monica Boulevard hustler than a classical god.

Ari wondered if the tears on his cheek were his son's or his own.

With this family, even the gods stood no chance.

67

High-Maintenance Homeless

Pepper practically leaped into the car when Marion came to pick her up for Maya's Garden Tour.

"How'd the kids like the statue?" Marion asked.

"Made it their bitch in less'n fifteen minutes. I dunno what Ari was thinkin.' I swear that man's gettin' more bad-tempered an' silly every day."

Marion shrugged. "Happens with age."

Pepper was so baffled by her husband's behavior that she didn't notice Marion's hair until they hit Sunset. It was upswept and wavier than she'd ever seen it. And the highlights were all wrong. They were pink. "Fuck me. How are *you* doin'?"

"Me? I'm fine! In fact, better than fine. The Muircroft Foundation kicked in three million for the hospital last week, and I've got meetings lined up with five more. You know I really think we should maybe forget going after individual donors . . ."

She wasn't about to talk about herself.

The rest of the way to Maya's, Pepper kept sneaking glances at her friend in the of hope of getting a true assessment of her state, and she didn't like what she saw:

Marion was wearing the same Hugo Boss suit she'd worn to the donor lunch they did together four days ago. It had a stain on the right cuff then and it had a stain on the right cuff now.

And her nail polish looked like she'd applied it herself.

"I assume you heard the Jack Powell went independent, surprise, surprise," she said. "After weeks in office. I think that's a record."

When the sunlight hit Marion's face from the side, Pepper could detect the faintest hints of crow's-feet at the corners of her eyes. They didn't look bad. It was just that no one Pepper knew on the West Coast had lines.

"Give him a month or two and he'll roll over to the other side, no doubt," Marion continued.

"Ain't that fraud?" Pepper asked.

Her friend had definite signs of being upkeep-impaired. Still, nothing to worry about.

Yet.

"There's about twenty voters' groups already forming to sue him for fraud. Thank God our side still has a wide majority."

It was then that Pepper noticed the backseat. "What the heck's all that shit back there?"

"Oh, I'm changing hotels," Marion said quickly, drawing her hand across her forehead then forcing it back down on the wheel. "Being at the same hotel as that gala . . ."

"Not the best of memories," Pepper finished for her.

"And I know everyone means well, but between Richard's desperate lawyers hounding me and concerned friends keeping tabs, I haven't had any time to process. So this may sound strange, but in order to get some undisturbed transition time, I'm keeping my location a secret for now."

Again, the hand to the forehead.

"Oh, honey, I get that so completely!" Pepper said, patting her friend's (rock-hard, supertense) forearm. "Shit, if it was me, I'd be in some South American country with no extradition deals right now, 'cuz Richard, Tawnee, *and* Lyndy would be dead by my hand. So whatever's best for you. As long as ya check in once a week."

"Promise. Uh-oh, here we go . . ." said Marion as they turned on to Maya's street and found it blocked by a sea of cars waiting in line for valet. At least a hundred people were massed around the front gates.

"Fuckin' mob scene! An' they ain't all here 'cuz Maya pimped 'er yard."

Ahead, through the crowd, they could make out the flash of cameras going crazy.

"Is it cool if I park by the service and we slip in?" asked Marion. "I'm not really up for photos these days."

Pepper was already dialing Vlad on her cell.

She kept her eye on her phone as Marion kicked a roll of toilet paper back under the front seat.

As they waited by the gate for Vlad to show up, Marion made a mental note to hide the toilet paper in the trunk with the pillows, sheets, bedspread, towels, blankets, bathrobe, slippers, and toiletries she'd lifted from the maid cart when the hotel had impounded the contents of the bungalow. And she had to dry-clean this suit!

Lyndy had no idea how deeply she had wounded Marion the night of the gala.

Not only had she been made to look the pathetic fool, in order to save face Marion had been forced to pledge away three months of her allowance.

She was sure Judge Volker would have attached some sort of rider covering her supplementing living expenses *on top* of her monthly allowance, *if* NFS & etc. had fought for it. Instead, the faithless misers had remained passive in an effort to break her spirit. They wanted to coerce her into entering a loony bin. That geezer Simon Sacks had even put a lien on the insurance payoff on her barbecued wardrobe to cover the Home Shopping Network expenses.

And she knew that Zephyr was hardly about to replace her clothes. At least that's what her daughter's secretary had said in a text message—their only form of communication these days. Any other requests were answered: "You've spent three months' allowance. We will resume contact in four."

The only clothing Marion had managed to get away with (besides the Hugo Boss) was what she'd been able to stuff into her purse (hotel security busted Xiocena's fat-lady charade) and her "sentimental jewelry" case (which she'd tossed out a window and into a garden bush while security was breaking down the door and pushed past the sofa she and Xio had leaned up against it). She just wished she'd grabbed more wisely.

You could only go so far in February with a beaded gown, five sleeveless tops, and a tangle of stretchy exercise clothes; although, as it turned out, she was finding that going without underwear was very invigorating. Maybe Crystal was onto something.

Marion had been living out of her car.

For the past two weeks.

Even dirt-cheap hotels were out of the question. Her car would be stolen or stripped overnight.

And she'd rather get shiatsu from her backseat than crabs from a Magic Fingers bed.

Xiocena had offered to put her up at her apartment, which was in a more savory neighborhood, but the parking wasn't security and the Lexus didn't exactly blend in. Marion just couldn't risk it.

Marion needed to keep the car intact and in her possession.

How else could she keep up appearances?

Or friends?

And she had a hospital to build.

She couldn't very well arrive at the Four Seasons by bus, then ask a potential donor to put millions into her "fiscally responsible" hands.

The city-council zoning hearing against Richard (aided by Senator Jack "Pick-a-Party" Powell) was in three weeks, and even though Pepper, Patti, and Maya had helped her inch nearer their goal, they had yet to hit $450 million in their fund-raising.

The Westside could only be milked for so much and all Marion's nonlocal contacts were in her *Black Book* in her safe in the closet in the house on the property from which she was commanded to remain a minimum of one hundred yards away.

They needed to hit the $500 million mark and get UCLA to take over. If they failed to do this, Carita Memorial Hospital would be dead in the water.

Marion was reduced to applying for a loan from what her late uncle Jerzy had always referred to as "The First National Bank of Broke."

So far she'd pawned the beaded gown, three pieces of sentimental jewelry (and the happy memories that went with them). The pawn money bought a sexy suit from Moschino (for male-donors-only lunches), a garment-district wholesale parka, gloves, running shoes, socks, a blow-dryer (which, after twenty years of professional blowouts, was harder to manipulate than she'd remembered), and a black rollerball pen (which could double as an eyeliner if the one in her makeup bag ran out). The rest of the pawn money she saved for gas, which wasn't too bad an expense thanks to her hybrid Lexus, disposable phones (bought hot off the street), and cash lunches for donors.

Marion made a point to book lunch reservations at hotels that stocked her favorite toiletries. She was now an adept maid-cart bumper.

She assuaged her conscience by reasoning that her acts of thievery were only making up for all the years she'd brought her own toiletries on vacations, and thanked her stars the purse she was carrying at the time of her eviction was the big Bottega Veneta woven tote. You could fit a boatload of stuff in there and still have room for two toilet-paper rolls and the contents of the breadbasket.

Regrettably, happy hour wasn't what it had been in the eighties. She had yet to find a "spread" that went beyond a dish of organic spiced nuts. (Must be lean times for students.)

Finding a safe place to overnight was easy. Xiocena and her coffee buddy, who Marion learned was named Lourdes, had put out the word on the Housekeeper Network that Marion needed a place to crash. Each day at four o'clock, she received the address of a vacationing Westside resident, their gate code, and the times she'd have to arrive and depart to avoid gardeners or other staff.

This magnanimity had been bestowed because the women of the Housekeeper Network had heard that Marion was dedicated to building a hospital with a large trauma unit downtown.

It was also motivated by the fact that they also hated *putas.*

Even though the alarms were always turned off, Marion never ventured into the pool houses adjacent to the driveways where she parked the Lexus she slept in. Not even to shower or pee. She was acutely aware of how awful it felt to have one's home invaded by a stranger. Beverly Hills gas stations had some very nice restrooms.

Upkeep was a different story.

The prospect of being left without upkeep chilled Marion's soul. It had nothing to do with that self-help-book crap about "not-loving-yourself-if-you-weren't-perfect-within-society's-narrow-definition-of-beauty, blah, blah, blah." She'd studied those self-help-book author's photos on the back jackets and had yet to see a man or woman who was as ugly as she'd been during her first twenty-five years. Growing up, Marion had developed a deep and abiding love and respect for herself that had shielded her from all the humans who judged her appearance as "malformed." As far as she was concerned, you couldn't discuss the experience unless you'd been there.

Theory was nice but human nature tended to elude such formulations. Marion had considered her first plastic surgery as an "equipment upgrade" that got her to another level, one she wanted to play on. The minute her bandages came off, her formerly stalled real-estate sales skyrocketed.

Eat that, self-help books.

If she'd needed a bone through her nose in order to make enough money to get Zephyr back, she would have done it.

Richard would have never *looked* at her if she hadn't transformed her appearance. It didn't make him fall in love with her. But it did get him to *look*.

A wealthy man's definition of beauty was essential life-or-death knowledge for a Trophy. Marion knew her world and the qualifications for admission into it all too well. Billionaires' *second* wives didn't keep husbands or make MAJOR INFLUENCE contacts cavorting around the beach in Ibiza with billowing jowls and pounds of cellulite.

If they *did*, she'd have made sure to acquire them.

It was the same deal as her car.

But her car was brand-new.

And Marion wasn't.

She'd had no idea how fast skin changes without the benefit of HGH, biweekly lasers, exfoliation treatments, plumping salves, private trainers, Power Plates, circulation massage, hydrotherapy, and expensive vitamins. She didn't want the "equipment" to disintegrate.

So Marion had begun to spend part of every day stalking an ever-widening circle of department-store makeup counters, gathering samples like a squirrel. This, unfortunately, meant that she had to subject herself to letting a "makeup artist" paint her face, often resulting in her leaving the department store looking like she'd just walked off the stage after playing the title role in *Turandot*. More than once, she'd frightened small children and broken the heart of that poor, nervous middle-aged panhandler in the Nordstrom's parking structure.

He thought he was hitting on a transvestite.

Yes, it was a brave new world.

She was also spending time at an ever-widening circle of gyms that gave "free trial memberships," but dispite her best efforts, her skin was beginning to smell like bacon. Mostly, she walked (jogging sags the skin) on the bike path at the beach at dawn to avoid sun exposure. She would have tried the public showers down there as well, but on the day she'd planned to check them out, she left her purse in the Lexus and couldn't come up with the "protection money" demanded by Bob-the-flasher.

In desperation, she'd mastered the mysteries of self-serve car washes, discovering that the pressure hose was great for shampooing (and lower-extremity cellulite prevention if you had the place to yourself), and that while hotel butter pats worked as well as Armoral, their *smell* was distinctly different.

She also learned Laundromat survival: always keep an open bottle of bleach within reach to fend off the pervs and avoid all offers of unfamiliar fabric softener unless you're a fan of undocumented skin reactions.

Still, a mere two weeks without her maintenance program and she was already showing signs of . . . ugh, just the thought gave her wrinkles.

And her hair and nails were on their last legs.

Marion had become a member of the high-maintenance homeless, a niche group so small it lacked both Web site and target-audience magazines.

Keeping up appearances was kicking more than her ass. She needed to get creative and consolidate.

As Vlad opened the gate and let her and Pepper join the flow of guests on the side path of the estate, Marion almost began laughing.

Here she was, walking a five-thousand-dollar-a-ticket garden tour in which she'd have the time to view only one of the twelve gardens.

She needed to leave early to make a one o'clock job interview for a practice-model opening at Culver City Beauty Academy.

68

Trophies on Tour

"Pointy fingers at two o'clock. Prepare for gossip an' incomin' smears."

Pepper was giving Marion a heads-up about the fact that Chloe Gelson and Lily Horowitz were walking toward them from the opposite direction on the path. Finding it ironic that Chloe was practically holding hands with the same woman she'd verbally assassinated a mere month ago, Marion bit back a chuckle and braced herself for the usual ensuing personal-space invasion. (And Chloe's trademark fire-engine-red lipstick, which had a tendency to stain everything in its wake.)

But instead of a lipstick smear, Chloe gave her a forced smile and a silently mouthed, half-second "hi."

From a distance of five feet.

Then she curled around *Pepper,* making a show of the fact that they were friends. "Okay, don't look now," Chloe purred conspiratorially as Pepper adjusted her light-colored jacket out of range of the other woman's lipstick. "But I think Savannah Langdon accidentally wore her *daughter's* dress today! I mean, any more back fat and she might as well stamp *USDA* on her shoulder!"

"And *I'm* standing over here to avoid the lightning bolt that God's about to send down on her head any second," Lily said to Marion, and giggled. "I think my boyfriend, John Byers, is working with your husband now. They went to that lunch together last Tuesday."

"The media luncheon?" asked Marion, seamlessly avoiding making the obviously uninformed woman feel awkward. "I heard the Brazilian delegation—"

"There's *Nars Vanderhoon!*" Chloe interrupted, suddenly clutching Lily's arm as if alerting her to a fire. "That architect I was raving about? Now's your chance to talk to him about the house you're planning to build. This is perfect!"

As she hustled her newly wealthy new buddy away, Chloe tossed a "'scuse us!" over her shoulder, like an afterthought.

Pepper made sure to check her jacket for lipstick stains, raving under her breath, "Shit-smearin' star fucker! Think I give a flyin' fuck about *her* opinion of another woman's body? An' who the fuck is she ta judge? There's not exactly a line formin' ta put *her* mug onna Clairol box, glass-house-living, stupid, shallow motherfucker! C'mon," she said, grabbing Marion's arm and escorting her toward the Hanson manse. "Let's go see how Maya's handlin' the invasion."

"Thanks," said Marion, putting an end to her friend's heartwarming attempt to avoid the obvious. She didn't need to say anything else.

Both women knew exactly what had just gone down.

To an uninformed observer, Marion's brief exchange with Chloe would have appeared casual and meaningless.

To a Trophy, it was like a dying canary in a coal mine.

Star-fucking women like Chloe approached all human beings with only one thought in their minds: How can I *use* this person for myself?

Right now, apparently, Marion Zane *wasn't useful.*

Claire strolled out of the shade of Maya's sycamore, oak, and ponderosa-pine-forested drive and beheld a sunlit fairy-tale setting, complete with cottage. She never would have guessed that beyond that mass of trees stood this magical glen! Just like one could never guess that underneath her platinum ringlets were originally brown hairs or that underneath the pink wool coat she had on a Betty-Boop-does-S&M black rubber romper.

Thank goodness Nicky Dupre forgot to take her coat from the car when Claire drove her to her baby shower last night! Claire wasn't up to greeting her peers wearing a reversible codpiece that converted into a strap-on. Craig had said the romper was "playful" as he'd forced her into her car this morning.

Claire didn't want to play.

Nicky's lovely pink wool coat perfectly covered up Craig's romper without looking like it was overclosed. As the wife of Billy's absolutely gorgeous African-American producing partner, William Dupre, Nicky socialized regularly with the Prices, and Claire had yet to see her in an outfit that wasn't *tasteful*. Deep in her heart of hearts, Claire yearned for *tasteful* clothes. Looking at the coat, she imagined that Princess Grace had probably worn something like this.

Feeling more like her secret royal self than she had in a while, Claire teetered down the path to the cottage and slipped inside the white picket-fence gate. She toed across the pebbly stepping-stones (which wasn't easy in studded ankle booties with six-inch-dagger heels) until she rounded the side of the cottage and entered the front yard, which was bursting with tulips, daffodils, and hyacinths.

She could be happy living here, in this cottage in a glen. Fairy-tale secret princesses living in cottages sang songs with human-voiced rabbits and chickadees. They didn't have to outrace fashion; they had only one dress. And they had mean stepmothers instead of mean stepdaughters. Claire would trade Haley telling her that her hair "looked like maggots" for a poisoned apple any day.

The cottage looked so cozy. And from the smell of wood smoke in the air, Claire knew it had a cozy fire burning inside. Too bad all the shutters were closed. She wanted to continue the fantasy just a little while longer. Maybe take a nap by the hearth, eat some porridge . . .

Claire stole a glance at the crowd gathered around the manse to make sure no one was looking as she crept up onto the cottage porch. Its cheery green wooden door practically whispered, "Come in, come in!"

The ogre who threw open the door did not.

"Toilet in backyard!" Dudayev boomed, sending Claire skittering across the stepping-stones and back up on the path, where she almost slid smack into Nicky's gigantic pregnant belly.

Claire's face immediately matched the color of the coat. "Oh my gosh, I'm so sorry I borrowed your coat without telling you! I can give it back if you need it—"

"Please! Keep it," Nicky said in her tough-girl accent. "I'm sweating like a fat man and it hasn't fit me for two months. Did Craig put you in another scary one?"

Claire unbuttoned and opened the coat for a second before Nicky practically crushed her yanking it closed.

"Shit! One look at that thing and I almost went into labor! I don't care if I picked the thing out, you're wearing that coat until you undress in the dark tonight. Alone. By the way, is there a head in there? I gotta take a piss something fierce."

"Backyard," said Claire, taking Nicky's arm and guiding her back up the path. "I had a nice time at your shower last night."

"Me too. Until I learned that it totally fucked me."

"What do you mean?" Claire asked, flabbergasted. "I never attended such a beautiful shower!"

"Right. *Attended*. Past tense. It's over. And I *didn't* invite my mother-in-law."

"But you said she couldn't come."

"Well, *wouldn't* was more what I was thinking," confessed Nicky. "Willie's mom has hated me from the second we met. Not because I'm white, but because I come from South Boston. In other words, I was born poor. She and Willie's dad come from fancy-ass old Atlanta families. She faked a heart attack when she found out I'd stolen her cultured pearl of a son. I almost didn't get married when she refused to attend the wedding. So naturally, I left her off the list that I gave to the shower hostesses."

"If you did it on purpose, why do you even care now?" Claire asked as they entered the backyard.

Nicky sighed. "She had a change of heart this morning! I practically broke water when the old bitch called to apologize. Probably still hates me, but doesn't want to miss out on the grandma action. Anyway, she wanted to know 'when the shower was' because she wants to come out for it," moaned Nicky, waddling to wait in front of an occupied Porta Potti.

Claire gasped. "And now it's too late!"

Nicky tapped her nose. "So of course I spazzed out and said something like, 'You didn't get your invitation? Oh, dear! It's this weekend!' I'm thinking there's no way she could drop all her southern civic-society shit and fly out."

Claire gave a bigger gasp. "And she is?"

"I am totally fucked. Now I have to throw myself an emergency Atlanta-quality baby shower, when I can barely bend my fingers."

Suddenly the toilet door burst open, revealing Patti Fink in rubber

Gucci Wellington boots, jodhpurs, blouse, horse-bit belt, fur scarf, and blazer. "Did someone say they needed help with a baby shower?"

"Oh, Patti, would you? It would save my not-so-skinny white Irish ass!"

Nicky shut the door on the Porta Potti before Claire could warn her. By the time she got out, Patti's project-embarking endorphins were flowing full blast.

"I'm envisioning a melding of cultures: black Atlanta with an Irish twist!"

Meanwhile Lyndera Montgomery Wallert was disembarking from the Bel Air Garden Tour judges' minibus and clipping smartly down the cedar-lined driveway with her clipboard ratings list poised.

She didn't care that she was entering the property of the mongrel that ruined her coronation, or that she might run into her or the few remaining fans of Zane.

She couldn't wait to give Maya's garden a low grade and prevent it from winning jackshit.

Even if she hadn't been a judge, the unexpected delight of catching a glimpse of her vanquished enemy and her bimbo-hick sidekick departing the grounds as the judges' minibus pulled up was worth all the trouble of daring to tread upon enemy territory.

Marion looked like shit. And she was driving herself! Things couldn't be going so well.

Thank goodness her own Montgomery gumption and courage had compelled her to fulfill her duties as a judge. The weaker-blooded might still be in seclusion, licking their wounds. Although Lyndy had to admit that it had been traumatic to lose her dignity and her historic camellia trees in one and the same night, still . . . two weeks was enough.

The crown she coveted remained, as of yet, unclaimed.

Charitable organizations all over town were panicking over the Zane marriage breakup and the dent that it might make in the size of their future coffers. If Lyndy played her cards right, they'd soon be begging for assistance. No one in L.A. possessed contact lists as extensive as Lyndy. (Except Marion, but she was locked up in the divorce penalty box.) Ass-flat or no ass-flat, the BHC Gala had gleaned seven hundred Gs. No other event (with the exception of Marion's uncouth Throw-Down) had raised that much in years!

And this *was* L.A.—a town where memories faded fast when the bottom line was at stake.

Yes, all she had to do was make like a true Republican and rely on audacity to see her through misfortune.

There was a reason she'd worn her lucky Ralph Lauren power suit today . . .

The sight of Lyndy Wallert judging gardens, her Montgomery head held high, would give the ladies a vision of leadership and power at a time when crisis had made the TOP ripe for her picking.

Pausing where the trees opened up to reveal a view of the entire property, Lyndy scratched down her first caustic comment: *Inappropriate and contrived at conception. Still inappropriate and contrived eighty years later. One simply cannot attain a British Isles garden with California vegetation! The results are a mishmash at best!*

And that was only the beginning. Honestly, whoever heard of a Scottish hunting lodge with palm trees and bougainvillea mixed in?

Just then, Lyndy spotted yuccas growing in formal British-style planter boxes anchoring the patio of the manse.

This was going to be fun.

Patti Fink had left the two Stage I Trophies to hang out with Mica Turtletaub, who was one of the judges. She wanted to talk about the ground cover Maya had put in the maze. Mica was a virtual encyclopedia of flora and her answer would be extensive and fun. Plus, this was a time when Patti could draw Mica's attention to the uniqueness of Maya's garden. But most important of all, Patti wanted Mica to point to the ground.

Because Mica gave good bracelet.

It was a pass-it-on-for-luck thing she had. That, plus Mica's grandfather had been one of the coolest jewelers in the world and she had piles of one-of-a-kind stuff spilling out of two vaults.

Ten years before, Patti had seen Mica wearing a pair of divine vintage thirties Deco creations: ribbed frosted crystal encased in smooth gold.

She'd admired the jewelry and complimented her friend—just once.

Mica gave them to her as a gift the following Christmas.

Three years before, Patti had admired a stack of carved onyx wonders dotted with tiny diamonds.

She received them on her birthday the following year.

Ever since, Patti always made it a point to get Mica to point. So far, she hadn't worn bracelets on any of the occasions when they'd met. Today, Mica's sleeves were rolled all the way down, but Patti could detect *bracelet bulges*. Poor Patti knew they were there, yet she couldn't view her potential Christmas gifts as long as Mica kept her sleeves rolled down. How on earth could she admire them? Hence the need to draw attention to the ground cover.

Although at the moment Mica was in her element discussing dichondra, so far she had failed to point her finger to the ground and cause her hidden treasures to slide down her arm. Patti could hear them seductively clicking against one another under Mica's woven jacquard, and their vintage bracelet mating call was too good to go unheeded. She decided to suddenly trip and fall. Then Mica would give her a hand up and a bracelet down. Her plan would've worked perfectly if Matthew McConaughey hadn't also been in the maze at that second.

"Oh, wow! Patti, are you okay?" Matthew asked.

In all of her most extreme fantasies, Patti Fink never once said "Shit!" under her breath in Matthew McConaughey's arms.

His hand immediately went to her back and the expression on her face turned arch. "Flying without your parachute again? Naughty girl!"

Uh-oh.

Maya wanted to hang her head out the attic window and scream, *Go back to the fucking garden, you stupid looky-loo fuckers!* at the people massing around the ballroom with their noses pressed to the glass.

But one of them was a judge.

When Pepper and Marion had visited her up here, it was getting bad, but now it was ridiculous. They were three persons deep out there!

Marion hadn't looked good. And that sucked because Maya had wanted to talk to her about the pressure Tom was putting on her to get pregnant. She'd missed almost five weeks of Diaghilev's happy hour already. Maya thought this was going to be her chance to get her friend alone.

From the way Marion looked, she'd decided no way would she approach her. From the way her face looked, something was wrong. Maybe it was just old-fashioned heartbreak and grief, but Maya thought she'd seen panic there as well. She'd have to keep an eye on her friend—instead of keeping an eye to her living-room windows!

She'd worked her ass off to make the entire grounds perfect, but all the people touring wanted was to catch a glimpse of Maya or her husband.

(Maybe she should tell Tom to go roll around in the maze.)

She'd been hoping to escape and go check out her competition. But the crowds were too thick for Vlad to manage around the garage. She'd been relegated to secret people-watching from the third-story attic window.

Unfortunately, the people she watched the most were pregnant.

There was one now, with a big swollen belly. It was Nicky Dupre, a young wife. She was standing along the camellia-tree alley that the boys had put in and that Lyndy Wallert was now trying to pull out.

(!!!!!)

The people spying into the manse were barely able to jump away from the living-room French doors as Maya blasted out.

Lyndy had successfully extracted one camellia tree and was working on number two when Maya's hand shot out and stopped her from rocking the trunk.

"What-the-fuck-you-think-you-do-you-crazy-bitch?!"

"I'm reclaiming stolen property," Lyndy hissed, trying to bump Maya out of the way so she could continue with her project. "These are *my* camellia trees! I should have known it was you who stole them after that assault the other night!"

Maya had easily five inches and thirty pounds on Lyndy. Plus, she was in flats. She bumped back, sending Lyndy wrapping around the tree trunk like a tether ball. Still, Lyndy hung on like a terrier, and the women continued to struggle.

"Crazy bitch!" yelled Maya. "Did your brain squirt out along with fake-ass jelly? My gardeners *buy* trees! I see receipt!"

Quite a crowd had gathered by this time, including Patti and Matthew McConaughey. He was "assisting" her back to her car and informing every person who asked what was wrong: "Spina bifida—without a parachute!"

But at the sight of the Lyndy/Maya confrontation, Patti immediately seized up with a "cramp." Luckily, Matthew stopped to allow her to recover because Patti wasn't going to miss this confrontation and would have kneecapped the actor before allowing herself to be budged.

"There are gardeners now!" Maya pointed, keeping one hand on the tree.

Sasha and Dudayev were also in the crowd. After Maya's allusion to them, they were trying to make themselves small.

"Sasha? Dudayev?" Maya called. "Did you buy trees from nursery?"

Both men nodded, wide-eyed like schoolchildren.

"You think I'm going to believe your lying Slavic sycophants? These trees are Millicent Miniever Doubles! The variety hasn't existed in nurseries for twenty-five years! Now unhand my property!"

"Your ass has not existed in twenty-five years!" growled Maya. "You're fucked in head and make mistake! My gardeners don't lie!"

At this point Vlad had joined the party. He took one look at Sasha and Dudayev and rolled his eyes. Then he made the mistake of trying to defuse the situation by putting his arms around Lyndy's waist and plucking her away from the tree. "Madame, I'm sure you and Mrs. Hanson can settle your differences peacefully tomorrow. Allow me to escort you back to your vehicle and . . . *Ow!*"

Lyndy had sunk her teeth into his forearm. She jumped to her feet and opened her red Hermès Birkin. It took her two seconds to fish out her cell. "That makes two assaults and a theft. I think that's enough for the police."

Sasha and Dudayev were about to jump in, but at the mention of the word *police,* they froze in their boots.

Vlad was about to try another kind of restraint, perhaps something more effective, like clocking the woman across the jaw—or a choke hold—but Maya signaled for him to refrain.

Lyndy had drawn blood from her antagonist.

Now Maya's eyes narrowed and she spewed forth a string of curses in Chechen.

"I hope you don't expect me to understand that gobbledygook," Lyndy said, chuckling, as she dialed the Beverly Hills Police Department's direct line. "*English,* Maya. In this country we speak *English.*"

Now Maya was *smiling* as she cursed.

"Perhaps you should have taken a Berlitz class before your guttersnipe genetic code rearrested itself. Then again, what can you expect from a half-breed, foreign—"

Wham!

The base of the tree Maya was wielding caught Lyndy upside her head, sending her sideways into the crowd and her cell phone flying into the air to land next to Dudayev's right boot, where it was promptly ground to plastic shreds.

Maya chased Lyndy all the way to down to the gate, where Vlad took over and turned her out to the waiting paparazzi.

On her way back to the house, Maya gave Sasha and Dudayev each a subtle low-five.

69

Needing a Break

Caught my husband by the old oak tree,
Cheating with Susie with his hand on her knee!
He said if I leave him his heart would break.
How many emeralds did it take?
One, two, three, four,
Call Harry Winston! I want more!
Five, six, seven, eight,
Now I want some real estate.

Patti Fink was skipping rope with Jimmy-the-trainer at Melrose Muscle, a cool new celebrity-filled gym. She wanted to get nice and hot before a stretching session she'd scheduled with Bobby-the-masseur. All that spina-bifida faking had ended up by really hurting her back.

And she could think of no better place to get hot than between the benches of Adrian Grenier and Snoop Dogg in the men's weight room.

The thing about exercise was that it increased Patti's blood flow and oxygen to her brain, which inevitably resulted in thinking. Right now Patti was thinking about Lou, which led to thinking about the lawsuit his adult children had brought against them, which led to Lou's terrific test results.

The main argument his adult children had made in their lawsuit against Patti and Lou was that he was "feeble, frail, and near death," meaning an old guy on his deathbed couldn't possibly make coherent decisions, meaning Lou's naming Patti as sole beneficiary of his $9-billion-or-so estate was null and void.

Patti had thought that argument was crap. Especially since it seemed that his "equipment" had woken up. Without Viagra.

She had told the judge as much, but he wouldn't listen, and she'd been forced to drag poor Lou to his entire panoply of specialists and doctors for extensive physical testing.

Happily, the test results had smashed those pesky arguments to smithereens. Lou's delighted doctors reported (in court!) that aside from needing a little postcancer help with respiration, her husband was as fit as a fiddle and improving by the day. Lou was even well enough to begin walking around the house with a cane. They gave him over ten extra years, maybe twenty!

Bottom line: Lou and Patti could expect to win the lawsuit with the adult children by the end of the month.

(And Patti could expect to start receiving *stepmother* presents from the adult children by Mother's Day.)

Unfortunately, thinking about Lou's terrific test results led to thinking about Ricky-the-surfer:

What was she going to do? Now her paramour's calls had begun to include offers to come over and keep her company during "the deathwatch." He wanted to "hang out" in her kitchen so they could "catch a quick bone" between bedside vigils with Lou.

"We'll tell his home-care nurses I'm one of those grief-counselor dudes," Ricky had suggested. "They'll *never* suspect a thing!"

Or maybe he could go for a jog . . .

Patti promised herself that if she ever got out of this mess with Ricky-the-surfer, she was going to take a paramour break. At least for six months.

Maybe seven. After all, Lou was walking . . .

Luckily, at the sight of Snoop eyeing her bust bouncing between bench presses, Patti stopped thinking because the show-off-and-flirt receptors in her brain had been stimulated, resulting in her accelerating her rope revolutions and skipping until she looked like she was inside a giant hamster-cage wheel.

If there was one thing Patti Fink was good at, it was skipping rope. She'd been cardio-skipping daily since her *Star Trek* years, meaning further back than she ever wished to consider, meaning she possessed a stamina level that would burn out most prizefighters.

Too bad she was wearing her wedding ring! Jimmy-the-trainer was slack-jawed at the sight of her, and both Adam and Snoop had stopped pumping. In fact, every man in the weight room was now staring at her.

Even Matthew McConaughey, who was now walking toward her.

Uh-oh.

"There you are, Patricia!" he greeted. "Your secretary said I might find you here. And here you are!"

Patti stopped skipping so abruptly she almost decapitated herself, *but* Matthew didn't look as concerned as she might have predicted. Not even when she bent over lamely at the waist, muttering "Ow."

Instead of rushing to her aid, he held up an eight-by-ten blowup of their Success Patient picture from the gala.

"I wanted to give you this," he said, before tearing the picture in half and letting it fall.

Matthew had vanished from the weight room before the pieces hit the ground.

Staring at the torn eight-by-ten, Patti Fink resumed thinking, which resulted in her becoming acutely aware of a behavior pattern that she desperately needed to change for her own good. Making a solemn promise to herself that she would, indeed, make that change, she straightened her rope and faced her still-attentive male audience.

"Sorry about that," she sighed. "He's been taking the breakup pretty hard."

As she resumed skipping, Patti thought about her promise:

To become more aggressive with her hairstylist and demand redder hues in her eyebrow tint.

After all, a girl's gotta be true to herself.

70

Beverly Park Blending

The valet helped Nicky Dupre's extremely proper Atlanta-matron mother-in-law, Adelia Dupre, out of the car under the Italianate porte cochere in front of Patti Fink's twenty-one-thousand-square-foot Beverly Park Italianate mansion. He attempted a handoff to Nicky and Claire, but "Miss" Adelia, as she was called, refused, swatting them away like flies.

"I'm still aboveground and ambulatory, thank you." She planted her hands on her hips and gave Patti's ever-growing edifice a one-second once-over, sniffed, and pronounced it "faux."

"Unlike the *real Italian mansions* that Michelangelo built on Peach Tree Drive in Atlanta," whispered Nicky to Claire as they trailed the older woman. "Shit, I hope the old bat doesn't ruin Patti's party."

If she had been listening (and cogent), Claire would have warned Nicky that *ruining* Patti's party should be the least of her worries, but her head was preoccupied making up happy new lyrics to the tune of the fairy god-mother's song from *Cinderella*. So she just smiled and nodded.

> *I'm in a bubble! Assholes can't hurt me,*
> *Bibbidi-Bobbidi-Boo!*
> *Take one every four hours and whaddayagot?*
> *Bibbidi-Bobbidi-Boo!*

"Is this Mrs. Fink a close friend of yours, Nicole?" asked Miss Adelia, mounting the limestone steps.

"More than a friend, she's a saint. Right, Claire?"

Again, Claire nodded and smiled.

"How would you describe her entertaining style?" Miss Adelia continued.

"Style?" asked Nicole, sidekicking Claire for assistance that never came. "Ah, I'd say 'traditional.' Patti just helped *Claire* give her first dinner party. William said Claire's husband, Billy, was thrilled and that it was a total success, right, *Claire*?"

"So beautiful!" exclaimed Claire.

Actually, she was commenting on the pretty dewdrops glistening on the leaves of the potted gardenias. They were winking at her!

Claire was having one of the best days in her new Secret-Rainbow-Princess-with-stepkids life. Today, she'd finally discovered the perfect strategy for combating Katia-the-nanny-from-Hades.

> *Birdies and bunnies, kitties and rainbows,*
> *Bibbidi-Bobbidi-Boo!*
> *I have pink toenails, la, la, la, la, la!*
> *Bibbidi-Bobbidi-Boo!*

Her strategy was working so well she didn't have a care in the world. (Who would, in such a wonderful, shiny place?)

Even when Patti's doorbell rang to the tune of a hip-hop version of "When Irish Eyes Are Smiling," a male model dressed like the Lucky Charms guy answered the door, and Miss Adelia began spouting biblical prophecies of doom, the protective marshmallow fluff surrounding Claire's feelings remained intact.

And the same fluff had protected her that morning at breakfast, when Katia had objected to Eva sneaking a piece of bacon from Claire's plate, "Because your stepmother's social life has surely made her a hotbed of contagious disease."

Remaining perky really pissed Katia off.

Such a perfect, effective strategy!

Claire even had a secret name for her new strategy:

"Xanax plus."

So when Claire walked in and saw Patti's airplane-hangar-size living room, she wasn't alarmed. Not one teensy-weensy bit!

Food makes your bot-tom fat! Alcohol makes you
*   snooze!*
The thingamabobs that do the job are
Bibbidi-Bobbidi-Boo!

Accepting a mint julep from a "Riverdancing" waiter in a kilt and a Huey Newton T-shirt, Claire wandered off, leaving Nicky trying to focus on something that wouldn't cause her to miscarry. It wasn't easy:

True to her word, Patti had incorporated the cultures of both parents-to-be into the shower theme. The result was a hellish amalgamation of rapper style, Celtic fetish, and Black History Month.

The tablecloths were southern-barbecue shack-style plastic red-and-white checkerboard. Towering out of the magnolia-blossom centerpieces were three-foot-tall stone effigies of the Celtic pagan goddess Sheela-na-Gig, who welcomed shower guests in her traditional posture: squatting and using both hands to hold open the lips of her gigantic gaping vulva. Being a good pagan, Patti knew that no goddess should stand alone, without offerings at her feet, so she'd wrapped candy bling necklaces and rosaries around potatoes and piled them at each effigy's base.

All place settings sported a Waterford shot glass of whiskey, plus a Colt 45 forty-ouncer in a brown paper bag. Party favors of Louis Vuitton–logo purses stuffed with Dior sunglasses, Moon Pies, CDs of U2 and Lil' Kim, and St.-Christopher-medal-lookalike automobile air fresheners sat on top of each purple satin-covered chair. The walls were hung with velvet paintings of Martin Luther King, Aretha Franklin, and Rosa Parks, interspersed with genuine bullet-riddled IRA posters.

Taking it all in, Miss Adelia downed her mint julep (as well as the one she snatched out of Naomi Campbell's hand) and clamped her fingers like a bear trap around Nicky's wrist to prevent her from bolting.

"Okay, the real truth is that I hardly know Patti Fink," Nicky blurted out.

"That's good," said Miss Adelia evenly. "Otherwise I'd wait until my grandbaby was out and then I'd cut your ass up."

Thus saying, Miss Adelia released Nicky's wrist . . . in order to snatch away Naomi Campbell's cigarette (as well as her pack).

Nicky, being pregnant, refrained from smoking and drinking.

Until she was alone in the powder room.

Claire, meanwhile, preferred the hard stuff: whiskey shots and candy bling necklaces. The sugar went with the fluff in her head.

> *I married Bil-ly! He thinks I'm sil-ly!*
> *Bibbidi-Bobbidi-Boo!*
> *Green gophers go golfing and babies blow snot!*
> *Bibbidi-Bobbidi-Boo!*

She'd put away three shots and was going for four when Pepper and Maya flanked her seat at the table.

"Sorry, kid," said Pepper, gathering up the rest of the candy necklaces and tossing two to Maya. "The menu's either corned beef an' collard greens with oatmeal hush puppies or fish an' chips with somethin' Patti calls 'Ghana sauce.' It's a matter of survival."

The word *survival* reminded Claire that her feelings were in danger of returning. Holding her chartreuse stingray clutch on her lap, she flipped up the flap, felt around inside until her hand closed around the Xanax bottle, flipped off the lid, and slipped out some strategy.

Feeling as sly as a pussycat, Claire then discreetly knocked the pill back with another whiskey shot and sat back.

Well, maybe not that sly because Maya and Pepper were staring straight at her.

"An' what kind of candy was that?" asked Pepper.

"Yes, little one," said Maya, taking Claire's pulse. "With eyes like two piss holes in snow. Tell us what you just blend with whiskey."

Claire was sitting between the wrong two women to give "Bibbidi-bobbidi-boo" as an answer.

As Stage II and a half Trophies, Pepper and Maya were charged with the feeding and care of the herd's young. In other words, they were veterans at "sobering up." A quick check of Claire's clutch produced the Xanax and Maya and Pepper launched into action:

Pepper spiked Claire's water with the Ipecac syrup she carried in case of child poisoning while Maya took up her station by the powder room. Claire showed up as soon as the corned beef hit the tables. Ten minutes later, she was returned to the table with her stomach emptied and feelings unhappily returning. Two Coca-Colas removed all traces of nausea and

Pepper ended the exercise by volunteering to drive her home. (After she lost the coin toss.) The whole thing took less than fifteen minutes.

"I had a prescription for those," Claire said, sulking and ducking while Pepper took 360-degree shots of Patti's decor with her cell. (For Marion, who was "unable to attend.")

"Oh, we're sure ya did, hon. So did the rest of the women eating steamed peas an' shittin' in diapers on St. John's psych unit. Maya, can you get me another shot a' Nicky's mom lookin' at Patti like she wants ta snatch 'er bald-headed?"

Maya obliged, using her own cell to shoot. "Next time we catch you with pills, we use Antabuse."

Claire gave up and dozed off for the remainder of the dining portion of the party.

When she awoke, she saw Miss Adelia playing the spoons next to Snoop Dogg and thought she was hallucinating.

"Don't be frightened. Is talent competition," said Maya, laying a hand on Claire's shoulder so she wouldn't run.

"Talent competition?" asked Claire, coming out of her haze.

"Patti got Snoop ta MC," added Pepper. "We're playin' 'Nicky's Party Got Talent.' Each table picks one representative. Winnin' table gets prizes."

"Talent competition?" repeated Claire over the applause for Miss Adelia.

"See big pile of bracelets?" asked Maya, directing Claire's gaze to a Riverdancer who was holding a platter of diamond-studded Buccellati cuffs. "Those are prizes we will not be winning because X-rated talent does not count. Now, everybody take straw."

While Maya held out a fistful of swizzle sticks for the women at the table to pull, Claire was beginning to galvinize back to life.

If there was one thing she could do, it was sing.

Long before her Secret Rainbow Princess Promise, Claire had her eye on the prize of competing for Miss America, a goal that demanded not only beauty but extraordinary talent. Since two, she had been winning her way up the pageant ladder with her voice, and had also been studying with the best vocal coaches in the state. Even pageant judges had said that Claire Crespi was the one to watch when they heard her sing. She'd had a real shot—before her parents got divorced and money became too precious to waste on such luxuries as coaches. The same went for plane tickets, entry fees, and gowns.

Even with no coaching and her only practice that of being the featured soloist at church, Claire had nailed the Harvest Queen crown.

At that moment Snoop turned his attention toward their table. "And which of you honeys will be performing for prizes?" he asked.

Pepper looked at her short swizzle. "Anybody got a maraschino-cherry stem?"

But Claire was already standing.

Once a pageant competitor always a pageant competitor.

She didn't care that she was in a roomful of well-documented talent, or that Brandy Balatine, Miss Universe from sometime in late nineties, was seated at table five.

As far as Claire was concerned, her honor was at stake.

"Dogg," she announced, "my name's Claire and I'm going to sing."

And then little Claire Crespi from Winamac, in Pulaski County, Indiana, parted her collagen-pumped lips and belted out the most yearning and soulful and life-revealing rendition of "God Bless America" that anyone present had ever heard in their life.

Claire sang out about years of shattered dreams still buoyed up by the hope that someday she would be special enough to be loved like a princess. A Secret Rainbow Princess Promise that could still come true, *had* to come true in this town of dreams.

She was awesome.

With a tear in his eye, Snoop Dogg threw the cuffs to their table before she'd even gotten to "from sea to shining sea."

Women were still on their feet applauding when Snoop broke into "Georgia on My Mind" and waiters brought in Patti's grand finale:

The three-by-three-by-three-foot swollen white belly cake with an Afro-American baby doll bursting out of a tiny incision (close enough to the pubic line to be hidden by a bikini bottom in the future) stole everyone's horrified focus . . . and as a result, it was only Pepper and Maya who happened to notice that Claire had fainted into her oatmeal hush puppies.

"I assume you're doing a C-section," Miss Adelia said to the cake-knife-wielding Nicky, between puffs.

71

Oogey-Boogey

"Hey, Mama! Wanna sit on my face?" asked the scruffy homeless man who was, at that moment, trapped in Marion's headlights as he staggered in the crosswalk. "If you gimme a ride in that fine car, I'll give you a mustache ride! Deal?"

"Thank you for the lovely and generous offer," Marion said through her partially lowered window, "but I'm afraid I'll have to decline, due to previously arranged engagements."

Just because her station in life had dropped, Marion saw no reason to avoid opportunities to engage in civilized conversation. This wino's syntax was a vast improvement on that of the students at Culver City Beauty Academy earlier that day. He was behaving better too . . . Oops, scratch that. He was unzipping his pants.

"Maybe you'll trade for this: I'm hung like a Kentucky—"

"No, no! I'll take your word for it. Yes, I'm sure you have a *most* impressive penis, but, oh, look at the light . . . Bye now!"

Yeah, definitely "going down." And going nuts as well.

Actually, for fifteen minutes Marion had been driving around in circles, trying to locate the Zane downtown property in order to do some sort of *Gone with the Wind*/Tara thing—which seemed rather lame at the moment, but had made complete sense when Marion was buying toilet paper at the 7-Eleven and noticed that her three-weeks-on-the-street appearance had alarmed a young mother enough to alert security.

When a 7-Eleven security guard stops you in line to inform you he doesn't want "your kind" using the alley Dumpsters for a toilet, well, a girl needs to reaffirm her purpose!

But that impulse to convince herself that she still had something of value to offer in this Chutes and Ladders game of life had somehow gotten her hopelessly lost on the streets of downtown L.A. (Well, that and the fact that she'd freaked out and disabled the GPS system two days earlier.)

The annoying disembodied male voice kept telling her that she was "going the wrong way!" when the GPS-prescribed route suddenly became congested and she was trying to find a way around the gridlock. (No shit, you friggin' satellite bleep! I should be going to Mustique, but I need to find a Laundromat! Shut up! Shut up!)

Nuts.

That's what happens when you go without rapid-eye-movement sleep for over a week as a consequence of having to wake and drive to a new location every three hours. Marion had never thought she'd reach a point in her life where she'd actually miss the luxury of being allowed to sleep a full night in the driveways of strangers. But here she was, tooling around downtown, with the rest of the homeless.

Her Lexus hybrid had been busted out of the Westside.

Evidently, an overzealous Neighborhood Watch block captain had recently done some tree trimming on her property (in order to check out her neighbors' new upstairs addition). When, in her zeal, she happened to stand on her toilet to better surveil the neighborhood, the block captain noticed the roof of an unfamiliar car parked just inside her neighbors' gates. The sighting turned into the latest Holmby Hills urban-legend mystery instead of front-page news only because the block captain's housekeeper, a network member, "accidentally" knocked off her glasses and broke them. Then "accidentally" disabled the household phones. And cell phones.

The cliché was right. It was all about who you know.

All about contacts.

The idea of contacts got Marion to thinking about her *Black Book*. She wondered if it missed her. Xiocena had told her that Richard had thrown Tawnee out of the Zane compound, but not before she'd repapered the closets. Poor lonely little *Black Book*. There were so many new entries she wanted to feed it.

Like which parking facilities were the safest to spend a few undisturbed hours in. Especially that well-lit parking structure in Santa Monica with the orange-scented disinfectant covering up the wee-wee and barf smells in the stairwells, bathrooms, and elevators. That was a find! She could get almost six hours of sleep in a row before a cop knocked on her car window, wondering if she had OD'd.

Lyndy would have gotten a kick seeing her rousted like that.

Speaking of Lyndy, Marion was still having a hard time accepting her as the mastermind behind all the rat fucks of her recent life. The minute she'd seen Tawnee spotlit at the gala (and Lyndy grimacing at her like the bichon guy), she'd figured out that her erstwhile friend was acting on feelings that had been building for years. But what she couldn't figure out was *how* Lyndy had been able to pull the whole thing off. She certainly couldn't see Lyndy knowing about drugs like Rohypnol, much less *buying* them:

"Pssst! Yes, you, with the institutional haircut and the regrettable oversize trousers! Do us all a favor, pull up your pants and sell me a pint of that date-rape substance. Uh-wh! Keep your distance! I haven't had a tetanus shot this year. Now hold your breath and drop it in the sanitary container."

Couldn't even picture it.

In these past three weeks, Marion had reviewed (several hundred times) her history with Lyndera Montgomery Wallert and concluded that she had no one to blame but herself.

When she'd first convinced Richard to purchase the entertainment companies and move to L.A., Lyndy had been as friendly to her as she'd have been to any potential ATM: parceling out a few charity invitations and condescending hellos as long as Marion was willing to pony up a donation and kiss the ring. And Marion didn't mind because she was a Stage I at the time and busy studying as many hostesses, philanthropists, and tastemakers as she could, the same way she'd studied successful real-estate brokers and sorority girls—not in order to usurp their positions, but to get a handle on how to operate in her new company town (without vomiting).

The turning point had been the Oscar de la Renta dinner Lyndy had invited her to. After Marion received that Lake Como invitation, Lyndy had been all over her like she was made out of Barneys New York Complimentary Parking Cards, offering to squire her around town like the gatekeeper to Hollywood and calling her night and day. In other words, she had wanted to become "close." Marion didn't have the benefit of a Trophy mentor to warn her that women like Lyndy were only capable of being "close" in the *Machiavellian* sense. Being the cootie girl in high school, she'd never been included in any group of girls and had therefore missed valuable lessons in social warfare, such as the one that tells us that "there can only be one queen bee in a hive." Plus, to be honest, she'd been too distracted by her newfound MAJOR INFLUENCE.

In the Trophy-wife world, being travel-with pals with a designer was the status equivalent to a football player winning a Heisman or an aspiring starlet a Supporting Actress Oscar. Marion came back from Europe as a Stage-II-with-a-bullet. Exclusive invitations filled her mailbox and jammed her phone and she now found herself hobnobbing with artists, politicians, and international celebrities. But the best part was that people were willing to get behind her. For the first time in her life, Marion was able to champion a cause or fight an injustice—and win. Heady stuff for someone new to the game. Lyndy had just somehow blended in with all of it. It wasn't as if she was the only woman who suddenly wanted to be Marion's friend. Lyndy was just the one who put in the biggest effort.

Ah, those golden days of innocence!

Even after Marion had witnessed enough casualties to become smart enough to bond with women in possession of healthy agendas like Patti and Pepper and Maya (correction: aside from numbness, Patti had *no* agenda), Marion still kept her friendship with Lyndy because a crabby asshole who sanitized her hands every five minutes and was snobbish to the point of being comical added a nice counterpoint to the group. Lyndy was a Stage III whose bark was worse than her bite, as far as Marion was concerned. Sure, she'd heard the story about *how* Lyndy rose to become a Stage III, but since it had supposedly taken place *before* Marion had arrived in L.A., she wrote it off as urban legend with the rest of the gossip.

And by that time, she was a Stage III herself.

Thanks to her *Black Book*, she'd been able to accomplish feats of heroism that elevated her in status while alienating no one, especially Lyndy. She'd figured anybody who'd wanted to come after her would have done so already. And admittedly, Marion had thought that no one *could* come after her. After all, she'd kept her nose clean along the way, making zero social enemies and keeping her secrets close to the vest. She'd risen *not* by being competitive but by simply doing her own thing.

And that was her mistake:

She'd bought in to the illusion of "bulletproof."

Which got her thinking about Richard.

Because she'd made the same mistake with her marriage.

At first, Marion wondered if her awful turn of fate was perhaps God punishing her for breaking up Richard's first marriage. The fact that the ex was a closet lesbian didn't exactly excuse Marion's behavior; she'd broken up a family, even if Mommy was doing her secretary and using poor Richard like a cash cow. Maybe Dickie Jr. would have turned out better . . . Nah.

She'd brought the disaster upon herself, thinking that the love, mutual respect, and history she shared with Richard (and lack of a prenuptial) would fend off any outside entity with malicious intentions. Frankly, she'd always thought that if the threat arose, it would be in the form of another woman who was after Richard, not a psycho-revenge-monkey-socialite like Lyndy who was after *her*. And if the unthinkable should ever happen, well, she had NFS and etc. in her corner. Bottom line: Marion had thought she was safe. Same old cocky "bulletproof" illusion.

Which got her to thinking about Zephyr.

Because she'd made the same mistake there too.

She'd thought her secret was safe. So safe she could put off dealing with it. Especially after she'd gotten rid of all those awful lying gossipmongers and . . .

Uh-oh. The engine of the hybrid Lexus was dying. Under a freeway overpass.

Oh, shit, oh please, oh no, oh please, oh, don't run out of battery!

She'd already run out of gas and was depending on the battery to get her to a gas station. But all the gas stations had been too scary to stop at. Where she was stopped at now, though, was, alas, even scarier.

Marion immediately cut her headlights and removed the key from the ignition to preserve the starter. Besides, there was no OnStar emergency service that was going to check on her. That had been canceled with the Bluetooth phone in order to take that Greenwich Foundation delegation to out to lunch.

Marion wanted to kick herself. Not because she'd been too sleep-deprived in recent days and too pampered in her past to realize that a hybrid could go only so far with no gas, but because she had refused to fence the Portofino brooch and purchase a new AAA card.

She'd refused because it was the last little happy bit of her husband she had left.

Even more than her Key to the Kingdom. (Which wasn't really a key at all anymore since it wasn't getting her in anywhere she wanted to be.) She'd locked the engagement ring up in the hotel safe, just as she had every night, thinking she'd be sly and get *it* out before she was forced to get herself out. She wasn't and hadn't. And considering her recent movements, both she and the ring were safer being apart. Old Simon Sacks was probably thinking of a way to convince Zephyr to sell it right now. If he hadn't already sold it himself. And in the end, losing it really didn't bother Marion a bit because Richard had let her pick it out herself.

But it was Richard who had picked out the brooch.

On that trip where she'd surprised herself and gone against all her instincts by falling in love with the big goof. She'd never regretted it. Even now. Even if Richard was so stupid as to allow a rat fuck to turn him into a traitor.

(She still loved him.)

All she had left were the memories that went with that brooch, memories of the first time in her life that she'd ever felt safe. She'd dropped the mask and told her whole life story to Richard on that Portofino trip—sparing no gory details. And it had made him love her even more.

Well, you can't put a brooch in a gas tank.

Marion whipped out her disposable cell phone and called Xiocena to announce that she was stranded.

"I told you keep more gas in car!" scolded her ex-housekeeper. "I want to see who's at the Elton John party!"

Marion had completely forgotten it was Oscar night.

What a difference a year makes . . .

"Where are you now?" asked Xiocena.

"Well, that's a good question . . ."

"Aieee! Why you kill Mr. Bossy?!"

(That was their name for the male GPS voice.)

"Because he deserved to die! Hold on now." Marion craned her neck to look around. "I think I'm underneath the freeway turn before Echo Park. Or maybe the one to Pasadena . . . Or is that Eighth up there, after all?"

"*Madre de Dios!*"

Marion thought she heard other voices on the line besides her maid's. "Are you alone, Xio?" she asked.

"Oh, no. I have big fun party with Hillary Clinton and Jennifer Lopez! What you think?"

"I think I'm going to have to get out of the car, take a look around, and get back to you."

"Aiee! Nooo! Don't hang up! I lose you! It no safe!"

"Fine, fine! I'll keep the line open."

Marion slipped on her cheap black parka, opened her car door, and stuck her head out to look around.

Oogey-boogey.

Whoops! That's just my reflection in a puddle.

Marion's sanity wasn't the only casualty of sleep deprivation. Her appearance had taken a body blow as well:

When the instructor at Culver Beauty Academy was discussing the day's assignment that morning, Marion had been particularly exhausted. She thought she heard the word *coif* before she passed out in the shampoo bowl. When she woke up, she discovered, to her horror, that the instructor had actually said "Goth."

Marion's four-process claret-auburn locks had been indelibly transformed into jet-black locks, with jagged jet-black bangs slashing across her forehead (give or take a few fluorescent-green streaks), and her eyebrows and fingernails had been dyed and painted to match.

It was hard enough to remain positive and look on the bright side when lack of HGH was causing the hormones to leak out of her body like a punctured balloon. But it was damn near impossibly hard when you looked like a character from a Japanese manga book.

The only bright sides she could come up with at the moment were that as a Goth, she no longer had to *try* to look tough at the ninety-nine-cent-store parking lot, or while patronizing public bathrooms, and that the barbed-wire-with-the-entangled-bloody-heart temporary tattoo she was currently sporting made her jewelry-free neck look less bare. Plus, she wouldn't be having any pesky potential-donor lunches anytime soon.

Or city-council hearings.

"*Good evening honorable council members, Senator Powell, Mr. Mayor, fellow citizens, today I plan to put forth a compelling case as to why designat-*

ing area number 6158 a hospital zone is a compassionate—hey! Hey! Let me go! What is this? No! Not the straitjacket. Noooo!"

That's why she'd wanted to find the Zane downtown property.

To say good-bye.

Now all she wanted to find was gas.

Marion tucked her strip of cut-up blanket around her neck like a muffler over her three layers of leotards (which kind of went with the look, come to think of it) and got out of the car.

Seeing no danger, she headed for the corner along a glass-strewn strip of sidewalk that bordered a small building surrounded by a metal slat-woven chain-link fence. Slats were missing in patches and she could see through to the asphalt yard, where she sensed movement not more than two feet away.

It was coming from a woman, curled up strangely in the doorway of the building. Taking a closer look, Marion could see a little hand sticking out from underneath the woman—what looked like a child's hand. Then she realized it was a mother curled protectively around her toddler. They were sleeping and shivering in their sleep.

And here she was whining about having to sleep in a hundred-and-fifty-thousand-dollar car.

"Mrs. Zane? Mrs. Zane!" barked the cell.

"Shhh!"

Marion didn't think twice about taking off the parka. She scrunched her hand through the chain link and tapped the woman, who startled warily as Marion pointed to her parka and tossed it over the fence. The mother caught it and wrapped up her child. A girl around three.

Would she and Zephyr have suffered this fate if she had kept her?

She wished she'd brought her purse. She wished she had some money in her purse to give to the woman. The woman's shoes were no more than bedroom slippers, so Marion slipped off her running shoes and tossed them over too. Then, because running shoes are no good without the cuff-less socks that make your legs look longer and don't leave a little ribbed sock-cuff line dented in the skin above your ankle, she took off her socks and tossed them over. At that point she wished she could also toss the Lexus over the fence.

The woman smiled and made an exhausted gesture of thanks, then crawled under the parka with her daughter.

Marion wrapped the blanket strip closer to her neck and picked her way to the corner, but found that all the street signs were missing.

They were probably put to better use—as housing material.

"Sorry, Xio. Still looking," she said into the cell.

"Okay."

Figuring freeway signs were probably less likely to be missing than street signs, Marion crossed the street and scrambled up the littered embankment that led to the on-ramp, clutching her strip of blanket to her throat at the top to keep it from being ripped away by the cold blast of traffic wind.

She was grateful that she was still flexible enough to lean back and make out the words SANTA ANA on the gigantic green sign tower. She wasn't grateful when a discarded half-full fast-food drink hit her on the side of her face.

Marion lost her balance and rolled back down the embankment and onto the sidewalk where she'd started. Seeing stars, she sat up and took a moment to assess the damage. Aside from the weeds, trash bits, and a freezing neck from the drink she judged to be Pepsi, she was fine.

Then again, maybe not.

Something was in her mouth. Spitting it out, she realized it was one of the veneers from her front teeth.

Nice. Goes with the look.

So did the tears emphasizing her kohl-rimmed "smoky" eyes.

As her vision began to clear, Marion found she was looking down the street at two fuzzy boys trying to jimmy open the door to her fuzzy Lexus. They were (obviously) not pros because they were using something that looked like a fuzzy screwdriver, not a fuzzy slim-jim. But then one of them scratched the fuzzy paint—

"Hey! You boys get away from my car!"

Marion scrambled to her feet and trotted toward the boys to shoo them away. But as they stopped jimmying and straightened up, her vision cleared enough to make out two baby mustaches and she realized that the boys she was shooing away were *big* ones.

They were sixteen or seventeen—an age when the male body's testosterone output triples. And they were taller than she'd thought.

And they were staring at her.

(Sizing her up.)

"Hey, Xio, I'm in kind of in a predicament here, Xio . . . Xio?"

The phone was dead.

Now the very clear big boys with baby mustaches were swaggering toward her. Smirking.

Marion was starting to turn to run for her life when her bare foot stepped down on a sliver of glass, sending a sting up her leg.

And she realized she was tired.

Tired of running, tired of losing, tired of a world that mocked philanthropists and made developers rich while mothers and kids slept in doorways.

Marion was so tired she was crazy.

There was a two-foot piece of broken pipe on the edge of the embankment. She grabbed it and advanced on the boys. And as she advanced, she banged the pipe viciously on the cement pillars and walls of the underpass.

"You think you can take me?" *Bang!* "Then let's go!" *Bang!* "But you better think about the fact that there's no nearby trauma center!" *Bang!* " 'Cause I'm telling you you're gonna need one before I let you take my car!" *Bang!* "See, I've got nothing else left to lose!" *Bang!* "Except maybe more estrogen!" *Bang!* "So c'mon!' *Bang!* "I'll grind your bones between my teeth!" *Bang! Bang! Bang!*

Mistaking Marion for a meth-crazed hooker, the boys thought better of attacking her and jogged away.

She watched them until they were gone. Then she calmly opened her car, got in, relocked it, and looked at the pipe in her hand.

And then she screamed.

Toward the end of her scream, she caught her reflection in the rearview mirror and noticed the budding wrinkles—sure to bloom without the ministrations of lasers and Botox and other products indigenous of low-stress, high-economic lifestyle. And she saw her dark veneerless front tooth. And manga hair.

And Marion realized she was looking at Baba Yaga.

"Baba Yaga" was a favorite cautionary tale told by all Eastern European grandmothers and parents in order to scare children into behaving. Baba Yaga was a crone with iron teeth who flew across the night sky in a big black cooking pot, looking for bad little boys and girls to eat. She would bang her fire poker on the pot, making sparks and screaming at the top of her lungs: "Bring the wicked, bring the cruel, I will put them in my stew! If after dark you're in the street, I'll grind your bones between my teeth!"

Yep. She'd turned into Baba Yaga. Scaring bad little (big) boys. (The original Baba Yaga was probably a homeless woman in Kraków who got tired of taking crap.)

Knowing her best shot at attracting police attention was to appear to be peacefully asleep, Marion closed her eyes and passed out.

A hand rapping on her driver's-side window awakened her.

But it wasn't a cop.

No. She *recognized* this hand.

It was easy, even though the hand had a new expensive manicure. And as Marion mentally plugged the hand into her time line of the last two months, she realized she'd been right in thinking that Lyndy hadn't acted alone.

Because the hand she was looking at was capable of *anything*.

And she knew it before she got the key in the ignition and she got the window down and the face of the waitress came into view:

Because the waitress's hand was wearing a heavy gold bracelet, a bracelet on which she could see a wolf sinking its fangs into a rabbit.

Oogey-boogey.

Verna Hale had added fat to her cheeks. She'd had her nose, lids, and jawline done too. Her skin had been chemically peeled and her hair was dyed dark.

But the hungry look in her eyes and her shark smile were the same as they'd been all those year back.

"Evenin', blood sausage."

Verna's voice was unmistakable too. No wonder that in assuming the role of the "waitress," she'd made her voice sound hoarse. Otherwise, Marion would quickly have recognized the grandmother of all rat fuckers.

"What happened to your old face?" Marion asked. "Burn off when you went to hell?"

Verna scowled. "Australia. Which is essentially the same thing. Shit, Marion, we were all set to watch those kids play with you." Verna looked over her shoulder and yelled, "Weren't we, Donnie?"

Marion followed Verna's gaze to a large man with a long-lensed camera, leaning on a van across the street. She recognized him too. He was the other "caterer" from the blow-job party.

Which explained both "Pinky" and the crazy spending.

"You drugged me," Marion accused Verna. "You drugged Richard and Tawnee."

"Yes, yes, and yes," Verna replied smugly. "Well, Tawnee actually gets off on the stuff, so technically she doesn't count. Plus, she's a regular employee of mine. 'Course, she's been pretty useless since you turned her into *roadkill*! Lyndy almost had to use a glue gun to keep her chin on."

"So you're working for Lyndy now," Marion sighed.

Verna hummphed. "Other way around, doofus! *I* contacted *her*! And only because I needed inside information from someone who hated you as much as I. No, my little blood sausage, Lyndy was just another tool. Albeit an extremely useful one! I thought you'd last indefinitely on thirty thousand bucks a month! Thank God she's a sadist and came up with the idea of asking you for money to keep you suffering in the spotlight. And thank God you were too proud and status-conscious to turn her down. But there are lots of tools out here in L.A. and I plan to use them all when I take the rest of you Trophies out one by one. *I've* been planning this for years!"

Make that four *"bulletproof" mistakes.*

"Years? Instead of having a life? How sad."

"Don't you dare pity me, you homeless hypocritical freak!" hissed Verna. "I saw just how far that pity went when I stopped being Mrs. Fred Bowman!"

"Hate to date ya, but that was before my time."

"Collective reference." Verna sneered. "You all drop people like hot potatoes. Or banish them down to digereedoo-land. Now, where was I? Oh yes, me, planning for years, in the land of sun overexposure and frightful cuisine. Do you know how hard it is to separate someone like you from their money? I corresponded with at least fifty U.S. lawyers about it. First, I had to wait until your spook went on vacation . . . His name isn't Ivan, you know. What is he? Ex-CIA or something?"

"Ex–German military." Marion yawned.

"Yeah, *right*. Well, he's not yours anymore," snapped Verna. "Next, I had to get you and your hubby divorcing. Not an easy feat. You were supposed to leave when you caught him in bed. He was supposed to split when the poodle thing went public. What kind of doormats are you two? Don't answer. Then I had to make you look crazy—"

"What if I had chosen to go into treatment?" Marion asked.

"You? No fuckin' way! You ran your ass way too high up the flagpole! As long as there's breath in your body, you won't jeopardize that! And you can see how well that pride's workin' for ya. Piss in anybody's bushes lately?"

"No, but you'll be crapping in senior diapers when you're done serving time for the charges Richard and I bring against you."

Verna let out a malicious laugh. "Yeah. Like he's gonna take your call. He's not even in the country! He took that big private plane-that-used-to-be-yours to that big private yacht-that-used-to-be-yours in the Caribbean and won't be back until your city-council zoning hearing. The women are probably coming out of the woodwork to ambush him down there. I bet you even know some of them. And even if you did get through to him, he'd have you in a straitjacket before your deflated lips could say Yves Saint Laurent!"

"Wanna wager on it?" Marion asked. "You're forgetting that you crashed a television series and two movies of his when you went after those actors with your lies."

Verna locked eyes with her and slowly leaned down until their faces were level. "I don't gamble, blood sausage. I *work* for my money. You're not going to call Richard *or* the police about me. Not unless you want to see an extensive photo diary of your adventures in homeless land splashed all over my new Web site, blog, and supermarket tabloid."

Across the street, Donnie waved his camera proudly while Verna straightened and preened in a way Marion would have found laughable (if she hadn't been buckling back from the first yip). Still, she wasn't going to let this viper see her sweat.

"See, Verna Hale died in Australia," her enemy continued. "I even burned my fingerprints off—ow! I'm *Beverly Linton* now. Publisher and owner of Red Hand, the new gossip-empire brand that's going to sweep this country by storm. I've got enough deals in place and Australian dough backing me to become a national power broker within a year! The model is city-specific. I'm going to offer scoops on celebrities alongside stories on local swells. It's genius!"

" 'Beverly' is a seventies name," Marion reminded her.

"Fuck you! Everybody will read my work because everybody hates the rich, which is where *you* come in, blood sausage. You hold more secrets than the Vatican and Pentagon combined. Unless you want to be the lead schadenfreude story in my L.A. flagship launch, you're going to feed me some of that gossip that you've been hoarding for yourself all these years. I'll start with your juiciest and milk you for one secret a month after that. I figure you're good for at least three years of scoops, by which time you'll get yourself a new rich guy and some much-needed appearance work because I'm going to pay you one million dollars to seal our deal!"

"Now it's my turn to say 'fuck you,'" Marion retorted, wincing through her teeth.

"Aw, feeling pressured, are you? Tough titties. It's not as if you can reinvent yourself this time; you're a little long in the tooth for that. What are you going to do? Go back to real estate? Maybe with some schooling. But you'd have to leave town. No, you're only qualified for one job: socialite hostess. But there's not a lot of call for such a position without a wealthy man. And you won't be getting many dates if I saturate this town with your sad nasty photo spread . . . So what will it be, blood sausage? Secrets or starring role? You have one week to decide."

"One week?" Marion asked as the yellow lights of the underpass glinted off the wolf bracelet while Verna tapped her nose. Marion's hand closed around the pipe she was holding and she calculated the upsweep she would need to make in order to crack it across that spot.

And then things happened very fast.

Marion heard the 1968 367 turbo Camaro coming before she saw it almost take Donnie's legs off, causing him to jump backward and bang his head into the side mirror of the van. He went down hard.

Then the classic flaming orange muscle car, with two white racing stripes on its hood, did a three-sixty at the end of the street and headed straight for Verna Hale, who dove away low, like a volleyball player trying to pick up a spiked ball.

Marion braced for a crash, but before it happened, the Camaro screeched to a stop next to the Lexus. And when Xiocena blasted out of the passenger side holding a can of gas, she gave Marion a clean view of Pepper, wearing a *fabulous* Dennis Basso evening gown, behind the wheel.

72

Trophies on Wheels

"Git yer ass in here!" Pepper yelled.

"What about Xio?" Marion yelled back. As weary as she was, Marion didn't want anyone else to drive her Lexus. After all, she'd fought menacing children off for it. (And besides, the bed in the back wasn't made.)

"She's gonna follow soon as she dumps 'er can! Marion! GIT IN NOW!" commanded her friend.

The Mommy voice did the trick and Marion got out of the Lexus. But as soon as she opened the Camaro door, she froze. Patti and Maya and Claire were in the Camaro's cramped backseat, also wearing fabulous evening gowns. (Well, Claire's looked like it was made out of shredded wheat, but once the girl unfolded from Maya's lap, Marion figured it might look better.) Marion wasn't prepared to face *anyone* as the manga version of Baba Yaga, much less *extremely glammed girlfriends*. It was like getting into the clown car and discovering all your colleague clowns were supermodels.

In that moment of hesitation, she felt a card being slipped into her hand from below. Looking down, she saw Verna Hale crawling like a roach away from the Lexus, and a second later Pepper was yanking her in and closing the Camaro clown-car door. Marion tucked the card into her bustier as she slipped on her seat belt. But not before seeing the scrawled phone number on the card and and the words *One Week!* scrawled beside it.

"So how many pictures did those paparazzi get?" asked Pepper, peeling up the freeway on-ramp.

"None," Marion lied. "I think they wanted directions. How did you know where I was?"

"NSA spy technology," Pepper replied. "Still got some friends left in D.C. I planted a chip in yer last cell phone so we could track you from the setup at Xio's house. Claire, can ya move that head so's I can see better?"

"*Track* me?" Marion asked in surprise. "Whatever on earth possessed you to—"

"You wore the same suit twice in one week," said Patti, matter-of-fact, by way of explanation.

"We *had* to shake down Xio," added Maya, by way of conclusion.

"All of you?" asked Marion, staring at Claire. She hadn't thought that the young Trophy was exactly in her lifeboat.

"No, just Maya, Pepper, and me, but Claire was at *Vanity Fair* with us when Xio called in the code red, so we filled her in," explained Patti. "By the way, Patti Hansen looked *gorgeous* tonight! Do you know who she goes to for—"

Marion interrupted. "You *filled her in*?"

"Well, Lyndy went rabid and we needed a fifth," reasoned Patti.

"Who are *we*? The New York Knicks?! No offense, darling," Marion said to Claire, "but we're fairly new friends . . ."

Claire stared back through bleary eyes. "My husband is still in love with his ex-wife, my stepchildren hate me, and they won't let me have any more Xanax because I'm abusing," she croaked, indicating Maya with her thumb.

"Okay, we're *better* friends, but—"

"And you were the first L.A. person who was kind to me."

"And she knows she will suffer if she blabs," added Maya.

"More than I already am?" moaned Claire.

If she only knew, thought Marion, giving up and turning to Pepper. "So, *how much* did Xio tell you?"

"Everythin,' hon. And we don't care, we love you."

"And fuck you for not trusting us!" added Maya.

"That whole dumping-the-broke-ex-wife is so nineties!" added Patti. "Besides, you'll get it in the end."

Those were the three nicest things Marion had heard in a while. She quickly rolled down her window, hoping freeway air would push her tears back in.

"Sorry," she said.

"Is okay," said Maya. "Just don't do again. We need you."

"Even with that hair," added Patti. "Did it get you into any clubs? Ow, Pepper!"

Pepper grinned and honked the Camaro horn, which played "Dixie" as Xio, in the Lexus, blew past them on the freeway.

"I still can't believe she gave me up to you guys," Marion said as she waved.

"Shit, Marion," Pepper scoffed. "Yer always sayin' it takes a village. Xio just got tired a' bein' the only friggin' villager."

"At least she's not the only Goth," Marion replied.

"Well, we'll soon remedy that," Pepper said, brightening.

"Why? Where are we going?"

"Beach house," said Patti. "There's a clandestine A-list trauma team waiting to make you presentable enough to be seen in daylight and take care of the two days' worth of dermo, plastic, and hair and beauty-salon prepaid appointments we've set up. You can sleep through the whole thing. I always do."

"I add emergency dentist in morning," Maya suggested, after noticing Marion's damaged veneer. She made a note on her BlackBerry.

"Aside from the veneer, did it ever occur to you people that the way I look might be intentional?" asked Marion, flipping her jet-black hair.

The Trophies didn't stop laughing until they hit the coast highway and Maya made Pepper pull over to get the Porfidio white tequila out of the trunk. Then they laughed harder.

By the time they hit Big Rock, Maya and Pepper were snoring in the back bucket seats and Claire was behind the wheel.

"So," Claire asked Marion shyly, "Zephyr's your daughter?"

"Yep. You're about the same age."

Claire attempted a smile. "I don't know if it'll make you feel any better, but I could never hate my mother."

"I said you were the same *age,* not the same person. But thanks, that was sweet."

"Zephyr has really *big* shoulders," piped up Patti from the backseat floor hump.

Marion ignored her. "I was young," she said, hearing a sigh and watching the moon run along the dark water to her left. She wished she'd known all of them back in those days. She held Verna's card with her cell number on it on her lap.

"If you want, I've got an extra set of eggs. Ow!"

"You're usin' way too much spray," Pepper mumbled.

Marion flipped the card over. *ONE WEEK!* she read again, and shivered. Then she tucked the card into her décolletage.

73

Coyote Ugly

P atti wasn't exaggerating. Her back house had been converted into the beautician's equivalent of a chop shop and Marion was seized by technicians the minute she set foot inside. Luckily, after she'd showered and salt-scrubbed, they managed to do most of the repairs from the memory-foam-mattress bed and she awoke the next day with passable hair, hands, and feet. At least that's what Xiocena's voice hovering above the thick moisturizing mask they'd covered her face with told her as the straw attached to a latte was pushed between her lips.

"Your cuticles take two hours alone," Xio said, placing Marion's hand around the cup. "It good to see you clean. You was coyote ugly."

"On the inside as well," Marion added. "It was disrespectful of me to make you keep secrets and I apologize for running you ragged this last month."

"'S okay. I no get scared till you go off network radar."

"Don't worry, Xio. No one will go off with your new tracking system," Marion said. Pepper had told her that she'd donated the NSA stuff to the Housekeeper Network for immediate resale.

"Sí. We chipping Yolanda's husband next week."

"Heaven help him," said Marion, handing the cup back to Xiocena as one of the beauticians peeled off the mask and swiped remaining bits away with a cold-cleanser-soaked cotton ball. Xiocena leaned over to pick a bit or two out of Marion's (joyously auburn) eyebrows.

"I see Miss Zephyr yesterday. She meet Mr. Sacks at compound."

"Did you manage to hide the Harry Winston box?"

"Yes, but he find it. That man is part demon."

"Only the good parts. So another one bites the dust."

"No. *Miss Zephyr* no let him take. *You* must take as sign. Mrs. Zane, you want your life back? Start with your daughter."

At that moment the beautician began to scold Xiocena for making Marion cry.

"I screwed that up permanently," she whispered, after she recomposed herself enough to undergo micro-radiowave massage. "My little girl is lost to me!"

"Bull caca," Xio replied. "My mother mess with my head from grave! There is *cord* there, between mother an' child. All you do is pull."

Marion wasn't so sure. "If I pull on Zephyr, I'll end up with a cord wrapped around my neck. She hates me, Xio. She thinks I was embarrassed to have a bastard!"

"Then tell her truth! *Your* truth!"

"How?" Marion asked. "She won't even enter the same room with me, let alone listen to anything I have to say. After all these years of lying, it's too late."

"There must be way! *Pull on the cord!*"

"Lie still, I'm doing décolletage," scolded the beautician. "You can't leave the house with these age spots!"

Lying back in the pillows, Marion thought about cords. And as she thought, she played with a strand of her almost-auburn-again hair. And as she played, she found the strand to be amazingly strong, considering the hell it had suffered. Stubborn little thing still wanted to be wavy. It had to be genes . . .

Son of a bitch!

There *was* a way to make Zephyr hear the truth. Unfortunately, it would require one hell of a coyote-ugly cord.

One she couldn't chew off, no matter how hard she'd tried.

It was a long shot. But it just might work . . .

Marion sat up abruptly. "Xio get me the phone! And use yours to call the Trophies and tell them I want to do a conference call in one hour! Screw pulling! We're going to *yank* that cord"

"Aieee!" Xio waved a fist in the air. "Now we cooking!"

"But what about your spots?" asked the horrified beautician, dodging the cell phone Xiocena had tossed to Marion.

Marion shrugged, "They'll never go away," she said, dialing long distance. "Runs in the family."

74

Road Hazards

Trapped at the back of the restaurant, Zephyr drummed an impatient rhythm on her seat as Patti and Pepper nibbled their entrée salads and scrolled through cell-phone photos of their children. Maya was off table-hopping with a contingent of Italian filmmakers. Without looking up, Pepper suddenly grabbed Zephyr's hand and patted it still.

"I still don't know why we had to have lunch. We could have done this at the bar," the young women groused. "That's what I always do here. It's twice as fast."

"Oh, stop bein' such a goddamn utilitarian, Zeph!" Pepper chided as she speared a perfect geometric stack of goat cheese and beets. "We raised you better than that. Ya can't approach everythin' in life like yer late ta class an' only got time ta grab a Starbucks."

"We didn't ask you out to lunch just to do an update on the hospital," Patti cooed over the rim of her kir royale as she snuggled closer to Zephyr and attempted to organize her hair. "We wanted to see *you*. And share a lunch experience with *you*. Here. At Spago."

". . . your temple of old-school Trophiness," finished Zephyr.

"Well, you have to admit, the visuals *are* good, darling," Patti returned, still cooing.

"Yeah, like those two dinosaurs at table five? Vintage suits and brooches! Whoo!"

"What is Zephyr whoo-ing about?" asked Maya, returning to the table and sitting down.

"She's mockin' the old school," Pepper informed her. While Zephyr looked away, she snuck a peek at her watch and made the internationally recognized sign for "Keep her talking."

"Unwise to mock Spago old school," said Maya gravely.

"That 'dinosaur' on the left is Victoria Sanger," said Patti in reverent tones. "*The* Victoria Sanger, principal shareholder of Sanger Multicorp. Since Foley Sanger's death in '86, she's singled-handedly controlled the biggest chemical producer after Dow. Imagine! She came to this town as a chorus girl—"

"—and like most of this front-room widow scum—no offense, Patti—screwed herself rich." Zephyr smirked.

"While erectin' five parks, a university, an' fifty-five permanent scholarships." Pepper smirked back. "What have *you* done lately, pumpkin?"

"Victoria forced Sanger Multicorp to go green before it was cool thing to do," added Maya, signaling a waiter for coffee. "She push through acquisition of four chlorine plants last week, just to retrofit smokestacks to keep mercury from atmosphere. She fight off two hostile takeover and win."

"Toe-to-toe with the big boys," continued Patti. "And she's lunching with Josephine Green, who pretty much bankrolled the women's movement and Choice, making it possible for you to 'take care' of that sophomore-year 'emergency' of yours—"

"God, Patti!" groaned Zephyr.

"—and go on ta law school," added Pepper, "They almost lynched 'er in Kansas. She still gets death threats from nuts. You stand on her battle-scarred shoulders, missy. Those two're dinosaurs, all right. T rexes."

"Spago is not for bar-stool sitting," finished Maya.

"And neither am *I*, in this skirt with no underwear." Patti chuckled. "Ow!"

A commotion near the entrance bar heralded Claire's arrival (caused by the fact that her gigantic tote bag was made out of four armadillos, which, through the wonders of taxidermy, had been gruesomely stitched together). Ignoring the stares, she bustled in breathlessly and plopped down next to Patti.

"Hi, everybody. The-valet-was-crowded-so-I-parked-behind-a-van-on-North-Crescent!" she said, loud and a little too forced, causing Maya to roll her eyes while Zephyr blew an exhale of relief and flipped her briefcase up onto the table. "Did I miss anything?"

"I'll send you my notes," said Zephyr, opening her case. "And remember to genuflect at table five when you leave."

"Just give us the total, smarty-pants," said Pepper, peeking over her shoulder. "You can fax us the donor lists later."

Zephyr pulled out a spreadsheet and, reading it, sighed. "Okay—four hundred and seventy-two million. I hate to break it to you guys, but unless you come up with twenty-eight million more in two weeks, you're losing UCLA and the zoning hearing. Since I work for the other side, I shouldn't even be telling you this, but Senator Powell's going to attend."

"Oh, screw that ol' turncoat! We'll get the money. Maya, get the check," Pepper said, grabbing her purse and stuffing the spreadsheet into it.

"How?" asked Zephyr. "Even Patti can't come up with that much money now, because of Lou's lawsuit."

Patti didn't seem too concerned. In fact, she was gossiping with a woman at an adjoining booth rather than answering Zephyr's question.

"We are optimist," Maya shrugged, tucking cash into the folder that held the restaurant bill and handing it to the waiter. "This was good. We do again, after hearing."

With the exception of Patti, the Trophies stood up.

"Wait!" said Zephyr. "I haven't even told you the big bad news!"

Patti whipped around. "That Lyndy Wallert had surgery for ass-cheek implantation at BHC last week, under the name of 'D. Gibson'? *Ow!*" Then she took her cue from the rest of them and stood up as well.

"No!" said Zephyr. "You guys, I'm sorry . . . but Richard is insisting that *I* be the one to present the arguments against you at the hearing . . ."

"Yeah!" Patti shouted, jumping up and down and clapping her hands.

"I'm sure yer gonna be brilliant, sugar!" Pepper said, linking arms with Zephyr and easing her up from her seat. "Lookin' forward to it."

"Me too," said Maya, taking Zephyr's other arm and guiding her toward the exit. "Did you valet?"

"You know I don't," said Zephyr, in confusion, as she was moved through the bar and Claire opened the door. "You guys aren't taking this seriously. I mean, you'll have to return all the hospital-fund money if you lose!"

"Easy come, easy go," said Patti as they all piled outside and surrounded Zephyr like a glove.

Pepper ruffled Zephyr's hair. "We'll walk ya ta yer car. Where'd ya park?"

"Way around two corners on North Crescent," said Zephyr, starting to walk away. "You don't have to go with me."

"I-parked-there-too!" said Claire, again sounding a little too forced.

"We insist," said Maya as she and Patti took Zephyr's left flank while Claire and Pepper took her right. "Safety in number."

Zephyr knew better than to argue with this group, so she allowed herself to be led. "I usually park on Clifton Way for Spago, but there were cars in all four spots today. It was weird."

The Trophies smiled—all four of them—until they turned as a unit onto Clifton Way and saw the tow-truck driver hooking up Patti's Rolls-Royce while a BHPD officer looked on from his squad car.

"Hey!" squealed Patti, before Maya sidekicked her and forced her to pass the lifting Rolls as if nothing were wrong, meanwhile continuing to guide Zephyr down the block. When Zephyr looked at her questioningly, Patti squeaked, "Aren't you glad you didn't park there today?"

"No shit," said Zephyr, trucking toward North Crescent and quickening her pace. "Forgive me if I speed up, but I have to make a three o' clock."

After ten paces, Patti suddenly peeled off from the group and ran back to defend her Rolls. "Um, I think I left my cell at the restaurant! Later!"

Patti Fink had her own system for dealing with parking tickets. It was called "Magical Thinking." Her Rolls had seventy-eight outstanding violations gone to warrant.

For under-quota, overcaffeinated officer Frank Dunfield, BHPD, the sight of Patti's Rolls was like finding El Dorado.

He had Patti cuffed before she could complete her first curse word.

Pepper remained in formation for another ten steps then looked back and saw Patti in bracelets. Three more steps and then she peeled off, running back to save her friend, yelping, "Whoops! I think I parked back there! See ya, Zeph!"

But Officer Dunfield had no desire to play tug-of-war with his bust of the week and managed to cuff Pepper before he and Pepper turned Patti into a wishbone between them.

Maya made it halfway down the block with Zephyr and Claire. She didn't want to screw up the mission.

But she also didn't want to miss getting a picture of Patti and Pepper in cuffs.

Thus, shouting, "Whoop! I need my thing. Bye!" she too peeled off and ran back to the tow truck.

Officer Dunfield cuffed her after she jumped on the roof of the squad car to get a better angle for her photo.

Claire was next; peeled and ran without saying a word.

Zephyr turned the next corner and, as she always did, never looked back. She was too busy wondering if the van with the blacked-out windows she had noticed when she parked had dinged her bumper as it wedged behind her Prius.

The van with the blacked-out windows hadn't parked behind Zephyr's car by chance. Inside, Marion was lying in wait, and when at last she spotted Zephyr approaching, she freaked.

"Oh no! She's walking alone!"

"Is no matter," said Sasha, who was keeping watch, with her, as he tore a length of silver duct tape off a roll. "We take her anyway."

Both he and Dudayev were crouched near the back doors, ready to spring.

"You don't understand!" Marion protested. "The others need to be here to help!"

"We do this before. Many times," said Dudayev, dabbing a spot of chloroform on a cleaning cloth. "And don't worry. We be gentle with your daughter."

"Oh, I'm not worried about her," whispered Marion, biting her lip and preparing to wince.

Moments later, while the martial-arts-trained Zephyr was ruining Sasha's sex life for at least a month and blacking out both of Dudayev's eyes, Officer Frank Dunfield, BHPD, was trying to stuff what looked like a four-Trophy centipede into the back of his squad car. (Dispatch thought he was joking when he called for backup on a woman armed with armadillos.)

Prisoners of Love

"*Saaay*, Officer Frank!" said Maya, snapping another cell flash of Patti, Claire, and Pepper smashed to her left while Officer Frank Dunfield, BHPD, pulled away from the curb and recounted the cell phones in his lap that he'd already confiscated. Six? Wait a minute!

"Officer Fra-ank!" squealed the Trophies.

Flash.

"I'm going to have to ask you to stop that flashing back there, ladies," the officer told them.

"Who's designing your uniforms nowadays?" asked Patti, ignoring him.

"Wouldn't know, ma'am," Officer Dunfield said. "Really, ladies, that flashing has got to—"

"And could you change the station to something more upbeat?" Patti asked politely.

"No. This is a police car—"

"Officer Fra-ank!"

Flash.

"Ladies—"

"Can the police chief eat shellfish?" Patti asked, for no apparent reason that the police office could detect.

"What?"

"Officer Fra-ank!"

Flash.

"Because I'm planning a dinner at Crustacean for the city planning commission in order to get them to change their ruling on my third-story cold-storage closet."

"Put the cell phone down!"

". . . and I heard that the chief, what's his name, Curry? I heard he has high blood pressure and I heard that that goes hand and hand with—"

"Car sixty-seven, come in." It was dispatch. "Do you copy?"

"Shhh!" said the beleaguered officer. "Dunfield here. Copy."

"We have a suspected armed robbery suspect headed your way south on Beverly. Description: five-foot-ten Caucasian female armed with a . . . a . . . *porcupine! Hee, ha hoo-hoo, ha!*"

"Officer Fra-ank!"

Flash.

"As long as we're pulling over, could ya pop into Canter's an' grab four Evians, *glass* bottles?" Pepper asked.

It took officer Frank Dunfield, BHPD, ten minutes to confiscate the seventh cell phone.

Sasha and Dudayev limped away from Patti's guesthouse while Marion rechecked the ropes (for the hundredth time) that tied Zephyr to the memory-foam-mattress bed inside. As she waited for her daughter to come around, it occurred to her that she hadn't had the luxury of spying on Zephyr while she was sleeping since the girl was fifteen. Her skin had really cleared up.

Try as she might, Marion didn't see much of her own features in her daughter. And that was a good thing. Zephyr's father had been cute (for a gargantuan asshole). Even the wild hair was more like her father's. No, the only thing mother and daughter shared at the moment was teeth grinding. But it was a start.

"Arrrgh! *Fuck!*" Zephyr snarled ten minutes later, almost taking off Marion's nose. "Are you out of your mind?! Yes! What a stupid question!" She looked at the ropes tying her to the head- and footboards and started to struggle.

"Easy does it," said Marion quietly. "You're in Patti's guesthouse at the beach."

"And you're going to be locked up in loony land!" Zephyr snarled. "You and those fucks who grabbed me! And the out-to-lunch bunch! This is it! You can't take this back, Marion! You better let me go now or—"

"I'll let you go as soon as you stop screaming and listen to what I have to tell you," said Marion in the same quiet voice.

It took about a half hour before Zephyr was able to hear the truth in what Marion was saying.

When at last Marion apologized for being a chickenshit for not telling Zephyr that she was her mother, she told her about her fears. The fear of making her daughter suffer. And the fear of losing her. It was the reason behind all the opportunities she had missed. And even as she finally fessed up, she knew it was a shitty excuse. Because all along it had really been selfishness. It was lying.

She told Zephyr that the three-year-old she tried to tell was frightened and that the thirteen-year-old she wanted to tell was depressed. And that the adult was still depressed. So saying, she now realized that she hadn't spared her daughter at all.

"And that," she said, "is what will always haunt me. Because I love you. I screwed up and I'm sorry."

Zephyr had the exact reaction she'd expected.

She remained dry-eyed and unmoved. And she hid behind her lawyer mask.

"Can I talk now?" she asked.

"Sure."

"You're forgetting one apology you owe me: for dumping me off on your nightmare parents. You abandoned me, Marion! You *knew* they were assholes! Your dad was a misogynistic drunk and your mother was a religious kook! And that makes your whole 'fear' and 'rejection' defense fall to shit. Where's your apology for handing me to the same people who'd abused you? Slip your mind?"

"Oh, I won't apologize for that. I was just a kid. I was tricked into it."

"Bullshit. And fuck you."

Marion had expected that reaction too. She swiftly crossed the room and opened the door to the living room. "Okay, you're on," she said.

An old woman in a traveling dress shuffled in.

Zephyr went berserk. Marion had expected that too.

"Who in the . . . oh, man. No. No! I am not going to be tied up and forced to listen to this asshole too!"

As Zephyr raved, the old woman turned to Marion and pointed a bony finger. "Are you sure I'm going to make my flight home? I'm not staying! I'm not staying in this demon's-nest city! I am a child of the faith of the apostles, harlot! You harlot to the beast—"

"You'll cut that out if you want me to keep paying your rest-home tab, Mom," Marion interrupted. "Now tell her the truth."

"Oh, great. You're *supporting* her? *Her*? Just so you can drag her out and make her *lie* for you?"

Marion had to restrain her mother from slapping Zephyr.

"May God curse you both!" she spat. "I do not lie. I am a child of the Holy Christ and the Blessed Virgin, and Satan shall not stain my lips with lies!"

Marion looked at Zephyr. "Threatening to kick her out of her rest home might get her on a plane. But I think Mom's more worried about getting that two-acre flat lot with an ocean view in heaven." She turned to her mother. "You *do* want to get into heaven, don't you, Mom? So don't you think it's time you confessed the truth?"

Then Marion opened the door to the other bedroom in the guesthouse. "Okay, you're on," she said.

The thought of another person seeing her tied up almost caused Zephyr to resume ripping out curses, but when she saw the priest enter, she held her tongue.

"This is Father Michael McKay," said Marion.

He was also Patti's brother-in-law from her second marriage.

In seconds, Marion's mother was all over the priest, kissing his cassock and begging him to take her away from the belly of the beast, blah, blah, blah . . .

Marion looked at her daughter. "She's not going to blow her escrow this close to closing."

Then she turned to her mother. "Keep your hands to yourself, understand?"

Then Marion left the room and shut the door.

And Marion went into the kitchen and made herself a blood-sausage sandwich. With *Zane*-brand blood sausage. Flown in from Cleveland.

Marion relished every bite because blood sausage always took her back. Back to when her thirteen-year-old daughter had shown up shattered on her doorstep and she'd finally felt compelled to try her hand at delicatessen work.

As her parents' rival.

Overnight, Zane delis started popping up across the street from all of her parents' own deli franchises. The rival Zane delis had more delicious food, bigger and better menus, bigger and better minute-wait seating with rock rooms for teens and cozy dining areas for adults, no-charge delivery that was faster than that of her parents' delis, seemingly hundreds of employees, and best of all, unlimited capital.

Mom and Dad were wiped out in two years.

Dad drank himself to death in four.

Mom lost her mind in five.

And for some reason, Marion chose to take care of her then, putting her mother in the finest Catholic home in the country, and she'd been taking care of her ever since. She hadn't known why she'd done it at the time and she couldn't tell you why now.

Pesky coyote cord.

Who knew it would come in so handy?

At the Beverly Hills Police Department, Patti used her one phone call to reach Lizzie-the-decorator to tell her to do something about the ugly fabric in the station house.

Then, between asking for different colors of fingerprint ink and objecting to being photographed in "such cruel lighting," she managed to stall her booking (and Officer Dunfield's Taser) until the mayor of Beverly Hills could rush in and save his *biggest fund-raiser.*

Evidently he'd received a call from within the station house. From a cell phone that was registered to Patti Fink.

Then, as always, Patti wrote a check.

All charges against the other Trophies were dropped as well. But Patti, Pepper, Maya, and Claire decided to stick around because Lizzie-the-decorator had ordered takeout from Crustacean and "no one could *ever* resist those noodles!"

Officer Frank Dunfield had to dig the Rolls out of impound during his dinner break. Luckily, he returned to the station house just in time for the big group shot.

"Officer Fra-ank!"

Flash.

76

Going Public

Marion walked along the tide line of Broad Beach, unconcerned that the tar globs accumulating on her feet were surely wrecking her latest pedicure. She was too engrossed in assessing her progress (and besides, Patti had a girl coming to the guesthouse at 3 P.M.).

The second they'd untied her, Zephyr was gone like a shot and then Marion's mother had grabbed her driver and was gone like an old shot, and Father McKay . . . well, he had a shot and blessed Marion and her hospital project. And then he was gone too.

But Marion felt at peace with what she had done.

Xiocena was right. The mother-child cord was still there. Even the coyote cord with her *own* flipped-out mother.

The whole time the old bat had been mumbling archaic terms for prostitutes and cursing her daughter and granddaughter to spend all of eternity in the regions of hell's lower GI tract, Marion found herself wondering if her mother was getting enough nutrition. And secretly yearning to be understood and forgiven.

Damn, that mother stuff was powerful.

Zephyr had always been bullheaded. As a teen, she'd suffered wearing a pair of too-tight boots for almost three weeks before she finally admitted she'd bought the wrong size.

Marion had time.

Her problems with Richard had time too. She had no choice. He was out of town.

But Verna couldn't wait.

And neither could the hospital fund-raising.

Verna was right. It *was* too late for Marion to reinvent herself. Mainly because she didn't want to. Marion *loved* being a socialite hostess and could give a rat's ass whether that was PC or not.

Besides, she was more than just a socialite hostess.

She was *the* socialite hostess on the West Coast! A billionaire Stage III Trophy with entertainment industry glamour; one of the most powerful and influential links on the food chain.

Normally, what with her resources and contacts, raising $28 million in charitable donations in two weeks would be a piece of cake. She'd've done it single-handedly.

She couldn't think of any other profession where an individual could do that on her own.

Two weeks to raise $28 million or bye-bye UCLA and zoning permit.

If only she had her *Black Book*. Marion was sure there was a source in there somewhere that could help her get her hands on that kind of money.

Her *Black Book* had sources for everything. It was a means for living excellently. Unlisted numbers, e-mails, addresses, and information on the world's best, most exclusive, and effective individuals and services gleaned from Marion's life experience. It put perfect action at your fingertips.

Everything from art-restoration experts in Chicago to fashion designers in London to hairdressers in Prague. From secret embassy numbers to military experts who could smoothly deliver anyone from any catastrophe, to the finest doctors in every country on the globe who could treat and medicate every problem, to detectives in South Korea, to OPEC officers in Qatar! The finest florists in Paris; unlisted private clubs in Munich; lawyers in Nice; the best Porsche mechanics in Germany, who would fly anywhere in the world on eight hours' notice; one-hour-perfect-custom-Savile-Row-trained tailors from Hong Kong, who, once given your measurements, would ship overnight anywhere in the world! She had the numbers of and access to most of the most influential people in the United States as well as the cell-phone numbers of their assistants. There was a club connecter in Dubai who could hook you up anywhere anytime, a fixer in Argentina who'd direct your bribes to the officials who'd grant your freedom, a silversmith in Denmark who could forty-eight-hour-copy any flatware pattern, a dentist in Botswana who could repair any chip, and a bartender in Mozambique who would fly to Botswana and make what was, as confirmed by Marion herself, the best damn martini on the planet . . . which you'd need after your dental work, done smack-dab in the middle of the Kalahari desert, was finished. (And all this from someone who was a dyed-in-the-wool tequila girl!)

All for a price.

The *Black Book* was definitely not for the slim of wallet. And no one else had ever actually seen it, save for Richard and Ivan. But *everyone* in Marion's circle had heard rumors. She hardly went a day without hearing an allusion to it. And over the years, some of the richest people on earth had come to her seeking sources to save their dinner parties, artwork, cars, hairdos, vacations, fortunes, children, or simply their own asses. Sources that they'd guessed came out of her *Black Book*. Hell, forget rumors, there were legends about Marion Zane's *Black Book* . . .

(!)

And hey! Maybe some of those richest people on earth would *pay* to skip the middleman.

Maybe they would even *pay to have it all to themselves* . . .

Up until one month before, the *Black Book* had been carefully guarded and constantly updated. It would need updating again and several secretaries to handle the research calls . . .

Damn, those project-embarking endorphins felt good!

Saved again, by the *Black Book*.

Of course she'd have to get her hands on it first.

77

Entering and Breaking

Pepper took the small black plastic box out of the back pocket of her jean miniskirt and checked the battery pack to make sure it was connected.

Maya was impressed. "Where you get that?"

"My 'Universal-Gate-'n-Garage-Door Opener'? Made it in self-defense. M' husband thinks we're gonna get invaded by li'l brown men." Pepper held the box at arm's length and wanded it along the edges of the Zane-compound service-entrance gates, in search of the sensor.

"He's afraid of aliens?" asked Marion, tucking her again recognizably auburn hair in her black knit Stüssy cap.

"Day laborers," Pepper sighed. "Knucklehead changes our codes every three days! It's pretty simple. Works onna binary system—"

"Shhh!" cautioned Vlad. He leaned out over the driveway and let his eyes sweep the shadows for signs of unwanted witnesses. (And let Marion, who at the moment was suffering from an advanced case of "pelvic congestion," have a nice perv on his rock-hard round ass, tantalizingly encased in black spandex running tights.)

Mr. Clean, Mr. Clean, can you make my kitchen gleam?

Seconds later, Pepper's device overrode the Zane-compound service-gate code with a bleep and the gates started to move.

"Open sez me!"

Vlad turned (the front view was even better!) and flung a penknife with deadly accuracy at the security-camera wires, slicing them neatly in half.

"Is everybody ready?" whispered Marion. "Patti? . . . Patti!"

Timing was a critical factor in their mission to rescue the *Black Book*. Xiocena had informed them that they had a window of opportunity only between the hours of nine and ten-thirty. Most of the staff was gone at this time, but Jeff-the-majordomo and Roger-the-chef would be stuck working overtime, doing an inventory of Marion's vast collection of china, crystal, and silver at the behest Simon Sacks. Therefore, the alarms on the mansion's exterior and downstairs wouldn't be armed.

But Carter and Gary would be on night security at the gatehouse.

That meant two sets of two men to distract. Happily, all of the Trophies had developed advanced skills in this area (although there was much arguing over who got to distract whom).

Maya, Pepper, and Claire were taking Gary and Carter. They needed to get into the gatehouse so Pepper could disengage the upstairs motion-detector beams.

Patti was going to distract Roger and Jeff while Marion and Vlad made their way upstairs to (hopefully) locate the thumb-recognition safe in Marion's closets and extract its prisoner. In the hope of lulling Roger's volatile nature, Xiocena had "accidentally" uncorked a few bottles of excellent wine before she'd knocked off work at six.

Sasha and Dudayev were still on the injured list after their tussle with Zephyr and thus unavailable.

Vlad finally discovered Patti checking the fit of her new black Prada ski jumpsuit in a gutter puddle and barely managed to yank her and her matching backpack through the last sliver of closing security gates.

"Why you bring that?" asked Maya, poking at Patti's pack.

"You have your ways of distracting and I have mine," Patti sniffed, splaying a hand across her bosom. "Actress, remember? It's my costume change."

"You still mad you no get to wear mini," teased Maya, referring to Pepper, Claire, and herself, who were all clad in tight, tiny outfits and heels topped off with fur coats and jackets.

"Oh, any old ho can make that work! My job is more—" Patti began.

"Jeezus, will you two quit?" whispered Pepper. "We went over this a million—"

"Maya! Pepper! Claire! Back lawn—go!" hissed Vlad, grabbing Marion and Patti and hustling them up the service drive.

Claire, Maya, and Pepper adjusted their makeup and headed in the opposite direction.

"I still don't think I can be convincing enough. I've always had perfect health and I've never even *seen* someone have one," complained Claire as the three women picked their way across the (replanted) back lawn.

"Bullshit. Yer just mad ya got the short straw," Pepper chuckled.

"This is good spot," said Maya, elbowing Pepper in the ribs and indicating a security camera in a tree that was aimed at them. "Claire, is that diamond on ground in front of your shoe?"

"Where?" asked Claire, bending over and looking.

"Down there. Oh! You knock it down in grass!"

Claire bent all the way over, eagerly combing the lawn in front of her toes and completely unaware of the fact that she was mooning the security camera.

Pepper stifled a snort.

"Now they come quick," Maya assured her.

Once Marion had made sure she wasn't treading on a machete, she slowly straightened up through the pittosporum bushes and joined Patti and Vlad, who were peeking in her kitchen window. The honed white marble countertops, prep islands, and chopping blocks she was used to seeing overloaded with Roger's creations were now forlornly bare, save for a few inventory lists.

Patti pointed at two empty wine bottles in the sink and grinned. "Good sign!" she whispered. "Let's go wait at the door."

Vlad grabbed her by the belt, "Wait. They could have used for cooking."

"*My* wine?" asked Marion indignantly.

"And *her* staff?" asked Patti incredulously.

"You must be joking," said Marion.

At that moment, as if to prove her right, Roger came lumbering into the kitchen swilling the rest of his glass, followed by Jeff, who was dangling his empty one between his fingertips. Neither man looked particularly pleased, but both looked blotto.

"I *told* you she doesn't keep the Tiffany demitasse in the dining-room breakfront," whined Jeff, checking the inventory list. "It's down there in an unmarked crate or mixed up . . . somewhere."

"Who gives a fuck besides the lawyer-of-the-living-dead?" growled Roger, disappearing into the staff dining room. "Making me stay here like a stock boy! *Merde.*" He returned with a full bottle of wine, set his glass down heavily, and refilled it. "Marion *always* used the Limoges, even on the boat. Richard didn't even think about china this trip . . . because . . . because he doesn't . . . *have her taste!*" Roger swiped at his eye with the back of his hand before consuming the contents of his glass.

"Aw. He misses you," whispered Patti.

"He misses the boat and the bikinis," whispered Marion as they watched Jeff stoop down behind an island.

"Let's just keep going. Little help?" he asked.

Roger scowled and bent toward him, and together they hefted a crate into view then lifted the lid.

Jeff counted dishes while Roger refilled his glass for him. "Two, four, seven, eight, ten, fourteen—no, wait . . . ten, twelve . . ."

"We go to the door," whispered Vlad before moving away.

Marion tried to follow, but Patti wasn't budging.

"Is that the Villeroy and Bosch you use between the Oscars and spring? Because I'd like to borrow it for this dinner I'm doing for the planning commission . . ."

Marion gave her a shove.

Vlad silently cracked the kitchen door a hair and they all watched Jeff scribble down a dubious total on the inventory list. Roger regarded the crate and rubbed his back.

"Leave it for Charlie in the morning," he said. "Let's finish with light stuff tonight."

"Hokay," said Jeff, slurping at his newly refilled glass before shuffling after Roger toward a door at the base of the tower staircase. "That new wine's good."

"Like you would know," said Roger, opening the door and revealing the continuation of the tower stairs, leading down to the basement.

As they descended, Vlad and Marion slipped into the kitchen and out to the foyer and started creeping up the grand staircase.

Patti scampered the other way, up the tower staircase (after grabbing a dish out of the crate).

When Maya saw Gary and Carter charging across the lawn in her direction, she tapped Claire on the back. "Oh, look. Is not diamond. Just piece of glass."

"Mrs. Papadopoulos? Mrs. Hanson?" said Gary, slowing to a very shocked walk.

"Maya. Don't-make-me-feel-old. And this is other end of Claire," Maya purred.

Pepper immediately started surveying the back lawn. "Well, they could walk the floor an' the tent back here, but they'd have ta crane in the set."

"What are you doing here?" asked Gary. He caught Carter smiling at Claire and elbowed him.

"And how'd you get in?" Carter asked, suddenly all business.

"We're location-scoutin'," Pepper replied, letting her jacket fall open and allowing her cleavage to do the rest. "I know it's late, but it's the only time we could all get together. We need a place ta hold a fashion show fer charity."

"A fashion show," repeated Carter, growing hypnotized by her breasts.

"Yeah, a *lingerie* fashion show benefitin' low-income kids . . . uh, 'Undies fer Underprivileged.'"

Maya rolled her eyes.

"Ever hear a' it?" Pepper asked.

Carter shook his head no.

"Mr. Zane is out of town," said Gary, taking hold of Maya's arm and motioning for Carter to take Pepper and Claire. "I'm sorry, but we're going to have to escort you out."

"Can ya do it around the opposite side a' the house?" asked Pepper. "I wanna see where to put the Porta Potties."

The three Trophies allowed themselves to be led toward the front entrance of the compound, maintaining a constant chatter about their fashion-show layout and avoiding the kitchen side of the mansion.

"You still didn't tell us how you got in," said Gary as they neared the front gate.

"Oh, Marion gave us the code," said Pepper casually.

That brought Gary grinding himself and everyone else to a halt alongside the guardhouse. "We changed the codes," he said, eyeing them suspiciously. "Does Mrs. Zane have the *new* ones?"

"Did Maya tell you she was *modeling* the 'Undies' in the fashion show?" asked Claire after receiving the internationally recognized signal for "Girl, that's your cue!" from Pepper.

"Is really pretty stuff," said Maya, letting her fur car coat fall open and giving the guards an eye-popping view of her tiny vintage Alaia stretchy tank that barely covered her crotch. She used her hands to outline her breasts. "There is little red satin push-up bra," she breathed as Pepper peeled off and slipped into the guardhouse. Next, Maya outlined her loins. "And itsy-bitsy red satin G-string that tucks up between the bum cheeks. What were you asking?"

"Uh-huh," answered Gary, whose blood had rushed away from his brain.

Carter made a stretch that turned into a flex. "Ahhh. Had a really good weight session today. Been working out with my old *Navy SEAL* unit. Mmm. I like to keep in shape because—"

"Where'd Mrs. Papapapadopoulos go?" asked Gary, without taking his eyes off of Maya.

"Oh, she had to pee," answered Claire.

"Where?"

"In there."

Gary followed her gaze. The sight of Pepper through the guardhouse window snapped him out of his trance.

"First we run, ohhh, twenty miles, thirty miles . . ." continued Carter, until Gary whapped him and pointed to the guardhouse.

"Mrs. Papadoupoulos! Mrs. Papadopoulos, we really can't let you in there!" Gary yelled as he and Carter rushed the guardhouse with Maya and Claire on their heels.

Inside was a ten-by-six-foot room with a security console, two chairs, multiple screens, a coffeemaker, computer set-up, and a bathroom. Pepper was fiddling with the alarm system but spun around when everyone piled in.

"Sorry, false alarm," she said with a shrug.

Gary gently took her arm and started guiding her to the door. "We have to keep this area restricted since—"

"I need to pee," said Maya, lunging for the bathroom (and almost colliding with Carter, who had his hands full of the porn pictures he was hastily removing from the walls).

Gary gathered Claire's arm in his other hand. "The rest of us can wait outside."

At that moment Pepper sidekicked Claire, who suddenly buried her face in her hands and sobbed, "Oh, won't somebody tell me which gun to buy!"

"Which what? Why do you need a gun?" asked a bewildered Carter. "Um, I'm sorry, I didn't get your name . . ."

"Claire! Claire the loser!" she sobbed, while Pepper went back to work at the console. "I'm sorry, but I'm just so confused! It's my husband's birthday tomorrow and I want to give him a really good handgun, but so far, ten different people have recommended ten different guns and I just don't want him to get hurt! Wah-ha-ha!"

While both of Marion's security guards instantly weighed in on their personal choices of weapons, she and Vlad crouched at the top of the grand staircase, waiting for the cat's cradle of red beams at their feet to dissolve.

At the opposite end of the Zane mansion, Patti Fink was in position on the second-floor landing of the tower staircase. She peeled off her jumpsuit and opened her pack as she watched Roger and Jeff lug another crate of dishes out of the basement.

Inside the guardhouse, Pepper was frantically trying to differentiate systems when Maya came out of the bathroom.

"Well, thanks a lot, we can go now," said Claire, cutting off Carter's agonizingly detailed description of a Heckler & Koch P30.

Seeing Pepper give the internationally recognized sign for "NOOO!," Maya sidekicked Claire, who gave a frustrated sigh before commencing to spasmodically jerk her body and roll her eyes.

"Oh, no! She's pitchin' one a' her fits!" cried Pepper, going back to the console.

"Oh, my God!" cried Gary, catching Claire as she fell back into his arms. "They didn't cover this in my CPR class!"

Carter helped him ease Claire down to the floor of the guardhouse.

"Quick! Catch her tongue before she swallow!" yelled Maya, to buy Pepper more time (and a few great pictures for herself).

Claire immediately started trying to spasm and shimmy away from the guards, but Gary caught her by the feet and dragged her back.

"I'll hold her jaws apart!" he told Carter, who was rolling up his sleeves.

Pepper had the beams disengaged a minute later.

Ten minutes later, she and Maya decided to let Claire know about it.

Feeling her way in the dark, Marion had no problem leading Vlad down the colonnaded corridor and the hall of the family wing, but she grew confused upon entering what she'd thought was the master suite. "I think I got turned around," she whispered. "This floor feels like the guest bedroom . . . Richard and my rooms are carpeted. Can we just switch that penlight on for a second?"

"Keep it low," Vlad advised, passing the light to her.

Unfortunately, Marion didn't keep it low and thus was able to discern the five big swipes of orange paint samples that were defacing the antique-silk-padded wall of her master sitting room. And the unlit neon wall sculpture of a kitten that could only have been chozen by Tawnee.

It burns! It burns!

"Are we in right room?" whispered Vlad, snatching back the penlight and switching it off.

"No. But we're going in anyway," she whispered, stifling her scream and taking his hand.

Marion later learned that Tawnee had also banished the silk plush carpet in the master bedroom after she tripped over a silver beanbag chair and landed with a bang on the black hardwood floor.

Roger and Jeff swayed slightly as they stared up at the ceiling.

"That was not the pipes," said Roger, stumbling backward and pulling open his cutlery drawer.

"We should call the guardhouse," said Jeff, trying to remember where the phone was located.

"Yes. And remember not to get your skirt wet when you sit down to pee." Roger sneered and raised a wicked-looking cleaver. "A child can divide a Holstein with this blade."

"Will it stopa bullet?" Jeff slurred.

"No, but your vagina will. Come on, there are two of us!" The red-eyed giant clamped down on Jeff's wrist, hauling him behind as he lurched toward the tower staircase. "No one!" he growled, taking a chop at the air. "No one disturbs the kitchen of Roger Dufau!"

The bang was Patti's cue.

She shook out the fringe on the sleeves of her white vintage dress (once worn by Stevie Nicks in concert!) and tucked a hair that was sticking to her white face paint into her flapper-style headband. As she leaned out over the spiral stairs, she caught a glimpse of her reflection in the tower casement window and was pleased to see she'd painted a perfect 1920s moue on her lips.

Eat your heart out, Gilda.

If that child bride had looked only *half* this good, she might have stayed off the roof.

Roger and Jeff were too startled, terrified, and shit-faced to move. Dimly uplit from the glow of the kitchen light spilling into the stairwell, Patti indeed appeared to their eyes to be a spirit.

"Holy God, it's the old-maid ghost," Jeff croaked. "I was h-here when she ch-choked on her peanuts in the l-laundry room."

Roger let his cleaver clatter to the floor and crossed himself. "Old and *hideous!*"

Patti was not amused.

"Are we in closet?" asked Vlad.

"Yes," whispered Marion.

When he broke away from her, it took her a minute to figure out that he was feeling the walls for her safe.

"Uh-uh," she whispered, pulling him into the next closet, where he broke away again and began the same exercise before she could stop him and pull him into the next closet.

––––––

Back in the guardhouse, Gary and Carter were trying to get a computer printout on the Heckler & Koch. Back on the guardhouse floor, Claire was sitting up, guzzling her third glass of water, trying to wash away the bacon taste of Carter's knuckles from her tongue and memory.

At that moment Pepper whacked Maya and pointed to the third multi-screen above the console. Security camera three faced west and included a view of the tower's second-story casement window. Its screen was currently framing an image of Patti-the-flapping-ghost.

"Ho-ly smokes!" Pepper yelled as Maya planted her pump on Claire's chest and pushed her back down. "She's seizin' again!"

"Man, I'll never get this printed," Carter said, rolling up his sleeve.

In the tower stairwell, a mesmerized Roger and Jeff swayed drunkenly below Patti's apparition, who was now trying to strike a more youthful pose.

"She must have been ninety when she died," Jeff murmured, taking Roger's hand.

Roger nodded in grim agreement.

Now Patti was just plain offended!

As this was going on, Marion pulled Vlad (who was now muttering in disbelief) through the third closet and makeup room and into the last closet. "It should be on this wall," she said.

Vlad switched on the penlight.

It burns! It burns!

Shielding her eyes from the sight of Tawnee's sunflower wallpaper, Marion helped Vlad feel for the safe.

Back in the tower stairwell, Roger had fetched some more wine and he and Jeff were now seated on the floor, staring up at a pissed-off apparition and passing the bottle back and forth.

"No one will believe this," mused Jeff.

Roger nodded. "It's like looking at a mummy."

Patti reached into the darkness and unscrewed a lightbulb from a sconce.

Vlad cut the last of the wallpaper away from the safe, spit on the thumb-recognition screen, and wiped it off with his sleeve. "Okay."

After a squeamish hesitation (and a dirty look from Vlad), Marion pressed her thumb to the screen. Instantly it came to green life as the metal panel slid back.

What was it that John DeLorean said? Oh, yeah.

"Better than gold!"

Marion felt the Stage III power surging back into her body as she once again held her *Black Book* in her hands. After Vlad spit some more on the safe (eeew) and stuck the wallpaper back, they began to feel their way out of the master suite.

"What the hell are you doing?" Marion whisper-moaned as they met up with Patti on the second-floor landing of the tower.

"Improvising!" Patti hissed, before hurling fistfuls of lightbulbs down on her disrespectful audience.

Jeff and Roger tripped over each other as they ran screaming out the front door.

Boo!" said Pepper, letting Vlad, Marion, and Patti out the service gate. At the sound of Jeff and Roger screaming across the front lawn, they all dove into the van with the blacked-out windows and Maya drove them away.

After the initial celebration inside the van, Claire sat back and resumed massaging her aching jaw. "What took you so long?" she yawned.

"Don't feel bad," Patti sniffed. "My two drank themselves blind!"

"Well, our diversion wuz gettin' desperate," countered Pepper.

Patti regarded Claire rubbing her jaw and could come to only one conclusion. "Marion," she whispered. "She's a *really* good friend."

Pepper, riding shotgun, looked back at the *Black Book* Marion was clutching to her breast.

"So that's the famous *Black Book*," she mused. "It really does exist."

Marion nodded. "Free at last, thanks to you," she sighed.

Suddenly Pepper reached back and snatched it out of her hands. "Good. I wanna see what it says under *my* name in there!"

All of the Trophies wanted a turn.

Broad Beach Daylight

Marion had never thought to ask her mother what exact time of day she'd been born (at least not until her mother had become too far gone to remember). So, "I *said*, morning and stop bothering me!" was all she had to work with. It made astrological profiles difficult. But since they really weren't that important to her, and her birth records had been destroyed in a fire, she'd let the question go. Besides, she was positive she'd been born at dawn. It was the time of day she cherished most.

At dawn, she could hear herself think. It was a time when enough of the world was still quiet and tucked away to allow her to receive the sensation that she was having a private encouragement session with the growing light. For Marion Zane, dawn felt like hope.

And at dawn on this particular day, she felt very hopeful indeed, watching the growing light illuminate the *Black Book* on the coffee table in front of her.

She'd just finished a conference call with brokers in Dubai, Los Angeles, New York, London, Paris, Rome, Cape Town, Tokyo, and Toronto. All of them had forgone sleep for the call. She'd faxed two selected *Black Book* pages to each of them, just to whet everyone's appetite:

The first page featured listings for a strike force in *Yemen* next to an amazing *y*odeling troupe from Switzerland (who'd perform *anywhere*, at any function), next to Yummy Cupcakes, the exquisite Santa Monica custom-order bakery with the fourteen-page menu.

The second page listed the *Black Book*'s alphabetized directories of categories.

It was a serious table of contents.

The private sale was set to take place next week.

Today's dawn had convinced Marion that she should do some publicity before the sale. Maya had offered her publicist. And she felt that all the bondo and bodywork the Trophies had compressed into this week for her shouldn't go to waste. Some buzz might sweeten the bidding.

Marion turned the *Black Book* over in her hands.

It contained everything a ridiculously wealthy person would want to know. (Especially if one could decode it.) Everything.

Except for private painful secrets, confessed in confidence by her dearest friends.

As she watched the light gently falling on her book, Marion thought about the Trophies and replayed in her mind the looks of relief and gratitude on their faces when they'd read their own entries in the *Black Book*. (Well, Patti Fink's expression was a little miffed when she learned that Marion had fabricated her age as thirty-five instead of twenty-eight, but please, it was supposed to be a book of fact not mythology.)

Her dearest friends. Ready to go above and beyond (and bizarre) in her support. Her lifeboat. Marion Zane thought about her dearest friends.

And she wondered which one of them she'd choose to betray.

Even though it was a foggy day, Marion could tell that the sun had fully risen. Dawn was over.

She'd been up all night, poring over every single entry in her *Black Book* biography section, as if she were combing for nits (thank you very much for the indelible memories, six-year-old Dickie Jr.), determined to find, then hoping to find, and then, finally *praying* she'd find something, anything, that was a juicer story than the one above:

Maya's forced prostitution and sterility.

Or Pepper's tampering with United States attorney's evidence in an international weapons-smuggling case. And perjury. And conspiracy to obstruct justice. And . . .

Or Patti Fink, wife of Louis Erhardt III, and murderer.

There wasn't a single one. Many of the biographies in the *Black Book* included mitigating circumstances (euphemized or in code, of course), but only Marion Zane knew where those Trophies' skeletons were closeted. She knew enough to be able to provide evidence and prove that the secrets she'd painstakingly gathered were true:

Wanda had witnessed Patti's hit-and-run. (Why else did anyone think she kept a maid with a bad back? Patti was crazy. Not stupid.) Any of the private detectives in the *Black Book* would be able to locate survivors and former patrons of Maya's brothel in Grozny. And Pepper had told her the exact lines she'd erased. Forensic examination would find what was written underneath.

Los Angeles was going to be Verna's launch town. Trophy scandals would have local flair. They'd be eaten with a spoon.

Atta girl, now you're thinking like Verna.

And that was unthinkable.

But the alternative was unthinkable as well. The photos Verna had of her, and they alone, would brand her a freak. (Even though she'd only relieved herself in bushes twice.) And the shots of her swinging a pipe at sixteen-year-olds . . .

Baba Yaga.

Was she willing to give up Stage III Trophy status?

Her husband?

The hospital? Let's not forget about that. Desperate efforts this week had turned up another $8 million, but even if they did get the rest of the money, everything would crumble once Marion was exposed as crazy penniless Baba Yaga. Was she ready to give up any other chance to make changes for the better using MAJOR INFLUENCE, now, when she was so close to her goal? Hell, the money was as good as in her hand. Was she ready to give everything up?

No.

She hadn't sunk to sleeping in doorways, but she'd tasted it. And that's where she'd end up after she finished serving years and years and possibly *years* (because she'd really go crazy; it ran in the family) in a rubber room! Judge Eli Volker wouldn't hesitate this time . . .

Just when you thought you couldn't yip anymore . . .

The *Black Book* was open to a page that listed a twenty-four-hour worldwide rescue team. They handled anything from lost passports to hurricanes to rebel uprisings. Maybe they could drop her off in New Guinea.

No. No more running.

She was determined to stay a Stage III Trophy. Verna knew all about that determination—from personal experience. That's why she'd bet the farm on Marion giving up a secret.

Marion too was a well-honed survival machine. Every obstacle that had ever come between Marion Mintz Zane and her own personal agenda had *always* ended up as roadkill. And information was Marion Zane's shield and sword. She didn't get her strength from the Zane downtown property.

Information was her Tara!

It's all who ya know . . .

And maybe *who ya screw* . . .

79

Sympathy for the Devils

After taking five minutes to allow her eyes to refocus on objects both near and far in the real, that is to say nonvirtual, world (such as Patti's shirtless twenty-year-old stepson Klaus, who'd just sauntered in to check the connections on her new printer), Marion slipped her readers back on and resumed surfing on her new laptop.

What a difference three days had made! And the Internet! And a world-class publicist! And Marion just couldn't tear her overstrained eyes away.

It was sort of like watching what happened when someone dumped a bucket of black food coloring into a swimming pool (thanks again, Dickie Jr.). The publicist had selectively leaked a release on the upcoming *Black Book* private sale to a few key entities. Within a day, every corner of the blogosphere knew of the *Black Book* sale, and unauthorized *Black Book* Web sites were multiplying like bacteria. By the end of the second day, even conventional news organizations were commenting on it. By the morning of the third, Marion had been forced to flee Broad Beach by fence-climbing reporters and was now ensconced in Jorge's currently unoccupied room at the Beverly Park estate (the Hondurans had turned the guesthouse into a nonoppressive sweatshop in order to warehouse and rework Patti's castoff clothing). Plus, Marion needed to be based in town to handle the action:

The publicist and all of the brokers were getting swamped with inquiries. Two Las Vegas casinos were vying to hold the *Black Book* sale on their premises. All the auxiliary hype the news was causing was almost freakish. Like the black food coloring in the swimming pool.

When Marion had first gotten wind of the chatter, she'd thought the free publicity coup would turn out to be a favor for Carita Memorial Hospital. But the story that was catching fire rarely mentioned the proposed hospital as it moved up into prime-time mass consciousness.

Marion Zane, billionaire socialite hostess extraordinaire, whose extreme connections were about to be put on the auction block was the story.

It seemed that everybody liked the idea of being extreme-connected and living excellently.

It's all about who you know . . .

While Marion was reading authorized and unauthorized articles about the *Black Book* in Beverly Park, six thousand miles away, Ivan was reading the logo on the Izod shirt logo his prey was wearing through a Zeiss scope.

He was on a high Andalusian ridge, overlooking the second of his old partners' two-thousand-acre rancho near the town of Cortijo Grande, Spain. Steadying himself on a stump, Ivan reset the bolt of his Mauser SP66, held his breath, and squeezed, wondering if his marksmanship skills were as proficient as they'd been in his mercenary days.

They were.

Back in Beverly Park, Marion stopped surfing to open her latest e-mail and learned she had less than an hour to pack for Chicago.

Good.

The *Black Book* story needed to be directed back to the hospital. Back to the fact that people living within blocks of Los Angeles City Hall did so without available trauma care. Friggin' *refugee camps* were better equipped!

And it was happening all over America. This wasn't an issue for MAJOR INFLUENCE, it was an issue for EXTREME MAJOR INFLUENCE!

Marion Zane was going on *Oprah*!

What a difference three days made.

Three days ago, Maya's publicist had become *Marion's* publicist. Because Marion, *not* Maya, was going to be paying the bills. Because three days ago, Marion had received access to the million-dollar checking account Verna Hale had set up for her. Because Marion had made a deal with the devil and had become a devil herself.

Three days ago, Marion Zane had caved.

But don't forget: she's our devil!

She wasn't proud of what she'd done. Ivan would have never approved. But this time Ivan wasn't around to "take care of things." Well, actually, he was taking care of things, ironically enough, by *not* being around.

Anyway, inexcusable or not, time had run out. Simple as that.

That ol' MAJOR INFLUENCE's got me in its spell!

The *Oprah* broadcast was going to air three days before the *Black Book* sale. The Black Book sale was going to take place three days before the zoning hearing.

And the zoning hearing would have one fewer supporter present. (Possibly three.)

80

Being Professional

"Could you hold the child a little tighter? He's not made of glass."

No, not glass, thought Maya. The squirming little one she held against her barely concealed breasts felt radioactive. And delicious.

She was shooting an ad for a new Lancôme perfume launch that was aimed at young mothers who had no intention of going the matron route.

What better way to say "I'm still a wild fuck" than to wear a perfume advertised by Maya, buck naked, except for five-inch Azzedine Alaia (master of fuck-me) pumps, holding a naked baby whose foot barely covered her Brazilian-waxed pubis and whose arms were provocatively squashing her abundant tits?

The baby's name was Max and he had just downed a bottle. He was groggy and sweetly compliant. Or, as the photographer put it, "Who wouldn't be?"

Maya loved holding the baby. She hated that she loved holding the baby. She hated that her baby yearning was so strong she thought she might break in half. So strong.

There was a time when she'd actually felt lucky. When she saw other models go through the pain and hassle of arranging abortions because their asshole boyfriends refused to wear rubbers, or when they suffered horrible infections from botched IUDs.

Now she wanted a baby as much as she wanted to breathe. And she didn't want to lose Tom. He didn't want to adopt. Wouldn't hear of it. Because he loved her, he wanted a baby made out of them.

How much would he love her if he found out she was a lie? How much would he love her when he found out that she'd allowed him to believe the myth her first agent concocted: that she'd been "discovered" in a Russian orphanage. How would she explain the damage to her womb when the fertility doctor checked her out at the appointment Tom had made for them? The appointment that was in *two days* . . .

Tom was going off on location after that. With a young, ripe leading lady. The girl was a lousy actress, but that wasn't her true profession anyway. She had a well-publicized history of carving men away from girl-friends and spouses. The gossip rags called her "The Chain Saw."

At any other shoot, Maya would have told the photographer to "fuck off" for telling her how to do her job. At any other shoot she might have thrown a light stand or two. But he was right: she was resisting and it was showing. But if she gave in, she might not be able to hold back. That was her predicament.

Still, this was work. And Maya was the best. And resisting the urge to luxuriate in cuddling Max was like trying to hold off a wave or a swollen summer rain cloud . . .

After the session, Maya lunged for her waiting vodka shot. She had bit through a huge section of her inner cheek in order to hold back her agony and she didn't want it to get infected. She was damaged enough already.

81

This Ain't "It"

"Nope, nothing tomorrow," Craig sniffed, over the bad connection. "At least the publicist and I have nothing scheduled. So aside from dinotopia on Tuesday, you've got the week off."

"Dinotopia?"

"The Society for the Preservation of Historical Homes. You're the only board member under seventy-two. You can style yourself for that one too, Eddie. Those gals can barely differentiate between light and shadow."

"What about night events?" asked Claire, still amazed that her normally manic schedule had opened wide. "Are you sure there's nothing?"

"Nope. Nothin' shakin'. And that's a good thing, Eddie, because my advice, if you ever decide to take my advice again, is to *lay low*. You went out on your own and now you're paying the price."

Craig was still furious that Claire had dared to wear Nicky's pink coat in public. Claire had to admit there had to be some sort of connection between the two occurrences, because ever since the garden party, the invitations had dried up.

And the red carpet incident at Billy's movie premiere had been beyond embarrassing. When the photographers had asked for a single, she'd let go of Billy's arm and posed. Then the photographers had motioned for her to get out of the way. They'd wanted a single of *Billy*, not her.

"Craig, you have to believe me, I was *cold*," Claire attempted to explain for the hundredth time.

"And now you're not 'it.' You know, you still don't really get what you've done, Eddie. Your restoration is going to stress every single ounce of my styling-muscle fibers to make you 'it' again. I'm going to have to train and take supplements because my body isn't prepared for the strain. So do me a favor and stay at home for two weeks, under your bed, with the curtains closed, while I figure this out. Capeesh?"

And then Craig hung up.

Out of the game.

And out of the family. Then again, she had never really been "in" to begin with.

Claire decided that Craig's call was pretty much confirmation that her new-er strategy, a secretly renewed stronger Xanax prescription, wasn't working at all. (In fact, no amount of meds would have been enough for her that day.)

When Claire saw the girls and Billy in the den, and the coffee table brimming with goodies, she assumed that Billy had brought home a movie and had decided to join them in watching it. And when she saw Brooke starting to shut the door, she called out, "Hold up! You've got a straggler!"

Brooke had looked at her like she was a complete stranger.

"We're having a family meeting," she announced, adding (in case Claire was thick), "That means *family* only."

Trying to catch her husband's eye, Claire only managed to get a glimpse of the smile across Katia's muzzle before the door was shut in her face.

And the lock was turned.

She was in the bathroom reading her PDR (sorry, Maya, but my life is scarier than your threats) when Billy came in with the meeting results.

"Cookie, we had a discussion and, um, well, I need you to do the girls a favor. Actually, me a favor too."

"Sure, Billy, anything you want. I'm your girl!" she'd answered as sweetly as possible, thinking that they'd wanted their lunch boxes cleaned out again. Or another load of towels. Lately, Claire, under the influence of her secretly renewed stronger strategy, had concluded that maybe menial domestic work was the new way to win her stepdaughters' hearts.

But her husband's request required a different kind of cleaning.

"Since Pam, uh, my ex-wife, lives a minute away, I mean, all girls need their mothers a lot, and since my ex has unlimited visitation rights, we think she should, uh, be allowed to come here, if they need her."

This request, due to the influence of Claire's secretly renewed stronger Xanax prescription strategy, required that she take a moment to think before responding:

Wow. The evil queen wanted to storm the castle and the prince wanted his princess to lie across the threshold like a damn welcome mat while he lowered the drawbridge. That wasn't in the fairy tale.

She should say no.

And yet . . .

It *could* be a way to draw her and the girls closer together. If her stepdaughters saw her being gracious to their mother, they'd have no excuse to think of her as an enemy. And frankly, she had been wanting visual proof that the woman existed. So it wasn't entirely the influence of Claire's new stronger strategy that had made her say:

"Of course, sweetheart, I think it's a great idea."

Billy had blown out a grateful sigh and had even kissed her forehead.

"Great! Thanks, Cookie! What a relief! Because you know how Pam gets. I was getting ready for a shit storm! You're the best!"

Then he reached for his wallet.

"I have no idea how long she'll be, so why don't you catch a movie? And here's something in case there's time to eat."

There wasn't a strong-enough pill.

On her way to the car, Claire ducked her head into the family room and said good-bye just to rub in the guilt.

Her only response had been an anxious wail from Brooke: "Oh, my God! She's *still here*? Mommy's coming any second!"

Claire drove down the driveway, but she didn't go to the movies. Instead she turned around and parked in the shadows of the biggest hedge she'd ever seen. With a perfect view of their gate.

She needed to see the ex who was still in love with her husband, because she had the feeling that her husband was still in love with the ex.

She ended up seeing more than she'd bargained for.

When the Hummer pulled up to the curb, Claire didn't expect to see Pam get out, much less wait until the very young guy she was with get out of her passenger seat and come around the car to take the wheel. She certainly didn't expect to see Billy's ex give a long, deep, wet one to the very young guy either.

(Okay, strike that in-love stuff.)

There was more unexpected stuff to observe.

Pam-the-ex was thin. Very thin.

Her long hair was thin too. It was the coarse, overbleached, straightened-one-too-many-times kind of hair that said, *I'd really rather be brown and curly and some protein wouldn't hurt either.*

She wore overhip teenager clothes that she no longer filled out.

And too much fad jewelry, and sunglasses, even though it was dusk.

And then something else broke through Claire's renewed stronger-strategy-that-was-evidently-useless when she saw Pam unsuccessfully punch the call-box buttons, throw up her hands and curse, dive into her purse, produce a card, finally get it right after two tries, and fume as the gate opened, obviously too slowly.

Something else broke through when she saw Pam turn back to the very young guy and say loudly, "This'll be short. I'm not going to let those little bitches make this a habit."

What had broken through was:

Pam was put out that she had to see her kids.

The next thing that had broken through was:

Pam used to be a Trophy wife.

Now Pam was a neurotic ex-wife who didn't want to deal with her age—or anything else, for that matter.

And Claire had needed to ask herself:

Was this going to be her future too?

Later, when Pepper'd called to make a lunch date for next week, Claire had been purposely vague.

She didn't know if she was going to be sticking around that long.

82

Dark Moon Arisin'

*T*his *Greek fever is gettin' scary,* thought Pepper as she watched Cooter and Maybelle stomp out of the living room in tears. Their tears usually *destroyed* Ari! They made him nervous to the point where he'd give in to just about anything, no matter how many times he'd been played. Cooter was turning him into Gumby at three and Maybelle disarmed him earlier!

But just now, Ari had coldly broken their little hearts, causing *real* tears without batting an eye. Well, she wasn't sure about the eye batting. The whole time he'd been informing the family that he'd canceled their spring vacation at Atlantis and booked them all on what sounded like a cruel and rocky holiday in Crete, he was staring out the window at Baphy-the-statue. He *still* was. It was creeping her out, making Pepper almost wish she *had* found drugs when she'd raided his medicine chest this afternoon in an effort to figure out what was wrong with him. She'd darned near lost a sister to methamphetamine, but at least she had *experience* with drug addiction. At least drugs would explain this behavior!

The Greek fever was progressing too. Closed-eyed sex, babbling on the phone for hours, and now, endless statue staring! They were up to three statues out in the damn yard (actually, four, but Maybelle had drawn a happy face on Apollo's "wiener" and he was out getting cleaned). What the hell was going on with this man? Greek people didn't act like this. *Weirdos* did! Ari'd been staring out the window and sipping at funky firewater ever since he'd come home!

He looks like a statue himself!

"Nice goin', Zorba," Pepper said to her husband-the-statue's back. "So who made this decision, you or your new best friend, Mr. Ouzo?"

"It is time they learned the true meaning of Easter," Ari said quietly.

"Forgiveness? I wouldn't wanna hold m' breath."

"They will love it," Ari insisted. "In Harakas Monofatsiou, Easter Sunday is celebrated by burning an effigy of Judas Iscariot on a giant bonfire. All over the island, you'll see villagers on their donkeys, gathering firewood. And the children can help gather wood too."

He's gone crazy.

"Um, I don't think they're ready ta trade shark tanks an' water slides for a burnin' man an' blood-colored eggs. An' speakin' a' Easter, when's the last time Ari Papadopoulos set foot in a church?"

"Last week when I registered Janos for Sunday school."

"That's not fair!" hollered Jerry, coming in to see what was going on. "I'm only half Greek!"

Ari turned in a flash and shot out a finger out at his son. "You're my son and you're Greek and you're getting confirmed and that's final!" he roared. "And how *dare* you raise your voice to me?"

"How dare you act like a stupid-head bully?" said the little boy, sticking out his chin, despite his shock.

That was it. Ari hurled his glass at the machine-cut quartz-paneled wall surrounding the fireplace and it exploded into a fine crystal mist.

At Ari's first step, Pepper instinctively moved in front her son like a shield and locked eyes with the stranger in front of them. "Jerry, git on upstairs, hon," she croaked. "Daddy's not feelin' like hisself tonight."

But Jerry was her firstborn. And he sensed danger around his mother. "Not if he's gonna hurt you instead."

The words might as well have been a mirror of Ari's soul. And for a split second Pepper saw that her husband didn't recognize his own reflection.

"That's ridiculous," he muttered, fingering the medal lying underneath his shirt before dismissing them with a wave and stalking off to his study.

Pepper felt her son lean his forehead into the small of her back.

Holy shit, she thought as the sound of Ari slamming his door and throwing the lock echoed back down the glass halls. *I'm back in Kentucky!*

In her now-Papadopoulos-subsidized apartment, Mariah, in a trance, dribbled three circles of bull's blood around a phallic-shaped candle containing painstakingly gathered fingernail clippings and strands of Ari's hair. (She'd followed him to the barbershop and managed to surreptitiously plunder the wastebaskets.) Lighting the candle, she muttered a final incantation before being released from the trance and collapsing.

A half hour later, she opened her eyes and focused on her bedroom's indigo walls and the work she'd completed. The seven-hour trance had left her hungry.

In the kitchen, Mariah consumed three large glasses of water and a pear while forking garlic-free lamb souvlaki out of a Tupperware container into a saucepan on the stove. It was left over from the lunch she'd served Aristotle Papadopoulos earlier today.

Just before she initiated their first kiss.

In four days, when the moon becomes full, he would come to her home for dinner. And she would finally seduce him and seal the spell, binding him to her forever.

And then, on to the next Papadopoulos brother.

The phone rang just as she tucked into the meat; she checked on the number as she chewed.

Right on time.

After pouring herself a glass of dark retsina wine, and washing down her mouthful, Mariah punched the speaker button on the phone.

"Good evening, Mr. Kousakis," she said.

83

Dude!

"Aw. Mrs. Erhardt, that's not a good—"

"Oh, come on, Joseph."

"A man could get killed."

"Don't be silly! You're thinking too hard."

"I'm thinking I don't want to die."

"Oh, just give it a shot. C'mon. Bam! Now!"

"No way! I am not going to guess your age!"

Patti looked at the other security guard inside the north gatehouse of Beverly Park. He was shaking his head without looking up from his book. Patti drummed her fingers on the steering wheel of her Aston Martin DB9.

"Okay," she began, "what if I was a stranger and I ran the barrier? And you had to call the police and give a description of me. What would you—"

"What kind of car?"

"Huh?" Patti asked. "Doesn't matter."

"Well, it does, because a Smart Car, like Mrs. Pollarde's, wouldn't break—"

"A Hummer. What age would you tell the police?"

"We'd notify internal security personnel first. Does the Hummer have plates?" asked Joseph.

"Give it up, Mrs. Erhardt," yelled the other security guard without looking up. "Joey ain't playin'."

"You all look twenty-one," Joey finally said, but it didn't satisfy Patti.

"Twenty-one like Cissy Pollarde, or twenty-one like Janet—" she began.

"Mrs. Erhardt!"

Thanks to the drunken observations of Jeff and Roger, Patti had spent the entire afternoon augmenting her face with Botox and fillers. The amount of cattle required to manufacture her lip collagen alone met the qualifications for membership in the Texas Ranchers Association. Patti herself would qualify as a weapon of mass destruction if she soaked her temples in the right aqueduct.

In order to prevent telltale bruising or swelling, she'd made her dermatologist spend fifteen minutes massaging every single poke point with ice and the results were smoother than she'd ever experienced. But since bruises had a nasty habit of sneaking to the surface, sometimes hours after a dermo visit, Patti spot-checked her face in the rearview every few minutes during the ride home—in case she needed to apply the emergency liquid nitrogen propellant she kept in her glove compartment.

Preoccupied thusly, she didn't notice a silver truck with multiple surfboards in its bed parked across the street from her house.

And she didn't go into her house by her front door because she'd parked at the east entrance in order to have a glass of punch at the big farewell barbecue party for Alexandra and her mother, two of the backyard Hondurans who were finally moving out on their own.

The mother, it seemed, had a flair for stand-up and had shaped her experience as a mudslide refugee into a lucrative act entitled "Locas Rich Bitches." A UTA agent caught it at an open-mike night in Silver Lake and secured the mother her own show on the Zane Enterprises–owned Spanish-language radio network. It was already predicted to be a hit by both critics and the kingmakers of the Housekeeper Network.

Patti made so many toasts that she was mildly in her cups when she finally entered her house to the sight of Lou carrying two glasses of scotch toward the living room, almost causing her to aggravate her injection sites by breaking into tears of joy.

He was walking without a cane.

Marveling at Lou's ability to balance scotch and maneuver his tank stand at the same time without spilling, Patti tiptoed up behind him into the living room as he handed a glass of scotch to Ricky-the-surfer, who was at the moment, sitting on the couch.

That was when she fainted dead away on the floor.

"Dude!" Rick pointed out to Lou. "Your wife's down."

Patti revived on the couch, waking up to see Ricky's face hovering over her.

Wow. It wasn't just a dream!

And then she fainted again.

The second time she revived, Patti beheld Lou. With a gun in his hand.

(!)

WWII or I?

And then she fainted again, dead away.

The third time Patti Fink opened her eyes, they focused on Ricky-the-surfer again.

"Patti, don't pass out!" he cried. "This scotch is amazing!"

"Okay, if this is heaven, I get to change that shirt," she said, wincing at the purple-and-brown tiki print Ricky was wearing.

"No way! You're not dead. And neither am I."

Patti dropped Ricky's hand and put a cube from his glass on her forehead. Lou was nowhere to be seen.

"I been stalk-parking across the street for three days," Ricky continued, "keeping deathwatch just in case you needed company or a sympathy bone." Ricky broke into a naughty smile. "Drove in on the wrong side while the guards were checking out this lady's Smart Car. Then this morning, I was taking a leak on your wall and looked over and I saw the old dude come out and get the paper. And he didn't look dead. And he didn't look about-to-be-dead. So I got, like, major confusion, so I jumped the wall and knocked on the door to ask the old dude to hurry up and croak because I was in love with his wife. And Lou was happy to see somebody that spoke English, so he invited me in . . . Patti? Patti? Whoa."

The fourth time Patti revived, she was still looking at Ricky.

"Patti, stay awake. I couldn't do it," he said. "Because now . . . I'm in love with *Lou*."

"This is *definitely* not heaven," Patti said, seizing his scotch and downing it.

"Not man-on-man love, but major-dude-admiration love. Lou is one seriously awesome dude! Did you know he both shredded and toked with the Duke?"

"Of Windsor?"

"Kahanamoku."

"Whoa."

"I can't rip off the Lou dude's woman," Ricky went on. "That would be seriously not righteous. And I'm sorry, but we can't get married either." With that, he uncrumpled his cocktail napkin and offered it to her. "Sorry for the trauma. Here."

Patti used it to cover her sudden screams of joy and relief.

Ricky shook his head sadly. "I knew you'd be bummed."

"It'll take time," she said, after composing herself. "Whooo! I had the strangest visions when I was out."

Ricky giggled. "You thought we were in heaven."

"And I saw Lou with this very big gun."

"Yeah, he got it from some dude named Nippon at some club or something called Iwo Jima. He was underage and lied to get in."

(!)

WWII after all!

Patti almost levitated them both off the couch.

"Whoa," say Ricky. "You shouldn't get up yet."

"Let-me-go-you-don't-understand! Lou is clever!"

"The gun wasn't for us," Ricky explained. "It was for crowd control."

"Huh?"

"The rave out back is getting pretty festive. Hear it?"

Patti had thought the loud music was coming from Klaus's room. And outside the living-room floor-to-ceiling windows, she noticed two men moving around, exchanging punches. "Whoa."

"And Katsume has a history midterm tomorrow," Ricky informed her. "But the Lou dude wasn't gonna wuss and narc on his own party. Besides, the cops have this button they can push that tells them the phone number of who made the call."

At that moment two shots rang out, coming from the backyard. But they didn't seem to dampen the mood of the party; in fact, people started cheering and the fight continued.

Then Lou appeared at one of the massive glass patio doors and let himself in. He had the gun in his hand and his portable oxygen tank in his Dunhill shoulder holster.

"Hey, sweet stuff, welcome back!" he said, sidekicking the man who was winning the fight so he could shut the door all the way.

"Um, I hate to tell you this, Lou dude," said Ricky-the-surfer, "but your rave is still raging. You're gonna have to shoot more than two people. Or maybe the sound system."

"Nah, shot in the air." Lou shuffled over to a massive amber-inlaid console table, opened a drawer, and put away the gun. "Right now every home owner in the park is calling the cops and hiding under their beds."

Sure enough, the sound of sirens coming from all directions grew progressively louder and the men outside stopped fighting and ran.

"Heh heh," said Lou, glancing out the closest window. "Look at 'em go! So," he said, shuffling over and smacking Patti's thigh as he sat down, "I see you met the kid. Did you know he can surf?"

Patti nodded and hoped someone on her staff was sober enough to hear her ring for more scotch.

"Lou dude, you never finished the Baja story!" said Ricky, plopping down at Lou's feet like a disciple.

"Oh, yeah, the trip with Bob Mitchum? Had to fight my way out of a brawl. Ever heard of a donkey bar?"

Patti watched her former paramour hang on her husband's every word. And she found it hysterically ironic that when the staff member brought in the cocktail tray, it turned out he was one of the two jokers who'd just been fighting in her backyard.

Whoa.

Boo!

Richard Zane watched the twenty-by-ten-foot wall-to-wall home-theater screen descend from the ceiling and felt his lower back descend and relax in concert with it as he settled deeper into his command chair. The rest of the room was filled with wide, down-filled couches and chaises, but he preferred his custom reclining seat, back row, center, slightly raised, overseeing the room. In control with the controls at his fingertips. He continued to watch the screen click into place as he swiveled his elbow to the right, picked up the remote under his fingertips, and then aimed it at the screen and depressed his thumb in order to dive into eleven days' worth of TiVo treats.

Nothing happened.

Richard clicked again. Still nothing. Looking down, he realized that the object in his hand wasn't his old familiar friend the remote but something foreign and smaller and heavier.

Goddammit! Friggin' Kenny!

Richard now remembered passing Kenny-the-Zane-compound-in-house-technician puttering around downstairs as he was departing for his vacation. But he'd been too preoccupied (or depressed) to stop and ask the guy what the hell he was doing. Every time Richard saw Kenny, it gave him the willies because the guy had a nasty habit of *updating* electronic gadgets. Dammit! He liked the old remote! He was used to it! Now he had to start all over again with this new alien ray-gun-shaped thing. Richard leaned back in his chair and tipped his head back toward the door.

"Marion!" he yelled. "C'mere, hon! Do you know how to . . . !"

Oh, God. He was doing it again.

This was why he'd gone on the trip in the first place!

He'd wanted to let the Caribbean sun and salty air burn away, and the warm wind blow away, these emotions that kept on emanating from the female side of his brain. He needed to get clean and acclimate himself to not having Marion around because he was beginning to feel like a damn amputee! What a joke. He'd returned early because the boat trip had only made him feel worse.

At every island port, single women were gathered around like starving jackals, ready to pounce on his rumored soon-to-be-eligible billionaire bachelor ass. He was lonely, yes, but not for *strangers*! It got so bad he was using bodyguards just to go ashore. That one dock-monster jackal had actually jumped onto the lower deck of the *Triumphant* before the boys had managed to get the gangplank down! Spider-Man in a halter top!

Thinking a visit with his little girl would cheer him up, he'd invited Crystal to join him. She was happy to oblige, but when his daughter arrived, she was attended by an eighteen-girlfriend posse and they all partied nonstop at all hours of the day and night. Some of those gals had even hit on him. Nobody got the message. The last thing he'd wanted to deal with was more women!

Worst of all, he couldn't be on the boat without thinking about one woman. Marion. Every time he crept up on deck, he half expected to see her standing there smiling and giving directions to the crew or sunning herself and looking tasty. Or getting ready for dinner in their stateroom or even shaving her legs in their bathroom.

He used to love watching that.

Now he felt like he was being haunted.

He really missed her.

He really missed her vagina.

The thought of being alone and vulnerable in bed with another woman right now was just plain scary. Maybe there was a clinic somewhere. Marion had ruined him!

If only she hadn't gone crazy.

Yet, he recalled, she hadn't looked crazy at Frank Greene's . . . Flame-blowing-pissed-off-dangerous perhaps, but not crazy.

Unfortunately, he had a pile of receipts from the Home Shopping

Network, half a stuffed poodle, and one pretty damning photograph that said otherwise.

So he'd abandoned ship a week early.

Then, as it turned out, home wasn't any better. He'd arrived late and just wanted to rest, but Tawnee had fucked up the master suite so bad he hadn't slept there *before* he'd left, so he wasn't about to return to it now. He didn't want to go back to the sleekness of Dickie Jr.'s black-and-gray low-lit room, which had been designed solely with sex on the brain. Crystal's room was too foofy-girlie. This was his house and he was starting to feel like Goldilocks. He didn't want to sleep in *any* of the upstairs beds, and the halls were haunted by Marion ghosts!

When he'd realized he was probably going to have to sell the compound to escape all the Marion memories, he dumped down to sleep in the media room in despair—the popcorn smell was still on his skin even after a shower. Now, back in the same media room, he was hiding from work and attempting to escape into the last bastion of peace in his amputee world. He just wanted something to take his mind off the fact that he was going to have to start his life all over again without the one person who gave it meaning. But no! His old friend the remote had been replaced with this ray gun!

It did feel kind of cool, though. Had a nice heft.

Richard sat up in his command chair, popped the drawer in his command station, and removed a pair of readers. The ray gun couldn't be that difficult to figure out; he was an adult. He owned a media empire.

Ten minutes later, he'd gotten the thing to go on, but he couldn't get past the home menu.

"Mr. Zane?" a voice called. "There's a Senator Powell on the line."

Shit!

He hadn't canceled that temp. She'd tip everybody off that he was back in town! "Ah, listen, ah . . ."

"Evelyn."

"Right. Evelyn. I'm not really up to taking calls, yet. I'm not really in town, yet. Just tell the senator that you were mistaken and that I'm still away. I'll see him at the hearing."

"That's what he wants to talk about, Mr. Zane."

Richard went back to his remote. "Tell him to tell it to Zephyr Mintz! And hold the rest of my calls, please!"

"Okay, okay." Evelyn turned and left.

Richard decided he hated all remotes.

Marion was always the the one who knew how to work these . . . !

He had to stop thinking about her!

Richard clenched his fist in triumph when the home menu disappeared and Oprah Winfrey's face filled the twenty-by-ten-foot wall-to-wall home-theater screen.

Moments later, Richard clenched his sphincter in shock when he saw Marion's face fill the twenty-by-ten-foot wall-to-wall home-theater screen.

She looked good.

Really good . . .

85

Pain in the Ass

O *oh-la-la! Just look at those mounds! Hold on to your heads, boys, they're gonna be turn-ing!*

Lyndy was almost finished recuperating from her surgery and eager to take her new ass out on the town.

Tomorrow! Tomorrow!

She'd have to designate a new gay best friend, one who knew all the cool clubs, by sundown. She'd go nuts restraining her new butt until a wedding or benefit came along.

Because my butt is ready to strut!

She was already going stir-crazy lying prone on her stomach with two drainage bottles hanging off the sides of her ass, despite the Frette sheets. Thank God Max had gone off to South America on his dry cleaners' retreat! His comments during the first few days had been merciless.

Lyndy adjusted the angle on her hand mirror to get a better view of the doctor's fine work.

Baby got back!

It was positively the prettiest, perkiest little bootie she had ever seen! Round and high and life-affirming! You could serve martinis off it! (Tee-hee!)

And all of her asshole Montgomery cousins—the ones who got to live in the mansions and had the nannies and the ponies and expense accounts and the chauffeurs and the clothes, the ones who used to look at their poor little satellite cousin Lyndera as though she wasn't really an actual part of their lauded, landed, and lustrous bloodline, the ones who used to play with Cousin

Lyndera up until puberty, then suddenly became hyperaware of social stand-
ing and began to consider her "outside of their crowd," the ones who excluded
her from their parties and made fun of poor Cousin Lyndera's "square butt"
behind her back—those motherfuckers could FUCK OFF AND DIE OF LEP-
ROSY!!!!!!!

Because poor Cousin Lyndy not only had as much money as they did! Now
Cousin Lyndy was the most-lauded and definitely best-butted one of the
bunch!

Lyndy wanted to shove her new butt up her cousin's blue-blood noses.
She couldn't wait for polo season to start.

Even all the public humiliation and theft Lyndy had suffered last month
faded into mere nuisances when she gazed upon her new ass.

And the TOP seemed as attainable as ever. Marion Zane had vanished,
and according to Lyndy's spies, no one was making a move to claim the
crown. There weren't any dynamic enough Stage IIIs and all of the domi-
nant Stage IIs were touring colleges with their kids at the moment.

The time was still ripe for a takeover. And when everyone got a load of
her new ass and the male attention it commanded, well, they'd be so envi-
ous, they wouldn't be able to help themselves from getting amnesia and
gathering at her feet!

"Right, Prince Matthew?"

The old chow dog stopped licking his privates and raised his head in
drooling agreement.

Lyndy settled back down onto the sheets, picked up the TV remote, and
began channel-surfing and daydreaming about herself on the dance floor
and her return to the TOP, and all of a sudden she realized that she really
had to be dreaming because only in a crazy dream would she now be seeing
that awful new-money ex-vampire Marion Zane as a guest on the *Oprah*
show. Yes, it had to be another Vicodin nightmare because Marion looked
far too well and Oprah was giving her far too many compliments and using far too many flattering terms, like *connected, skilled, premiere philan-*
thropic socialite hostess of Los Angeles, and as far as Lyndy was concerned,
that was *her* title and she really needed to pinch her arm because who
would ever want to linger in such a repulsive dream and why could she feel
the pinch and why wasn't Marion Zane's gorgeous and flawless face disappearing from her eyes and why was she beginning to sting from pinching
so hard and drawing blood from the pinch and . . .

Lyndy leaped to her feet on the bed.

"NOOOOOOOOOOOOOOOOOOOOOOOOOOOOOOOOOOOOOOO!" she screamed.

It's a lie! Marion Zane does NOT possess the skills of Emily Post, Elsa Maxwell, and the Vanderbilts combined! I DO! MARION ZANE LEARNED THEM AT MY FUCKING FEET! THOSE ARE *MY* SKILLS! *MINE!*"

And when Oprah had the audacity to tell Marion that she could "start a new career as the new Martha Stewart or Google-for-rich-people with all of her contacts," Lyndy began shaking her fists.

"CONTACTS? *CON-TACTS?* WHAT KIND OF CRAPPY RESEARCH ARE YOU DOING ON THIS SHOW? I, LYNDERA MONTGOMERY WALLERT, HAVE *CONTACTS*! MARION ZANE HAS *VICTIMS* THAT SHE SUCKS! SHE'S A VAMPIRE! THIS IS FRAUD! I SHOULD SUE!"

Lyndy shook so violently that she dislodged one of her drainage tubes, and it and the bottle that was attached to it popped out and landed between Prince Matthew's paws, where they was enthusiastically gummed then rejected.

Lyndy was so consumed by her screaming rage and hatred toward Marion Zane that she didn't notice she was missing a drainage tube and bottle until the *Oprah* segment was over and she had taken a double dose of Vicodin. And even then, she didn't notice until she accidentally dropped the pills on the floor. When she finally spied her drainage tube and bottle, she picked them up and shoved the tube back into the hole on the side of her new ass without washing it because she was too busy desperately calling every gay man she knew in search of a dance partner.

Because there had to be at least one portion of the universe that Marion Zane hadn't already poisoned by her presence. One little portion where poor Lyndy could reign . . . One!

86

Behaving Appropriately

fter taking a deep drag of the Turkish cigarette, Maya directed her exhale toward the space behind the bar. The green LED light from the telephone lit the edges of the churning smoke and she imagined it to be a shadowy bartender. She toasted him with a slight nod before knocking back the shot she imagined he'd poured for her. There was, however, nothing imaginary about the syrupy iced vodka that was sluicing down her burning throat. In Chechnya, the Russian alcoholic beverage was referred to as "liar's blood." It was an appropriate name.

Maya had the gift of the con. The need for survival had forced her to hone her skills upon the sheets of Grozny and on the streets of Istanbul, Belgrade, Zagreb, and Milan. No lie detector could find out the secret of her past. She'd passed with flying colors in Budapest, when Dudayev had fucked up on timing and she'd been apprehended at a crime scene. East European police love their lie detectors. Maya loved them too. They had exonerated her as an innocent bystander, when in fact she had not only blown the safe, she'd also been the one tossing down the jewelry from the window of the building she and her cohorts had broken into.

Becoming a model was a natural extension of being a con artist.

To this day, she'd never been caught in a lie.

And she'd never suffered a moment's guilt.

But a few days ago, when she sat in the doctor's office and looked into the excited, expectant face of her husband, she knew she couldn't con him.

She loved him too much.

And what had happened to her in Chechnya deserved more respect than a faked fertility-test result.

When the doctor came in to see her and Tom, fully prepared and paid off to play his part with falsified results, Maya reached out, took the print-out from her hands, and tore it in half. Then she took her husband home.

And she told him everything.

She might as well have stabbed him in the stomach.

Tom could not believe how much of her past life she had withheld from him. He was horrified to learn that she'd undergone such nightmares, *but* he and Maya were "supposed to be soul mates." And it seemed to his so-called soul mate had conned him into thinking she was someone else entirely.

He could not believe she had allowed him to happily anticipate a family. A family that she would provide him! And to think—he'd had to jerk off in a cup!

He also couldn't believe they had *gypsies* living in the cottage.

Finally he ended up just crying and saying "I don't know my own wife!" over and over, turning the words into a mournful chant.

Tom left in the morning, still red-eyed, for location. He wasn't due there for another week. He didn't wake Maya up to say good-bye.

And even though that had been three days ago, and even though to-night Marion had tried to coax Maya out for six hours, Maya wasn't ready to leave the rumpus room of the manse.

It was dark down here.

And there was a bar. With vodka.

It felt appropriate.

87

Calling Out the Big Guns

Pepper stubbed out her doobie as she pressed her universal gate opener at the alarm control panel in her bedroom and watched the sleek stretch limousine with its trail of baby Town Cars slide up their statue-studded hill, thanking the Good Lord, her lucky stars, and sweet baby Jesus that Marion Zane was off the streets and back on her game.

One more night with Ari like that last one and Pepper would just pack up the kids, buy a trailer, and turn into her mother. (Okay, not a trailer.) And come to think of it, but for two more daughters and she'd have the same amount of kids as her mother. The similarity was too close for comfort.

Pepper had to admit that she was a little pissed that it was Marion who came up with the idea and not herself. 'Course it was hard to think when a Greek-fever victim was clunking around downstairs trying to stuff half a goat carcass into her oven. It smelled like somebody had burned a carpet.

"Fight fire with fire," Marion had said. "If he wants to get in touch with his roots, help him out."

At least Ari wasn't too xenophobic to cancel his game of golf—which had been invented by Scots, not Greeks—with Alice Cooper this morning. Pepper was relieved about that; she wanted some alone time with the fire she was about to light under her husband's ass.

From her bedroom, she could see that the stretch limo and its Town Car train had come to a stop. The Russian wolfhounds were first out of the cortege followed by a flurry of fussy valets and refrigerator-size bodyguards toting matched sets of Hermès luggage. By then, Pepper's own sticky welcoming committee was pouring out the front door and mobbing the limousine.

"Nana!" they yelled.

Mercedes Papadopoulos, mother of Ari, was the epitome of an old-school Euro jet-set diva. Pepper decided that her mother-in-law must have had her sons when she was a toddler because she didn't look a day over forty. Most American women born with Mercedes's large aquiline nose would have lopped it off in shame, but Mercedes carried it with regal hauteur, allowing it to be the defining element of her beauty. Both Helmut Newton and Avedon had been obsessed with her face and statuesque figure, which, frankly, still looked good in a topless bikini.

The grande dame of Greek high society presided over Swiss ski resorts in the winter and Mediterranean yacht marinas in the summer. The rest of the time she'd show up on TMZ.com—hunting grouse in Scotland, dancing at a ball in Venice, being pampered at spas in the Black Forest, attending museum openings in Paris. Mercedes was a Trophy wife who had attained a level that American women couldn't reach in their wildest dreams. Patti Fink had actually curtsied to her once at a Christmas party.

Mercedes could charm the pants off of most jaded royals and spoiled rock stars.

She could also turn you to stone with one look. Ari's father hadn't nicknamed her "The Gorgon" for nothing. And Ari stood up when she entered a room.

Because Mercedes Papadopoulos didn't suffer pretenders or fools.

And she took her family seriously.

Very seriously.

She had fired up the G5 the moment she got Pepper's call, and now here she was sweeping into Pepper's home asking, "What's with the statues? Has Ari gone gay as well as insane?" After briskly greeting the grandchildren then dismissing them to play with her dogs, she draped herself in a chair in the breakfast room and laser-focused her attention on her son's marital woes with her favorite daughter-in-law.

Pepper gave precise, vivid details, including the glass he'd smashed against the fireplace wall and his demands for adherence to Greek Orthodox religious tenets.

Mercedes listened to everything stoically. Then she took a long pull on her Campari and soda and asked, "Darling, has Ari by any chance been wearing a red string lately? On his wrist, finger, around his neck?"

Pepper racked her brain to remember.

"Now that you mention it, I saw some sorta red stuff 'round the clasp of his Poseidon medal. I figured he just snagged it on a sweater. I've been meaning to pick it out—"

Mercedes nodded knowingly and announced, "He's fucking a Greek."

Pepper couldn't speak.

"Or he's about to. It's magic, darling. Those island bitches still know that old stuff. She's probably from Crete. They take a string they've soaked in their menstrual blood and—"

"Jee-zus!"

"Let's just say there's some nasty witchcraft afoot. I had one come after Alexandros twelve years ago and she almost succeeded in taking him away from me. Thank the gods I had an old laundress from Chania that year! She figured out what was going on."

"That motherfuckin', cheatin,' son of a—"

Mercedes interrupted again. "Before you castrate my youngest son, you need to know that he really has no choice in the whole thing. He's literally under an enchantment."

"I don't believe in fairy tales," Pepper scoffed. "But I'll show him the enchanting end of a baseball bat if he thinks he's goin' out on me!"

"I'm not saying he shouldn't be thrashed," Mercedes said equably. "But, my dear, you have to ask yourself if you're willing to lose him *completely*. Because that's what will happen if you simply lash out at him and don't address the real source of the problem."

Pepper knew that anyone else would think this crazy. A mother's desperate, albeit creative, excuse for her son being a dog. But Pepper had grown up with grannies whispering about "love spells." She'd seen hill women sprinkle hog blood around a dead apple tree and circle it, singing strange chants. And she'd seen the very same tree come back to life. It had borne huge, scarlet apples. She'd seen people lay hands and heal the sick.

"Oh, I'll do more than address her . . ."

"Good girl! The first thing you need to do when he comes home is get that string off! I buried Alexandros's in a jar of sea salt and dropped it into a volcano. Next, you need to identify the Greek interloper and drive her away. Who are the Greek women that are currently in your circle?"

"That could be anybody!"

"Start with his calendar and secretary. Ari is incurably anal about his schedule. As a child, he'd make 'appointment' lists before breakfast, and was afraid that time would disappear if he didn't organize it."

"And when I find her?" Pepper asked.

"You don't need crosses or silver bullets," Mercedes answered. "Just confront her and make it clear that her scheme has been foiled. There are lots of other fish in the sea. She'll just focus her energy elsewhere. Avoid looking directly into her eyes, though. They lay curses that way."

Although Mercedes was famous for air-kissing just about everybody, she saved her genuine embraces for family. Pepper knew this about the woman, and so threw her arms around her in gratitude.

"I won't castrate yer boy," she promised. "Least not till I get a couple more babies outta him."

"The more the better! And speaking of grandchildren, I've got toys, chocolates, and age-inappropriate DVDs burning a hole in my bag. And tell the drivers to stash the cars around back. I want to surprise my poor boy."

Mercedes rose and headed for the children's wing.

Pepper checked the time and finished her Coke.

There was just enough time to make it to Ari's office building and be back before he finished his game. Luckily, the head janitor of the building had a crush on her.

She was glad she'd TiVo'd the CNN coverage of Marion's *Black Book* auction.

She was going to be a very busy girl for the rest of the day.

88

Passion After Fashion

As Patti Fink shuffled along the corridor of the L.A. County Museum behind the rest of the fashionistas who made up the Los Angeles Costume Council, she wondered if there would ever be excitement or passion again in her life.

Ricky-the-surfer had gone the way of the dinosaurs (which meant he now had cocktails with "Lou dude" regularly on Thursdays) and she had elected to go on a paramour-free diet for a while.

Most of the Honduran gardener's family had moved out of the backyard tent city. The one sister who remained had started to make a nice living for herself deconstructing and reconstructing Patti's castoffs and selling them to local boutiques. She had ascertained early on that Westside rich ladies thought ragged designer clothing with a bit of junk trim or silver paint tacked or daubed on instantly transformed them into youthful rebel sprites. The parent company of Free People had tracked the young woman down and hired her as a style consultant.

With Patti's stepson Günter's help, Felix-the-driver had secretly downloaded, copied, and printed Patti's address file and sold it to two entities, one loyal to the Democratic Party and one to the Republican. The sale made him enough money to return to Honduras and purchase his own house *and* a new moped.

He had sworn off cars forever.

The rest of her Honduran campers had disappeared after Lou's raid, leaving nothing more than tent-imprinted albino grass patches as proof that they had ever resided in Beverly Park.

With only five stepkids in the house at the moment, the place was practically a ghost town.

Patti had been hit especially hard yesterday. It all started when she had looked out her bedroom window to see Lou chatting in the backyard with Sumner Redstone and Warren Buffett. They were seated around the converted Greek Orthodox baptismal font Patti had smuggled out of Turkey, sipping drinks and reenvisioning tax codes.

The fire pit in the backyard table had been blazing so hot that the Italian lava rock was glowing red. And the latter, Patti had noticed, was treacherously close to *Lou's oxygen tank!*

Patti had practically flown out of the house, wearing nothing but a G-string and T-shirt, to shoo her husband out of harm's way (and, however unintentionally, prevent a stock-market crash).

The rescue had aroused Lou and one thing led to another, and before she knew it she was late for a post-tea, pre-cocktail reception for Gillian Landro's babywear launch, and in her haste, she hadn't looked at the purse she'd flipped to Wanda to stuff with the requisite phone, card case, Red Vines, panty change, stun gun, perfume, makeup, and prayer beads.

At the valet, she discovered she had grabbed a bag that was wrong with her outfit.

Disastrously wrong.

This season's bags were constructed of soft leather. Hers was constructed *hard*! She was wearing layered, sheer pastel, high-fashion Comme des Garçons. Her bag was brown croc classic Asprey! They didn't mix!

For the first time in her life, Patti avoided the photographers, slipping in through a side entrance. She ran into Gillian before she had time to wrap the bag in a napkin. After a moment of exchanging pleasantries during which Patti expressed her excitement about viewing the onesies, Gillian was pulled away by her publicist. But not before she remarked, "Great bag."

Great bag?

Gillian was a goddess of style! Wasn't the bag *wrong*?! And then, to compound her confusion, almost every person she met that night had something nice to say about her ensemble or the bag.

Patti's whole world had taken a downturn from that moment on.

Could it be that fashion didn't matter any longer?

What now? What matters now?

Certainly not the pre-WWI European coronation gowns she'd been seeing in the boutiques. They just weren't as riveting as she had hoped.

Instead of schlepping around the museum, Patti thought she should be celebrating with Marion when the *Black Book* was sold today. It was bound to bring in big dough (and big press).

Lucky Marion Zane. Now, that girl had *passion*! Marion *sacrificed* for her dream of building Carita Memorial. Patti had seen her eyebrows and the burns that had been left by the waxing lessons she'd been forced to endure during her stint at the Culver Beauty Academy. Marion Zane "gave of herself" light-years beyond cutting a check or making a list. Then again, Marion knew she had something worth giving.

Patti looked at the aged finery in the museum costume department. She wondered if anybody would notice if she switched the handbags of the Lithuanian countess and the Swedish queen. In fact, she was about to try it in order to see if the docent caught on, when she heard a strange noise coming from an exhibit that was part of a "women's history" show.

When she turned the corner and entered a darkened room, Patti found that the noise was coming from a documentary film currently in progress. It was about a group of women from a small coastal fishing village in East Africa. An oil company had paid off the government to obtain the drilling rights to the village's adjacent bay. The installation of, and daily spillage from, the oil rigs ended up killing all the fish in the area and coating the mangroves with a deadly fungus. The local wells were poisoned as well.

When the fishermen complained, the government told them that the oil company had brought great wealth to their country. As per usual, the "great wealth" went to select government officials, while the villagers went hungry and became ill.

When the fishermen complained further, their government told them that the oil rigs would mean jobs. Shortly after, foreign workers were brought in.

When the fishermen formed a protest, the oil company had armed thugs fire tear gas upon the protesters and beat the ones they caught or put them in jail.

The women of the village had had enough. Their men were destitute, their children were starving, and their ancestral home was dying. In the dead of night, they manned their husband's boats and seized control of an oil rig, bringing production to a standstill.

When the oil company sent thugs to remove them, the women fought them off, wearing rags tied around their faces to combat the tear gas.

When the oil company and the government called out the local navy, the women stood up en masse and bared their breasts.

They bared their breasts.

In East Africa, a woman baring her breasts at a man is a great shame. The women were "shaming" their country and its naval forces. No African man would dare go against them.

The navy turned back.

Word of the shaming spread on the wire services and in order to restore production and save face, the oil company agreed to train the fisherman to replace the foreign workers on the rigs. They also cleaned up the wells and started to employ pollution controls in the bay. A small percentage of the company's profits would be invested in bettering life in the village, building schools and improving medical care.

The film showed the women stoically baring their breasts and chanting into the barrels of the navy gunboat.

All sizes and ages. They looked immortal.

Patti took in the faces of the sailors as they beheld the sight. She had enough experience in New Age teachings to figure out that the breasts were also home to the heart chakra.

The women were blasting the sailors with their hearts. The sailors and thugs and oil-company personnel and government officials could not help but look inside their own.

Patti watched the film nine times. She could feel herself standing alongside the African women . . . her beautiful breasts blazing in the sun.

89

Mama Knows Best

When Ari caught sight of the abomination, he slammed on his brakes so hard that the Bentley fishtailed sideways off the driveway and onto the lawn, where the wet grass almost sent him skidding backward down the hill and on top of his neighbor's roof.

I am in hillbilly hell!

His statue of Dionysus had been decapitated.

And castrated!

This wasn't one of his son's exuberant accidents. This was a direct assault on Ari's authority.

This was his hillbilly brats' payback for the canceled Atlantis vacation!

Looking up the driveway, he could see that the blasphemy wasn't limited to merely one of their father's new antiquities. Every single god lining his driveway was missing both head and phallus.

On his way up to the house Ari crushed two bicycles, two scooters, assorted helmets, kneepads, a skateboard, and a baby carriage. (The Barbie Jeep withstood three direct hits and was allowed to live out of respect for its tenacity.)

"Pepper!" he bellowed, blasting in the front door. "Bring me your children! Bring them before me right now! Pepper!"

"We're all in here, hon," called Pepper's voice from the den.

Good. The den had only one entrance and exit. The hillbillies were cornered. He'd give them a vacation they wouldn't forget. And it wouldn't be in

Greece either. He'd save Greece for his new mistress and send the whole lot of them to Orthodox day camp! Or perhaps that old military camp took kindergartners . . .

As he stormed through the living room, Ari looked out at what was left of the god formerly known as Baphyrus and tore at his waistband to yank off his belt.

Defy his authority! He would teach these hellions the price of their crimes!

Jerry, Maybelle, Cooter, and Chevelle didn't even turn around when Ari kicked the door open. They were sitting on the floor on either side of a huge armchair, facing the wall-to-wall screen, watching some sort of home movie that had been shot on a yacht.

The yacht was enormous and looked strangely familiar to Ari, but at the moment he was more concerned with administering paternal justice. And he was quaking with rage. "You dare destroy my statues?" he began, in a menacing whisper.

His question didn't get exactly the response he expected. None of the children except Maybelle even acknowledged his presence.

"Shhh!" said Maybelle by way of acknowledgment.

Such insolence! He'd get their attention!

Ari doubled the belt.

"Oh, they didn't bash up them statues. *I* did."

Pepper was sitting in a chair next to the door. She had Jerry's baseball bat across her lap.

Ari turned toward his wife, dumbfounded.

But he didn't lower the belt.

"They'll be easier ta transport ta the dump with the heads off. Loppin' off the family jewels was just for fun."

He probably would have struck her then if her words hadn't halted him in his tracks. "Transport my statues to the *dump*?!"

"Before the plaster melts into your lawn. Honestly, Ari, the next time you're tempted to go filling the pockets of charlatans, do your bank account a favor and run the dealer's name by a family member who actually knows a thing or two about Greek antiquities. That's what the Athens Museum does, when they're not borrowing from my personal collection."

Ari's belt hand dropped to his side like he'd been caught stealing coffee cake.

And Pepper relaxed her grip on the bat.

"Mama?" he asked in a small voice.

Mercedes's regal head swung out from behind the armchair, and as he looked into her Gorgon eyes, her youngest son seemed to enter into a state of suspended animation.

Pepper had always marveled at how her mother-in-law kept those updos so perfectly piled. You could never see a single bobby pin. It all just bubbled up out of a lone satin headband.

"Put your clothes back on, you're in the presence of ladies," Mercedes scolded, ruefully looking at Ari's belt.

Ari felt ashamed and promptly shoved the belt back in its loops and buckled it instantly.

Now Mercedes unfolded from the armchair and advanced on her son. In Chanel ballet flats, she was equal in height. She kissed him formally on each cheek and then slipped her hands around to the back of his neck. With a flick of her nails, she whisked his Poseidon medal off for examination.

"This is no way to treat Uncle Fanourios's medal. Pepper, would you clean off this filth?"

With another flick of her nails, Mercedes cast the medal to Pepper, who gasped and almost dropped it.

Lately, Ari had taken to wearing his undershirt 24/7, so she hadn't really seen the medal in a while.

The entire chain was braided with rotting brownish-red string.

Ari felt his body relax. And he had the sudden sensation of being very, very grateful to see his mama. A smile spread across his lips.

Because he knew he was her favorite.

"This is a nice surprise, Mama," he said.

And now Mercedes encircled him in embrace.

Pepper dropped the medal into a diaper wipe and shoved it into the pocket of her jeans.

Ugh! These Greeks didn't fuck around!

She had plans for the string.

And she had plans for the statue dealer whose address was on Ari's calendar, next to the space for 8 P.M. tonight.

Ari looked up at the big screen. It was a home movie from a cruise on his parents' yacht; there were his brothers and his father.

"I thought they'd like to see a little footage of their heritage. Here's your father now."

The children broke into delighted screams of laughter as the camera panned to reveal Ari at age six.

"Daddy! You were a porker!"

"Oh, Daddy! Look how fat you were!"

"*Big-boned*. And be nice!" Mercedes giggled.

"It's okay," said Ari, sitting down among them. Chevelle and Maybelle instantly claimed his lap, but his arms were long enough to ruffle his boys' hair. "Daddy *was* a little fatso back then."

Astonished, Pepper looked at Mercedes, who winked.

On-screen, a gorgeous, statuesque woman in a Brazilian bikini bottom swept the little fat boy up in her arms and covered him with kisses. She was topless.

"Mama!" said Ari, instinctively trying to cover Jerry and Cooter's eyes, without success.

"Oh, let them watch!" said Mercedes. "It's just a part of the human body! If you lived on the French Riviera, they'd see breasts as often as elbows!"

"Yes, Mama, but we're not French, we're Greek."

"Actually," Mercedes told her, "you're more French."

Ari almost pitched the girls off his lap when he turned around.

"I'm all French, your father's half—"

"B-but your maiden name is—" Ari stuttered.

"Forged. For the sake of family tradition and stipulations of a certain very large trust fund. Just like Grandmama's maiden name," Mercedes continued. "In fact, the only real tradition in the Papadopoulos family is that all the men marry *non*-Greek women who are terrific bullshitters! My real name is *Levy*."

Ari's jaw dropped. "I'm Jewish?"

"Jerry, Cooter, I need you to tear your eyes away from Nana's boobies an' come with me onna errand," said Pepper. "Besides, she and your daddy got some talkin' ta do."

"Aw, Mama."

Ari continued to stare at his mother as his daughters reclaimed his lap and jostled for position. Pepper collected her sons, then pecked her husband on the top of his head. On her way out, she leaned in to Mercedes and whispered, "If I didn't see it with m' own eyes . . . thanks."

Mercedes made the internationally recognized sign for "Shhh!" and winked again.

90

Rites of Passage

A dream is a wish my heart makes
Blah, blah, blah, blah, blah
De, de, de, de, de, da, dum, de
Whatever the wish I can keep
Have faith I forget the words now
My rainbow de, de shining through
Da, da, da how my heart is grieving
I will go on believing
The dream I will wish will come true . . .

"Ah, ah, ah, BULLSHIT!" Claire sneezed as she packed her things. She took her time.

Billy was at a film festival, leaving her plenty of time to pack. Katia had gone to the store and it didn't matter that her stepdaughters were still here. Haley was in bed sick, and Eva was off sulking somewhere. Brooke had broken into a victory dance when she saw Claire hauling the suitcases to the master bedroom.

"Hi! You ready fer lunch?"

Pepper was standing in her doorway.

"Pepper? Oh, my God. Oh, I am, ah, so sorry. I thought I said I *didn't know* about having lunch today."

"But I *do* know," said Pepper, who took her Stage II "care and feeding" duties very seriously (especially since Maya was unreachable). She stopped looking at the suitcases and, employing a mommy grip, pulled

Claire out of the room. "C'mon down in the kitchen. I make a mean tuna melt."

Claire burst into tears. "I'm not happy here! Everyone hates me and I hate me too!"

"Didn't your mama tell you not to make any decisions onna empty stomach?"

Thinking about it, Claire realized she had done precisely that.

"An' don't worry 'bout yer girls. Jerry an' Cooter'll keep 'em occupied."

From down the hall, they could hear screams erupting.

Downstairs in the kitchen, Claire told Pepper everything over tear-dampened tuna melts (and a few beers).

She also told Marion, who joined them for lunch via speakerphone.

The Wynn, a hotel in Las Vegas, was covering the no-longer-private *Black Book* sale/auction which would begin at 8 P.M. sharp. They could catch her on the live coverage on MSNBC!

After hearing all the reasons why Claire didn't fit in her new roles as mother and wife and was never able to fit in anywhere socially, Marion took a minute to think (and deal another hand of baccarat) before saying, "What was different, in Winamac, between you and Billy?"

"I don't know. I suppose I was more sure of myself there," sniffed Claire.

"Obviously. Weren't you working for him?"

"Oh yes. I was his liaison to the city. I told him where to shoot and who to talk to and places to park and what to blow up. Stuff like that."

"Mmm. And who seduced who?" Marion asked.

Claire blushed.

"Chee dith," said Pepper, finishing off the second half of her sandwich.

"Okay." Marion clapped her hands. "First things first: get rid of the nanny."

"But Billy won't fire her!" Claire waited. "She works for Pam!"

"Then Pepper will."

"On it," said Pepper, sneaking a bite of Claire's tuna melt.

"Next, young lady," Marion continued. "I think it's not a matter of 'you fitting in.' It's a matter of you—the *real you*, not some ass-kissing, nanny-and-stepchild-and-ex-wife-whipped, style-morphing mouse."

Claire gasped.

"Sorry, darling, but Billy was on the market for some time. He didn't marry a girl from L.A. He married a girl from Winamac."

Claire's wheels began to turn. And the tuna melt was leaching the remaining "new strategy" from her system. "A *Harvest Queen ambassador hostess* from Winamac," she corrected.

"Exactly," said Marion. "Don't feel bad. This is a rite-of-passage. When a Stage One finally figures out that all that geisha shit isn't working for her."

"It means yer ready ta move up ta Stage Two!" said Pepper brightly. "Kick ass on the sale, Marion!"

"Keep your fingers crossed," Marion told her. "Good luck, Claire. You too, Pepper, with that other thing that gives me the chills just to think about."

"Thank you!" Pepper winked.

When Katia showed up in the kitchen and demanded to know who was going to clean up the flooded playroom upstairs, Pepper hooked her by the elbow and hauled the nanny into the den, where she promptly poured her a shot of Jim Beam.

"Okay, name yer price," she told her.

"What on earth are you talking about? Who are you? Are you the mother of those two creatures upstairs?" snapped Katia.

"I said, *name yer price*. How much is it gonna take ta make you go away?"

Claire, who had been listening to this exchange from the other side of the door, almost fell through when she heard Katia say, "Two hundred thousand."

Pepper nodded. "Just a minute, I'll be right back. Sure, pour yerself a refill. Ain't my booze."

Moments later, she emerged from the den with a corkscrew. "Okay," she said to Claire. "Which one do you hate the most?"

Claire was alarmed at first because she thought Pepper was talking about her stepdaughters, who appeared to be losing the battle with Pepper's sons, judging from the noise upstairs.

But Pepper had already moved into Claire's now le Quinne–decorated living room and was taking stock of the walls.

Claire pointed to a nine-by-six-inch painting of a pug dog. "Start with that one," she said.

As Pepper went to work, unframing the painting, Claire decided that her day was getting better by the minute.

As Katia was hauling her suitcases, along with an armload of rolled-up art, out of the house, Craig-the-stylist was hauling an armload of dress bags and store packages into it.

He and Katia crossed paths at Claire's front door.

"You're next!" declared the nanny.

"A couple more shots and that Adam's apple will go down," Craig repeated over his shoulder as he draped his load across the chest in the entry. "Eddie, I think I just concocted a miracle!" he said dramatically, unzipping a nine-hanger bag and rummaging around in it. "I have in my hot and huge hands three samples of—" He stopped when he saw Pepper's Miu Miu boots step into his line of sight next to the bag he was leaning over.

He followed them all the way up. "Hey, chick-o'-stix!" he said, attempting to be dismissive. "Fancy seeing you here. Shouldn't you be home breeding or leaking, or whatever it is you do when you're not out carpooling?"

Pepper zipped Craig's bag back up for him. "I'm here to give you the heave-ho, button eyes."

"It's not up to you! I am here to help Claire!" Craig sniffed, not budging.

"Yeah," said Pepper, collecting some bags. "I remember how much ya *helped* me back when I first got here. Think I'm still payin' the bills."

"Aren't you late for an episiotomy, or something? Come on upstairs, Eddie, we've got some major surgery to perform," Craig said, snatching his bags away from Pepper.

Claire walked to her front door and held it open. She drew herself up into her best pageant three-quarter stance and broke into her best Harvest Queen smile. "As we say back in Winamac: 'Get the fuck out.'"

Craig didn't need to be asked twice.

At this juncture, Pepper hollered for her boys, who trudged downstairs looking disappointed.

"The big one's eye shadow only *melted* in that Easy-Bake Oven," grumbled Cooter.

"Yeah," said Jerry. "It didn't explode at all."

"Well, it ain't a *microwave*, sillies!" said Pepper, ruffling their hair. She turned to Claire. "This house is now clean. Rest is up to you."

After saying good-bye, Claire headed upstairs to check on Haley.

She was in charge of the girls now.

Claire was met in the hall by Brooke, who was brandishing her cell phone. "I'm calling my mother right now to tell her you just drove Katia away!"

"Nobody drove anybody," Claire said, passing her and heading into Haley's room. "Six canvases did the trick."

"Katia said not to disturb Haley!" cried Brooke as Claire flipped on the light.

"Katia isn't—" Claire stopped.

Haley didn't look good. Her face was flushed and her head was tilted at a funny angle, like she was gulping for air. Claire ripped the covers off her bed and felt her head and underarm.

"Did Katia say your sister had a fever?" she asked, flying into the bathroom and tearing open the drawers and medicine chest. Locating an electronic ear thermometer, she dashed to Haley's side.

"Get away from her!" Brooke screamed. "I'm calling my mom!"

Ignoring the girl, Claire sat Haley up. The child was listless and could barely keep her eyes open. Her temperature was 104.9 degrees! Claire started pulling her pajamas off.

In the background, she could hear: "Mommy, this is Brooke. When you get this message, please, please come over quick because—"

Brooke suddenly dropped the phone and flung herself on Claire's back, grabbing at her hair and pulling her away from her sister. "What are you doing to her?! Don't take her clothes off, you freak!"

Claire had begun her childhood in a split-level house in a nice suburb of Winamac. But she'd finished it in an apartment. *Downtown.* The change in location hadn't been wasted on her. She snatched up Brooke's fist in one hand, got ahold of her neck with the other, and planted a knee in her chest. And Brooke froze in fear.

Claire spoke quietly and directly. "*You* have been watching too much trash TV and spending too many hours on the Internet. Your sister is sick. Go into that bathroom and run a tub of tepid water . . . now."

Then Claire let her up.

"What's wrong—"

Claire was already stripping Haley down and lifting her. "NOW!"

She turned to Eva who appeared sucking her thumb at the edge of the bed. "Eva, we're going to be in the bathroom. I need you to stop sucking and get me a head of cabbage from the refrigerator."

Eva quickly complied.

Claire then grabbed Brooke's cell and dialed 911.

When she hung up a few moments later, Haley started to seize. Not the comic imitation Claire had done at the Zane guardhouse, but the very scary, very real thing.

Claire twisted a dry washcloth over her hand and clamped down on Haley's tongue and lower jaw so she could breathe. Then she deftly lowered her into the water, then climbed in with her to keep her from injuring herself.

Brooke started up again with the screaming.

Claire dealt with her quickly. "Shut up and grab that bowl! DO IT! Start pouring water over her body . . . don't worry about me, I'm already wet!"

Just then, Eva returned with one of the big cabbages Katia used in the foul-smelling stew she was always cooking. Claire put a big leaf on Haley's forehead. It was limp in under twenty seconds.

"Eva, we need to change these as soon as they get soft. Don't stop until the paramedics get here. Then go open the front door."

Eva went to work alongside Brooke.

"Brooke, turn on the cold water. Don't stop pouring the water . . ."

Claire started CPR.

All ambassador hostesses had been required to take the course.

Eva went through the whole cabbage before the paramedics arrived.

Turned out Haley had a peptic ulcer with internal bleeding.

The paramedics told Claire that Haley would have died without her quick thinking.

And the look on Brooke's and Eva's faces told her that her stepdaughters were now hers.

91

Dancing Queens

"Ya know, that new rump of yours would look a lot hotter if you weren't scratching it every five minutes," Lyndy's partner told her.

"And your mouth would look a lot better without my Jimmy Choo planted between your teeth, so why don't you shut it and dance us closer to the center of the room," she replied.

"It's your bar tab, sweetie. Follow me!"

Lyndy was living her dream.

She was taking her new bootie out on the town and shakin' her stuff on the dance floor.

All the boys' heads were turning too.

She just wished they were turning her way instead of toward the shirtless young man in the white jodhpurs and boots who was dancing with her.

And she wished they weren't the only ones dancing. What was wrong with the boys in this bar? She had been promised that Fubar was a crazy place. Fubar was supposed to be fun!

And she wished her butt didn't feel so frightfully itchy as it healed.

It must have been because of all the healthy blood rushing through it.

It was redder than a Georgia ham.

Flushed and ready for fun!

Even Max had taken the butt bait. He'd been all over her this afternoon, until he saw the Brazilian wax she'd undergone in honor of her ass freedom. "Good God, Lyndy," he exclaimed. "What have you done?"

"It's called a Brazilian! I'm feeling frisky!"

Max blanched. "I'm feeling frightened. I could lose my keys in there!"

And that is why Max hadn't been invited out on the town tonight.

Just then, Lyndy caught herself scratching her ass. It was healing full speed ahead, all right. *Healing.*

Not *infected. Oh no-no-no-no-no-no-no!*

She was too busy living her dream.

Lyndy checked her watch. It was almost nine o'clock. "After this song, I want to go to a straight club. I don't want my new equipment to go to waste!"

"Are you sure?" asked her partner. "The ones that're open this early have much brighter lighting."

"Just shut up and dip me," she told him.

"Only if you promise that the G-string stays on."

"Now!"

As Lyndy Wallert was dipped down and threw her leg up to the ceiling, she decided that she'd have to find a new gay best friend.

ASAP.

Craig-the-stylist wasn't that good a dancer.

92

A Very Full Moon

Aristotle was late. He must have been entangled at home.

But Mariah was sure of her spells. They were as strong as those she'd cast upon all the other helpless fellows. Ari would come, eventually.

He had no choice.

Mariah was anxious to see him. She had spent the early evening between worlds while the ancient succubus took possession of her body. The spirit was ravenous in her now and she could barely contain it.

"*Soon,*" she told it. "*Soon you shall feed.*"

Mariah added a final dab of oil to her bosom. She fluffed her luxurious, dark-as-night mane. No earrings, which could be dangerous if the spirit became wild. Her skirt and blouse would come off with a tug. She wore no undergarments.

The footfalls on the stairs to her apartment were light.

Her man was eager. Her charms had worked well.

He wouldn't be disappointed.

Mariah flung open the door without waiting for his knock.

Instead of Ari, she was face-to-bust with the most beautiful woman she had ever seen in her life.

Pepper never once looked into Mariah's eyes as she beat the living shit (and succubus) out of her. (And ground the charms, candles, and other "stalker crap" into the garbage disposal.)

She did use a cross, though. Her Lori Rodkin Maltese diamond ring left a cookie-cutter outline below Mariah's fractured right eye socket.

It went well with the newly shaved head.

To let the witch know she meant business, Pepper forced one of the punch-closed eyes open wide enough to see the doll she'd made out of Mariah's hair and fingernails, and told her that if she wasn't on the next flight to Athens (or wherever the fuck she came from), Pepper would start in with the pins.

The doll was old-fashioned hill-country revenge.

Mercedes hadn't been the only mama Pepper had called.

As Pepper was leaving Mariah's apartment, Pam-the-ex arrived at Beverly Hills Central Hospital, nearly *two hours* after Claire had managed to finally reach her and tell her not to hang up again and that her daughter had just had emergency surgery but was stable and whole.

Pam's makeup was perfect.

She waltzed past Claire and into the ICU as if Claire were invisible.

Didn't she want to know where her other girls were?

Or to speak to them? Pam couldn't possibly have reached Brooke and Eva by phone.

Since only five of the eight bedrooms in Patti's children's wing were currently occupied, Patti had come by and collected them for the night.

No wonder Billy's daughters were mean.

After watching Haley sleep a bit and talking to the doctors, Pam was starting to leave—without even speaking to Claire.

Oh, no you don't!

Claire grabbed Pam by the wrist and with her best ambassador-hostess polite-but-firm-tour-guide tone of voice said, "Right this way. That exit is closed."

Claire was lucky she'd stopped relying on the "medicine-chest strategy."

One more week of Xanax and company and she wouldn't have outweighed the ex.

As she was being dragged into the nurses' lounge, Pam made the mistake of asking, "Where is my husband?"

"*My* husband is flying in from Toronto. My name is Claire Price and I will be your tour guide to your new reality . . ."

And Claire read Pam the riot act.

And made the ex her bitch.

At ten-thirty, Billy rushed in, kissed his "Cookie," then rushed to talk with the doctors and sit with his little girl.

And after he was finished, Claire grabbed his wrist. "Right this way . . ."

And after she was finished reading him the riot act in the nurses' lounge, Billy locked the door and made love to her on a ring-stained Formica table.

And Claire knew that her husband was hers.

Right about the time Claire was getting coffee rings on her backside, Maya, drunk in the basement rumpus room, was calling Tom's location hotel in Quezon City, in the Philippines.

Again.

He hadn't checked in yet.

And Maya thought about how she'd never visited that part of the world.

The Asian part.

Because part of her was Asian. On her father's side.

What was her father's name again? Oh, yes, Wen. And he was tall. Some Chinese people are tall. The ones who live away from the fucking toxic factories and cities with brown air and water that stunts growth and shrinks testicles, but her father was born in Hong Kong, which is fucking polluted. His height came from an African-American basketball-player father. She was in Japan, once. She felt like a giant freak. Her father must have felt like a giant freak in Hong Kong. That's why the Yugoslavian basketball scout on the sex holiday had seen him so easily. Wen was the result of a basketball player's visit to a brothel in Hong Kong. Thanks to Grandma, brothels were in Maya's blood. Which is why she'd never visited Hong Kong. Lots of basketball players and models come from Yugoslavia, so Wen must have felt more normal there.

What was she thinking, again?

Oh, yes. She'd never been to the Philippines either. She'd come close on a Victoria's Secret shoot. How close was Australia to the Philippines? She'd have to look on a map. But since there weren't any maps down here in the dark, she'd have to imagine the Philippines, but hopefully not the part of the country where her husband was fucking that blond, fertile, lousy actress. Maybe just the deserted parts. With grass. But what was she thinking? Australia. They have kangaroos. It is upside down from here. But no one stands on their head. Well, that one model did, but the photographer still didn't give her better lighting. Maya knew many photographers. They had cameras . . .

The phone rang.

Vlad's voice came over the speaker. "Tom is on the phone. He's calling from Hong Kong."

"Bullshit. Tom is fucking lousy actress in part of Philippines. I don't want to visit there," Maya slurred.

Vlad finally broke down the door and put the phone to her ear.

"Oh, Maya, girl!" she heard. "Hey, baby. First, I'm sorry. I'm sorry. I'm sorry I left crazy. I love you so much it was a lot to—"

Maya interrupted. "Hey, you sound like Tom! He was my husband. Once. Many years ago. But he left to fuck lousy actress. Somewhere near Australia . . ."

"Oh, boy. I'm so sorry, girl."

But Maya didn't hear him. She had passed out facedown on the couch.

Vlad picked up the phone. "I *tell* you she is down here long time."

"Could you do me a favor, buddy?" Tom asked. "It's about three in the afternoon here. Do you think you can dry her out in, say, six hours? I have some gigantic-amazing news. But she should be sober to hear it."

"I will want bigger Christmas bonus."

"Sure. Wait! I don't pay you."

"Is joke."

"Can you do it?"

"Yes."

"You know a part of me still can't believe I've got gypsies in my cottage."

"And another part think it cool."

Vlad hung up and with little effort hefted Maya over his shoulder like a very long sack of grain.

A sack of grain that needed dry toast, borscht, a gallon of water, three or four espressos, and several much-needed soapy, cold showers.

He would make sure Sasha wore a cup.

———

While Vlad, Dudayev, and a well-armored Sasha were giving Maya her first of several soapy, cold showers, Marion Zane was watching the closing of the not-so-private *Black Book* sale at the Wynn Hotel in Las Vegas. Not the bidders. The bids. The casino actually had them posted on a big board and MSNBC had provided its own set of graphics.

After 11 P.M., the field had narrowed to nine bidders: two from Dubai, rumored to be members of the Saudi royal family; two from France, one rumored to have created duty-free shopping; one from Italy (and we know who lives there); one from Thailand rumored to be royal; as well as three from the United States, two (the U.S. broker had a big mouth) rumored to be members of Skull and Bones.

By 11:30 P.M., France and Thailand had dropped out, as well as one of the bidders from the United States.

By 11:45 P.M., it was Italy, one Dubai, and one United States. The bidding ping-ponged upward from there, fast and furious.

The crowd at the Wynn was naturally rooting for the United States bidder. The section of the casino where the sale was being broadcast was so extremely boisterous that Marion had to switch to headphones in order to follow the sale. And she held her BlackBerry under one of the headphone earpieces so Patti Fink could follow the action from Los Angeles.

The bidding slowed down around $15 million. That wasn't enough. Marion was beginning to wish she had stashed some of her big jewelry in the thumb safe at the Zane compound before the separation—but that was like wishing she wasn't separated and believed loony because one of those Swiss bank accounts would have covered the remaining money she needed for the hospital fund, no problem.

That's when the handsome man with the card approached her. He was tall, late forties, ice-blue eyes, and chocolate curly hair. With big clean hands and a nice ass. (Marion couldn't help it.) He started to talk to her, but it was too hard to listen.

All she remembered were the words *magazine, products,* and *partnership.*

When Marion signaled to Blue Eyes that now wasn't a good time (but that if he wanted to turn around, flex, and stay, it was okeydokey), he handed her a card. As she put it in her new Fendi clutch, he disappeared.

Oh, well. *Back to the sale!*

At 11:50, the bidding began to move. Seventeen million.

Then, in what was a complete shock to the crowd, Dubai dropped out. Marion had pinned her hopes on Dubai being capricious and illogical enough to skyrocket the price. Her heart sank as she nervously urged the Vatican (whoops!) and the United States to hang in there.

Almost midnight and not high enough—$18 million . . . $18.5 . . . come on, be greedy! Nineteen million.

Ahhh! Why did she have to pay the publicist out of her own money? Because she hated asking her friends for it and they'd given enough . . . Maybe she could beg Ari's mother—no, she'd given already and his brothers were cheapskates and . . . Ahhhh! There's a higher bid . . .

Nineteen-point-five million and thirty seconds until closing and . . .

YES! YES! TWENTY MILLION DOLLARS!

LADIES AND GENTLEMEN, THE UNITED STATES OF AMERICA HAS JUST WON—I MEAN *BOUGHT* THE *BLACK BOOK*!

Jeez, we'll get patriotic about anything.

Who gives a rat's ass? We can partner with UCLA!

Marion gave her old friend a good-luck kiss and got a little misty as the armed guards representing the broker and buyer ceremoniously took possession of the *Black Book* and left the premises. And she said good night to Patti Fink, who was now doing damage to her inner ear (having already ruined her outer one).

And the news reporters closed in. And the interviews began.

They weren't asking about what she was going to do with the money from the *Black Book* sale.

They weren't asking about the hospital.

All they were asking was the same question:

Who bought it?

Marion wished the hell she knew.

While Marion was being interviewed, Ivan was coming up for air on Bora at Hotel Bora Bora, his favorite of the Aman resort chain.

Ibiza would have been lousy this time of year.

Having spent what he considered enough time at sea, he had chosen one of the poolside *farés,* the native Tahitian hutlike dwellings, rather than a bungalow built above the water. The pool *farés* were also more private, just in case his two lovely guests grew tired of sunbathing topless and wanted to to do it completely nude.

He probably could have checked in with Marion by now, but he really wanted Jeff to win the betting pool that the Zane-compound staff had started.

He had another week to go.

And even though he had eliminated the death sentence that had hung over his head for the past fifteen years, which meant he no longer had to be in hiding and could do as he was wished, he would be returning to work for the Zanes.

He liked his job.

Luck had brought them together. Luck had kept him alive.

After all, Gregor von Wolfen was dead. After killing the four Colombian assassins who had attempted to kidnap Crystal in Tikal fifteen years ago, he had placed their bodies outside the obnoxious Zane daughter's hut and stripped the corpse that most closely resembled himself. Next, he donned the corpse's clothing, charged into the Zane brat's hut, and tied up the nanny and brat. He then left the hut and faked the sounds of a deadly scuffle outside. Re-dressing himself in his own clothes, he tucked his identification papers into the corpse's pockets and effectively "killed" Gregor von Wolfen. Then he reentered the hut as a "hero" to free the obnoxious Zane daughter and nanny.

He didn't take the name of the assassin in whom he planted Gregor's identification papers. Or that of any of the other assassins he'd dispatched. They were simply displaced criminals who had stopped working for generals and chiefs of intelligence in order to work for drug lords.

Ivan Annatov had been a notoriously skilled Russian spy. He was by far Gregor von Wolfen's most dangerous quarry and worthiest adversary. After he had stalked him for two years, and engaged him in three unnervingly vicious confrontations, it was by sheer luck that "Gregor" had finally eliminated him.

For the man who was Gregor von Wolfen, taking the name "Ivan" was a "trophy."

At the moment, while his guests showered in their *farés* and unpacked their bikini bottoms, Ivan was strolling down the palm-shaded path toward the Matira Terrace for lunch. He definitely needed refueling. It had been a long night.

Hearing a commotion at the Raititi Lounge, Ivan popped his head in and saw an American family watching MSNBC and cheering because an American had "won the *Black Book* sale."

Ivan's first thought was that he was glad he'd copied that listing in Marion's book, the one for that twenty-four-hour worldwide rescue service.

He didn't change his departure date. But did make a few phone queries. (He *could* have taken the next flight out but, after all, he did have *two guests* whom it would be discourteous of him to abandon.)

While Ivan was making the best use of his time, and of his guests, Maya was hugging a toilet and screaming at Sasha to stop trying to blow-dry her hair while she was puking, and screaming at Dudayev that he must always read the expiration date on the container of sour cream before making borscht.

Then Vlad walked in with the phone.

It was good to know that Tom was still her husband.

It was mind-shattering to know that he was with Maya's own *grandmother* in Hong Kong! Did she know, Tom asked her excitedly, that her *grandfather* had been a *Harlem Globetrotter*?

Grandma owned a casino now. Communist-sanctioned.

It was universe shattering when the heavens seemed to open and Tom said to wait a minute, there were two people who wanted to talk her, and suddenly Maya's *mother and father* got on the phone. It was quite an emotional reunion, to say the least.

Maya's parents turned out to be very much alive and living with Grandma in Hong Kong.

It seemed the Russian soldiers who had run the internment camp in which her parents had been placed liked to play basketball.

When the Russians released her parents, they had searched desperately for Maya until they traced her to the Grozny brothel. There they were told that their daughter had perished in a bombing raid.

When Wen, Maya's father, was eventually deported from Chechnya, he was glad to have hung on to his Hong Kong citizenship. Which was now Chinese citizenship. So, he told Maya, all three of them moved in with Grandma.

Three?

(Here there was a brief interlude for stomach evacuation.) When Maya got back on the phone, she was informed that her mother was not happy to have learned that Maya and Tom had allowed gypsies to live on their property.

THREE?

Then Tom was back on the line to explain things.

The morning after Maya discovered that her husband had left, she'd called Marion in despair. Luckily, Marion remembered that Tom was going off to shoot one of *Richard's* movies. On a hunch, she contacted the pilot of the Zane Enterprises' G5 jet (who'd always been *so* grateful for the lovely sweaters she sent him each Christmas), and sure enough, Tom was indeed traveling on the Zanes' plane and was willing to speak to her. Tom told Marion his version of the story, and requested that she let him work it out with his wife on his own.

Marion told Tom that from what she'd gathered from listening to both him and Maya, she wasn't worried about their marriage. And that to her, he sounded mostly upset about learning that he'd be unable to have a child by his wife. Then she gave him two pieces of advice. Advice that she'd wished Maya had taken years ago.

Her first piece of advice was that he consider tracking down what was left of Maya's relatives. That meant looking in Chechnya, Hong Kong, and maybe even America. Perhaps, she cryptically suggested, he could find a relative willing to provide "the next best thing" to Maya's DNA.

Her second piece of advice was to call a wonderful private detective service she had listed in her *Black Book* (which she'd just happened to have lying open on her lap as she spoke).

Tom had decided to take that advice and had told the detectives that since he was going to be shooting in the Pacific, they might as well start looking in Hong Kong, because Maya had said that her grandmother—

THREE! WHAT THE FUCK DOES *THREE* MEAN? WHO IS *THREE*? MY MOTHER, MY FATHER AND *WHO* MAKES *THREE*?

That was when Tom asked, "Maya girl, would you like to speak with your sister?"

93

News Flash

Marion knew that the city council was going to rule in Richard's favor before Zephyr had even finished her argument.

Her daughter had presented a convincing case. (Naturally, she had *always* been gifted.) She'd started with the convenient and compelling example of the King/Drew tragedies (with accompanying requisitely gory details), and then argued that the proposed Carita Memorial project could face a similarly doomed path. Then she gave comparative listings of overruns and defaults by a staggering number of hospitals and trauma units throughout the state and the nation—and, of course, the costs to taxpayers as a result. *(Thanks, insurance industry, big-box stores, and Big Pharma!)*

Next, Zephyr offered traffic reports and statistics on accidents where ambulances were involved, which, in Marion's opinion, were not her daughter's strongest arguments and should have been left out.

(At this point Marion felt like a latter-day version of Dr. Strangelove, as she had to sit on her hand to keep it from shooting out and brushing the hair away from her daughter's eyes.)

Then, came the "March of the Insulted": legions of deeply saddened and wounded reps from local hospitals, including Mercy and Angeles Hope, took the stand, beating their breasts in outrage and claiming they could easily shoulder the needs of the community and that Carita's death, though a terrible tragedy, had clearly been an anomaly. Blah, blah, blah.

Zephyr didn't take a single shot at her mother. Eli Volker had freed Marion's finances from trustee control when it was revealed that some of her alleged Home Shopping Network telephone orders were had been *recorded*. An investigation (Ivan's idea) by NFS & etc. revealed that they had been placed by a person with a hoarse voice that obviously did not belong to Marion Zane. (Upon hearing this, Simon Sacks actually *knelt* in apology.)

Still, Zephyr *could* have "accidentally" skipped the earlier ruling that had branded her mother "unfit" into her argument. She hadn't.

It might have frayed down to a mere thread, but the cord was still there.

Yes, Zephyr had made a brilliant case.

But Marion's case had been better.

(And it struck her as predictable but disappointing that after all the hoopla over the *Black Book* sale, there was barely any coverage of the city-council hearing. Only the same old local cable channel that covered all the city-council hearings. Did O. J. do something again?)

Marion's case should have been a national concern.

She had packed the city-council chambers with victims of delayed care that had resulted from a lack of trauma facilities. From a lack of hospital facilities. From inane requirements from hospital lawyers and insurance providers and budgeting directors that took precedence over human life.

She had packed the city-council chambers with residents who had to live in substandard conditions in order to be able to feed their families.

She had packed the city-council chambers with former skid-row residents from other cities who'd benefited from low-cost psychiatric care and adult education programs. The hospital Marion envisioned would provide that psychiatric care. The community center she proposed would offer adult education, yoga, and anger-management courses to ease the tensions of poverty, as well as a safe day care and a sports and recreation facility for kids.

She discussed the proposed hospital clinic, supported her proposal with statistics on the benefits to taxpayers and businesses if people could receive affordable preventive care and stay healthy instead of turning to trauma centers for nonemergencies or when their health had deteriorated to a hopeless point.

She had all sorts of stats in her favor.

She had health workers from around the country in her favor.

She had UCLA.

And she had the Trophies sitting supportively by her side. Maya, Pepper, Claire, and Patti. They were all respected, politically minded, philanthropically disposed women who swung a ton of weight in the Los Angeles community. Pepper sat on the boards of four organization—for under-privileged children, victims of sexual assault, women's shelters, and teen substance-abuse recovery. Maya was the environmental movement personified. Claire had wisely settled on only one charitable activity, public school arts programs, and Patti Fink gave shit tons of money to everything.

Strangely, Patti Fink seemed a little over-the-top about the hospital—even for Patti. She referred to her friends as "sisters" and the city as "our village" enough times to frighten even Al Sharpton. And what was the deal with the African jewelry she was wearing? It really didn't go with her pink Versace suit.

African jewelry aside, Marion was well supported. And she'd made a better case than Zephyr.

But it wasn't the weakness of Zephyr's argument compared to her own that told Marion the city council was going to rule in Richard's favor.

It was the *faces* of the city councilwomen and -men as they gazed at her soon-to-be ex-husband, sitting in his power suit on the other side of the room and avoiding Marion's eyes.

When they looked at Richard, the council members had the same expression on their faces as a potential Trophy has when she gazes at a potential husband.

Politicians always sucked up to the husband in divorce situations. It was in the manual.

Marion wished the city-council members knew that almost none of them would have received a dime of Zane campaign contributions if she hadn't begged Richard for funds on their behalf.

They also didn't know she had no prenuptial.

They also didn't know that blue-eyes-with-the-good-butt (whose name, ironically, turned out to be *Tushman*), the man who had approached Marion on the night of the *Black Book* auction and given her his card, had offered to partner with Marion in creating her own Martha Stewart–like style empire. (Because the rich just kept getting richer and needed to be re-mined as a market.) He wanted to make her a "brand." Marion was supposed to give him an answer tomorrow and she was leaning toward saying yes. Tushman's tush was that good. (And she'd always wanted to see her name branded on the walls of a stainless-steel-paneled safe room.)

Eventually, Marion would have access to enough dough to purchase another site for Carita Memorial, albeit an extremely downscaled version of the hospital. Downtown properties the size of the Zane property, and possessing the same central location, were few and far between. Who knew when another one would come along? Could the community afford to wait ten or twelve years or even twenty years?

Bottom line: they'd put up a good fight, but the big dream was over.

And why wouldn't Richard look at her?

She'd heard reports about the women in the Caribbean. Had he met someone else?

Guess that meant they were over too.

Zephyr was winding up her argument with a "Joint Coordination and Jobs—Not Disasters and Debt" bumper-sticker-like slogan. It was an easy sound bite and Marion could see the city-council members virtually inscribing it on their lips for press use later.

What press? Just the lone cable camera operator remained.

The council members were conferring with one another.

And Marion was braced for the worst . . . And wondering when it would stop hurting.

Patti Fink was squeezing Maya's hand black-and-blue. She just knew they were going to win. They were going to win for the people. The people who were dependent on others and had no voice. The people who contributed hard-earned wages to social security and received nothing in return. The people who were told they were citizens but were, in reality, victims. Victims of the whims of a bureaucracy that would betray them without blinking an eye. Just like the corrupt East African government officials she'd watched in the movie at the museum.

She and her fellow "tribeswomen" were changing that today. They were bringing justice to the people. They were ushering in a new age of community and commitment.

They were bringing love.

She just wished they didn't have to do it on this awful blue carpet!

Maybe she should flag down that security guard and ask him to do something about that horrible overhead lighting . . . Or that weird feedback.

Or was it groaning?

"What? What did they rule?!"

No! NO! They couldn't rule in favor of Richard! They couldn't! To do so would be saying that the will of the people, their hopes and dreams and lives, didn't matter. It would be saying *they* didn't matter . . .

Not again!

Never again!

She'd promised herself *never again*!

Why is everybody standing up to leave? Why won't they stand together and fight?

WHY IN THE HELL WON'T SOMEBODY DO SOMETHING?!

It was then that Patti Fink heard a *call*.

And she knew she finally had something to give.

And she knew she had truly magnificent gifts.

The *call* was an African chant.

And it swelled inside of her until she couldn't contain it any longer . . .

Suddenly Patti Fink kicked off her Manolos and climbed onto the top of her chair.

And at the top of her lungs she screamed:

"SHAME ON YOU!"

The council chambers fell silent. The city-council members, already standing, hoping to get a chance to shake hands with Richard Zane before making a hasty departure, froze.

"SHAME ON YOU!"

Patti screamed it again. And again. And again.

Her scream became a chant.

And as she screamed, she opened her suit jacket.

Nothing else mattered. In that moment, she was immortal.

With one rip, her shell broke open.

And even with the horrible blue carpet beneath her feet, and the horrible light above her head, her beautiful breasts were *blazing*!

These assholes were going to feel the power of her heart!

She continued chanting as the security guard made his way across the room toward her.

Maya couldn't believe the irresponsibility of the doctors in this town. First Claire and now, apparently, one of them had been a little too generous about Patti Fink's prescriptions. It was bad enough that the hospital had been turned down by these politburo-style motherfuckers! Now Patti was having a bad drug reaction . . . in public!

The security guard was getting closer.

Maya didn't want her friend to be arrested again. This wasn't Beverly Hills. Who knew what medications Patti was holding in her purse? Or what a pee-pee test might reveal!

But what to do? Patti looked manic. Like she might kick out Maya's teeth if Maya tried to pull her down!

Well . . .

It wasn't, Maya suddenly thought, as if the public hadn't seen her tits a million times before, in ads and layouts. Figuring that a little scandal wasn't going to cramp her style (and in reality, nothing could, after she'd received the best news in her life), Maya shot to her feet and jumped up onto her seat just like Patti.

And she whipped off her Tom Ford Men's ruffled tuxedo shirt.

"SHAME ON YOU!" She hollered.

Let that fat-fuck guard try to wrestle both of us down!

Inside the aging remote van, the director of the local cable-news station dropped his latte and burned his leg. He was just getting ready to go out on another boring, dust-bowl city-council hearing, then schlep the van back to the station and then plan tomorrow's dust-bowl night, then go home and try to get it up to resume work on his now six-year-old unfinished novel . . . he hadn't gone to film school for this.

But then he saw Patti screaming and stripping off her top in the city-council chambers and the sight of her rekindled a long-forgotten fire in the belly of the remote director. There were boobies on remote camera one. Beautiful boobies! Right before his eyes! Boobies that could help his career bust into the majors! Sports coverage!

And to think that that weirdo, Kavi-the-cameraman, who was inside the council chambers, the *only* news camera on the premises with exclusive live coverage of a set of career-rocketing boobies, had just opted to refocus his camera on the carpet and was asking him, the only remote director, what to do!

What would *any* red-blooded American newsman do? His duty! The public has the right to know!

The remote director frantically got on the line with the station programmer and swore to her that he'd marry her or give her his parking space or anything else she wanted from him, including a kidney, if she didn't break the connection.

And she said okay, she was going to go with it!

Then the remote director kicked awake the reporter who was sharing the van with him and shoved him out the door.

Lastly, he swept the latte off his plastic stool and fitted his headset on for the long haul.

"Screw Janet Jackson legislation," he told Kavi-the-weirdo-cameraman, "we're cable! PUSH IN ON THE BOOBIES!"

Normally, Pepper wasn't a competitive woman. But ever since that skank statue seller had tried to hex her husband, she'd been feeling a little feisty.

And, as it happened, she too had a mighty fine set of jugs.

Easily, the biggest among the Trophies. And, at that particular moment, her milk wasn't threatening to let down.

She could see that the security guard was getting closer and was about to lay his big mitts on her friends! So, fuck it . . .

Pepper tossed off her Dolce & Gabbana jacket and the spandex tank underneath, popped the lock on her nurser . . . and out sprang the Girls.

"SHAME ON YOU!" She hollered along with Maya and Patti.

Normally, Claire *was* a competitive woman. She had cut her teeth on beauty pageants. And pageants, mind you, were a far cry from tea parties. Before her parents' divorce, she had been a flexible and cunning contestant. If she happened to see four little girls in the Peewee Princess Regionals wearing double-lace cuff anklets, she begged until her mother ran to the local fabric shop and added triple lace to hers. If the girls in the Little Miss Bluebell Nationals were listing themselves with two middle names, she made up three. If the Junior Miss Texas had glitter hairspray in her kit, she'd steal the can and replace it with paint.

That's how competitive Claire was.

And so, when she saw that she was the only one in a lineup of beautiful women who still had her top on, something knee-jerked inside her. Anyway, her breasts were the *youngest* . . .

Off came the Ralph Lauren Jessica white cashmere suit jacket and navy silk bow blouse.

"SHAME ON YOU!" she hollered, adding her voice to the chorus.

M arion was already mentally working out a list of other downtown land-holders and wondering which one of them had a penchant for redheads when she noticed that the hearing had turned into a Russ Meyer movie. (Or an *early* John Waters?)

What strange new hell was this?

She was right-flanked by topless chanting friends.

(!)

Bending her knees in preparation for her first-ever attempted backflip (to elude what was surely the path of the Martian radioactive gamma rays that were no doubt sizzling her friends' brains and inducing them to turn themselves into a Scores lineup), Marion suddenly remembered that her topless chanting friends were also lunatics. This behavior was not out of the range of their possibilities. They knew what they were doing. This was their "Plan B."

Marion was touched by their loyalty.

A little grossed out, but touched.

But what was happening with Zephyr? She could her her daughter coming toward her and . . . could it be that she too was unbuttoning her shirt? It was one thing for those kooky broads Marion called her friends to flaunt their knockers, but it wasn't the kind of action a mother should condone in her own daughter! Yet there was Zephyr, bare-breasted, now standing next to Marion and chanting "SHAME ON YOU!"—and doing so despite a judgment that had just been granted in her favor. As far as Marion was concerned, it was the loveliest sight she could ever hope to see as a mother. Her daughter was taking *her side*.

And the cord SCOOORRRRES!

But Marion Zane wasn't so swept up in heartwarming if somewhat grossed-out feelings that she didn't take a moment to weigh the effect that flashing the council would have on her chances of becoming a "brand."

Hmm . . . Fergie got toe-sucked, but afterward she still got Weight Watchers. Paris got a TV series and a Burger King commercial after her Internet video, not to mention a perfume gig and other stuff like paid appearances, and all after serving very little jail time. Nicole shrank down to next to nothing and still had a baby. Pamela got a movie, a series and a USO tour, and more unlasting marriages. Lindsay's got so much talent and public adoration she'll work forever no matter what trouble she gets herself into. Britney Spears will roll merrily along even if they have to use animatronics in her videos. Every single male actor since Robert Mitchum has kept on working after an arrest. (Okay, Pee-wee Herman had to stop for a while, but now he seemed to be popping up on-screen every time she turned on her TV.) Martha was a "brand" and got two series and saw the rest of her kingdom expand after once behaving the way that no less than over half of the male large investors in America behave regularly.

And *that idiot-son-of-an-asshole had gotten his cowboy ass reelected.*

Marion concluded that neither nudity nor crime would hamper a celebrity's plans. And after paying that publicist a fortune, she herself was a celebrity. Flashing the council, she therefore decided, would generate the perfect buzz for the "brand."

The public would never forgive her for the recent poverty she'd known or for living out of a car, but they'd relish the illegal impulsiveness of flashing. Anyway, Marion had had a vitamin-C and salt-glow treatment at the spa last night.

Her skin was perfect.

She was a Stage III.

And she had a great set.

She couldn't let her daughter flash alone.

And she couldn't let the rest of these Trophies show her up.

And maybe this was her last chance to catch her soon-to-be ex-husband's eye . . .

Marion Zane's Chanel suit jacket had a snap front.

And nothing underneath.

And so . . .

"SHAME ON YOU!"

The rest of the audience on Marion's side of the chambers picked up the chant and in a stadium wave of emancipated areolas, the women took off their shirts. Young and old. All sizes and shapes. All creeds and colors. Even a transvestite got into the spirit, but he was soon booed down by the men who were seated across the aisle. Within a matter of moments, the entire audience was on its feet.

The city-council members sat frozen. Not one of them wanted to be the council member who called the police on the impassioned women who were screaming and rending their shirts so that a hospital could be built.

It just wouldn't generate good press.

This ruling had been *supposed* to fade quietly into the background.

And the women were barring the doors, anyway. The head of the city council told the security guards not to contact the Parker Center. The last thing they needed was the police showing up.

"SHAME ON YOU!" the council members heard all around them.

Soon the security guards, joining the spirit that had invaded the room, backed off and began enjoying the view.

Thanking the gods of news coverage that there were no minors present in the hearing room who might change the cheery flavor of the events that were unfolding into something possibly dicey, Kavi-the-cameraman and the remote director in the van got down to business. They were a local station covering an important decision and therefore felt it was their civic duty to feature the nicest pairs of indigenous boobies: namely those of the Trophies, a gorgeous Korean woman in the eighth row, seven lovely Latina women in the third (who were part of a larger group that seemed to be a club of sorts), a bagwoman of indeterminate age, and, surprisingly, an African-American grandmother who had to be at least sixty. Arlen-the-reporter was giving the on-the-scene, up-to-the-second coverage of his life. Nevertheless, he remained but a disembodied voice situated off camera as the women continued their now-dithyrambic chant.

"SHAME ON YOU!"

Just then, Marion felt a sudden tugging at the hem of her skirt, and looking down, she saw her soon-to-be ex-husband crouching on the floor.

(Mercy!)

Richard wasn't, by nature, a croucher. Then again, she wasn't, by nature, a flasher.

She saw that Richard was motioning to her to join him.

Well . . . first she was going to slip her suit jacket back on.

"What can I do for you?" Marion asked, careful of her ankles, which were in danger of getting stomped on by Ravi-the-cameraman.

Richard was staring at the brooch on her suit-jacket lapel: two generously rounded hearts of polished crimson coral, joined together and pierced by a Cupid's arrow of gold and pavé diamonds. He looked like he was going to cry. Strange. Marion had honestly thought she'd have lost him to another woman by now. (He was, after all, a leg man.) Then she watched him unfold a battered eight-by-ten photograph and offer it to her, saying, "I guess I just need to know why."

Marion looked down at the photograph.

Eeek!

The only thing she recognized was her head.

Marion's first thought was:

You've got to be kidding.

And her second was:

I wish I was having that much fun. Then and now.

And her third was:

Richard couldn't possibly think this was real!

But when she looked into his eyes, she saw he did think that. And Marion Zane's Stage III rhino-skinned, battle-scarred, beat-to-shit Trophy heart went out to the poor guy.

Not totally, of course. But enough for her to say:

"Sweetheart, may I borrow your readers?"

One close look was all she required.

Verna Hale's shady sidekick, Donnie Watson, should keep his day job as a thug.

"Here," Marion said, handing her soon-to-be ex-husband his readers so he could put them on and catch the best light on the photo she was holding.

"Since when do I have a tattoo of the starship *Enterprise* on the inside of my left . . . you-know-what?" she asked her soon-to-be ex.

That was when Richard Zane reached inside his coat.

And handed the *Black Book* to his wife.

94

Fade-Out

Max Wallert reached for the remote and slowly teased it out of his wife's hand.

Finally!

He'd had to double-dose Lyndy with Nyquil before she'd nodded off. The way she'd been running around at night it was no small wonder she came down with this nasty cold. Feeling chilled and wanting the heat on and another blanket, then feeling overheated and wanting a cool cloth, then feeling chilled again . . .

What was the name of that guy down in hell that got his liver torn out every day? Max suddenly wondered. Anyway, their maid had knocked off early that night and right now he felt like that guy.

Then, suddenly, Lyndy's moaning had switched off.

She didn't look good.

She was breathing funny too.

Max decided to call the doctor to come over and have a look at her.

Right after he checked the scores.

But as he flipped toward ESPN something made him stop and flip back.

Max Wallert was a boob man.

He watched for almost five minutes before he realized that he recognized the heads on top of the boobs.

"Lyndy! Hey, Lyndy!" Max yelled, shaking his wife none too tenderly. "You have to wake up and see this! Marion Zane is topless on TV!"

That was the one name in the universe that could have coaxed Lyndy out of her delirium enough to open her eyes.

What see saw was Marion Zane, topless, in the middle of the bedroom big-screen, flanked by all her vampire friends, who were flaunting their breasts as well. And behind Marion was a sea of topless women.

And they all looked good.

It was the last image Lyndy saw before she slipped into unconscious-ness. "She *would* have to show up my ass . . ." she muttered as darkness claimed her.

95

Winning Trophies

With a well-trained eye, Ivan scanned the Zane downtown property for troublemakers. Even though there was police protection, he'd hired Sasha and Dudayev to handle certain possibly unruly elements of the mob of paparazzi that was due to descend the second the Zanes arrived. Maya's comrades had experience with that sort of work. Meanwhile, all the official ceremony photographers were already inside the reception tent with Marion's publicist.

Ever since the city council hearing last month, where *Zane v. Zane* turned back into just plain Zane *and* Zane, paparazzi had been hounding Marion wherever she went, hoping for a comment on what was now being referred to as "The Flash-Down." It was still the most downloaded clip on YouTube.

On Tuesday, Carter had caught some paparazzi stationed in the big monterey pine, and last night, Ivan had personally plucked two off the neighbors' newly remodeled back house.

Ivan knew how to get through the hedge.

So did Xiocena.

And Lourdes.

No troublemakers so far.

The groundbreaking ceremony for Carita Memorial Hospital was due to begin in half an hour, and among those who had been invited, only the Price family had just now made it to the prereception with the local elected officials. And since the officials were elected ones, they were anxious to keep the Zanes and their friends in their camp, because ever since the

Flash-Down, all sorts of people were considering running for office. The officials' jobs had been "glammed." A bad thing in this town of fame and fun seekers.

Ivan knew that the rest of the Trophies were late because they were attending Patti Fink's pre-prereception, which featured a cornucopia of entertainments and refreshments that were intended to reflect the diverse cultural backgrounds of the residents of downtown Los Angeles.

Ivan hoped everyone made it out alive.

His prayers were answered by the windshield glints of an oncoming caravan of hybrid, electric, and alternative-fuel vehicles. Ivan counted the glints.

All Trophies accounted for.

The Flash-Down had been heroic enough to bump Pepper up to Stage III status. She didn't need to care and feed the young of the herd anymore. And she didn't need her mother-in-law to tell her that Ari needed to be allowed to take responsibility for some things. From now on, if she ever felt compelled to take over and take care of anything, she'd find a way to manipulate or do it in secret. It was good for her husband's spirit.

It didn't hurt his prostate any either, because she got knocked up with Jed's "Irish twin" as soon as she took Jed off the tit. She wasn't showing yet, but the pregnant woman's volatile appetite was already setting in and she was glad she'd brought that big Dolce & Gabbana tote to the ceremony. It was able to hold six of Patti's kung pao pork burritos. Pepper sneaked a bite of one and watched her kids pile out of a hydrogen-powered Escalade while the nannies cleaned the food off her husband's neck with diaper wipes.

He'd wanted to take charge of the driving. And Maybelle had eaten a whole plate of Patti's jerk goat and fries. Live and learn.

Ever since Ari had found out he was a mutt, her husband was back to his old continental self. Although he hadn't gotten off his Greek-statue kick and was now taking private classes on ancient Greek art with a docent from the Getty whom Marion had found for him. After all, Ari, as Mercedes's favorite, was destined to inherit quite a few real statues.

He'd be embarrassed now if he knew that Baphy-the-homosexual-river-god was still on his property. When it came time for the plaster statue's removal, Pepper found she couldn't part with it and had stashed it halfway down the back hill.

Because Pepper liked to keep trophies herself.

And Jerry needed something to shoot with that damn air rifle.

Ivan needn't have hired her comrades. Maya, also now Stage III, was doing a pretty good job on her own, biting the heads off any of the paparazzi who dared aim a lens at her nineteen-year-old baby sister, Sonya. She'd even managed to bean a fence climber who was trying to crash Patti's pre-prereception with an empty Colt 45 forty-ouncer in a brown paper bag. (Proving that all was not just for the Irish. Skid Row needed representation at the pre-prereception as well.)

Sonya was the spitting (and stunning) image of her older sister, except she wasn't so sweet-natured. As a result, Vlad had had to stay up more than one night patching the weekly shoe-dings that were constant appearing on the head of Ming, his employers' new brother-in-law and Sonya's much-abused husband. The hormones coming through Sonya's body in preparation for her "implantation" were making her cranky. And on more than one night, Ming and his two-year-old son, little Wen, had had to seek refuge in the cottage.

Maya was shocked that her sister had married so young and already had a two-year-old child. Vlad, Sasha, Dudayev, and Tom were shocked that anyone would *want* to marry as nasty a customer as Sonya, or even risk bodily harm by getting close enough to her to father a child.

The whole family had insisted on staying with Maya and Tom for the duration of the upcoming pregnancy and birth. This was both a blessing and a curse: Maya's mother, Lladya, insisted on doing the cooking because she didn't trust "gypsy" cuisine; and Wen loved working the gardens. As a result, the comrades were freed up to engage in "other pursuits" and such duties as looking after Grandma May-May. At this juncture, Grandma May-May was teaching Sasha and Dudayev how to play mah-jongg and giving them tips on how to improve their bookmaking business. But only *after* skinning them for eighteen grand.

Maya now knew where she'd gotten the gift of con from.

Meanwhile, Tom had found a buddy for Laker games and a kindred geek spirit in Wen. Maya, however, wasn't pleased with their plans for set-

ting up a theater-size screen, outdoor projection system, and heated ga-
zebo at one end of her meadow for weekend "sports nights."

A very large hole in Maya's heart had been repaired.

She was going to have a baby of her own.

And she had her parents back. In fact, she had a whole new, big family.

Maya now began her mornings with tears of joy instead of memories of
nightmares.

And every day was a gift. (Although her mama was starting to get on her
nerves, throwing out all of Maya's "liar's blood" and Turkish cigarettes.)

The cottage was getting very crowded at night.

And Wen was getting his ear bent with complaints about "Mama's
bossiness" while he walked the back meadow in long strides, with his
daughter at his side.

Marion surveyed the new Zane Enterprises project from within what she
now knew was *not* the safest place in the world. (No marriage was truly
safe.) Still, Richard's arms were her *favorite* place.

And ever since he'd learned to his horror that he'd allowed himself to
be rat-fucked and had betrayed the love of his life, Richard held her in her
favorite place every chance he got. (When he wasn't on his knees apologizing.)

He wanted to make it up to his girl.

Buying back the *Black Book* had been a good start. Marion hadn't been
too hard on herself for not guessing that her husband was the buyer. Even
though she'd known he was a member of Yale's Skull and Bones secret
society, the guy *had been* trying to put her in the loony bin. At least, she'd
thought so at the time of the sale.

Marion wanted to make it up to *herself*.

She decided not to take on any new projects for a while. (At least, for the
first two weeks.)

Then she took Tushman-the-good-butt up on his offer—*on her terms*.

The magazine and Web site Tushman proposed received only selected
Black Book listings; they didn't get *Marion*. Not the Marion Zane
"brand."

Marion already had a job: Trophy Wife.

And she was good at it.

"Is everybody here yet, honey?" asked Richard. "Because if they are, let's get this thing over with. I think I'm feeling the revenge of Patti's 'refreshments.'"

Marion flicked open her Chanel croc clutch, took out her husband's vitamin case, and handed him a little purple pill. "There's water in the reception tent, sweetheart."

With a quick smooch, he hurried away.

Richard's stomach was bearing the brunt of his punishment for not trusting his wife. His stint with Tawnee had left him with excess acid.

Marion wished she hadn't shared that fact with Patti Fink. Now Patti was trying to track the girl down in order to hire her to go after her least-favorite adult stepson, the litigious one.

Marion squinted against the sun to watch the unmistakable silhouette of Patti Fink, in a crepe de chine flamenco dress by Yohji Yamamoto topped off with an enormous Russian sable hunting hat, awkwardly disembark from her hybrid bus and pose for paparazzi before leading a battalion of assorted stepchildren and "friends" into the reception tent.

Marion could tell that Patti's paramour-free diet was just about over. Although the beautiful young man at Patti's elbow did speak Spanish, Marion doubted if Spanish bullfighters were truly representative of downtown Los Angeles residents. (Lou and Ricky had bonded with the members of the pre-prereception mariachi band and they'd all stayed behind at the Beverly Park estate to make sure none of the Bosnian folk dancers moved into the backyard.)

Patti herself had become something of a folk hero on the Westside now. She had both fame and respect. The double whammy.

One of the niche magazines Marion had launched with Tushman-the-good-butt had the goal of funding, teaching, and sourcing "Women as Activists." And Marion had put Patti at its helm as managing editor. It was going to be a never-ending project for Madame Fink and she was taking to it like a twenty-year-old with her first Neiman Marcus card.

For the first time in years, Patti Fink was unleashing her passion. Already she had created or identified no fewer than 1,300 blueprints for taking action and effecting change. And 1,299 of them required no disrobing. She'd christened the magazine WAM (Women's Activism Magazine). The name was simple and preferable to *Activist's Sourcing Service,* or worse, *Compiled Ladies Integral Training,* the other titles that had been considered.

With sales of Marion's sources from her *Black Book* acting as a *WAM* foundation fund, Patti Fink was becoming both an activist fairy god-mother and something of a brand in her own right. But she needed to shorten the time she spoke during her weekly downtown community seminars. She had a tendency to ramble. For hours.

And Patti finally made it into the pages of *Playboy* magazine.

She wasn't the centerfold. But she got her own page in a retrospective article about "The Women of *Star Trek.*"

An editor had seen the YouTube footage of the city-council hearing and made sure he attended Patti's photo session personally.

"After all," reasoned Patti, "Gloria Steinem started that way, and look at her now."

Marion didn't have the heart to tell her pal that the famous feminist had been a Playboy bunny *waitress,* not a pictorial. The *Playboy* pics had made her friend happy. Almost as much as the paparazzi attention.

Hell, the woman had impersonated a ghost for her.

They had all been there for her. Her Trophy girlfriends.

And then there was the Housekeeper Network. Marion set up a health-care program and an emergency fund for her "local." And now had a standing Monday lunch date with Xiocena and Lourdes—as girlfriends.

Good girlfriends can get you through hell.

Didn't Pepper say that once?

Guess the whole key wasn't impressions or props but being able to take the risk of trusting other women . . . even with all the ugly stuff.

Okay, *almost* all of it . . .

At that moment Marion Zane spied an undesirable guest who, just the same, had been issued an invitation and a press pass. And she was coming her way.

Marion also had the bejesus jigged out of her by Ivan, who materialized at her side before she could even think about thinking of him.

The undesirable guest arrived at the same time and promptly asked in a familiar, hoarse voice, "Can you get the ball rolling on the dedication of your latest shine, blood sausage? This sun isn't good for my skin. And not yours either, from the looks of those crow's-feet."

Marion wasn't going to dignify that with a response.

"I'm waiting for a few more guests to get here, Verna."

"Well, don't look for Jack Powell, he's toast since the launch. By the way, I'm guessing *somebody* here is going to be the subject of the lead exposé in the next edition of *Red Hard*'s tabloid magazine."

Although he appeared stoic, Marion could feel Ivan restraining himself at her elbow. It was probably killing him that Verna had been able to get her boot on his employer's neck because he hadn't been around to stop her.

And she hoped he'd taken some comfort knowing he'd saved her ass, even in absentia.

It had been in a moment of despair and frustration at the Broad Beach guesthouse. Marion had thrown the *Black Book* across the room and something she had stashed behind the back-cover lining and forgotten about fell out.

In that instant she knew Ivan had put it there.

And she instantly knew it contained a secret she'd be willing to sell to Verna Hale.

It was the memory stick Ivan had wrenched away from the thug who'd been trying to blackmail Jack Powell.

What she didn't know was that it contained *two* secrets. At least not until she viewed it.

Not only did it show Jack Powell pummeling a girl, it showed that the girl he'd been pummeling had been . . . Carita, Xiocena's niece.

Luckily, Xio had wanted payback more than a hideous keepsake of her niece's degradation. She let Marion dance with the devil.

But Marion wasn't worried about giving Verna a secret this month or ever again.

Ivan was back now. Things would work out.

Marion shrugged. "Nobody here is a story for you," she said to Verna.

"If you're thinking about Lyndy Wallert, think again," Verna hissed.

Okay, that was weird.

Of all people, Marion thought that Verna would appreciate the irony that it had been drug-resistant bacteria that had finished Lyndy off in, of all places, the *Montgomery* Wing of Beverly Hills Central Hospital; she was surprised Verna hadn't included the story in this month's launch issue of her supermarket tabloid.

"Lyndy was my best friend back in the day. She was my only friend after the divorce," Verna continued. "And she's off-limits. Screw it! I'm going to pick a candidate myself."

As Verna stalked into the reception tent, with Ivan stalking after her, Marion was struck by a strange notion:

Verna *still didn't know* the truth.

If she had, she wouldn't have found anything "friendly" about the woman who'd caused her destruction: Lyndy Montgomery Wallert.

Back in the day, the BHC Gala had been *co*-chaired by Lyndy Wallert and Verna Bowman. Both women were rumored to be in contention for the BHC Foundation presidency. It was a prestigious position that would bump either one of the two Trophies up to Stage III status.

Then, out of the blue, Fred Bowman fell in love with another woman and dumped his wife of five years.

Verna was knocked out of the marriage, the presidency contest, and the whole damn Trophy scene.

Lyndy became president of Beverly Hills Central Hospital Foundation.

Clearly, Verna never did learn who the "other woman" was.

Once Marion had her *Black Book* back, she'd done a bit of research on Lyndy Wallert. She wanted to know why the woman hated her so much.

She soon found the answer between the lines.

If Lyndy would destroy another person for a hospital presidency, how would she feel about someone who'd stolen Oscar de la Renta from her? And stolen the entire Westside as well?

Marion checked her makeup in her compact. Yep. There were a few lines in the corners of her eyes. She'd *earned* them weathering this storm.

They were her trophies and they were staying.

Not all of them. But she did want eyes that could smile.

(Besides without so much Botox, your cheeks didn't fall.)

(Yet.)

Right now her cheek looked like she had been in a knife fight, a result of the crimson gash Chloe Gelson's lipstick left on it at Patti's pre-prereception. In fact, the telltale signs of no fewer than five different colors were there. Marion fished a tissue from her clutch.

Oh, yeah, the star fuckers. They all came back.

Once word of the Zane reconciliation hit the streets, the MAJOR INFLUENCE was cemented back in place.

Going on *Oprah* hadn't hurt either. (Even Verna Hale told her that she admired that strategy.) Breaking through the society-magazine ceiling and achieving mainstream mass-media attention in the name of a cause definitely bumped up a Trophy wife's status. (Marion was surprised that Lyndy had never tried it.)

As she looked at herself in the mirror, it occurred to Marion that she could have turned into either one of those women, Lyndy or Verna: destroying others for a living . . . or reducing her world to one of regret and vengeful fantasies.

But there was one big difference between Marion and the Vernas and Lyndys of this world:

Marion Zane wasn't an asshole.

Marion saw her husband exit the tent and she forgot about Verna and Lyndy.

Because Richard was walking with her daughter.

And her daughter had, for a change, excellent hair.

And she didn't want to waste her energy on caca anymore.

Zephyr bussed her mother on the cheek and quietly said, "Hi, Mom." She was still uncomfortable about appearing in public as Marion's daughter. And she wasn't going to hide it.

The notion that she was the Zane-empire heiress had definitely caused an increase in ribbing at the office.

And Zephyr liked to keep a low professional profile, as did her colleague in the profession, Barry Shapiro.

They had a lot in common, those two. That's why Zephyr had always been Barry Shapiro's favorite Zane. And that's also why they were lovers. Had been for years. Zephyr had kept *that fact* very low profile.

Secrets were a family tradition, it seemed.

But even Marion didn't know every secret.

"Ready for showtime?" Zephyr's new stepfather asked her new mother.

"I am," her new mother replied. "But it's up to Xiocena. She's got the shovel at the groundbreaking."

Sasha and Dudayev were walking to the groundbreaking ceremony behind Verna Hale.

Because they wanted to measure her.

To see where she'd fit into the hospital foundation.

It was nice having more time for "other pursuits" now that Lladya was handling cooking and Wen was taking care of the gardens.

It gave them a chance to make up for the losses they'd sustained in betting against May-May-the-wicked-old-Chinawoman.

It was also nice that Ivan believed in outsourcing the disposal of his victims' bodies.

"We keep that bracelet," Sasha said. "It is real."

"And heavy," Dudayev happily agreed.

"The bracelet's mine, gentlemen," said Ivan, making both of them jump because the man had just materialized out of nowhere like a wraith.

He felt the bracelet was a worthy trophy.

"It's okay to come out now, girls," Claire called. "Pepper's boys went home with their nannies and tummyaches."

Brooke, Haley, and Eva peeked timidly out of the tent.

"I promise. Cross my heart and not hope to die."

Claire's stepdaughters came out of the tent, dutifully. And Claire thought it was wonderful that they trusted her.

She also thought it was wonderful that they knew better than to give her any shit about her requests or her corny midwestern sayings.

Claire ran a tight "tour" these days.

"That means you too, Billy. Turn the cell phone off now, please."

And Billy didn't fuck around either.

Because he wanted to fuck around.

As they walked to the site of the groundbreaking ceremony, several photos were taken of the Price family. Claire was happy that the girls knew better than to fight her stepmom-chooses-the-dresses-for-her-public-events rule. They looked perfect in their matching pink Ralph Lauren shift dresses.

Appearance was sooooo important.

That was why she'd made Billy wear a tie and a navy sport coat with gold buttons. He needed to look as important as he was.

And it was also why she'd chosen the pink cashmere Ralph Lauren shift with the matching cashmere coat for herself. It hugged her curves without looking slutty.

She wanted to give the community a good picture of who the Prices were. And nothing does that as well as well-groomed, obedient children.

And matching shifts.

It would tell everybody what a no-nonsense tight tour she ran.

In turn, people would want her to run other things.

Like galas and capital-raising campaigns. And fund-raisers for congressional aspirants.

She was meeting more and more of Marion's connections every day.

She wanted to study Marion Zane's every move.

It was best to always study under the best.

She was meeting with Marion's decorator next week, in fact.

She wanted her house to be perfect for board meetings and entertaining.

She wanted to redecorate in Classic American Splendor.

CAS always put people at ease. (But not too much.)

Marion had been right to tell Claire to stick with her own style. CAS was tasteful and that's who Claire was.

Their house wouldn't look like a fad freak had ripped them off.

(The way Nicky Dupre's house did.)

And Claire's house wouldn't look like a Perfect Rainbow Princess Castle either.

Because Claire didn't want to be that girl anymore.

Who the heck wants to be princess when you can be *Queen*?

After she made sure that no cameras were in range, Claire twisted the clasp on her fuck-you Hermès Birkin bag and addressed her perfect, tasteful family.

"Mentos, anyone?" she asked sweetly.

96

Continuity

The crystal bar glasses were right. But the champagne flutes were wrong. They had cuts.

"No, that's not the Murano," Marion said, dropping her bra and taking the glass out of Ivan's hand. "This isn't even mine, it's from catering. I didn't order this!"

"That weddin' planner's paddin' the bills," said Pepper, unzipping her dress and letting it fall. Even after giving birth to her sixth child, aside from a slight hood over the belly button, her body had snapped back as usual. "Marion," she scolded, "I *warned* you 'bout her!"

Ivan averted his eyes. Not to avoid the sight of Pepper in her underwear, but because *he'd* warned Marion about the wedding planner as well and didn't want to rub it in.

"They are all thieves," Maya pronounced, angling the bottle of warmed goat's-milk formula for her sister-surrogate's gift—her two-month-old son, Rex. "Is giant business."

"Fine, she's a crook. Say I told you to say it," said Marion, quickly handing the flute back to Ivan and leaning over to let her breasts fall properly into the nude La Perla bra.

Ivan already had told the woman. When the planner "accidentally" double-ordered the booze.

Not wanting to damage her manicure, Marion swung up holstered and turned for Ivan to help fasten the bra. He did. "Just tell the guys to get those back in their crates and—"

"I already did. And Jeff is retuning the Murano crates to the kitchen, since *your wedding planner* sent them back down to the basement. Mrs. Price is keeping an eye on the woman downstairs to prevent further disasters."

Normally, Ivan wouldn't have bothered Marion while she was dressing with tattletales about a stemware mix-up, but this was a very important occasion for her and he wanted to keep her calm so she could enjoy it, which meant keeping her totally informed.

And besides, the visuals were too good to pass up.

"Oh, Claire will keep her in line." Lately, she preferred to change clothes in private, a policy that included even Ivan. "Thanks. I'll finish up and go down and see Jeff."

"Very good."

"Ivan, you know how to feed baby?" asked Maya.

"Yes I do, Mrs. Hanson."

"Could you?" she asked, gingerly offering him her son.

Ivan made a smooth exchange and assumed Maya's seat on the fainting couch without disturbing the infant or moving the bottle from his lips. "How old is Rex now?"

"Two and half month; thanks." With that, Maya's own dress fell to the floor and Ivan (delightedly) noted that she still forsook undergarments. "He always drink so slow at end of feeding."

"'Cuz he's snockered on milk, like a li'l drunken sailor," cooed Pepper, soothing five-month-old Demeter (destined to be nicknamed Demi) in the carrier at her feet, and giving Ivan a nice shot of her backside.

"Could somebody get these, please?" asked Marion, indicating her fragile nails, then the garter-belt clasps above the stockings she'd donned.

"Allow me," said Ivan, tucking the baby bottle under his chin.

"Sorry to be so helpless," Marion apologized. "Xio's with Zephyr in the guesthouse. You're saving my ass."

Ivan remained stoic. "No problem at all. Turn around, please."

Suddenly the door flew open and Crystal Zane stomped into the closets, wearing a Nina Ricci blouse and nothing but Jimmy Choos below her waist.

"I can't *believe* I forgot my underwear!" she fumed.

Pepper immediately shot Marion a look.

"With four suitcases? Neither can I, sweetheart," said Marion, avoiding Pepper's eyes at all costs and turning so Ivan could fasten her other leg. "There's new in the third, right side, bottom left."

Crystal went to fetch the underwear and Ivan didn't bother looking at the visual. The girl was pollution.

The door opened again and Dickie Jr. nonchalantly strolled in, causing everyone to gasp and cover up.

"This cuff link fell out," he griped. "Need a little help."

"Get the fuck out, Mr. Peeper!" snarled Maya, throwing a shoe.

Dickie Jr. clutched his eyes and staggered dramatically backward into the master bedroom. "Ahhh! It burns! It burns!"

"Nice try, degenerate," muttered Crystal, stomping out in a new Dior G-string.

"You're welcome, sweetheart," Marion said to the empty air.

"Oh, like I'm supposed to know you guys would do a total wardrobe change between acts!" Dickie laughed from outside the door.

"Yes, you are," answered Ivan, who'd finished with Marion and was tucking sleeping Rex into his infant carrier.

"Hey," said Marion, "this is my first and, hopefully, last time to play mother of the bride and I plan on milking it. Anyway, my Oscar dress from the ceremony had black mascara tears all over it."

"Sor-ry!" sang out Patti from the back bathroom.

"Mine was spit-upped," added Maya.

"Mine wuz leaked out," added Pepper, which came as no surprise to anyone.

"And who wants to look like the mother of the bride," Marion continued, hopping into a shorter Chanel chiffon cocktail and offering her back for Ivan to zip, "when the band is smokin' insane? Have a seat out there, Dickie, and I'll be in to help you in a sec."

"Speaking of a little help," Patti yelled from the bathroom, "I'm having sort of a problem with these bikini-wax strips . . ."

Pepper almost caught her hip in her zipper and her baby girl started to cry. "God almighty, Patti Fink! Why're ya doing that now?!"

"I'm going to be *dancing*!" came the answer from the bathroom.

"Well, Marion's about ta have a house fulla people an' I'm tryin' ta play beat the clock with m' tits an'—shit!" There were two identical wet stains on the front of her blouse.

"Second closet, end of the Missoni," said Marion as Ivan secured the hook at the nape of her neck.

"It's in a very tender place!" bleated Patti.

Maya made a face. "My tits leak too!" she quickly lied back to Patti while shimmying into a gold cutoff Galanos.

"Coming, Mrs. Fink," said Ivan, striding back to the bathroom.

Someone had to help her.

Marion stepped into her Manolos, clipped twenty carats of diamond drops into place, and swept out to the bedroom, where Dickie waited, smirking.

"Are you sure that Ivan of yours even *has* a cock?" Dickie Jr. cracked as Marion recuffed him.

Marion looked up at him: "You made this hole bigger when you pulled your cuff link off," she said quietly.

Downstairs, Marion Zane clicked over to the old stairwell that led to the basement and peered down. The second Zephyr announced her engagement, Marion had rung up Seppe at Murano and ordered five hundred of their exquisite "reticello" flutes for the toast. But Zephyr had insisted on an intimate wedding . . .

"You only need to bring two hundred back up, Jeff," Marion called down to her majordomo.

The sounds of several men moaning floated up in reply.

"Dictatorial cow!" snorted Roger, frantically chopping pimientos like a mad hedge trimmer on the other side of the kitchen. "Let *her* try recutting two hundred garnishes!"

The wedding planner wasn't making many fans today.

So once in a while the *Black Book* was wrong in its recommendations? It wasn't often.

At the sounds of more wedding-planner curses coming from both sides of the room (and one comparison to the reproductive organs of a hyena), Marion backed out of her kitchen the same way she'd come in.

———

As Marion started up the tower staircase en route to the master suite, a startling flash of light from overhead almost caused her to lose her footing.

Who was taking pictures up there? The guests *couldn't* have made it back from Broad Beach yet! She was sure Patti had paid off the valets to stall them!

When Marion looked up, she saw only early-evening shadows in the empty tower. But when she looked back down at the steps, something flashed above her again.

Did that old chandelier have a short? she wondered

Marion clicked up the tower staircase to the second-floor landing.

But the lights weren't even on up there.

Strange . . .

Looking out the casement window, she noticed that dusk had fallen. It was spring, but the air was still chilly. Make that cold, almost frosty.

And the air was *vibrating*.

And Marion knew she wasn't alone.

Slowly, a figure started forming in the empty center of the shadowy stairwell in front of her. It looked like it was made of poofing sheets—no, poofing scarves . . . no, what did Patti call it?

Ectoplasm.

Great. You finally decide to show up when I'm expecting two hundred guests for a wedding reception.

But Gilda had already materialized into herself.

She was more beautiful and youthful than her pictures.

And she had a look of mischief around her pixie mouth and eyes.

There were seed pearls in the delicately woven lace of her sheer flapper frock. (Marion was glad she wasn't naked.)

And her shoes were . . . well, they were awesome.

Her jewelry was impressive. Especially the engagement rock. Apparently, Rutherford had loved her. (Before he met the Italian.)

Gilda looked at Marion expectantly.

What?

Gilda kept looking at her expectantly.

(Marion didn't have time for charades.)

Um, I have no more questions. I got it.

Gilda looked up to the cupola.

Yes, you jumped off the cupola. We went over this. Remember . . . last January?

(One of two months Marion wished she could forget.)

But Gilda was shaking her pretty bobbed head.

No? But I thought . . . wait, were you pushed?

Gilda was nodding her pretty bobbed head yes.

No shit? You weren't drunk or doing opium or any of that twenties stuff . . .

"No" shakes.

Then I was right in the first place? Did Rutherford push you?

More "yes" nods.

I gotta learn to trust my research . . .

Then Gilda smiled.

"Fifteen minutes, Mrs. Zane!"

It was Ivan's voice coming from deep inside the master suite, followed by a bloodcurdling scream. The last was from Patti.

Well, thanks for clearing that up, Gilda! Um, I gotta go now, it's getting ugly down there . . . Rutherford pushed you because he was in love with the Italian. Thanks . . .

But something in Gilda's smile was saying no.

The girl had a killer smile.

In any age, she would have been a heartbreaker.

Then suddenly someone else materialized . . . and this someone told Marion that Gilda was indeed a heartbreaker.

Next to the girl ghost, more poofy sheets were coming out of the air.

And they were forming into a man ghost.

Marion wasn't really in the mood to look Rutherford Wilson in the eyes. Or ghost eyes or whatever ghosts looked at you with . . .

She didn't have to.

The man ghost was younger and cuter than Rutherford.

In fact, the man ghost was a stone-fox-major-fine-hunk!

And he was wearing a chauffeur's uniform.

And he had his hand on Gilda's ass.

And she was ghost-giggling.

Oh! Rutherford loved you but you were doing . . . um, the staff?

And with a wink and a bright flash, they were gone.

It was completely dark outside now.

Trophies, Marion thought.

This town hasn't changed.

Another scream pierced the hallway.

"You've almost got it, Ivan! I'll hold her ankle."

It was Dickie Jr.'s voice coming from deep inside the master suite.

Marion sighed, turned, and quickly clicked down the hall.